WILD BASEBALL ROMANCE

MARI LOYAL

*For everyone who has lost
themselves in tragedy.
You can find **you** again.*

HEAT LEVEL AND CONTENT WARNINGS

Before starting this novel, I encourage you to first read this section to determine whether it's the right fit for your personal circumstances.

This book is closed door romance, which means there is innuendo, kisses are descriptive, and characters don't shy away from their attraction.

There is mild to moderate use of cuss words, particularly in emotional moments. However, there is no use of f-bombs, religious blasphemies, or known ableist terms.

The heroine is harassed by a man on the page multiple times. The hero lives with and manages anxiety. There is mild violence. Adult characters may consume alcohol on the page.

Visit my website mariloyal.com for general content warnings that apply to my books.

CHAPTER 1
AUDREY

LATE MARCH

Sometimes life is like baseball—in that it can suck.

But as every fan of a team who is playing worse than pee wees in desperate need of a nap, sometimes you just have to sit there and endure until the last inning. Even if you know that what awaits is a big L.

This is one of such occasions. I know it as well as I know my legal name, what with the fact that I changed it and all. The assistant of Charlie Cox, owner of the Orlando Wild team, is missing from his desk, which makes this all the easier for me. Without warning, I push the door of team owner's office open.

There is no one else in this building who would dare to barge in on the man upon whose whims hinge all our salaries. I have seen people actively cow away when he walks down the hallways, among them my roommates. It's probably a result of how he wiped half of the workforce the second he bought the team just five years ago. Unlike Hope and Rose, though, I have full immunity from getting fired.

The truth is that Charlie Cox is my father. However, Charlie isn't the protective kind of father, wanting to get his spoiled daughter a big present that will make her happy.

Baseball was supposed to be my refuge *from him.*

I thought going away to an ivy league college would put enough distance between us. After everything we had gone through at that point—losing my brother, followed by my parents's inevitable and very expensive divorce—I figured he would be better off living his alcoholic billionaire life without me in the picture.

It worked out for a while. I graduated from college, found my dream job at a professional baseball team without any connections, and even got a loan to buy a nice house and start fresh by my own, honest means.

Then five years into my new life as Audrey Winters—Mom's maiden name—Dad showed up again as the new owner of the team I worked on.

We've kept a careful truce since, consisting of pretending like we don't personally know each other while at work, and me blocking him from every other form of communication.

This is the moment all that is going to end.

Hope and Cade's relationship came out to light yesterday, and Rose is about to risk her entire career to help them. I can't just stand by doing nothing when I hold the figurative keys to the kingdom.

It just means that I'll have to give something up—something I've been getting quite comfortable with in the past few years.

My peace of mind.

Dad turns around at my entrance, cutting an impressive figure for someone who is sixty-three-years-old and has personally met the bottom of many a bottle. His phone is in his hand and Airpods in his ears, which makes me guess I'm interrupting a phone call. He may be negotiating the purchase of an entire country for all I care.

"I'll have to call you back," he says to whoever is on the other end of the line, a smirk growing on half of his face. "I'm afraid I have a very interesting visitor to take care of."

Like in all dealings with him, I can't help but feeling like a little bird hopping willingly into the mouth of a cat. I fold my arms and widen my stance, pretending like my heart isn't about to escape from my throat with how fast it's beating.

"Audrey," he says as a greeting, finally removing the Airpods from his ears. "To what do I owe this honor?"

"I'm here to make a deal with you," I respond, cutting to the chase because he and a panel of other powerful men in the organization are about to go into a conference room with Cade Starr to decide on the fate of his girlfriend, my roommate and friend, Hope Garcia, and whether dating a player is a violation of her employment contract.

I have zero confidence that panel's better judgement will prevail. Since when do men judge women fairly? And as much as Rose's fingers have the magic to make viral hits for the team's social media page, I doubt that public opinion alone will be enough to sway my dad, a man who doesn't even care about his family. The only thing he responds to is power, and no one but me has any semblance of it over him.

"Is that so?" His bushy, white-blond eyebrows rise, giving him the same air of cynicism from a robber baron of the Gilded Age. And yes, I've been watching a lot of historical shows. Anything to escape my reality.

Dad is old, *old*, and yet even older money, and has always conducted himself like it puts him above the entire plane of existence called the twenty first century. The worst part is that it's true, his rules of the game are completely different to anyone else's. I'm here to play by them, even at the cost of losing.

I take a deep breath. "I want you to guarantee Hope and Rose's jobs."

"Who?"

It's not easy, but I manage not to snark at him. I don't know if he asked the lil question to be annoying, or if he truly doesn't know.

"Hope Garcia, the training staff member who was found to be dating our starting pitcher, and Rosalina Mena, the social media manager who is about to blow it up publicly."

"Audrey, that's not how you make a deal. You have to make me care and also give me something in return." He shakes his head in mockery. "I thought I taught you better."

What he really taught me is to not trust him, but saying that aloud won't help my case right now.

"In exchange, I'll give you something you want." I make a strategic pause but Dad shows no signs of being reeled in. Finally, I say, "Direct access to me."

All along, that's what he's been angling for with buying the team and hovering nearby. Adam, my brother, has been dead for ten years already, and Mom moved to Paris the second her passport said Adalyn Winters instead of Adalyn Cox. I'm the last possible puppet Dad has left.

Rather than closing his jaws around me, the big predator in the room just shrugs. "How is that any different than how things already are?"

"Very different," I hasten to add, thinking my argument aloud. "I'll go with you to galas and country clubs, and pretend like we're a happy family like you want."

"Audrey, Audrey." Dad shakes his head like he's disappointed. "That's not what I want."

"Then what?" I ask even as I know the truth behind his words. If he'd really wanted a happy family, he wouldn't have been the one to destroy it in the first place. But instead of starting out with a high and dangerous bargain, I'd rather try on the lower end.

"What I want is for you to accept your inheritance."

My breath hitches.

That sounds good, right? Accepting a trust containing a multitude of businesses, among them a whole professional baseball franchise, billions of dollars in cash, jewels, properties, holdings, stocks, and bonds is probably anyone's dream.

But it's my personal nightmare, because it comes with strings attached. The kind you'll never be able to cut.

"We've already talked about this," I remind him. In fact, that was the subject of our very last fight before I went to college on his dime, before I decided that cutting off his money supply was the only way I could free myself from him.

Back then, I believe that the words I used were *hell* and *no*.

"I recall." His amusement raises the other corner of his mouth into a full smile. "But surely you don't expect that a few soirees will be enough for me to forgive your roommates."

I bristle at that—not at the fact that he does know who Hope and Rose is. "Forgive? That word would only apply if they had offended you directly."

He places a hand on his chest, right over the place where his heart is missing. "I am personally offended. Look at them, trying to sink the reputation of my team, when I kindly offered them their jobs in the first place."

"They're not in breach of their contracts and you know it."

Ignoring that resounding argument, Dad just says, "That's my bargain. Take it or leave it. Either you accept your inheritance with everything it entails, or I let HR take care of your little friends."

Wow, I didn't think I could hate my own father any more than I already did, and yet I just unlocked a new level of vitriol for the man.

Grinding my teeth and squeezing my fists, I ask, "Can we change the terms of my inheritance? I'm happy to leave most of it to the trust or something as long as I don't have to…"

I can't say it.

My throat closes up and I have trouble taking in oxygen, like I'm allergic to the rest of the sentence.

Dad finishes it for me without a problem, though. "No, you will have to marry a man I approve of in order to get your inheritance."

My head swims. I regret power walking so far into his massive office because there's nothing nearby for me to balance against.

"But I'm willing to sweeten the pot a little. I'll guarantee that your friends will stay employed by the Orlando Wild for as long as they want, and I'll even make you the team owner a year after your marriage. How about that?" He stuffs his hands in his pockets, *aww shucks* like and not as if he's uttering absolutely unhinged words.

"Your definition of sweet and mine are very different, Dad," I say with a bitter taste in my mouth.

He checks his Patek Philippe watch, worth the entire salary of our All Star catcher. "I have a disciplinary meeting to go to in ten minutes, so tell me quick. Is that a no?"

Shit.

Even though my head races, I can't find a single way to solve this, and I knew from the beginning that I was going to be the loser of this deal. I just didn't think that Dad would charge me the full price.

But I have no choice. There's no way I can stand by and watch an injustice being done against my friends. They're like my family now—more than this man ever was, or than the woman who lives in front of the Eiffel Tower.

"Fine," I mutter, barely holding down the bile rising up my throat. "I agree to your terms."

The predator leisurely leaves his spot by the window, where he was sunning when I barged in. He stops before me, extending his hand for a handshake. The moment his hand closes around mine is when the commentators in my mind announce that I've officially lost the game.

CHAPTER 2
MIGUEL

My daughter hates baseball, which is an issue when I'm a professional baseball player.

Her arms are like two noodles wrapped around her torso, small and skinny but mighty enough to contain the explosion of her temper. The air conditioner blasting in the car isn't enough to cool it down. Even BTS, her absolute favorite boy band in the whole wide world—her words, not mine—isn't powerful enough to soothe her this time around.

As the South Korean pretty boys crone in the background about a mic that keeps dropping, I mull over what to say. If anything. I'm not sure if to apologize for moving her across the country for a new start with a new franchise, to a rental apartment, and finally to a new home now, with a new nanny in the mix.

When put this way, yeah, I'm horrible. Worst dad in the world. Not worthy of BTS.

It's for her own good, though. I squeeze my hands around the steering wheel, my shoulders bowing under the weight of my perma-guilt.

"I heard that we have a great ice cream place nearby," I say with a lot more cheer than necessary.

A whole stadium full of fans from a team that hates me can't rattle me, but Marty's mean glare almost makes me start sweating.

"And your new school has a pool." I stop at a red light and turn to her.

Her mouth is twisted into a sneer that makes her look like an angry kitten. Pretty sure this would be entirely the wrong moment to show any amusement.

"Hmph." She looks out the window, in case it wasn't clear to me how displeased she is.

Finally, I let a smile fly.

Martina Machado was born unimpressed by me ten years ago. It doesn't mean I won't spend the rest of my life trying. It's why I read enough parenting books to get a degree from it.

"Since this is a fresh start for both of us, why don't we redecorate the house?"

She perks up a tiny bit. But still doesn't turn my way.

The light turns green and I welcome the sign. It brings us closer to our new home, and also to Marty's mood changing. I can feel it.

The pretty boys sing about butter as we roll down a pretty residential street. The road has a canopy of old trees dripping some kind of moss, and if it wasn't so sunny it would feel like we're in another place that isn't in the middle of Florida.

From the outside, moving here makes zero sense. The Denver Riders are the defending World Series Champions and again a top prospect this year. I was on track for breaking my personal home run and stolen bases records. I was selected for the All Star game for the seventh consecutive year—also a franchise record.

Breaking all that momentum with a sudden trade is not only senseless, but also potentially a harbinger of bad luck.

Pero… I have a good feeling.

That also makes no sense. I'm an old school baseball guy who knows the power of his little rituals, like rubbing the golden cross that hangs around my neck to calm me down—which I do right as I turn us into our new residence. Nothing skewers routine more than moving to a brand new place with a different weather, traffic flow, and even a different path to the bathroom in the middle of the night.

I did it for my daughter, I've told the public, *so she can be surrounded by more people who speak Spanish.*

In truth, it's because she was being bullied at her old school, and hid it from me for a year. I only found out when I went to her class for career day, even after she had told me not to—which, by the way, she still hasn't forgiven me for.

"Here we are. Home, sweet home," I announce, parking in front of the cozy duplex townhouse that I bought for us. "What do you think?"

I wish I could see her face, but the house is by her window and all I can do is guess.

The house looks like something that belongs in New England, red brick and white trim, complete with a porch and a swing, and the greenest grass I've ever seen. Her room is upstairs and even has a windowsill that overlooks a big tree that the real estate agent says blooms yellow in the spring. Better yet, her new middle school is a short bus ride away and boasts some of the best rankings across the country not just in academics, but in wellbeing and environment.

Who cares about my streak? My daughter will be much happier here.

Okay, I also care about my streak. I just have to pick it back up. My hand rises to the cross to soothe myself.

I nudge Marty with my elbow. "Vamos."

Sighing, she unbuckles herself and opens the door. I turn off the car and show absolutely no sign of relief at the silence, instead making a quick circle around the car so I can take in her impression.

My daughter is a vault, though. She looks up at the house where we'll live together for the foreseeable future like it's the building version of me. Unimpressive.

Should I have bought one of the big ass mansions nearby? But I've always wanted her to grow up as normal as possible, even if her dad is an unmarried guy who plays with a ball for a living.

"Why don't you go in to explore?" I ask her, producing the house keys from my pocket and offering them to her. Her little mouth is a downward arch even as she accepts the offering, and she stomps up the red brick walkway to the entrance.

Placing my hands on my hips, I drop my head with a sigh and wonder how to make things better. Do I need to buy her a freaking pony?

The *sold out* sign catches my eye, the red of it in high contrast with the grass background. I would drag my feet if I didn't care about marring the perfect green blanket, but even when I'm careful pulling the sign off it damages that area.

It's another metaphor to my life. No matter how good my intentions are with my daughter, I inevitably screw up.

The noise of a door opening distracts me from my private pity party, but it's not from Marty coming out of the house. Rather, a woman steps out of the duplex next door, in a long-sleeved pajama top like it's not a million degrees and a hundred percent humidity. She yawns so wide that I can almost see her shoe size, and she scratches her head vigorously, making her mess of blonde hair even messier. If she notices the random 6 foot 4 guy staring at her from the yard next door, she ignores me.

I shrug. So what if our neighbor's a bit quirky? As far as Florida Woman headlines go, one who wears long-sleeved pajamas in the middle of Florida summer ranks as the milder sort.

I tuck the *sold out* sign under my arm and head back out to my white RAV4 to get our suitcases out and put the sign away. A soft little grunt comes from somewhere behind me and I try to ignore it… until it comes again. Glancing over my shoulder, I find the neighbor in a one-on-one battle with her mailbox.

"You—friggin'—" She's pulling at the mailbox's door with all the power in her body and it doesn't budge, but if she keeps going she's going to get herself hurt.

"Excuse me," I call out. "Can I help you?"

"I'm fine," she snarls.

"Okay…" I hesitate for a second, but I'm starting to put my money on her and not on the mailbox so I return to my task. My daughter's suitcases come out first and—

Something snaps.

The Florida Woman squeals.

It happens in slow motion. The mailbox finally opens— that's the snapping sound—exploding with more mail than the minuscule box should fit. She loses her grip on the handle and her bunny slipper slides off the edge of the sidewalk. Her arms helicopter around her but the outcome is inevitable. She's gonna start her day with a bruised tailbone. Unless I catch her.

Before my thinking brain kicks in, the one that rules over every reflex takes over. I'm not far. I can catch her right before she hits the pavement. I stretch out my arms. She can't see my heroics and keeps trying to save herself.

"Oof!" Me.

"Shit!" Her.

I see stars from one side as her flying hand lands a wild hit on my eye. Stunned, I don't exactly succeed on my quest and she falls anyway—on me. And I'm the one who lands ass first on the pavement.

After a still second where my face throbs in tune with my

butt cheeks, and the figurative dust settles, I run a quick inventory of the rest of my body parts and find: limbs, safe. Head, safe. Family jewels, safe. Pride, very much injured.

Neighbor gasps and scrambles off, finally turning to meet her failed knight.

And her jaw drops.

Not gonna lie, that's what finally makes me panic. "Please don't tell me that my eye is hanging out of its socket or something?" I ask, my voice an embarrassing octave higher.

She gasps. "You're Miguel Machado."

I snap my own mouth closed. I suppose she wouldn't care about that if my eye was doing really bad. "Um, yeah." I clear my throat, forcing my mouth back to normal. "Are you a baseball fan?"

"I, uh—S-Sorry." She pushes off her hands to get back up, the fight completely gone off her body as she stands there for an awkward moment, clutching at her pajama top. From this close, what seemed like boring polka dots in a light green background are actually tiny bunny heads.

She coughs a little and I look up at her face, and I'm met by the greenest eyes in the planet.

I mean, of course I haven't personally inspected the eyeballs of every person currently alive, yet the statement holds true when the perfect lawn behind her pales in comparison.

"Please don't sue me, I can't afford it," she blurts out.

My jaw drops for a second. "Shouldn't you at least ask if I'm okay first?"

"Are you?"

"Well, now. That sounds forced." I sit up and brush dirt off my hands. "Are *you* okay?"

After a moment, she responds, "I think I broke a nail."

"That's rough, buddy," I say, quoting a line from Marty's favorite cartoon.

"Did you just quote Zuko?" she asks with the same air of having heard someone recite every decimal in the number pi.

"Dad, there's no food."

The tiny and grumpy voice of my tiny and grumpy daughter captures my attention. I jump to my feet, give one last look at the awkward blonde, and give her an even more awkward wave that intends to portray both that I'm fine and that it was good to meet her, even though it really wasn't. She ducks and turns back to her scattered mail.

I touch my face and confirm that my left eye is in its rightful place, and even though the fridge is empty, I sure hope it has some ice.

"I know, honey. We'll have to go shopping later. First we have to unpack."

"Fine."

That's the fifth word she's directed at me all day, which is a huge improvement and tells me that she at least must've liked the house. As I wheel her suitcases up to the porch, I sneak another look at my neighbor who is now rushing to her own door, using her loose hair as a curtain to hide her face. My cheek twitches.

As far as signs go, this weird welcome to my new home shouldn't bode well. Yet the good feeling hasn't left me.

CHAPTER 3
AUDREY

"There's a woman who has been thoroughly kissed by her man," Hope announces as Rose joins us at the cafeteria for a little coffee break.

I say nothing, choosing to cradle my little ice coffee like it's my one lifeline, but discreetly noticing that Rosalina's cheeks are bright enough to pass as neon signs.

"How do you know?" she asks with an airy laugh.

Hope jerks a thumb at me. "It's the same face Audrey says I had when I walked in."

"Do you guys not do any work?" I ask in a droll, shaking my head. "Is sneaking around with your menfolk all you do these days?"

"Yes."

"Kinda."

"Feminism is dead," I announce.

Rose snorts, stabbing her cup with a compostable straw. "It's not dead, but no one said it had to be miserable and lonely, especially not when you've found true love."

I'm glad that at least I'm not the only one who cringes. Hope's shoulders also rise to shield herself from the sap.

However, she doesn't counter the point, what with also being besotted and all.

It's not that I'm jealous—even if I'm not building a compelling case right now. I'm actually so happy that two of my best friends in the whole world were fortunate enough to find two of the few good men among a population sample of four billion plus. Perhaps it should give me hope, or at least dial down my cynicism to a healthier degree. But seeing Hope and Cade holding hands and looking at each other like the secrets of the universe are contained in each other's eyes, or Rose and Logan stroking each other's cheeks tenderly like that little touch is all they need to keep their souls alive, hasn't fixed me.

And that's the sad part, I really thought it would. These four are the first examples I've seen in real life of what love and partnership is really supposed to be like. I guess I'm too far gone.

I rest my chin on my fist. "I have a random question for you two."

"Is it about work?" Hope's eyes light up. "Please tell me it is, there's only so much cringe I'm able to tolerate in a single day."

She better brace, then.

"I know it's very early to ask this, but I'm just curious…" I stretch the pause by taking a sip from my drink. The bittersweet taste is apropos. "If you end up marrying your beaus, will you change your last names or not?"

Hope freezes. "Whoa, I was genuinely not expecting that."

"Me neither." Rose swirls her cup to mix the milk and the coffee, humming under her throat as she ponders. "Hmm, I think I might keep my last name Mena, if only to protect Logan."

We both stare at her and I prompt, "What do you mean?"

"It might keep weirdoes off him if I appear as Rosalina

Mena on the screens once I'm officially part of the broadcasting team."

I snap my fingers. "That's the spirit."

Meanwhile, Hope clears her throat and ducks to speak at her straw. "Is it bad if I would want everyone to know that Cade has an owner?"

"No." Rose laughs. "Maybe that's the right answer for you two."

I lean back, staring at them with wonder. They don't realize how special they are, or how blessed their circumstances. That they found men who would fight stalkers and bad exes to protect them, and whom they would do anything in return for, is nothing short of a miracle.

Meanwhile, here I am, with a form printed and tucked in a manila folder at my desk to change my last name again to my dad's—arguably the worst specimen of the male species that I've encountered.

I'm not strictly of either camp, that every woman has to keep *or* change her last name. I think it should be their choice, based on circumstances like this. I wish I had a choice right now too, but I made a deal that I can't walk back without destroying Hope and Rose's happily ever afters.

Sharper than her fairytale princess persona would lead anyone to think, Rosalina turns to me. "Why do you ask?"

"Just curious." I shrug to downplay my interest.

Every line of Rose's gorgeous face tells me she doesn't believe for a second that that's all there is, but she chooses not to press further.

Hope checks her watch. "Well, I better go dig my elbow into someone's hamstring or something."

A snort escapes from my throat and turns into a laugh.

"And I better go edit footage of professional baseball players acting like children," Rose announces, pushing her chair back to stand up.

"You have the best job." Hope chuckles.

I also get up and tag along as we walk out. "What are we doing for dinner? Tacos?" I ask before we all veer in different directions.

"Oh, sorry." Rose gives me a sheepish look. "Since it's a rest day, I was planning on going to the South Korean BBQ place with Logan."

"And Cade and I are making dinner together at his place," Hope adds.

I guess I don't do a very good job at masking how bummed I am because I earn apologies and hugs. Sighing, I wave them off and turn the opposite way, toward the back offices where there's a corner reserved for communications and public relations. That's where I work, and also where unpleasant things await at my desk.

Once I get there, I push away the manila folder I've been trying to ignore for months and fire my laptop back up.

Dad's growing impatient. There's only so many times I can use the excuse that government bureaucracy is slow when I haven't actually submitted the forms yet. This morning I got a text from him basically ordering me to attend a gala with him tomorrow *or else*. He probably suspects that I'm dragging my feet and is going to change tactics into a more direct approach.

Nagging me for an entire night.

Ugh, one of my desk plants is showing some signs of sadness, just like my soul. I spritz some water on the little pot, wishing I could fix myself that easily.

I hadn't truly noticed how liberating it was to not be among the so-called high society all these years, if only going by the growing pit in my stomach. I wonder if I should make up some excuse like being on my period—I'm not—or having a severe case of diarrhea—can be arranged.

My computer pings with an incoming message and I pause from watering my desk plants to check it out. Karen Schmidt, my boss who doesn't exactly debunk the reputation her first name has garnered online, writes to me on Teams.

SCHMIDT, KAREN [15:23]:

Come to my office

I allow my expression to sour freely in the privacy of my cubicle. Hers is just a few steps away from mine. She could either drop by herself or ask like a normal person.

I find her typing on her keyboard like she's the busiest person in the entire Orlando Wild organization. "I'm disappointed in you," she says as her opening—loud enough for the entire office to hear, by the way.

Since it's not our first rodeo, I mutter, "Is that so?"

Finally she tears her attention from the screen and swivels on her chair to face me. "How is it that we've had the best hitter in the entire league in our team for almost a month already, and you haven't found him a campaign?"

I do my best to keep my expression neutral. "We already had one with Lucky Rivera lined up," I explain.

"That was already shot last week." She waves a hand, like the past shoot doesn't require more work afterward. "Bring me a proposal about Machado by the end of the day. And make it bigger and better than the previous campaigns we've ran. I'm sure your *SPORTY* contacts will be happy to support," she adds with a sardonic smile.

I guess she'll never stop being annoyed that I'm the one who got us the *SPORTY* sponsorship through Camila Puig, my college roommate. A good boss would take it as her own win, but not dearest Karen. Ever since she's been out to get me.

"You'll have it by the end of the week," I respond with a smile that would look friendly to HR, but raises Karen's hackles.

"End of today, I said."

I don't respond. If she could fire me over this disagreement, she would've fired me ten times over already. And I'd take the *SPORTY* account with me wherever I go.

Wait, maybe this isn't so bad. I can use the excuse of having too much work as an excuse to dip out of the gala early.

"There's only one problem," I mumble as I take a seat back inside my cubicle, resting my elbows on the desk and lacing my fingers. "Miguel Machado," I say against my hands. My new neighbor, who I gave a black eye to last week that has caused many rumors. And who still doesn't know that I also work for the Wild.

Somehow I've managed to avoid the guy both at home and here, and I'll of course deal with his agent to arrange a campaign. But eventually our paths will cross and I'll have to give explanations that I'd rather not share.

Then again that's my life, a circle of being forced to do things I don't want to. I tuck the manila folder with my name change forms in my purse and get back to work.

CHAPTER 4
MIGUEL

arty has a new nanny. Her name is Consuelo Gomez—sixty-one-years-old, with thirty six years experience taking care of kids, no criminal records, perfect credit score, recommended by our previous nanny back in Colorado, over two hundred five star reviews on the website of the top nanny agency in town, and apparently also cooks amazingly.

MI NIÑA BONITA

Dad stop worrying

Or I'll block you

What, she already knows how to block numbers on her phone? When did she learn that? She's just *ten*. I didn't know how to keep a damn Tamagotchi alive when I was her age.

I press my lips tight. It's fine. I'm fine. Everything's fine.

I type *I'll stop worrying about you when I'm dead* but Marty hates it when I'm a drama king—which is all the damn time. It's funny how I can be completely calm in a stadium full of fifty thousand screaming people, facing a ball that comes at ninety miles per hour with just a wooden stick, yet I have negative chill when it comes to my child. I hate that I have to leave her in the hands of strangers all the time, but even more for a frivolous thing like this.

Except I can't really say no to the owner of my new team when he invites me to some fundraising gala to show me off to donors. I'll probably retire from the Orlando Wild when the time comes, so I have to play nice.

ME

I'll check in again in fifteen

After hitting send, I wonder if she'll follow through on her threat to block me. Joke's on her, there are security cameras around the house, and if Consuelo were to not pick up her phone I'd call anyone from nine-one-one to the Army.

I tuck my phone in the pocket of my slacks and take in my surroundings again. No one would guess that this place isn't located in Manhattan but in Dr. Phillips, in the south of Orlando. There's more marble, gold, and crystal than I consider in good taste, but I guess the point is opulence. I'm by far the poorest person in this place, which is saying something when I have a seventy five million dollar salary. But I don't come from old money like these people—rather, I come from a hot and forsaken city in a country called Venezuela that these people probably couldn't point in a map. My dad was a high school teacher and my mom a secretary, and they had two kids who in turn managed to have kids of their own way too young. Not quite the pedigree that is expected in an event like this.

"Excuse me," someone says nearby. "Are you Miguel Machado?"

I don't even twitch at how badly my last name is pronounced, almost like saying mashed potato. I plaster on a friendly smile and turn to the stranger, a man in his fifties and in his cups. "Yes, hi."

"Wow, I'm a really big fan. Let's take a picture." Dude hooks his arm around my neck, forcing me to bend down uncomfortably as he takes a selfie that no doubt will be a blur.

"I see you've met Robert Munn," a familiar voice says. As I extricate myself from the tipsy man's hold, my team's owner strolls over, two champagne flutes in hand. "Robert here is a banker, and a very important friend to me."

A.k.a. a very wealthy potential donor that we need to schmooze. If we weren't here to gather funds for the team's charity, which provides scholarships and baseball equipment to orphans, I'd have peaced out a while back and headed back home to my own kid.

I shake the banker's hand. "Great to have your support for this important cause, Mr. Munn."

"Call me, Bob, kid," he says like I'm the one who's ten, patting my shoulder. A waiter walks by with a tray of colorful canapés that distract Bob. "Will you excuse me? I'm a tad hungry."

"Of course."

As the man chases after the little food, Charlie Cox takes his place and tells me, "Thank you for that, just humoring him for a few minutes probably got us a million dollars for the charity."

I blink slowly. I also donate to good causes, especially for the people back home, but I usually have to think about it longer than it takes to take a selfie.

Clearing my throat, I say, "No problem, I'm here to help."

"Here." He offers me one of the flutes. "Let's cheer to a successful night."

"I—Uh, I can't drink alcohol in the middle the season, sir."

"Wise." Cox nods, clearly unperturbed. "As it happens, I've been sober for a while so this is non-alcoholic."

"Then, thank you." I accept the offering and we clink the flutes. Before the silence gets too awkward, he speaks again.

"I'd like to introduce you to my daughter, but she seems to have given me the slip again." My eyebrows rise at the *again*, not only because it implies that she's done this more than once, but also at the disaffected way he says it with. "Like you, she doesn't really enjoy these things."

I choke on the bubbly.

Billionaire businessman and philanthropist Charlie Cox laughs like any other man. "You think I didn't notice? You've been checking your phone all night like you'd rather be elsewhere."

Meanwhile, I return the world's most awkward laugh. "Sorry, I'm just worried about my own daughter."

"Right, Martina, was it? Is she getting along at her new school?"

I don't know why I'm surprised that he remembers. When the first thing he asked me when my agent contacted his team was why I wanted the trade, I answered very honestly and didn't get much commentary about it in return. I figured that a player's family issues would be beneath the notice of a man whose focus is on the several zeroes in his bank account. Or bank accounts. Trust funds? Whatever rich people have, then.

"So far so good," I admit despite my own worries. "She's with her new nanny right now. Doing great. I think."

That causes the powerful man to laugh again. "So that's what has you so preoccupied."

Busted, and so I say nothing.

I'm saved by something catching his attention, and for a second I wonder if it's the elusive daughter. Instead, he says, "I just spotted one of my business partners. Shall we go get another million out of her?"

Cox only frees me after three more rounds of schmoozing, and only because he gets a phone call from some diplomat who was unable to attend the event. I leave my flute on a tray of used cups and find an isolated spot behind some potted plants.

I'm a tall dude and have no hope that I'm truly hiding, but hopefully it signals leave-me-the-heck-alone well enough. I take my phone out and my heart nearly stops when I see that I have a text from Marty already.

MI NIÑA BONITA

I'm still fine

The text came exactly fifteen minutes after I last said I'd check in. *This kid*, I think to myself, shaking my head.

ME

Good. Did you have dinner already?

MI NIÑA BONITA

Yes

She offers no further commentary, and so I text her once more.

ME

What did you have?

MI NIÑA BONITA

Arepa emoji

Hmm, maybe I'll also have one when I get home. The posh finger food is nowhere near enough to fill me up.

A burst of laughter nearby distracts me. My eyes travel over the potted plants to a group of people, all on the younger side of the invite list, but decked in outfits that probably cost twice what my car does. I'm about to return my focus on the cellphone screen when I notice something familiar.

I tilt my head, wondering how that can even be possible, when I spot her—the blonde woman who gave me the black eye I was forced to cover with makeup tonight, and who has been missing in action since.

I narrow my eyes. I better steer clear of her lest she gives me a second black eye, or breaks my nose instead.

ME

I'll be home early

We can watch some Percy Jackson before you go to bed

MI NIÑA BONITA

I already watched them all

"Ugh. Ruthless." I press my hand against my chest.

But can I blame her? I spend two thirds of my time traveling for games or training, and everyday Marty grows more independent as result. It's hard not to feel some type of way.

I'm about to text again when I hear something strange. "— Like, *bigger*, since the last time we saw you." The emphasis is what beckons my attention.

"Do you mean *fatter*?" another woman adds, laughing in a mean way. "Why, Audrey, you've really let go since high school."

Call me a drama king, but after what my kid has gone through, I'm so not here for the damn bullies. I tuck my phone away and prepare to leave my hiding spot.

My neighbor tosses her goldilocks over her shoulder and folds her arms. "And you guys are bigger douchebags than I remember, which is quite an impressive feat."

My feet stop. An amused snort comes out of my chest.

And finally the ultra green eyes lift to find me. They widen like she can't quite believe what they're registering, and a touch of alarm lights them up. Is it because she recognizes me as the guy she randomly boxed at first sight, or because it's clear that I heard the insults she's trading with these people?

What was it that they called her, again?

"Audrey," I say, recalling at the last second. I let my lips stretch into what's a surprisingly genuine smile, and every pair of eyes in the vicinity turns to my arrival. "Here you are, I've been looking for you all night."

You have? her large and expressive eyes convey. Next thing, she catches up to the ruse and plays along like a smart cookie.

"Miguel," she exclaims, a veneer of cheer falling over her face. I nearly double take that she knows my name, but she already knew who I was last week. "You owed me a dance so this is perfect timing."

"Shall we?" I offer my arm like I indeed have made such a promise.

One of her companions—rather, bullies—scoffs in open annoyance as my neighbor passes her by to take my arm. Her dainty hand grabs me with surprising strength, which tells me that she really wants to escape this group. And so I whisk her away.

To the safety of the dance floor.

CHAPTER 5
AUDREY

What is happening? What is my life?

Miguel Machado, a once in a generation baseball talent that most people can't dream of breathing the same air with, has not only appeared in front of me once... but twice. And for reasons that my brain hasn't caught up to, my hand is on his rock-solid arm, which I guess is a step up from socking him in the eye.

"Thank you for helping me back there," I say, my voice sounding foreign to myself. "I just have one question."

He hums from his throat, indicating that he's listening even as he keeps us moving farther and farther from my ex-high school classmates.

"Were you legitimately looking for me all night, or was that just a line to get me out of there? Because I already said I'm really sorry about the eye, but I can't afford to lawyer up."

"Considering how I still have full use of my eye, that something called concealer hides the bruise pretty well, and that I had no idea you were here until I chanced upon you getting bullied..." He trails off with a shrug, making my knuckles brush against the soft fabric of his suit jacket. "I'd say that I have no motive to serve you with papers."

"Whew," I voice in an exaggerated, yet flat way. "Also, I technically had it handled so I didn't really need your knight in shining armor services."

"I know you did. Let's just say that it was my own sense of justice what I serviced instead."

He slows down amid a moving mass of people. Suddenly, he tugs me in a way that I end up facing him. Next thing I know, one of his hands places mine on his shoulder before it circles my waist, resting in the middle of my back—which feels like nearly all my back with how enormous his hand is—and the other grabs one of mine.

"Wait." Tingles rush from my chest to every corner of my body—the bad kind. The kind that usually precede an embarrassment rash, because of course I can't be a pretty blusher. "What are you doing?"

Miguel's eyebrows rise. "We're going to dance."

As if he had bribed someone, the band reaches the last notes of a jaunty tune and begins a slower one. It takes me another moment to recognize it as Fly Me to the Moon.

I shake my head like a robot. "Oh, no. I don't dance. I just said that as an excuse to get away."

"Where would our honor go if people don't see us dancing?" he asks with an affected tone of voice and a twinkle in his eye that I don't understand.

"Uh, this isn't a historical ball where it matters who dances with who and how many times, you know?"

"Do you always challenge the people who are trying to help you so much? Because..." And here Miguel does something unprecedented. He leans lower—lower still—until he's so close that I can no longer see anything that isn't his massive shoulder. For a wild second I wonder if he's trying to kiss me. But of course he isn't and just whispers into my ear, "Your bullies are watching."

A shiver goes through my spine.

Am I creeped out that my ex-classmates are keeping tabs to see if I lied? Kinda, yes. Is my back cold? Very, but only because the heat that this man radiates has me well and toasty at the front.

Why does he smell so damn good, though? There's something familiar about it, and the name of the scent is lodged in the back of my mind where I can't pluck it out for my immediate satisfaction. Yet, there's also something even better that I can't pinpoint, but I'd like to because now it's going to nag me forever.

My lapse in self-awareness ends when I realize that I'm swaying. Or rather, he's making us move somewhat in sync with the classic song.

Oh. Wow. How did that happen? I ask myself.

I pull back from him slightly, trying to bring oxygen into my brain instead of deliciously intoxicating man-cologne. I'm glad he's just making us dance a little and not walking me down a plank or something.

It doesn't seem to matter that I'm the stiffest dance partner this guy has probably ever had, he has enough command of his own muscles that I probably look like a professional to the untrained eye. Peeking over my shoulder, I confirm that what he said is true, and the whole group of rich pests is watching our every move with avid interest.

It's no surprise that half of the people in attendance at this gala have been in my father's circle all our lives and comprise of his business associates, who in turn had kids I went to school with.

Tonight is the first time in years since I show my face in this polite society, so I was ready for some impoliteness in return. I just could've never foreseen how the scene would unfold.

Playing damsel in distress to an elite baseball player whose future smells of hall of fame wasn't on my bingo card.

Slowly, I drag my attention back to the front where Miguel Machado is watching me with some curiosity, and no obvious interest in suing the pants out of me.

I clear my throat, scrambling for some sense of normalcy, and say, "You really blended the concealer well." Then I cringe. Of all possible conversation topics, why did I choose that one? "Or your wife, I mean. You probably don't know anything about makeup."

His lips draw into a smile that forces back laughter. "I don't have a wife and my daughter's toy makeup kit wasn't good enough, so I actually had to get my makeup done professionally." He pauses for a moment, grinding me to a stop as well, and looks off into the distance. "Wow, that's a sentence I never knew would come out of my mouth. And I'm a girl dad—I've worn tutus."

He catches himself, eyes widening like he can't believe all that just came out of his mouth.

"Hmm." I press my lips. "Debating whether to tease you or allow you to keep your dignity since you've been nice to me."

"I would absolutely tease me if I was you." His face stretches into a full grin of contagious proportions.

Using my vast reserves of willpower to stay serene, I say, "You said tutus, meaning that this happened more than once?"

A snort from Miguel turns into a full blown laugh. "And here I thought you were gonna ask me what color it was."

I narrow my eyes in thought. "Definitely pink. Purple would wash out your complexion."

"It was black, actually. My daughter is kind of goth." He displays his pearly whites and dimples appear on his cheeks. They're more like the bracket kind than the dots one. "By the way, we haven't formally introduced each other."

"If we shake hands the vultures will know we're complete strangers but hi, I'm Audrey Winters, nice to meet you."

Miguel tips his head. "Likewise, or better now that you're no longer causing me bodily harm."

"I could still change my mind," I add offhand.

Ignoring that, he asks, "By the way, you never answered my question." I raise my eyebrows in confusion, and he explains, "Last week, when I asked if you knew me because you were a fan."

"Oh. That." I cringe a little. "I assure you I'm not a stalker. The truth is that I'm—"

"Audrey."

The new voice makes us stop dancing at the same time, and that's when I notice a few odd things. First, that the song must've changed at some point already. Just how long have we been dancing?

And second, that I lost sight of the most important self-preservation tactic of the night. The biggest threat wasn't my ex-classmates, but my dad, and now he's right next to me and I'm trapped in a man's arms—arms that are made of steel and heat, not likely to pry away easily if I try to run away.

Also, how pathetic would that look? It's not like I'm some Cinderella.

Sighing, I face my progenitor. "Dad."

This perks Miguel's attention. "Dad?"

"I see you've met my daughter," the older man says. "And perhaps I should also thank you for helping me locate her."

"Is that what you were doing?" I slide a suspicious look at Miguel, but dude looks confused.

"That's news to me."

I don't know why this is the moment when he decides to release me. His hand slides off my back and he steps back a polite distance, not that we were grinding on each other or anything, but definitely like he doesn't want my dad to think something's going on.

Stuffing his hands in the pockets of his slacks, Miguel looks first at my dad and then at me, no doubt finding that I have the same nose—girl version—and that I got my hair color from Charlie Cox. "Did I hear different last names, though?"

"It's a long, boring story." Dad waves his hand like the topic is unimportant. "She'll be changing her last name soon anyway, isn't that so?"

Great. The rash of embarrassment that I had somehow managed to contain is taking over. I regret wearing a dress that keeps the top of my chest and shoulders visible, because not even my loose hair will hide the angry, red splotches.

I brush at my skirt, trying to pretend like that's enough to rearrange my own thoughts and feels. "You're right, Dad. Let's not bore Miguel with those details."

I don't know the slugger very well, but the spark in his eye tells me that if he could, he'd grab some popcorn and sit down for the whole tale. No wonder my roommates say he has fit so well with the bunch of goofs that make up the Orlando Wild team.

"In that case, allow me to steal my daughter away so we can bore each other instead." Dad gives one of those curated laughs that sound warm and friendly to the untrained ear, and I know to just be a mechanism for him to get what he wants.

He offers me his arm, which, unlike Miguel's gesture earlier, isn't meant to help me out of an awkward situation, but the entire opposite.

"Of course." Nothing in his neutral expression prepares me for what Miguel says next, "Please enjoy each other's company."

My jaw slacks.

That little jerk. He could've pretended like I was the most riveting creature he's ever met.

But he did allow me to tease him earlier, so I mouth *touché* at him before Dad grabs my hand and steers me away. I do my best to keep my composure and not show Miguel or anyone else that I'm not comfy with my dad, even if it's the truth.

I huff. "Did you have to say that in front of a random guy?"

"Random?" Dad glances at me. "You two looked pretty chummy."

"Our definition of that word is clearly different. For example, anyone who sees us right now would think that we're a chummy pair of father and daughter, and they'd be completely wrong," I say with total calm.

That quiets him for only a brief moment. Dad isn't a guy to turn the other cheek. "That's going to change now that you're making public appearances with me again, isn't it?"

For once, I can't come up with a clever comeback.

Unlike Miguel, who took me away from annoying people, Dad does entirely the opposite. As he takes me on a seemingly endless parade of small talk with strangers and familiar faces—most of them undesirable—I almost wish I could go back to talking about tutus with Miguel Machado.

And that's when I have a sudden realization. No one at work knows that the team's owner is my dad—no one but the new guy who is getting chummy with my roommates, who are the very last people on earth I want this secret revealed to.

CHAPTER 6
MIGUEL

"Damn…"

My steps fall like explosions on the treadmill, my thighs pumping at my maximum speed. The trainers told me to push hard to establish a very clear baseline, and that's what I'm doing. My lungs burn, trying to send oxygen to my muscles at a violent pace. The altitude mask doesn't exactly make it a comfortable exercise either, but if that's not enough to confirm whether I'm going full throttle, the electrodes stuck on my bare chest around my heart probably give it away.

"Do you think he's human?" someone asks.

The response is, "definitely not."

I've heard a lot of yapping throughout my baseball career. One of the things that made me stand out since I was a kid back in my home country was that, despite my height and the weight that comes along with it, I was a pretty fast runner. That has definitely ensured my stolen bases record, but the less obvious thing is how having powerful legs is what has allowed me to bat the home runs that fans enjoy so much.

However, even though my legs are my secret weapon, my

real talent lies somewhere else. Namely, in being able to worry about my daughter no matter what I'm doing.

Practicing my swings? Meanwhile, wondering if Marty's liking Consuelo's food or if we should hire someone else.

Running workout? Wondering if summer school is going okay and whether she's making some friends.

Walking up to the plate with all bases loaded? Makes me wonder if she has realized that my walk up song is for her. I guess Mi Niña Bonita by Chino y Nacho would more widely be interpreted as a typical love song, but the only sweet princess in my life is Marty.

Except that these days she's more of a sour princess. At first I thought that it might be because she's not used to the new nanny, or that perhaps she wasn't as amazing as advertised, but after a week of knowing Consuelo I can confirm that she's everyone's favorite grandma, and that even though Marty loves her, she's still unhappy.

Which in turn makes me wonder if maybe things aren't going so great at school after all. Losing so much of the previous school year with the move forced me to sign her up to summer school, so she can start the new year at the same level. And even though the teacher assured me that their summer program isn't about punishment, maybe Marty's still taking it that way.

Franklin, the head trainer, tells me, "You can begin to slow down." He adjusts the speed a couple of notches lower, and I match the pace.

"Well," this loud voice I recognize as coming from one Lucky Rivera, the mood-maker for this team. "I'm glad I've seen this while this guy's already on our team, and not when he was still one of the Riders."

I work to even out my breathing the more I slow down. Of course, I've asked Marty here and there what's up. If home-work's hard, if her classmates are nice… But all she does is turn up her lower lip and ignore me. It's easier to have a conversation with a wall than when she does that.

I'm still breathing rough even as the treadmill is fully stopped. Hope Garcia, the only female physical therapist who I know is the starting pitcher's other half, makes for my mask but can't reach. I step off the machine and lower my head, the electrodes pulling uncomfortably at my chest hair.

Movement from the corner of my eye catches my attention, and it's Cade Starr, her boyfriend, motioning toward his eyes and toward me like I'll be in the crosshairs if I make the wrong move.

I start shaking my head but Garcia says, "Stay still." Something in her voice tells me that she's the one I really have to obey, so I stop moving.

A different thing catches my attention now, something gold and flowing. My mind immediately forms the image of my odd neighbor in the cinched black dress she wore at her father's benefit gala. No way that the elegant heiress to the Cox empire would come to the musty, stinky gym.

But I do a double take because sure enough, that's her—she of the unmistakable eyes.

I blink slowly. The vision of her in a fancy outfit swaying in my arms almost made me forget that she wore pajamas with bunny slippers when I first met her.

"Hey, Audrey," Garcia says while she ruthlessly tears the electrodes off me.

I try not to flinch. And fail. Someone else hisses on my behalf.

Worse than the pain, Audrey Cox—wait, Winters?—turns her attention down to my chest. I'm not really a shy dude, what with making a living out of my body, but I really wish she'd come at any other moment.

"Hey," blondie returns to the other woman, now raising her green eyes to my face. "Are you done with this guy?"

Garcia cocks an eyebrow. "I am, but I think my boss has a couple more baseline tests to take."

"That's fine. I can watch and wait," Audrey says, turning into the crowd without a backward glance. Now I'm the one whose eyebrow's twitching.

Hmm. Does it matter that watching has precedence over waiting?

I scratch my belly, for once wishing that I had absolutely shredded abs like some of the other guys here.

Instead, I touch the cross around my neck because you'd think I'm at a high stakes game instead of following pretty standard procedure. The upper and lower body strength tests go on without much fanfare—at least not from the staff. My new teammates are still watching like hawks and I know exactly what's going on through their heads: can they beat me? Can they run faster? Hit harder? Jump higher?

The answer in Spanish is: *no*.

But I'd like to see them trying. That's the fun part about baseball, a little healthy competition is what makes me better. I wonder if Marty will want to develop that skill in a sports club at school this year. Softball would be fun to play together.

"Excuse me." I freeze in the middle of toweling my sweaty hair and turn to find the owner's daughter behind me. She tilts her head back to look up at me. "I need to speak with you for a moment."

This is where, in my previous locker room, the guys would've started wolf whistling and catcalling. It's not everyday that a woman strides into the gym to single out a guy in the pack. But now that the testing show is over, the guys are going back to their own exercise machines like this happens frequently. And I guess it makes sense, since there's a female therapist and all.

I'm only a little unbalanced when I say, "Uh, yeah. Sure." I clear my throat. I'll get used to how things are around here eventually. I just hope this isn't a sign that my game is gonna go to the crapper since joining the Wild.

"This way." She motions at me to follow and I do. Glancing over my shoulder confirms that no one gives two shits about this scene. I guess they all must know the team owner's daughter too.

She doesn't take me far, just into the therapists's office, and away from the traffic. Folding her arms, she squares up to me, blocking the entrance with her back to the rest of the team. "I guess I should've told you I'm in the PR team when I introduced myself the other night."

I blink slowly, the picture of who she is finally starting to fall into place. "Cool," I say noncommittally.

She continues, "I dropped by to say that I called your agent to offer a promotional spot with *SPORTY*. She sounded stoked but still asked me to get your opinion."

I place my hands on my hips, and that catches her attention for a microsecond. "I'm listening."

"As you know, *SPORTY* is our team's main sponsor. They regularly feature our players on their magazine. In your case, they want to star you in an apparel commercial."

I raise my hand to my hair and find my towel still on my head. Not to act like the actual awkward turtle that I am, I pretend like I wanted to pat dry my hair all along. "That sounds cool"—Welp, did I just use the c-word twice in the same conversation?—"But we're pretty deep into the season and I don't want to jeopardize the team's focus."

"Completely understandable," the woman says in a business tone that matches neither the bunny slippers nor the fancy black dress. "That's why we'll set up the filming equipment in our facilities and work around the team's training schedule. They're used to it, trust me."

I bet, considering how focused they are on their workout

even though this blonde with knockout curves and stunning eyes is in their midst.

I'm going to say yes. Not because she's hot, but because I'm conscious that I have to play nice with the top sponsor and become synonym with the Orlando Wild. People can no longer think Denver Riders when they look at me.

"Fine. Yeah. Sure." I dry my face, hiding the cringe on my face with the towel. "Send us the paperwork."

"Great, thank you for making my job easier," she says in all seriousness and offers her hand out for a very belated handshake.

I make sure that my hand is dry before I return the gesture, wrapping my massive paw around her smaller, more delicate hand. Right as I start debating whether this is getting awkward and long, the woman grabs on tighter.

"Also, one more thing." She pauses. "Actually, two."

I can't help but letting my eyebrows fly. It's the first sign of uncertainty from her throughout this whole interaction. "What's up?"

"Have you told anyone?" she asks like I know what she's thinking.

"Told anyone what?"

Her eyes narrow. She squeezes my hand a notch harder. "About me being the owner's daughter."

Listen, I'm very bad at math—which is fine, because baseball is all about physics—and sure enough, my jock brain can't compute why this is important enough to cause a wrinkle between her eyebrows. "Don't they know?" I ask, testing the one theory I come up with.

"No." She leans closer, lowering her voice to what should sound menacing. "And they better not find out."

With my free hand, I slide the towel down around my neck for her benefit, to see the confusion on my face. "Why's that?"

Smiling in a suddenly too saccharine way she responds, "Not your business."

"Fair, but…" I point at my hands with my lips. "Can I take that back, at least?"

"Sorry." Audrey drops my hand like it's a burning coal and takes a step back. Then another. And she points at somewhere behind her. "Okay, I'm gonna go email the contract to your agent and… yeah."

"Wait." Now that my hands are free to be twitchy, I stuff them in the pockets of my joggers. "What was the second thing?"

"What—Oh, right." Her eyes blaze a trail down to my bare chest, my stomach, and stop shockingly low for someone who is virtually a stranger. She points with her index. "Your pants are about to fall."

With that, she twirls around and leaves.

I glance down and sure enough, my joggers are showing the waistband of my *SPORTY* underwear. As my face flames, I suppose that they'll be happy to hear from the PR lady that I've been a customer all along.

CHAPTER 7
AUDREY

A ginormous package sits outside the front door once I get home from the office. Fortunately, there are no witnesses as I walk up the steps, grinning like the evil clown of a horror movie who's about to commit murder. That's my intention—upon the mailbox that is the bane of my existence. At last I'll be able to replace it for a brand new one.

It's just way larger than I expected. Maybe this will be a job for more than one person. I palm around my pockets until I find my phone and send a text to my roommates, asking when they'll be home. Today is a rest day, so if I want their help I better recruit them today before they join the team on the road tomorrow.

That done, I better empty the damn mailbox one last time before I send it tumbling down the residence's trash container, where it belongs.

I skip around the package at the front and head inside to change into something comfortable and with short sleeves, it's the only way to brave the stifling cold of a June afternoon before the daily monsoon. I grab a tool set I don't know if I'll need, and walk back out to face the enemy.

In all fairness, this inanimate object is the lesser on my list of evils, but is really the only one I can solve.

Now properly armed, I pluck a wrench from the tool set and pry it into the lip of the mailbox door. To be safe, I check around me for any potential baseball players whose eyesight I could potentially jeopardize.

"Coast is clear," I mutter, finding that the only other sign of life is a gecko scampering across the hot sidewalk into a hedge.

Grunting, I pull at the door with all my might. This time the wrench offers enough grip that I don't have to struggle too hard. I don't even lose my balance as it finally opens—no one behind me would've been maimed. It also wouldn't have made me realize that Miguel Machado is a decent guy who just might keep my secret. And if not, I know where he lives.

Kidding. Or am I?

Among the pieces of mail addressed to me is an envelop that looks like it costs about as much as my monthly mortgage, signaling right away that this belongs to my dad's world. I tuck it in the back pocket of my bike shorts so that it can ruin my mood later. I stretch my neck, roll my shoulders, and crack my knuckles. Then I fish for the drill to tackle some screws.

"What are you doing?" a soft voice asks somewhere behind me, and since the last time something like this happened I nearly knocked someone out, I stop cold turkey before checking for the speaker.

It's a girl somewhere in her tweens, she's tall enough to confuse me. She clutches at the straps of a black sparkly backpack and I immediately know she's a connoisseur of taste.

Straightening out, I lower the drill and respond with, "Dismantling my mailbox, and you?"

"Watching you dismantle a mailbox." Her eyebrows rise a little. "What does dismantling mean?"

My lips twitch. I raise my drill and press the trigger once for added drama. "It means bringing down something that no longer serves a good purpose, and it can apply to many things. In this case, a mailbox that refuses to open."

Okay, I didn't think that was a masterful joke that could win awards, but I also wasn't expecting it to cast a shadow over the girl's face. She kicks at the sidewalk concrete with black Converse that are also sparkly and have hot pink laces. I was nowhere near this stylish when I was her age.

"Can school also be dismantled?" she asks in a calm and serious way.

I lose my previous train of thought and look at her more closely. I've only seen her once before, when she walked out next door to retrieve her dad, who I had just accidentally beaten up. So I can't say for sure but… her eyes look red and puffy, like maybe she's been crying. Slowly, I set down my tool to focus on the girl.

"I'm Audrey Winters," I say rather than answering her very pointed question. "I live next door with two other girls. We all work at the Orlando Wild with your dad, actually."

"Okay?" It's clear as day that none of this information means anything to her.

"And you are?" I prod gently.

Smart cookie that she clearly is, she says, "I'm not supposed to talk to strangers."

"That's good." I bob my head and shrug. "But you're also the one who started the conversation. It's only polite to let the other person know your name so they can address you properly."

She grunts and releases her backpack straps to fold her arms. "I'm Martina but I'll kill you if you call me that. I go by Marty."

That's a test if I know one, so I say, "It's nice to meet you, Marty. And to answer your question, generally the people who want to dismantle schools are not the good guys."

"Shucks." Her mouth turns into a little upturned u.

"Are people in your school being mean to you?" I ask with as much tact as one can possibly have with a child, while also having zero experience with children.

"No…" She drifts off, swaying a little in that way that only someone with a lot bottled up inside can. "People are okay, it's just…"

"School work is hard?" I raise my hand in defense. "I'm not judging. I hated like half of my classes because I just didn't get them. Biology was the worst. I assure you I've never once had to bust out the definition of mitochondria."

Marty blinks several times, like trying to make out what kind of adult breed I am. Are all adults supposed to spew pro-mitochondria propaganda?

"Well…" I lean forward just a little, all my attention on what's tumbling out of her mouth next. "It's just…"

"This is worse than a bases loaded, bottom of the ninth game. You're killing me, Smalls."

That makes her expel what is clearly a disappointed sigh, and I almost fear she's going to leave me hanging and turn into her home.

"There's going to be a mother-daughter tea party at school, but I don't have a mom so I'm the only one in my class who can't go." And now that it's finally off her chest, her big brown eyes start watering for what I'm sure is the nth time today.

Oh, shit. What do I do now?

I check my surroundings, trying to find ideas for how to calm down a sad kid. All I can think of is the freaking mailbox. "Hey, what if I distract you for a bit while you help me with this thing?"

One sniff. A swipe at her cheek. "Let me tell my nanny first."

"Yes, good idea."

As she takes herself up to the duplex home next door, I

grab at my cellphone on the other pocket of my shorts and text the group chat with my roommates.

ME

SOS Miguel Machado's daughter came back from school all sad and somehow I've volunteered myself to distract her. What do I do?

Responses come in record time.

DARLING HOPE

Obviously you distract her lol

ME

Thanks, captain obvious

PRINCESS ROSE

Marty? She's a hoot! Logan and I met her at Miguel's welcome party a few weeks ago

But wait a second. What do you mean she came home from school? I thought you were at OUR home, not Miguel's??

ME

Oh

Did I not mention that he's our neighbor?

DARLING HOPE

Wait WHAT

PRINCESS ROSE

EXCUSE YOU

HOW DARE YOU KEEP SUCH A JUICY PIECE OF GOSSIP FROM US

The sound of a door opening and closing pulls me away.

My phone is still buzzing with texts as I tuck it back into my pocket and wait for Marty. Her expression is still the definition of grumpy as she walks over to stop before me.

"Nanny Consuelo said I can be out for an hour before she calls me for dinner and to do my homework. And also that she'll be watching us through the blinds." Then she points at the house where, sure enough, the blinds shake after someone quickly steps away.

"I agree to the terms." I nod in agreement and then point at the mess we're about to make. "I assume you've never used a drill in your life, right?"

"Er, no." Her pretty eyes widen, though they're no longer sad or watery.

I grin, hoping that she can tell I was joking. "It's fine, that's the part I enjoy the best anyway. Just help me hold the evil thing while I unscrew it."

"You got it," she says like a little soldier, and we get to work. I succeed on my mission of distracting her until her dad arrives from training, and the most curious thing happens.

Her grumpiness returns in full force.

CHAPTER 8
MIGUEL

I officially like Consuelo. The second Marty walked home and asked her if she could play outside with a neighbor, Consuelo called me with a full report to ask my opinion. Granted, this time it worked out because I wasn't in the middle of a game, but also because said neighbor turned out to be none other than Audrey Winters-not-Cox.

Even knowing that, I'm unprepared for the sight that greets me as I get home and step off my RAV4. I circle the vehicle slowly, kinda hoping that my presence doesn't attract their notice—if only because someone could lose a limb if I break their concentration. Probably me, with how my record with the blonde goes.

"Okay, I got it as firm as I can," said blonde declares while simultaneously trying to hold a post and keeping as much distance as she can.

My daughter holds a mallet over her head. "Ready?" she asks.

Our neighbor scoffs. "I was born ready. Hit it."

Yeah, no. I'm thankfully still in time to prevent a trip to the hospital.

"How about I do it instead?" I ask from my driveway, and both of them turn to me like I must've teleported here. The shock in their expressions is exaggerated enough that it prompts me to ask, "What?"

"You're kidding, right?" Audrey's face twists in annoyance. "What if you get hurt for real? If that happens there's no way I'm keeping my job. Or my life."

"Right, Dad. Even I know better." My daughter shakes her head like she can't believe me.

I'm equal parts frustrated and amused, which until this moment wasn't a combination I thought possible. Placing my hands on my hips, I say, "What I mean is that I can do the thing by myself, and then there's no risk of someone hammering my hand or something."

Marty lowers the mallet. "Oh."

"No." Audrey shakes her head, the back of her hair swinging around while strands at the front stick to her sweaty face and neck. "I could never ask you to do this for me."

"But you could ask my daughter?"

Awkward silence ensues. I didn't mean it as an attack. Honestly, I just wanted to show her that her concerns are unfounded.

"Um, I didn't mean—"

"You know, you're right." She straightens out, releasing her grip on the post. "I'm just going to wait for my roommates and we'll get this done safely and in no time."

My chest deflates with a deep sigh. I continue my trek to round out the hedges that divide our yard from the sidewalk, and once I'm close enough I motion at my daughter to scoot over. Also, I take the mallet from her just in case. The last thing we need is her dropping it on her foot or something.

"What are you doing?" my neighbor asks as I take in the surroundings.

Her previous mailbox lies disassembled on the grass. The

shiny new one awaits for its rightful place, and it seems like the post that I'm now holding corresponds to the latter. She could've just unscrewed the old mailbox and loaded the new on the old post, but I guess that doesn't matter now.

I grab the top of the post and give it a stir, as if it was a big spoon and the dirt underneath was soup. I figure that if this is the best way to dig an umbrella into beach sand, it may work here. Glancing up at Audrey, I say, "I'm sorry. I didn't mean it as a dig. I just meant that if it's safe enough for my daughter, it's safe enough for me."

Her eyes widen. "Wait, you have a good point. Maybe this wasn't safe for Marty all along."

"I'm fine. I have all my fingers, see?" Marty raises them up for my view.

"It's a happy day." I grin.

Checking for a quick moment, I confirm that the post is as dug up as it's going to get. I reach for the mallet and give it a good whack, just to make sure that the mailbox is gonna stay in place. The bad news is that I've managed to disturb her pretty grass.

"Oops." I kneel down, reaching for the dirt to smoothen it with my hands. Next thing I know, Marty joins me.

We once did something like this, planting some flowers in our old Denver house a couple of years ago. The biggest difference—aside from the fact that Marty wasn't permanently grumpy like she is now—was that we were by ourselves.

I turn around in time to catch our neighbor also sinking to her knees, heedless that she's getting her knees dirty since she's only wearing shorts. Neither of us is wearing gloves, but somehow the one who surprises me about it is Audrey. It's not like I know her, yet I've clearly painted a picture in my mind that was all wrong.

Apparently she's really *this* Audrey, the one that wrestles her mailbox to submission in the dirt, and not the glamorous one that danced to Frank Sinatra with me. Rivulets of sweat trickle down her face like she's been going at this for a while.

"There," my daughter announces, sitting back on her haunches to brush at her hands. "What's next?"

"Now…" Audrey grabs the collar of her T-shirt, smearing dirt all over it as she wipes sweat off her face. She leaves a big streak of dirt on her cheek. "Now we screw the new mailbox on top."

"How's this? I hold it, you screw it, Marty passes along the screws," I suggest. Complaints don't rise immediately, so I take it as agreement. "Vamos."

Now that the post has been defeated, the rest of the work goes smooth and quick. Which is a bit of a bummer when I was starting to have fun. Marty and I stand off to the side, allowing the owner of the brand spanking new mailbox to give it a try and—

The thing squeaks like a rusted door in a horror movie. The three of us cringe at the strident noise.

"Marty," my neighbor says in a dark voice. "Cover your ears."

"Why?"

"Because I'm about to let out some very necessary expletives."

I snort and nudge my kid with my elbow. "How about you run on home to get washed before dinner?"

She grunts but recognizes that this is not a battle she'll win. With one last look of utter displeasure, she marches up to the house. Once she's near the porch, I turn to my neighbor.

"Let it out now."

"This freaking piece of shit." She kicks at the post.

I'm happy to report that it doesn't budge one bit.

"You had one job," she tells the inanimate object, raising a finger to make her point. "You were going to fix my whole life by opening easily."

I almost laugh but manage to turn it into a cough right in time. "Erm, it may still do its job if you just grease up the hinge."

She pulls back, her body relaxing even as her face gets redder. "Good point."

I motion at the mess around us. "Let's pick up for now, and I'll see if I still have a silicone spray somewhere."

"Thanks, you don't have to do that."

"Consider it my thanks for becoming Marty's buddy," I say as I grab the pieces of her old mailbox in my hands.

"Let me take this one." She reaches for the mailbox part, leaving me to carry the heavier post. It's a decent compromise, so I don't challenge it. After a moment, she speaks again. "So, about Marty…"

"Hmm?" I get to the trash cans first so I open one for her.

Grunting, she hefts the mailbox and tosses it inside with gusto. The look on her face is almost gloating as she brushes her hands off. I follow in her example and close the can.

"What about Marty?" I prod, now that we have officially ran out of excuses to be in each other's company. My kid and her nanny are waiting at home for me, and I have no doubt that this woman would rather hop in the shower than spend another moment melting down in this stifling heat.

She takes a deep breath, but it's not because of the climate. "I don't want to be a snitch, so I'm going to let her tell you what's going on, but there's something at school that upset—"

I take a step closer, a tinge of desperation moving me. "She's not getting bullied again, is she?"

"Again?" Audrey's eyes widen.

Now I'm the one releasing a verse of expletives in Spanish. I catch myself in time to not run my dirty hands down my face. "Shit, I thought this was a better school. Why is this happening again to Marty? She—"

"Wait, wait." Audrey leans to the side, appearing in my

field of vision right as it was starting to tunnel. "She's not getting bullied. It's something else."

"Oh." I still. "But she was upset."

"Yes."

"How bad?"

"There may have been some crying."

My eye—the one that is now fully healed—twitches at that. "Sobbing or no sobbing?"

"None that I could hear."

I exhale in relief. "Then it must not be so bad."

"Yeah, so talk with her."

I debate whether to tell her that Marty doesn't really want to talk with me these days, but that would be too much to burden my new neighbor with.

Fortunately, I'm rescued by the arrival of a car that parks by the curb, and Audrey exclaims, "Oh, that's my roommate. I'll see you around, Miguel."

"Right, see ya." As she starts walking away, I recall something. "Wait!" She turns to me and I can't believe how I got used to seeing the dirt smudge on her cheek. "You have some dirt around here." I motion at my face in the same area.

"Thanks." She wipes at it with the back of her arm. I press my lips tight not to laugh but she can tell I'm struggling. "Let me guess," she deadpans, "I made it worse, didn't I?"

"Yup."

"Ugh." She reaches for her T-shirt, except it's probably dirtier than her face is.

"Wait." I tug my T-shirt out of my joggers and turn the fabric around my hand before wiping her cheek with the inside. My neighbor blinks up at me but cooperates, which makes this less awkward for all parties involved. With one final swipe down to her chin, I declare, "There."

Our eyes meet and here's where it gets weird. We're way too close. I can make out each freckle that dusts over her nose, all of which are standing out more and more because it's too hot and also because I just did something incredibly cringy, as Marty would say. And if anyone else saw it, I'll never be able to live it down.

I jump away and raise a hand for a wave. "All right, see ya later neighbor. Thanks for everything!"

"Yeah, you too," she wheezes out.

I pretend like I jog up to my house every day, and not like I'm trying to run away from my embarrassment.

Real smooth, jackass, I tell myself.

CHAPTER 9
AUDREY

Call me a drama queen but when I walk into a door that is swinging closed because a coworker I thought would hold it open, doesn't, and I spill my iced coffee all over my blouse, is the exact moment I realize that today is going to suck.

"Oops," says Otto Berger, one of the therapists in Hope's team, and apparently that's all I'm going to get because he's already walking away.

Sighing, I have no choice but to let it go. It's not that I'm a pushover. Rather, people will find out any time soon that I'm the owner's daughter, and any whiff of attitude from me is going to come back to bite me in my small behind.

However, I do keep a mental tally. The way this jerk acted toward Hope was bad enough to earn him two strikes all at once. Letting a door close on me and spilling my coffee gives him half a strike—and it wouldn't be a strike if it was from literally anyone else. Half more and he'll earn himself the silent treatment from me forever.

After tossing my now empty coffee cup in the trash, I make a sad beeline to the PR and communications area. We always have a surplus of marketing material, and I find a team jersey in my size that can save the day. Unfortunately, I don't know if that fate awaits my formerly cute blouse in a delicate cream color.

"Ugh, freaking Otto Berger," I mutter to myself in the women's bathroom, having swapped tops and now attempting to wash my blouse with hand soap. Who would've thought that purple soap doesn't get coffee stains out?

I return to my cubicle with a sopping blouse I'll try to rescue at home, no caffeine in my system, an overload of annoyance, and zero desire to be here.

Still, since I'm a responsible adult who has bills to pay and integrity—and oddly enough wants to keep both—I boot up my laptop to begin my work day officially. I had actually made an effort with my outfit because I have a teleconference with Amelia Herrera, Miguel Machado's agent, to talk about the *SPORTY* campaign, but surely she won't be weirded out at seeing me wear the team's jersey.

An email at the top of my inbox stops me. For a second I'm transported back to school when I was called to the principal's office. Dad's assistant—who as far as I know isn't aware that we're father and daughter—is summoning me to Dad's office ASAP. It's the four-letter-acronym the one that sends my pulse skyrocketing.

This can only mean one thing—no, not that he's going to scold me or give me detention. Instead, he's probably going to make the big announcement. The one I've been dreading, where he reveals to everyone my best kept secret.

Sighing, I drag my feet all the way up to his office. The facilities have nothing to envy from a Silicon Valley company, with team spirit decor that doesn't border on tacky, open areas for chatting or playing a table game, more monitors than an airport showing clips from games or from the history of the franchise, enough plants to not make the place feel sterile, and more coffee machines than necessary. But the top floor of the admin building, where Dad's office is, boasts of serious money. Rumor has it that he modeled it after an opulent airport in the Middle East—marble, touches of gold, crystal, and priceless art.

I *know* that he did. If only because that's also how he decorated our home when I was growing up.

Well, not home. The house we were forced to live in when all of us were subject to his rule.

His assistant has all the air of a butler. The guy is in his fifties, with white hair and a mustache, and all he's missing is the monocle. He jumps to his feet while wishing me a good morning—glances very briefly at my jersey and dress pants mismatched combo—and opens the door to his boss's office.

Somehow I expect paparazzi to jump out at me, blinding me with camera flashes and overwhelming me with questions. Am I truly the long lost heiress? What made me be lost in the first place? Is it true that I've hidden my identity from everyone? Why does only a random player know and not my friends? What do I think they're going to say when they find out? Shouldn't I have told them myself?

Instead, it's just Dad and another man.

I do a double take. The feeling in my gut that today was going to suck intensifies. I know the guy. Adam, my brother, told me years and years ago to steer clear of him.

The butler assistant closes the door behind me, trapping me in a gilded cage with two hungry wolves.

"Audrey," my dad starts, sweeping a hand toward the much younger guy next to him. "You remember Henry Vos."

Unfortunately, is what I want to answer. Instead, I respond with, "Yes." It comes out drier than burnt toast, and I do nothing to fix it. I almost laugh at the horror that briefly flashes across my dad's face.

Henry Vos just chuckles. "Sassy as always, I see."

There's no mistaking the condescension in his voice. He also comes from a long dynasty of the ultra rich, whose family is just a smidge poorer than my father—and we're talking like maybe half a billion dollars less, which is a staggering amount of money, but just a percentage of each family's assets.

I blink slowly, giving no further indication of how aggravated his sole presence makes me. Adam and Henry were often pitted as rivals, since they were in the same class at school, and heirs to competing little kingdoms. But where my brother, flawed as he was, was genuinely a good person to the core, Henry Vos is the mustache twirling villain who'd rather toss poor people into the fire so long as his train can keep churning. Except he'll do it wearing Zegna and an exclusive cologne designed by the CEO of Hugo Boss, that Henry once bragged to Adam about.

None of that is the real reason why I can't stand him, though. During Adam's funeral, Henry's personal condolences to me included something I'll never forgive him for.

Maybe now that Adam's out of the picture I'll be able to make you my wife, huh?

And that was also the moment I learned why my brother couldn't stand him. Turned out that all along I'd just been an object to Henry.

My fists tighten, bile rising up my throat at the memory just as he starts heading over to me. This is way worse than Dad telling everyone that I'm his long lost daughter. If Henry Vos is here it can only mean one thing.

These two must be making a deal. Over me.

"It's been too long, Audrey," Henry's saying as he approaches. "The good news is that we'll be able to reconnect now that I'm back from Kuala Lumpur."

"Henry was starting a new branch of his father's business in Malaysia," Dad supplies helpfully, like that's supposed to impress me. If he'd given up his riches and name to become a monk I'd actually be impressed.

"Good for you," I mumble, casually stuffing my hands in my pockets right before he reaches out. I side step away from Henry's near circle and face my dad. "So, what did you really call me for?"

Freaking Henry chuckles at the subtle dig, where any other guy with an ego of the size of his would fume. That's why he grosses me out. If at least he was honest, I'd be able to openly tell him where to shove it.

"This is why." Dad motions at the other guy again and my heart stops. "Now that Henry's back, he wants to invest in the team."

"Oh." My voice falters.

"Disappointed that it wasn't you I came back for?" Henry asks me, showing all the pearly whites his parents bought for him. He's all blue eyed and blond—the dirty kind, unlike Dad and I—and for all intents and purposes, an attractive guy. If it wasn't for my brother, I might've become one of Henry's notches on his post.

Now that Adam isn't here, I only have my own means to protect myself with. Dad would gladly throw me at this wolf for his own gain.

I pretend like he didn't speak. "Invest how?" I inquire to Dad.

Henry's the one who answers. "I want to sponsor the team in exchange for ad placement for our new venture, an electrolyte tablet that can be dropped in water to hydrate you after a workout, and also into a glass of vodka for a perfect cocktail."

"Isn't that brilliant?" Dad asks, laughing in rich guy. It's the laugh of someone who can afford bad ideas.

I blink. "Is this finalized or am I here to bring up the potential partnership to the team?"

"It's a done deal." Henry shrugs. "Charlie and I just signed the papers. We just need you to onboard me, maybe give me a tour of the facilities." And here he winks.

Dad snaps his fingers. "That's a great idea. Audrey, why don't you take Henry around? The team is traveling today, so it should be no bother to anyone."

Yeah, it's a bother to me, though. I'd rather eat my coffee stained blouse.

Alas, I know how men like these react upon any female attitude. They're worse than an Otto Berger who would whine to anyone who'd listen. These two would use all their might to lean harder until they break what they want.

I make a big show of checking the time on my phone. "Fine, but I only have twenty minutes until my next meeting." That's actually true. Now I'm even more invested in getting back to my cubicle to call Miguel's agent.

"That should work," Henry says while offering me his arm. "After all, it's not the last you'll see of me."

There's no way he misses the goosebumps that break all over my skin, but I don't know if he understands which kind it is. I don't take his offering and speed walk through the facilities, wishing it would make time go by faster.

CHAPTER 10
MIGUEL

"Will you be okay while I'm gone?"

Marty sighs like she's seventy-years-old and has already lived a life, even though she's just zipping up her sparkly black backpack for school. "You always ask that."

I'm also zipping up my bag—the duffel one I pack as carryon for away series. Departure today is at a reasonable hour, so I didn't have to ask Consuelo to come over early to get my daughter fed and delivered to her school bus safely. I'm taking care of it before I go.

"That's because I always wonder the same," I explain before pointing at her plate. "Finish your breakfast."

This is a household that breaks its fast on arepa with cheese and eggs. Marty's plate is complimented by orange juice and mine by a green protein shake that tastes like death compared to the corn dough sandwich of my native country. Marty twists on her chair back to focus on the food, her now fully loaded backpack sitting next to her on my spot.

Leaving my bags at the door, I return to the kitchen to finish drinking my swamp shake. Yesterday Marty was the most excited I've seen her in a long time after hanging out with our neighbor. I didn't think it was the right time to bring up whatever's going on at school. But my kid isn't a morning person, so asking her right now isn't going to make her morning any worse than it always is.

"So…" It's funny how I have to gather my nerve for something like this. "How are things going on at school?"

She lifts her head from the arepa in her hands, watching me as I round the kitchen island. "School is okay."

"Are you making new friends?"

She shrugs.

"Give it time. Sometimes it takes a while for people to open up to you."

Shit. I walked myself into a conversational wall.

I let her munch for a while, buying myself some time to devise a new approach. But even though my brain races with possibilities, I'm modest enough to admit that I'm only really smart at the game of baseball and nothing else, and finesse requires wits that I just don't have. I end up going for the very direct approach.

"Anything difficult at school?"

She gives another long suffering sigh and sets the last of her food down on the plate. "Did she tell you?"

"Tell me what?" I tilt my head, a moment later realizing that if I really wanted to seem innocent, what I should've questioned was the who and not the what.

Her little mouth arcs with displeasure. "I didn't want to worry you."

"Do you not know me?" I cross my arms over the counter, lowering myself closer to her eye level. "All I ever do is worry about you, chiquita."

It embarrasses her when I call her *little one*, especially because she's always the tallest girl in her classroom—even over the boys, since they're still not teens. But what can I say? She's always going to be the tiny bundle of farts and puke I used to hold in my arms.

She pokes at her food with her finger, avoiding my eyes as she speaks. "There's going to be this thing at school that I'd like to go to…"

"Hmm?" My shoulders relax. That doesn't sound like much trouble at all. Of course I'll let her go to a school day trip or a pajama party with responsible parents or—

"But I can't, because I don't have a mom."

I freeze. You could hear a pin drop.

Finally I break. "Wait, what?"

"It's a mom and daughter tea party at the start of the new year. It's a school tradition," she says, her voice softer, like she's about to cry.

The swamp protein shake in my stomach threatens to spill over.

Marty has a mom—she's just in Doctors Without Borders, and last I checked was based out of Cambodia.

Lauren Smith showed up as a beautiful and fun woman at a nightclub. She was with other med school friends and I was with some teammates in the minors, riding a high after a commanding win against another team. One thing led to the next, and by morning we had no idea that we had just made the best mistake of our lives.

We agreed to see each other again casually until she was supposed to travel abroad for a semester, except that the morning sickness started hitting pretty early.

That changed everything. I considered giving up my baseball career, and the reason that didn't happen is because I'm not very good at anything else. There was a better chance of me being able to support my new family if I stuck to it.

Meanwhile, Lauren made the difficult decision to stay home rather than pursue her assignment abroad, and we settled into a somewhat domestic life for roughly a year, through the delivery, and the first few months of Marty's life. We had to start on the rotation of nannies since then so Lauren could return to med school in Denver, and so I could travel with with team.

Everything seemed to be working at first. Yes, we were chronically tired from bad sleep, my performance at games wasn't the best, and Lauren was exhausted all the time. We started considering marriage, even though I was just twenty-one and Lauren three years older, and we probably would've gone through with it if it wasn't for a big elephant in the room.

Lauren's post-partum depression.

She hid it from me at first, which was probably a sign that a marriage between us wouldn't have worked. The truth outed itself gradually—or perhaps I was too dense to notice it quickly enough. We had to call it quits when it became clear that she couldn't carry on with this life that she hadn't chosen.

Anyone would argue that I also hadn't, but I did recognize that I had it easier. I was still doing what I did best, traveling with the team and growing my career—even getting a lucrative first chance at the majors. Lauren was just as ambitious, but all her plans were stalling. She wasn't a silver spoon and all the debt she had already accumulated at med school was going to sit on her shoulders unrewarded.

So the marriage plans fell through, I let Lauren go for her own health. I figured that would be a better example of caring about others for our daughter down the line.

I became Marty's only parent, and my support system has consisted of a steady rotation of paid nannies and occasional visits from her grandparents from Venezuela.

I don't really regret being irresponsible during a night at a club where I met the mother of my daughter, because otherwise I wouldn't have the best thing in my entire life. But I do constantly beat myself over the fact that I alone am not enough for Marty. I can't fill Lauren's hole. And I can't spend as much time with her as she deserves when I'm too busy making sure that she lacks nothing. I'm simultaneously a decent father and a failure.

Right now, the pendulum swings hard toward the second one.

I try to temper myself and not show any reaction, but on the inside all I feel is a cold hand squeezing my stomach and pushing my breakfast up my throat.

"What if I go as your mom?" I ask with a thick voice.

She shakes her head, eyes cast down. "It's supposed to be girls only."

"And Consuelo?" I insist with a smidge of hope.

Marty shrugs. "Maybe? But she's just my nanny. I'm still going to be the only one without a mom."

I doubt it. I'm sure there's at least one more kid who is an orphan or with divorced parents and a mom who lives across the country. But even when that can be true, it doesn't negate my daughter's hurt.

What I'm about to ask is just a Band-Aid, but that's all I can offer her. "Isn't that better than missing out altogether?"

A.k.a. *isn't settling better than nothing?*

That's not one of the life lessons I ever wanted to pass along to my daughter. I don't play at the top of elite big leaguers just for my own self satisfaction. Yet it's not like I can produce a new mom for Marty out of the woodwork.

She lifts her little shoulders again and they stay quite high the whole time as I walk her to the bus. "I'll call the school and make the arrangements, okay?" I promise her as we wait by the curb, her tiny hand in mine. I pat it with my other hand, like I'm making an arepa.

"Okay…" she says, her usual grumpiness missing in action. I give her a big, sloppy kiss on the top of her head that would normally send her kicking and shrieking away from me, and she even lets me stay with her until she climbs aboard the bus.

I watch as it drives away, my heart hammering painfully just as I pull out my cellphone to call the school.

It takes a while to connect with someone, maybe because it's still too early, or simply because I'm being impatient, or simply because one can't always get what one wants.

But my mood comes crashing down even further when, instead of hearing an easy yes, what I get instead is, "I'm so sorry, but our policy for safety reasons is that only women with a proven kinship can join this event."

CHAPTER 11
AUDREY

There comes a time in every woman's life where she has to spend all her patience putting up with one man's shit.

That might as well be my biography, except this time around the culprit isn't my dad directly—indirectly, yes. He's the one inflicting me with this pain deep down. However, I'm specifically referring to Henry Vos here.

Now that the sponsorship contract has been signed, Henry has been coming to the Orlando Wild facilities like he has an employee ID, and Dad has allowed it. I'm currently trapped in a meeting room with him and my boss, and Karen is positively salivating about being in the presence of a guy whose face and other body parts have consistently been in tabloids since before it was legal for him to be photographed that way.

Look at that. I found the one thing that my father did right by Adam and I. He always managed to keep the paparazzi away from us, probably by wiring hefty sums to the tabloids directly. Otherwise, Karen would already know that I'm the team owner's daughter, heiress to a ridiculous fortune, just like the guy yapping across the table from us.

"—Do you think?" he asks with the gloating expression of someone who believes he just spat out a literal nugget of gold from his mouth.

"That's a phenomenal idea." Karen lets out a twinkling laugh I had never heard coming from her.

I purse my lips because there's no way I can tell them both where to stuff it when, in theory, they haven't earned such treatment *right now*. But they're both perfect for each other: apparently polite but vicious individuals on the inside.

"We could assign a cubicle in our office for you," she offers, leaning over the table because she can't stop her own impulse of reaching closer to him.

That's when my brain decides to pay attention, not to what she just agreed to, but what it implies about everything I zoned out about.

So, Henry coming and going wasn't a coincidence. He wants to have full access to the facilities. Karen's agreement is a joke she's the only one who isn't in on; Dad will support this in a heartbeat. They're really trying to socialize me to Henry, huh?

Or worse, is he trying to negotiate a buyout of the Orlando Wild from my dad? Because if that's the case…

If so… I'm going to have to scorch earth. There's no way I can let Dad do that.

My knee bounces and I check my watch. In twenty minutes I have a realistic excuse to high tail it out of here and not see any of these two people for a while. It's the one time slot I found in Miguel Machado's packed itinerary to discuss the logistics of the *SPORTY* shoot.

Unfortunately, my silence attracts their attention and it's Henry who hones in. "What do you think, Audrey? Would you also like to see more of me around here?"

Karen glances between us like we're in a tennis match and ma'am, this is a baseball facility, there'll be none of that.

I grit my teeth. I wish he'd have phrased that in literally any other way. No one is supposed to guess that we know each other, and there's no doubt my boss is starting to suspect something.

I channel my best impression of an ice cube when I say, "Why does my opinion matter in particular? I'm just one of many employees."

"Right." Karen offers more of that girly laugh and discreetly smacks my arm under the table. "I'm sure everyone in the building will be happy to have you around for this collab, it's going to be fantastic."

It's going to be a pain in the ass, is what.

Henry passed around free samples of his product yesterday, and the entire crew that composes the marketing, communications, and PR staff tried them while we watched the Orlando Wild on screens, playing the last game of the away series in Seattle. The biggest bummer of all is that his electrolyte tablets are actually tasty on their own, and even better in vodka. It *will* be a good collab for the team both financially and for the image, and Dad made it look like I'm the one who got the account, so I'll be getting a hefty bonus out of this. On top of that, the apple flavor was particularly good.

All of this makes me feel like I'm betraying my own values, ugh.

Henry chuckles. Either he can read my thoughts through the deadpanned expression on my face, or he's just amused by my obvious disdain of him. Like it's a little challenge.

I honestly don't know what tactic will work best on him, if acceptance or indifference. Somehow I have the feeling that neither of them will work *for me*.

"This has been very productive, but I'm afraid I have to leave early to prepare for my next appointment," I say with a heavy dose of sarcasm that makes Karen give me a sharp glance. From her point of view, yes, I'm being a completely unprofessional employee. I'm only slightly sorry.

"Great," she chirps, clapping her hands. "How about we start setting you up with a work space?"

"That would be amazing." He pulls himself up while buttoning his Tom Ford blazer at the same time.

I push away from the table, collect my iPad and Apple Pencil, and act ruder than I ever have by leaving without another word. This will get me an earful from Karen later, and honestly I'll accept it. I just don't want to spend any more of my energy on this guy today, especially now that I know I'll have to preserve it for however many days it takes him to play his little game here.

But what is exactly is Henry playing at?

I need to get the tea out of my dad. But how? I've spent years trying to cut off contact with him. I can't just walk up to him with big eyes and a pouty mouth and ask for information.

Also, I'm not prepared for what I might hear.

I bite my thumbnail as I walk back to my cubicle, not hard enough to damage it, but just to have something to do with my mouth that isn't screaming. Parking at my chair, I fix my eyes on the hanging plants inside my cubicle and try to look at things from a different perspective.

Maybe I should just start applying for jobs elsewhere. My friend Camila has extended an offer to work with her at *SPORTY* that, in her words, never expires. Then everyone around me will be new, and they won't even notice my name going from Audrey Winters back to Audrey Cox.

But I also quite like the life I've made for myself here, and the friends I've made.

What would Rose and Hope think of all this? I'm sure they'd say I'm being a fool—because, yes—but they'd also ask me how they could help. And them taking on a fight against my powerful father is the very last thing I want.

Like a plant, though, I need some hydration. I grab my tumbler and find it empty, which gives me a great excuse to pace. With my iPad, I make an excursion out of the communications department toward the nearby kitchenette. Miguel agreed to meet me around here, so I'll be ready in case he shows up while I'm in the middle of panicking.

A small group of people walk out of the kitchenette together, masking the sound of someone behind me. Only when I'm filling in my tumbler with ice does he show himself. By leaning against the counter like he owns the place.

"You don't have to be so caustic," Henry says, folding his arms. "That's actually what's going to make people think there's something going on between us."

I force myself to keep my attention ahead. "Is there? Something going on between us that I don't know about?"

Screw asking Dad. I'll try to get info out of this jerk.

"Would you like there to be?"

Damn it. Of course he won't cooperate.

I have enough ice now, so I stop dispensing and sadly turn to him. He's in the way of the water dispenser. "Of course not. Now, if you'll excuse me…"

He doesn't take the hint. Rather, he moves closer.

I'm so confused that I don't react at first. Guys don't just get in my personal bubble very often.

But when it becomes clear that he's going to continue, possibly until there's physical contact, I take a step back. Then another. And a larger one. And it's the one that makes me bump into a wall behind me, which Henry takes advantage of by corralling me against it, placing his hands against the wall until I can go nowhere.

"What are you doing?" I ask in a very low voice.

"Flirting." He lifts the corner of his mouth. "That's what I'm here for. And also for the brand sponsorship, I guess."

My mind races. Out of the two possibilities I had in mind,

one being that Henry was after the team, and the other that he was after me, somehow I wouldn't have bet my money on the latter.

"Why? I'm the only person in this building who knows the real you." I frown like my stomach isn't churning with sour bile. I clutch at my tumbler harder, a pastel green Stanley I've covered with Orlando Wild stickers that I'm not afraid of using as a weapon. "Can't you just go flirt with Karen instead?"

"That's why. I don't have to fake being nicer than I actually am around you." He leans lower and I glue myself to the wall. "I'd rather have a thrilling marriage with you than a bland one like our parents."

"Marriage?" I exclaim, my jaw dropping in uncertainty.

"You didn't know?" I hate the amusement that expands in his face. Now his whole mouth smiles and while his eyes also show a glint of amusement, it's a rather predatory one. "Charlie told my dad and I about your little deal with him over golf, and I might have made one of my own."

"No. Shut up. Move away." I shake my head and push against him.

He doesn't budge. "Think about it. You change your last name to mine, get your inheritance *and* mine, and you won't have to deal with your dad anymore if you don't want to. We'll be too powerful together."

"Move, I said," I all but growl, pushing at him hard enough to bruise.

"Audrey?"

The new voice is what makes Henry stumble back, and I manage to free myself from the physical trap.

Miguel Machado stands at the entrance of the kitchenette in his training uniform, stained with reddish infield dirt down the entire left side of his body, and his cap turned backward. His eyes are a light brown under the white office light, yet they darken as he glances at Henry and me, back and forth.

Relief washes over me. He's early, I'm sure of it. But if he'd been on time, who knows what Henry could have done. Or me. I could've smashed my tumbler against his head for all I know.

I nearly trip on my own feet as I rush over to the baseball player. "Miguel! It's so great to see you. Are you ready for our meeting?" I ask with a hell of a lot more pep than I intended.

Without tearing his eyes from the other guy, Miguel says, "Yes, of course. Sorry I'm late."

But he's not. And in my nervous state I almost blurt it out and blow it, when he's just trying to help me.

Swallowing hard, I grab at his arm—which I would never, under normal circumstances, do to a player. "Not a problem. Let's go." And without further ado, Miguel lets me lead him away at a punishing pace.

CHAPTER 12
MIGUEL

My spidey senses are tingling—and by tingling, I mean roaring. If I'd been a minute too late, I think I might've ended up witnessing sexual harassment. It already looked like a close cousin when I arrived, unless it was fully reciprocated.

I don't think it was. Audrey's face was pale and her eyebrows creased when she walked out of the circle of that guy's arms. That's not how she'd have looked like if she was enjoying the attention, or even if she was embarrassed about being caught with a boyfriend at work.

She also wouldn't be power walking away as fast as her dainty little shoes allow her. My shoes squeak against the floor while hers click-clack, which to me is the sound of uncomfortable footwear.

We bypass a couple of departments that are enclosed by glass and house mazes of cubicles, which leaves few witnesses. I'm sure the weird guy is watching, though, but I'm going to pretend like he doesn't exist.

If I turn and don't like the look on his face, I might do something to get me suspended.

Audrey pushes against a metal door and the air abruptly changes to something that feels like a humid hair dryer—also know as the great Florida outdoors. I turn my cap around, protecting my eyes from the relentless sun with the bill, until I get distracted by how her hair positively glows under the sun. Rather, it's like the sun descended to rest on her head.

Finally she releases my arm and keeps walking. I take a look around. I got a tour of the entire facilities when I joined the team but I don't remember this place. It's much larger than just a balcony, yet it's on the second floor of three, therefore it's not the rooftop. There are benches and plants all around, like this is genuinely somewhere that employees can hang out. Audrey sets her things down on a bench by the fence and leans her arms on it. Kicking my feet into gear, I join her and look down.

Ah, I know where we are now. Literally below us is the entrance to the admin building, and below us is the sprawling employee parking lot.

"Aren't you going to ask?"

I turn to Audrey. Her face is pinched and it takes me a second to figure out that it's not out of annoyance. The sun is hitting her right in the face. I remove my cap and reach over to place it on her head, lowering the bill so it shadows her face. She stays still even as I shift away and also lean against the fence.

"Do you want me to?" I volley back.

"I don't know," she responds in a low voice. "But I probably would. The scene you walked into wasn't normal and it's enough to make anyone curious."

"I did walk into our best pitcher and our only female therapist making out earlier," I say, trying for levity. It doesn't get even a twitch of her lips out of her, so I change tack. "I can lend you my ear if you want, but if you don't, I'm also good with just staying in silence. Or we can start our meeting instead."

Audrey casts a little glance at me. "Let's do that."

She pulls away from the fence and retreats to the bench, retrieving her iPad before she takes a seat. I turn and raise my arms to rest them over the fence, watching as she fires up the device and taps at the screen. My cap obscures her face as she looks for something on the iPad, and she makes a little *ah hah* sound.

Her face lifts but her words get stuck in her throat.

I raise my eyebrows when the silence extends further. Clearly she still needs a moment to compose herself.

Instead, Audrey sets the iPad aside again, knocking her tumbler and somehow not sending it tumbling down the floor, pun intended. "Fine, I'll talk."

"Are you sure?"

"Yes." Her face sets in stubborn lines. "You've already proven quite good at keeping secrets, anyway."

I bob my head in gratitude. I like being a man of my word. "I'm all ears and no mouth."

"You just talked, though."

"I mean"—I interrupt myself to snort—"That I'll listen and not say a word of this conversation to anyone."

"Ah." Audrey squirms and settles her arms on her lap. She's in a simple dress with a jean jacket, which looks surprisingly good with my cap on her head. "That was Henry Vos, an acquaintance of my dad, and a new sponsor for the team."

I make a humming sound from my throat so she knows I'm paying attention to what she's saying. She doesn't have to know that I'm also paying attention to her shapely legs. Good genes.

"I've never liked the asshole," she says, and there's enough anger in her voice now that I stop checking out her gams. "He's the kind who takes no for a challenge and not for the answer it is by itself."

"Wait." I stand up straight. "Did he do something to you?"

This makes her look up sharply, like she detected something in my voice that alarmed her. "Well, not this time."

"When?" I ask roughly. "When did he hurt you?"

"No, no." Audrey jumps to her feet, hands extended out. "It wasn't like that. He didn't hurt me physically—"

"Emotionally?" I tilt my face down and a strand of my hair falls over my eye. "Because that still counts."

She expels a harsh breath. "I guess. He tried to hit on me at my brother's funeral."

Every muscle in my body locks as tight as granite.

I replay the words in my head because I couldn't process them the first time. I didn't know that Audrey had a brother and lost him, but for someone—anyone—to be inappropriate during a moment like that?

What the hell?

Then I say it aloud.

"I know." She shakes her head, lifting her arms to cross them. "But trust me, I told him where he could shove it and I didn't see him again for years. Until now."

"Why now?" I can feel my lip twisting.

Audrey closes her eyes and tilts her head back like she's running out of patience just thinking about it. "Apparently my dad and Henry want me to be the next Mrs. Vos."

A beat goes by. Another. A third.

"What?" My jaw drops into the universal sign of *huh?* "Is this a telenovela?"

Deadpanned, she responds, "Yes, that is exactly what my life is. You see, I was trying to cut contact off with my dad when he decided to buy this team, that I was already working for. And it was fine—I was fine—as much as one can be near a father who traumatized the hell out of you, until he was about to fire Hope for dating Cade, and Rose for defending them on the team's social media account. So I had to make a deal with him so he'd leave them alone, and I think this is finally how he's planning to cash out."

Her nostrils flare as she finishes, and after much gesturing around she stays frozen while pointing an angry finger at the floor. The whole speech takes less than a minute with how fast she speaks, but somehow I was able to catch every single word.

"Whoa."

"Exactly." She snarls, throwing her hands in the air in exasperation. "Who else has to put up with something like this? It's ridiculous, it's bizarre, it's… it's…"

Her chest rises and falls. She looks up at me, not hiding that her chin is trembling and her eyes are watering. I have to use a hell of a lot of willpower to not pull her into my arms for a hug. I know that she needs one, but she also just got harassed by some asshole. I won't make any moves that she doesn't expect.

And so I ask, "What do you want me to do?" Audrey blinks hard, and the first few tears start to roll down her cheeks, splotchy with angry red. "Do you want me to just listen? Or call them every name under the sun? Or punch them in the face? Or hug you?"

She sniffs. "Why would you do any of those things for me? We're strangers."

"Are we?" I tilt my head to the side. "Here I thought we were on our way to being friends."

Lips still trembling, she says, "That's true. You did forgive me for punching you in the eye."

Meanwhile, I have to bite my lips not to smile. "See? That's what friends do."

A little snort escapes from her nose, but she doesn't deny it. She wipes her face with the back of her hands and moves away, which confirms that she doesn't want a hug. Instead, she takes a seat back on the bench and pats the empty spot beside her. I lower myself beside her, allowing enough space between us to feel comfortable, even if it means one of my butt cheeks is hanging in the air.

"Thanks for listening and also for getting upset on my behalf, that's enough for me."

Yeah, not for me. But I don't have a right to press.

I clasp my hands over my lap. "So, what are you gonna do now?"

"I don't know. I could get another job…" She drifts off, looking into the blue sky that's only marred by a few white streaks of cirrus clouds. I learned that a couple of years ago when I was helping Marty with her homework.

"I sense a but," I prod gently.

"I really like my friends."

I nudge her with my elbow. "Including me?"

"Yes, including my newly made friend, Miguel Machado," she says in such a dry tone that I can't help chuckling. For the first time today, it makes her mouth quirk with amusement, though. "And also, why should I uproot my life over this jerk?"

"Damn right. He's the one who should get packing."

"Exactly!" She smacks her thighs. "But how? How do I make him go away permanently? Like, I can't believe I'm going to say this, but this is the one time I've ever regretted being single."

"Huh? I'm not making the connection there."

She twists to face me, bending her leg over the bench. "Don't you get it? If I was already spoken for, these two wouldn't be trying to use me for a transaction, which is ironic because that's why I've always wanted to stay single. So I don't have to be manipulated by men."

"Now I can't believe I'm going to say this, but then… Why don't you just lie?"

She blinks up at me.

So I clarify. "Say you have someone."

"They'll want to know who it is." Her eyebrows crease.

"Lie about that too." I shrug, grinning. "Make someone up. He's 7 feet tall, a scientist for NASA, and you only see each other during the weekends. Bam."

"7 feet tall?" she asks, her mouth remaining open in confusion.

"I thought you'd be more impressed that he's a NASA scientist."

Audrey smacks me on the arm softly. "Stop. Unfortunately, it's not that simple. My dad alone is like a dog with a bone. He'll hire a private investigator to find out every detail of my alleged boyfriend if I don't give him enough satisfactory information. And I can't just magic a real one out of thin air."

That makes something click, but it's too weird to say it. I close my mouth and my teeth make a clacking sound that catches her attention.

Now she's looking at me funny, and I feel funny, and the thoughts in my head are funny—but not in a ha ha way, in an I-better-not-say-what-I'm-thinking way or else she's going to think that I'm as creepy as the Henry guy. But the idea keeps mocking me because, with different words, I had the exact same thought a few days ago when I found out that only a woman who is related to my daughter can join her for her school event.

I jump to my feet and pace away. "Nah," I say to myself. I grab onto the cross at my neck, and it's the only thing that keeps me from freaking out.

"What?" she asks from behind me, still at the bench.

"Never mind, we'll find another solution."

"Miguel, *what?*"

I stop pacing with my back to her. Slowly, I glance over my shoulder. "You won't like it."

"Trust me, I'll like staying curious even less."

I run a hand down my face and place my hands on my hips in the quintessential dad-pose. Leaning my head back to face the sky, I ask it to give me a sign about whether I should say this or not. An airplane flies overhead, and if that's the sign I don't know what it means.

Click-clacks take Audrey to stand before me again. She copies my stance down to the width of her feet. "Spill."

I draw in a deep breath. "I also have a problem."

"I'm all ears and no mouth," she repeats my own words.

I tap my fingers against my hipbones. "Marty told me why she was upset."

"Oh?" That makes her entire demeanor change. If anything, she looks even more worried now.

"Yeah, there's a school event that requires her mom so Marty can attend. But her mom is in Cambodia."

Audrey does a double take. "Not exactly around the corner."

"Right. So I asked the school if Marty's nanny could take her spot, and I was told no. Only women with proven kinship can join, for safety reasons."

"Whatever does that mean?" Audrey's face scrunches up.

"The student's mom or stepmom, an aunt, an older sibling, something like that. And Marty doesn't have any of those around here."

"Wow, that—" Audrey stops herself. Swallows. "You're not thinking—"

I jump backward, raising my hands up. "I told you it was going to sound creepy! We don't have to—"

"Wait." She blinks fast and I can almost see her doing some complicated math in her brain.

I scoff. "Forget it. The last thing I want to do is add myself to the list of creeps in your life. That's just not how I roll. I have a daughter too, you know?"

"Can I think about it?"

I clamp my mouth shut and look at her like she's the one

who has lost her mind, even though the wild idea was all mine. "You're not serious."

"I'm desperate. If I don't come up with another solution, this might have to be it."

"I—" Mierda, I'm about to say something even worse. "Okay?" It comes out more as a question because honestly I don't know what I'm doing.

CHAPTER 13
AUDREY

"Come inside, Barbie. That hat is not enough to keep you from frying."

I snort and just turn over my shoulder. Rose takes one peek at the visible lather of sunblock all over my face and starts chuckling. Yes, I look like a little kid whose overprotective mom went a bit too hard on the sun protection.

But this is a trick I learned from a severe sunburn I got when I was about ten, after sitting with my parents and my brother at a balcony seat in Monaco for the Grand Prix. The adults didn't mind the sun or the heat because they had alcohol to keep them entertained. Meanwhile, I was still in my obedient phase so when I was told *sit here*, that's literally all I did, and my chair was the one lucky spot that was in the sun the whole day. I probably owe half of my freckles to that occasion alone.

Yeah, yeah. I know. Boo freaking hoo.

"The plants won't water themselves," I explain in my driest tone.

Rosalina shakes her head, glorious curls framing her face

delicately. "You do know that there's practically a daily monsoon in the Central Florida summers, right?"

"Not this week, according to the weather app." I shift to hose the next potted plant. "Besides, it relaxes me."

"What are you stressed about?"

The way she asks makes me feel a little guilty, because there's absolutely no ulterior motive behind her question. Rose is clever and inquisitive, attributes that anyone would use to gain one cutthroat victory after the next in the way that my dad does business.

In contrast, Rose is one of the most genuine people I've ever met. If she asks you something, it's because she really wants to get to know you deep down. It's her secret sauce for making one viral video after the next for the team's social media, because she has the talent to bring out the truest form out of everyone. No wonder someone as closed off as Logan Kim fell for her so hard.

But I'm a vault.

More than once I've considered sitting Hope and Rosalina down for too-boozy margaritas, Trader Joe's snacks, our Costco blankets, and telling them everything.

And I mean *everything*—from the sunburn that happened out of parental neglect, to how my brother started sampling Dad's booze stash since he was a tween because he was also neglected, to how our parents still ignored him even when Adam was showing serious signs of addiction in his teenage years, to how that led to his death behind the wheel, and how that was the catalyst for me to finally leave home and become a family of one.

Also, to how I no longer feel alone since they've become my friends.

I bite my lip. Talking about all that would still not resolve the big issue for me—and non issue for literally anyone else—

that I can't find a way to cut my dad off without putting them at risk.

They'd kill me for it, and so I have to solve this on my own.

Or… or I take the lifesaver that Miguel casually threw at me.

I stiffen when I notice I'm practically drowning one plant, and move on to the next one. Conscious that Rose has been patiently waiting for me to say something, I break the silence with "just work. There's a new sponsor that is a pain in the ass and I wish he'd go away."

"I heard through the grapevine that he's some rich guy." I roll my eyes but she doesn't see that, and she adds, "Could he be brother-in-law material?"

I manage the feat of spraying my own feet, but even that isn't anywhere as annoying as the sudden urge to barf all over the backyard deck. "Ew! Don't curse me like that. I sincerely wish I could take back every year of my life I've known him for." Especially that moment during Adam's funeral.

When there's no response to that diatribe, I shut off the water hose just to confirm that she's not speaking and I just can't hear her. I find her looking at me in confusion, though.

"So you knew the rich guy from before?"

Oh. Crap. I did not intend to reveal that little bit. I was just so offended at the concept of getting together with that turd that I babbled.

I snap my mouth shut, schooling my expression while on the inside, I flip through any reasonable explanation I can give that won't wake up the curiosity of this friendly reporter.

Fortunately for me, some noise attracts our attention. It's not Hope coming to the rescue—she's with the team tonight. Rose's man is still recovering, so she's making a quick pit stop after work to change before going out for dinner with him.

The one approaching us is none other than our neighbor— little Machado, that is.

She slides her home's back door shut and comes with full purpose. Rose and I exchange a glance that seems to say, *are we in trouble or…?* This ten year old girl all but struts toward us, carrying some school tomes under one arm, and a Kuromi pencil case in her other hand.

"Hi," she says standing before us, watching my hose drip pitifully as Rose scratches her head.

She's the one who recovers to say, "Hi, sweetie. How are you doing?"

The kid responds in full honesty. "I'm about to pull my hair out, and you?"

Shocked, Rose pats her own hair protectively. "I'm good the way I am, thank you for asking."

I mask a snort with a cough. "What's got you so frustrated, Marty?"

"This." Her expression twists even more as she lifts up her books. The word *math* is written in bold, red letters that are unmistakable.

"Ah."

"I see."

Marty tries to fold her arms but fails, since they're busy. "Nanny Consuelo is good at many things. She makes a mean mondongo"—I blink at the unfamiliar word that she slides in with ease—"And is very nice, but she also can't do math."

"I'm sorry, sweetie, I'm a journalism major." Rosalina raises her hands in defense. "Let me know when you need to write an essay or something that's more about words, okay?"

They all look at me.

"I'm no rocket scientist." I shrug.

"Can you do fractions?" Marty rounds her eyes in a big, hopeful expression that has nothing to envy of the Shrek cat.

"I—er…" There's no way I can tell this cute kid no when she's looking at me like I'm her last resort. "I may need a moment to brush up on it before I try to help."

"Yes!" She pumps her pencil case-holding fist in the air.

Rose sends me an amused smile. "Surely this will keep your mind off your mysterious worries, huh?"

*

It works like a charm. Not only is my mind off my weird conundrum, and not only did I manage to evade capture from Rose's curiosity, but my stomach is also singing with joy after eating the most incredible soup I've ever had in my life—the famous mondongo—and I'm fully focused on defeating Marty's homework.

"I remember now," I declare after reading her textbook chapter like three times. We're sitting together at her kitchen table, while nanny Consuelo loads the dishwasher. "We used to do two big Cs like this to know what the operation was like."

I grab a loose piece of paper and jot down two random fractions that are going to be divided, drawing a big C from the top number to the very bottom one—the fourth—and then a smaller c between the middle numbers.

Marty leans closer, eyes wide like I'm showing her what stardust is made of. "And you do that every time?"

"Yep, until you don't need to draw the Cs anymore because you know exactly what to do." I slide her textbook with the math problems back to her. "Try it."

"Hmm." She gets to work, sticking her tongue out the corner of her mouth.

I smile. What a little weirdo.

Something grabs my attention from the corner of my eye. Consuelo looks down quickly at the glass that she's rinsing before putting it in the dishwasher rack. I push away from the table and get up.

"Can I help you with anything?" I ask the older woman once I reach her.

"It's fine, mija. I got it." I've been around enough Latina friends to know what mija means, and this woman is so grandmotherly that I almost melt.

"I would love to help. You did feed me for free, after all," I insist.

"Okay." She glances around. "Then, can you help me put the leftovers away?"

"Yes, ma'am." I start flipping cabinets open until I find some airtight containers and go to town distributing the leftover soup.

"You're very good with the kiddo," the woman says besides me, as she collects more used utensils from over the stove.

"I am?" I ask, not because I'm fishing for compliments but because I'm genuinely surprised.

She leans closer to whisper. "She seems to get along better with you than even her dad."

I shake my head. "In my experience, it's a daughter's duty to be a pain in the neck to her dad. Marty's just carrying on a long legacy."

"He's a pretty good fellow, though," Consuelo says, passing me a kitchen towel when I spill a bit of the soup on the marble countertop. "I don't actually understand why they don't get along when he loves her so much."

A little groan pulls our attention behind us. Marty's facepalming with gusto, and it's not because her homework is frustrating. "Dad is so embarrassing," she says.

Consuelo turns to me slowly, the wrinkles at the corners of her eyes intensifying with her amusement. Pretty sure I look the same.

"How so?" I prod with a light tone of voice, even though I'm curious as hell to see what ammo I can use to tease the unsuspecting All-Star.

"He's just so…" Marty makes the universal expression for yuck. "*Sappy.*"

Of all the things I could've expected, that one wasn't it.

Does she know that pitchers tremble when Miguel walks up to the plate? That he makes outfielders move back without even noticing that they're anticipating a canon blast from one of the most powerful hitters in the history of the sport? Does she have any idea how much my father had to shell out to entice Miguel to join our team?

And also, does she know that he's this untouchable giant everywhere else, but is a sap only for his baby daughter?

I think it's the cutest freaking thing. I wish my dad had cared a fraction of this for me.

"Besides," Marty adds, lowering her hands as she looks on at us. "I really hate this thing that he does…" Consuelo and I lean toward her, two very curious cats. "You know, where he tries to also be my mom because I don't have one."

Well, there goes Consuelo's and my amusement. That's just heartbreaking.

Tentatively, I say, "I heard that he tried to talk your school into letting Consuelo or him go to the tea party with you."

"I know. He promised he would." She looks down at her scribbles and pushes around her mechanical pencil. "But it doesn't matter. I'm not going."

I tuck my tongue against my cheek.

It's been at least a week since she first mentioned this, and clearly the poor kid can't stop thinking about it, which means she really wants to go. She doesn't want to be the odd one out, the kid who's different, the one everyone will point at and pity.

I've been there, albeit for an entirely different, also heartbreaking reason. It wasn't like my acquaintances were actually my friends, but they endured me well enough so they could hang out around my brother, who was the real star of the show. After he was gone, their tolerance turned into pity, and then into condescension and bullying. According to Miguel, his daughter has already gone through that. It would suck if it happens again.

I know what to do now. It's feeding two birds with one scone. Miguel's a good person, and he's also well off. He has no reason to get weird or greedy if I go along with his idea. Marty will get to not miss out, and maybe that gets him to score some points with her too.

And my own problem will go *poof*.

"Hmm," I say, and nothing more.

I need to talk with Miguel first. If he's still on board with the wacky plan of us pretending to be in a relationship for our own purposes, he'll first have to clear it with the school to ensure that I can escort Marty. And *then* we'll tell her that she's not going to be the odd one out after all. Not on my watch.

CHAPTER 14
MIGUEL

Being mic'ed up at a game is both an honor and a curse. Consuelo had just sent me a text when the broadcast team came into the dugout to outfit me with the mic equipment before the next inning. I know that this treatment is given to favorite players who are also not going to drop accidental f-bombs on live broadcast, but I really wanted to see what the text said.

Is Marty okay? Did something happen? Or is it a simpler thing like running out of toilet paper? Although that would also be horrifying.

"—Don't you think?"

Mierda, I wasn't paying attention to what the broadcast guy was saying. My lucky star is shining though, because this is exactly when the ball is hit my way.

"This is going long!" the announcer says in my ear and to everyone watching at home. "Machado takes off and—"

I stop listening, every fiber of my being focused on making the play. I can read the exact trajectory of the ball arching in the air, and after years and years of mapping the outfield of every stadium in the league, I know just where the projectile's going to land. The runner on first is shooting to second and even though there's no one on third, if I don't catch this damn ball they're going to get excited.

Not on my watch, son.

My thighs pump with the force of sledgehammers, my steps light on the green while I track the ball. I don't even reason it out—I launch myself at the padded fence, finding purchase against it to propel myself up one step, two. This is one of the softer fences in the pro stadiums, which makes this child's play. I reach with my glove at a full stretch, right in time for the ball to nestle inside my glove. I'm not sure how high I am, so I soften my knees for the landing and roll with it. The world spins and I let it, in the meantime reaching for the ball in my glove. The second that the green is below me and not above, I throw the ball at Lucky Rivera's general direction with all the power of my hips.

The ball is a white streak and the clever shortstop reads the play like we're of one mind. He makes the catch and slides head first to tag the runner trying for third. Laying on the base, he throws to first and with that gets the batter out too.

Noise explodes all around.

This never gets old—the rush of dopamine and serotonin and any other happy hormone that engraves every successful play in my soul. I can't believe I get to do this for a living.

"Unbelievable!" the guy exclaims in my ear, reminding me that I'm mic'ed up. "This is going to make the highlight reels for a week, and it all started with your superhero catch! How are you feeling right now, Machado?"

"Hungry." It's probably a better answer than saying how pleased I am to retire the inning this way, even if my shit-eating grin doesn't hide it.

The second announcer laughs. "You definitely deserve a snack for that play."

Something I've learned about the Orlando Wild is that,

since Spring Training, this is a team that is highly motivated by pizza—especially if it's paid for by the main catcher. I'm sure this inning will qualify for that special treat, and that alone is wroth bragging about.

However, if you've been a professional baseball player for longer than two games, you know that there's an unwritten code of conduct. You simply don't show other guys up, not even if you've just done something that's going to be part of baseball history.

That's the tricky part about being mic'ed up, that it makes it a lot harder to contain your own self-satisfied glee and not alienate everyone else in the league. I already have enough with how irrational some fans are on social media, so I have to rein myself in and be as bland as possible right now.

"Thank you, guys," I respond with a good natured chuckle, and pull out the receiver from my waistband as I head toward the dugout. As I turn it off, I breathe a relieved sigh out that I didn't screw up—the game or the broadcast.

And now for the main thing—I grab onto the pendant hanging from my neck. Players and staff alike manhandle me as I enter the dugout, and by rote I return the high fives, the ass pats, the chest bumps, slowly making my way deeper to the shelves that house the batting gloves and pads, where I also left my cellphone.

"Dude, that was freaking amazing!"

"You flew like two meters, bro."

"What are two meters?" someone asks. "I don't math."

Me neither, I want to say. Instead, I swipe my phone screen and find Consuelo's chat.

The pretty blonde neighbor is teaching math to your daughter, it reads.

I blink real slow. My body should relax now that I know this isn't life or death, but for some reason I can't. My blood stays running as hot as if I was still in the outfield about to fly two meters in the air.

"It's like six feet and a half and there's no way Machado jumped that high," a familiar voice says nearby—Logan Kim, who is joining the team again for the first time today.

"Someone should measure it because that looked pretty impressive," another familiar voice adds—Cade Starr, who's officially done pitching for the night after conceding only one run.

"You know," Lucky Rivera asks in an amused tone, "Those are pretty dangerous words in a dugout full of red-blooded and extremely competitive assholes."

That tears a snort out of me, and next thing I know a beefy arm is thrown around my shoulders. "Besides," Lucky laughs in my ear, "Tall guys have an unfair advantage, but it's all about proportions."

"Are we still talking about jumps or something else?" I ask.

He gasps in an exaggerated way. "Jumps, of course. Mind out of the gutter, you perv."

I shake my head, though a glimpse at the words *pretty blonde neighbor* on the corner of my eye gives me pause. Did she see my big, *big* jump?

Wait, the whole nation's gonna see it on repeat in any sports outlet, and I'm sure everyone employed by the team will too, from Charlie Cox to the guys who open and close the stadium doors everyday. Why would it matter if Audrey Winters specifically sees that I'm capable of an athleticism feat like this?

I tuck my tongue against my cheek. I'm not one of those guys who are in the business of denial. I know exactly why her opinion matters more than the team owner's or anyone else. She *is* pretty. She *is* good to my daughter. And I *am* a very simple guy.

This is bad.

*

"Be rational, Miguel," I tell myself while driving home after the game. It's well past midnight and the commute from the park downtown to home is calm. "Biologically speaking, you know exactly what was going on at that moment."

A cocktail of macho manly man hormones swirled in my belly, dimming my brain function. What little I had was fully spent on not screwing up during broadcast. I can't be blamed for making a new brain synapsis between my pretty blonde neighbor who was teaching math to my daughter, and feeling good after a bold play. I haven't read all the parenting and psychology books I have to pretend like I don't know what's happening.

"She's an attractive woman," I continue explaining to the quiet inside my vehicle, just as I turn into my street. "You've known that from day one."

And by that I mean the day she punched me in the eye. It was just reconfirmed when I saw her the next time, when she somehow ended up in my arms for a dance.

My chest does a thing. I thump it to stop it.

"Realistically, you'd be feeling the same way if you were exposed to another attractive, single woman."

Would I?

My eyebrows tighten a little. Yeah, admitting that makes me a jerk because women aren't interchangeable. I force myself to think of other beautiful women I've met before, from Marty's mom, to celebrities like the singer Celina, to the woman who asked for my autograph at Trader Joe's last weekend, and the fans who sometimes show a lot of cleavage to get players's attention. My chest doesn't do the thing with any of them.

"Okay, so I find her more attractive than others." I shrug. "So what? No big deal."

I park my SUV outside of the garage, trying to make as little noise as possible since Marty must be asleep. On days like this, when I took care of Marty's morning routine, Consuelo stays until late and waits for me awake. We've fallen into a good cadence and I know we're so fortunate to have found a nanny who not only is reliable and safe, but also flexible.

Gathering my duffel bag from the back, I shut the car door as carefully as possible and my attention strays to the duplex next door. The downstairs lights are on, which isn't surprising knowing that all the residents work for the same team that I do, which just finished a home game. Maybe Audrey saw the entire action from the comfort of her living room. I wonder if she's impressed.

"Stop. You're acting like a teenager." I shake my head.

I force myself to veer toward my door. With my free hand, I key in the remote code on an app that unlocks my house. Makes it a lot easier to elbow and shoulder my way in when I'm tired and sleepy after a game.

But then I freeze at the foyer. Consuelo waits awake for me, all right—across from my pretty blonde neighbor at the dining table.

Steaming mugs of what smells like chamomile sit between them, and they stop mid laughter to turn to me.

Yeah. That sound you hear? My chest doing the thing again.

This time it stays doing it, though, almost alarming me. It takes me a moment to remember that this is what it feels like when I'm nervous and I clutch at my necklace.

"There he is," Consuelo says, motioning toward me with a motherly smile.

Audrey pushes a gold strand behind her ear. "Welcome home, Miguel."

The strap of the duffel bag slides off my shoulder, and it falls on the carpet with a dull thud.

"That was a very good game and you must be very tired," the nanny says, picking up her mug and blowing on it. "I'll finish this quickly so I can leave you to get some rest." She chugs on the tea with surprising fortitude, considering how hot it must still be.

"Thanks," I say, still rooted to the spot and daring a glance at the other woman. If she's stayed here ever since the math lessons started, and Consuelo saw the game, then surely Audrey caught a glance too.

I shouldn't be tingling everywhere the way I am.

"I should also head home," Audrey says, pushing her chair back.

My muscles tighten like I'm bracing for something unpleasant. But I'm also standing in the way of the exit, so I tear myself off the spot.

Consuelo picks up the two mugs, saying, "Didn't you mention you had something to talk about with Mr. Machado?"

I pretend like I'm mic'ed up and can't express what's really going through my head by focusing on something less important. "Consuelo, I've asked you to call me Miguel many times."

"Give it up." Audrey chuckles softly. "I've spent the whole evening trying to get her to stop calling me Miss Winters because it makes me feel like I'm my mother, but no dice."

"Not my fault that I was taught respect." Consuelo says with a sniff, quickly rinsing the mugs under the faucet and patting her hands dry with her own apron. "I'm heading home now. Have a good night, kids."

Audrey turns to me with a sardonic expression and mouths, *kids?*

I press my lips tight. I'm also aware of the irony of being referred to as mister and kid at the same time, yet that's exactly what I am to Consuelo Gomez, who is nearly the same age as my own mother.

As I open my front door for her, I tell myself that I'm just being helpful, and not that I'm kicking her out so I can hear whatever it is that Audrey has to say. But as Consuelo passes me by, the smirk on her face tells me that she's not fooled.

"Drive safe." I wave her off, stalling on purpose so that I don't appear as eager as I am. I even wait until the woman drives off and I can no longer see the tail lights of her car before heading back inside and closing the door.

Audrey Winters waits for me leaning against my kitchen counter, her arms and legs crossed. For all intents and purposes, it seems like she doesn't even want to say whatever's on her mind.

"So…" I start, slowly advancing toward the kitchen and stopping farther than I normally would. I mimic her by also folding my arms.

She narrows her eyes a tad, the green jewels piercing. "You have a really good kid."

"I know." I tilt my head a little. "Is that what you wanted to talk about?" That's good. Friendly territory. Safe. Not disappointing at all.

My whole body itches. I want to go out for a run or shower again. There's no way I should be buzzing like this after a regular season game where the job was well done.

"Kinda," she answers after a beat, before running her hand through her hair in a way that leaves her bangs askew. "It's just that it got me thinking, which is usually never a good idea."

I cock an eyebrow, curious about where this is going.

"What if…" Audrey makes another pause and rocks on the balls of her feet. "We do it."

Chest.

Thump.

Brain.

Fart.

I say nothing.

She unfolds her arms to shrug, palms facing up. "I mean,

both of my roommates have executed ridiculous fake dating plans too. Obviously, this is different because we're friends, right? But that's actually going to make this work out better, because we'd never try anything weird on each other."

Something among all those big words makes my eye twitch. I replay them again and a record scratches in my head. "Hold on, you hit my brain out of the park early on and I'm not following."

She gives me a *seriously?* look. "Hello? You're the one who came up with the idea and I'm just agreeing to it."

Me? With an idea? I couldn't remember my name right now if she asked.

"Marty's so bummed and I really have no other easy way out." She lifts her chin. "So let's do it, let's be a fake couple."

"Oh," I mumble. So that's what she meant by *let's do it.* Of course. What else? Pfff. Clearing my throat, I say, "Right. Okay. Let's do it." I clamp my mouth shut since I unfortunately can't stuff my foot in it.

"One thing, though," she adds all businesslike. "You should call the school and confirm before we share the plan with Marty."

"Agreed."

She jerks a thumb to one side. "All right, I'm heading home now. Don't forget to stretch before you go to sleep, or whatever it is you do after games to rest properly."

"Thanks." I nod.

Audrey blinks at me for a second. "Um, okay. Bye."

"Yep." I wave at her just like I did to Consuelo, except Audrey's still standing in my kitchen.

Prickles of sweat break all over my skin, a portent to death of embarrassment.

In contrast, she's dignified as a queen as she makes her way out. I stay still, hoping that she won't decide to come back in and make fun of me for being the most awkward member of the entire Orlando Wild organization, even as I was wishing for her to see me as one of the best players instead.

When it's clear that no such thing is happening, and the faint sound of her door shutting reaches my ears, I pluck my phone and keys from my pocket, leave them at the counter— and drop to the floor.

"Uno, dos, tres…" I count the pushups in Spanish, which is what I do every time I know I'm going to reach a high number. It may be absurd, but if tiring myself out is the only way I can stop the sudden attack of my hormones, that's exactly what I'm going to do.

CHAPTER 15
AUDREY

A root canal. Waiting for three hours at the DMV only to find out you didn't bring one of the required documents. Your delivery driver leaving your food at some unknown house that is definitely not yours. An apprentice taking out your blood sample.

What do all those things have in common?

They're more pleasurable than brunch at the country club with my dad and his groupies.

You'd think that all these people who own entire portfolios of companies all over the world would have something more important to do than meet for brunch on a Friday to talk about their golf swings. I'm on my second mimosa and very glad that I didn't drive myself to the function, because alcohol is the only thing that will see me through.

My father turns to me with a beaming smile. "What is your opinion, Audrey?"

I have no idea what he's talking about, and I also doubt that my thoughts are really required. If I learned anything from my mother—and it wasn't much that was good, trust me

—is that the way to survive these functions is by blending with the background.

As response, all I offer is a wan smile and busy myself with another sip of the boozy drink. Dad's bushy eyebrows twitch, like he can't hide his surprise at the fact that I'm not cooperating. That's how I know I'm doing a great job.

The conversation ebbs a little after that, and he pretends like we're being called to someone else's presence. With my hand in his arm, he steers us away from the group, hiding in the relative privacy of walking in the periphery to whisper, "You're being rude, Audrey."

"Am I?" That brings a little smile out of me and I try to hide it behind my crystal flute. "I did agree to your terms of showing up to public events together, but it doesn't mean I have to enjoy them."

"If you don't appear like you're having a good time, how will people think that we're a happy family?"

I gasp in mock exaggeration. "Dad, you didn't say that lying to everyone was part of the deal."

He sighs and if I didn't know him, I'd think he was sincerely disappointed. "In any case, I would like to have a word with you about the status of your name change. But first, we need to appear social."

Then he stops us in front of Henry Vos and I realize this was just a little distraction that worked swimmingly. With my hand trapped in Dad's arm and throngs of rich, but sweaty people all around us, it's not easy to execute a clean escape from this situation.

He stops mid sentence in a conversation that seems to be about horses, to stare at me—or more specifically at the sliver of skin at my waist that my outfit reveals. I have to really exercise my willpower to not ram the heel of my hand into his chin. I wore this outfit because I wanted to at least feel cute while being miserable, not for his satisfaction.

He's still staring at my skin when he says, "Fancy running into you both."

As if he made a single lick of effort to find us, I think to myself, mumbling something incoherent that makes Dad tighten his arm.

"You were looking sharp out there in the green," he tells the younger guy, and turns to me. The twinkle in his eyes makes me wary. "Isn't that true, Audrey?"

I blink slowly. I will never praise Henry Vos, even if he was donating half of his fortune to charity because nothing that comes from a bad person is ever any good.

And so I take another swig of my mimosa, sadly reaching the bottom this time.

"I don't think your daughter is very fond of golf. Otherwise she would've joined us out there," Henry says, chuckling.

Dad gives me a sharp look like he can read my mind because, yeah, even if I freaking loved golf, I wouldn't subject myself to playing with them for any period of time.

My phone buzzes in the pocket of my skirt. It gives me a great excuse to pull my hand from the crook of Dad's arm, and I leave my now empty cup on a nearby table. "Excuse me, this is important," I say, blatantly lying through my teeth.

After producing my phone, I make a big show of stepping aside like I'm getting ready to talk with my financial advisor or something. Even better, the buzzing ends up being a couple of texts from someone I absolutely don't hate—none other than the man, the legend, the awkward turtle that is Miguel Machado.

FUTURE HALL OF FAMER

Big news, I came to the school to talk about the
event and there's a way we can make it happen

But

There's a catch

My lips twitch. Even though what I really enjoy is a drama-free life with my friends, and my plants, and my cozy house, and not having to put up with other people's mess, I find this situation with Miguel just funny. It's absurd and harmless in a way that makes me feel alive. Like I've taken a page out of the great Lucky Rivera playbook and am in on a massive prank.

It turned out that I didn't lie, then. This *is* important.

ME

What's that?

FUTURE HALL OF FAMER

The G-word might not be enough

ME

You're gonna have to get a bit more specific because there are a lot of words that start by G

FUTURE HALL OF FAMER

Girlfriend, I mean

They don't consider parents's girlfriends or boyfriends to be family enough

Which, who gave them the right to define what is family and what isn't?

Are Marty and I not family enough because it's just the two of us?

I assume that as a PR rep for the team I work for, you won't let me sue them, right?

Welp. It sounds like this poor guy is spiraling.

"Everything okay?" Dad asks, and I do as he does when he's interrupted by raising a finger and stepping even farther so I can make a call.

Miguel picks up at the fourth ring. "I'm sorry for my rant

interrupting your day" is the first thing he says as greeting. In the background, his steps fall in steady thuds like he's pacing.

I shake my head, wishing he could understand how unbelievable he is. "You're kidding, right? If it wasn't for your current existential crisis I'd still be stuck in one of my own."

His steps stop. "Why? What's wrong?"

Covering my mouth and ducking my face so that my hair hides it from view like a curtain, I say, "Brunch at the golf club with Dad and his ilk."

"Ouch."

"Yeah, so you figuratively did it again—coming to the rescue," I explain.

Miguel chuckles a little. "Glad that my suffering wasn't for nothing."

"So what happened?"

"I'm regretting my choices in life," he announces somberly. Before I freak out that he's meaning something like he regrets being a single dad, he adds, "Maybe I should've put Marty in a public school instead of a bougie, snobby place ran by judgy adults."

My shoulders sag in relief.

Guess the noxious fumes of expensive perfume, sweat, and colorful little beverages all around me were starting to make me forget that not everyone in my life is like these people.

Miguel's records and talent could've got to his head, yet here he is, once again trying to be a better dad today than he was yesterday.

I toss a side glance at my own progenitor, who is in the middle of laughing at something Henry has said. Knowing them, it's at the expense of the poor or something evil like that. What a contrast.

"Then, if I can't be your fake girlfriend, should I pretend to be your sister or your cousin?"

I can practically hear the grimace in his face as he says,

"Who would possibly believe that Americana Barbie and Ricky Martin Ken are blood relatives?"

That makes me bark a laugh that attracts a lot of unwanted attention. I turn around, facing a table full of hors d'oeuvre displayed between fresh flower arrangements and real pearls.

"Fair point," I concede, clearing my throat. "Does that mean that Marty won't be able to go to the tea party then?"

"Er, no. Remember when I said there's a way but with a catch?"

I blink, heat traveling up my neck the second I feel silly. "Right. What was that?"

"Well… When the principal was giving me a whole speech about how the purpose of the event is to strengthen family bonds, and how a father's girlfriend may not stay around long enough to become important in the child's life, I may have…" Here he makes a pause long enough that I have to prod him.

"Yes?"

Miguel coughs a little. "I may have said that we're committed enough."

"Don't tell me we have to fake marry now." A snort escapes from my throat.

"No, no." Another pause. "A fake engagement, though."

My jaw drops.

I guess the wide open mouth can be interpreted in many different ways because one of the servers asks me, "Caviar with crème fraîche hors d'oeuvre?" And he offers me a whole plate full of it.

"Er, no, thank you," I answer.

"Right," Miguel says into my ear. "It'd be wild. Too big of a lie. Maybe I can talk with Rose and ask her to pretend to be my sister? We do look like cousins or something."

"No!" I exclaim, now turning away from the server and, for

lack of a better alternative, I hide behind a tall potted palm. "That wasn't for you—I was turning down gross food."

"Oh."

Silence.

Did I just tacitly agree to cosplaying Miguel's fiancée?

I straighten and allow my sight to get lost in the distance, landing on someone's pink hat that looks like it has a dead flamingo on top, and probably costs twice an average sedan.

Honestly, in the grand scheme of ridiculous events in my life, how bad can this one be?

Besides, I reason while shifting my attention back to my dad and his new business partner—who is such a creep that he hasn't lost sight of me even while I'm trying to hide—this would give me a really solid alibi to free myself from their plans.

"It's not a big deal," I tell Miguel. "Girlfriend, fiancée… potahto, potayto."

His walking resumes. "Are you sure? Because I'm not Hollywood type of famous, but someone will probably say something that will end up on social media, if not the news."

I shrug, though he can't see it. "It's fine, I'm a PR professional and the whole point of this is so I can also spin it to my benefit." I peek again at the insufferable pair of men. "And I really need to benefit ASAP so I don't have to be dragged around to these things anymore."

"Hey, Audrey?" Miguel asks all of a sudden.

"Hmm?"

"Is that code for wanting to be rescued right now?" That catches me by surprise, and as my mind races, he keeps speaking, "Because I don't want to make the mistake that generations of mens have made in assuming that you can't take care of yourself, but it kinda sounded like you need a hand."

Something in me loosens—my spine, my soul, my hackles.

I'm not annoyed by his observation. It doesn't negate how

angry I am that my own father is still using me as his pawn and that my self sufficiency was so flimsy all along.

Rather, it recognizes that saving myself has been the way I have lived for years until recently, until I had a good group friends who are better people than me. Who made me see that getting help every once in a while isn't so bad.

Why is it so easy for me to do everything—and I mean *everything*, even sacrificing my own freedom—for my friends, yet it's so difficult to recognize that it'll be better to solve something with help than on my own?

It's taken getting to the point of peak manipulation from my dad to realize this. And for the first time in my life, I don't feel like a failure for reaching out.

"Actually, I'd appreciate some help. Any excuse to get out of here early will cut it."

"I can do that." I hear a raspy sound, like maybe he's rubbing his face and it has some bristles. "How's this? Let's explain the plan to Marty together over ice cream."

"Isn't she in school?"

"Yes, but I'm pissed at this place and want to leave. I'm sure she feels the same, right?"

"Perfect." I grin at the potted palm. "This is so gonna get you best dad award." And it's also going to improve my mood drastically.

We keep the call going just to give me an excuse to look unapproachable and too busy to have more vapid conversations.

In a record amount of time, I'm leaving this joint while escorted by a knight in shining sweats, his little goth princess, and a sensible SUV for a carriage.

CHAPTER 16
MIGUEL

"This. Is. The. Best. Day. Of. My. Life!" Marty exclaims, punctuating every word before taking a bite out of her ice cream.

Yes, a bite.

I watch fascinated at this strange little creature I call my daughter. "Wow, I've created a monster."

"I would say she's perfectly well adjusted," Audrey counters, licking her ice cream cone like a civilized person.

Welp, I too am a monster I guess, because I definitely shouldn't be paying any attention to the pink of her tongue as it carries chocolate ice cream into her mouth. I lower my focus on the sad fruit cup in my hands, stabbing a chunk of strawberry with more violence than necessary.

Audrey continues, not noticing my pause. "If any of my parents had pulled me out of school on a normal day and taken me to the ice cream parlor, I'd probably feel differently about them."

There's something weird in her voice, like she's trying to make light of something that really isn't. Usually when people do this, they're torn between wanting to share and not being pried into. And if dealing with a certain Logan Kim has taught me anything, it's that the best course of action is to wait until they're ready to share.

I play along by turning to Marty. "Is my bribe working? Am I your fave dad at last?"

"You're my only dad, Dad," she responds unironically, taking another bite out of the ice cream. How does that not make her teeth hurt? Who *is* she?

"I guess this is the only trophy you win for participation." Audrey's lips draw into a wide smile that shares all her pearly whites, and for the first time I notice that her two front teeth are slightly longer than the rest. There's something so charming about it that I can't stop staring. "What? Do I have something between my teeth?"

To save face, I point vaguely at her and say, "Yeah, a little something—there. You got it." The only thing she got is my full attention, damn it.

So, it turns out this attraction wasn't a sudden one-off the other night. I *am* a red-blooded straight guy who is into this woman. But the sky is blue and the grass is green—who wouldn't be into her?

She's smart—enough to teach my daughter math. She's kind—also enough to agree to this absurd plan, just so my daughter can hold her head high at school. And she's gorgeous. We're talking head-turning, double-take-inducing type of gorgeous. The guy behind the counter can't stop staring, and a woman who came in earlier also ogled Audrey like she was seeing a celebrity. My presence and Marty's hasn't deterred attention, because we're obviously not a real family and it shows, even though we're about to start faking it.

"Anyway," I announce, remembering the point of this little gathering. "Now that Marty will be able to attend the tea party, we have to get serious about how this is going to work. I'm all ears for your ideas, ladies." I lean back on my chair, folding my arms and glancing at them to pass on the figurative microphone.

Marty looks at Audrey. "Should I start calling you Mom?"

The blonde chokes on her ice cream.

I snort, but still reach for the napkins on the table to pass her one out of the goodness of my heart.

"Well, how else are my classmates going to think I'm normal?" my kid asks, missing the giant sized irony of her statement. It dries my amusement up and the balloon of guilt that permanently resides in my chest swells up again. It had been quite deflated while I basked in my success this afternoon.

"Normal is overrated," Audrey says in between coughs into the napkin. She wipes her mouth and reaches for my water bottle. I let her, clearly she needs it more than I do. "But maybe let's keep that for when we're in front of other people, okay?"

"Fine."

Audrey turns to me. "I have a ring that is going to work perfectly for the ruse."

"A ring…" I trail off, my mind gunning it at full speed like I'm trying to score on a wild hit that has low chance of success, just to reach her point. "You mean an engagement ring."

"Yes." She motions at her left hand. "It's a gold band with a green sapphire. No one needs to know it's part of a jewelry set that my brother gave me for Christmas once."

"You have a brother?" Marty wonders. "Should we get him on board with the plan?"

Audrey's lips twitch but don't form a full smile. "He would've been so on board."

Before I can form an apology in my mouth, my daughter continues like nothing's amiss. "And there's one more thing."

"What's that?" Audrey asks absentmindedly as she takes another lick of ice cream.

I'm displeased to report that my reason decides to make itself absent again thanks to that.

Marty checks out her surroundings, leans closer to her new partner in crime, and lowers her voice. "I heard that the mean girls wear matching outfits with their moms. Can we do that too?"

Audrey smacks the table in mock outrage. "Rather than doing it too, we're going to do it better. Let's go shopping!"

*

And this is how I find myself in the middle of a thrift store when normally I'd be training at the Orlando Wild facilities on a day off. I scratch the back of my head, confused but not upset about this turn of events.

Marty pulls out a garment from a rack, showing it to Audrey. "How's this?"

It reminds me of the goth tutu I once had to wear when one of her loose teeth hurt her so bad that she wouldn't stop crying, and I didn't know what else to do to cheer her up but dress up as a too buff, goth tooth fairy.

"Very stylish," the woman responds as she runs her fingers over the transparent folds of the skirt. They have something shiny on them, some kind of glitter. "I'm thinking this would look great with something pink."

"Ugh, pink is for girls," my daughter says like this is a personal affront.

Audrey turns a side eye my way and I raise my hands. "I'm not the one who taught her to hate pink."

She narrows those striking green eyes like she doesn't quite believe me, before returning her focus on my kid. "I think pink is for everyone who likes it, and I like it a lot."

My ever sharp daughter says, "Really? But I've never seen you wear pink. You're usually with something green." Here she points at Audrey's outfit.

I'm not the right guy to wax poetic about clothes, but I

kinda regret it at this moment. It would probably make my assessment feel more factual than thirsty. But the truth is that Audrey's wearing some kind of strappy top that is very tight against her *very* generous curves, but also leaves a gap before the matching skirt begins. The fact that the outfit has massive yellow lemons with crowns of green leaves on a white background doesn't minimize how stunning she looks.

I remain a silent, tongue tied buffoon as Audrey volleys back with, "That's because it's my favorite color, but it doesn't mean I don't like other colors."

It only stands to reason that her favorite color would be the shade of her eyes. No other compares.

"Prove it." Marty tips her chin up, eyes twinkling like she's challenging an equal.

And then to my surprise, Audrey Winters-not-Cox responds in kind. "Fine." She lifts one shoulder. "Let's go find me the pinkest outfit to ever exist."

"Fine."

"Fine!"

With each escalation they sound more and more amused. They stomp away in mock outrage, leaving me behind on the same spot by the girl's clothing section.

My heart thumps painfully, working way harder than it did last year when I won MVP of the league.

I place a hand on my chest and it does nothing to slow down the beat.

"Estoy en problemas," I tell myself under my breath.

But it's fine. This makes sense. I haven't let a woman into my life since Marty's mom. I've been really busy raising Marty and sustaining a career that can secure her future. None of that has changed, and the only reason why this woman has made her way in is because our lives simply overlap. We're neighbors and coworkers of sorts. We see each other everyday. Neither of us are making any extra effort here, like people who are dating would. I'm just confusing the closeness for attraction. Or rather, I'm confusing how close *and* hot she is for something more.

She deserves better than that. The second she catches me drooling over her like a dog, she's going to rightfully freak out and kick me out of her way. And that would hurt Marty, who is making a new friend in our neighbor.

So I stuff my hands in my *SPORTY* joggers and trail behind them, sticking around so they know I'm not abandoning them, but not really participating now that I've figured out what my place in this dynamic is. We're doing all of this for them, not for my hormones—rampant as much as the asshats are.

"How's this?" Marty pulls out a dress almost as long as she is, holding the hanger up high. "You should try it on."

I can tell by the twitch in Audrey's eyebrow that this isn't her thing, but she's not going to back down from a ten-year-old's challenge. She grabs it. "If it fits me, you'll have to try something that matches."

"Deal." Marty offers her hand and they shake on it.

In turn, I shake my head, fighting back a smile.

Audrey marches into a changing room and slides the curtain shut. Only then does Marty acknowledge my existence by grabbing my hand and dragging me back to the girl's area. "C'mon, Dad. We need to find me something that matches."

I bark an abrupt laugh. "Wow."

"What?"

"You didn't need to do all of this to allow yourself to wear pink, mi niña," I tell her, grinning.

She presses her lips into an arch and says nothing.

My daughter, the master manipulator, ladies and gents.

I'm not very helpful after that, though. Finding pink clothes is easy, but something that doesn't make her gag? Now that's the real challenge.

"This?" I ask, showing her a fluffy sleeved top.

Marty opens her mouth and points at her throat.

"Or this?" A pair of pink jeans.

"Dad, please. I don't want to look like cowboy Barbie."

"Excuse me," a third voice says, and we turn to Audrey wearing what I'd normally define as a monstrosity—a hot pink dress with hanging flaps on the sides. I'm sure they have a name. "What's wrong with looking like cowboy Barbie?" She motions at herself.

I really have to bite my lips hard this time. Pretty sure no one would appreciate to be laughed at in these circumstances. And the warning look she tosses my way tells me as much.

"On second thought," Marty says like it's no biggie. "Maybe that dress really wasn't for you."

That does it. I explode in the most unhinged laughter—great guffaws that bend me over and burn my eyes, giving my jaw the workout of a lifetime.

It takes them dropping me off in the men's section to calm my outburst down to sporadic giggles.

They don't show me whatever they get after that, but they're both pleased as punch on the drive back home. It tells me that whatever they picked is going to cause waves at the school event. My chest is about bursting as we get out of the car, even as we say goodbye to our neighbor, because I hadn't seen my daughter this happy in… ages.

She grabs my hand again and looks up at me like I'm no longer her enemy. "Today was the best day."

I let myself smile down at her with all the joy I feel, and my free hand reaches up to wrap around the pendant of my necklace, which I usually only do when I'm nervous.

And I realize that I am—I'm afraid that this moment will end. That this joy won't last.

Like the worst sort of prophet, I freaking bring the end of the calm with that thought alone, because suddenly there's a clear "what the shit?" coming from next door.

Normally I'd try to shield Marty's ears from the spicy language that I'd otherwise use in the locker room without a problem, but there's enough alarm in the three words that a different instinct kicks in.

"Audrey?" I call out in the quiet of the dimming evening.

The woman reappears in our field of vision, huffing, her eyes wide as she pushes her golden hair away from her face. "I —I can't get into my house. Someone has changed the lock."

My head jerks back, as if punched.

What the shit, indeed. Who would do that?

I don't know if I've said it aloud, because Audrey hisses and says, "I know exactly who did this," and reaches for the phone in her pocket.

CHAPTER 17
AUDREY

Dad answers exactly at four rings, and I manage to contain my anger enough to not spill another flaming word in front of Marty. "What the heck, Dad?"

"Good evening, Audrey. Did you like your surprise?"

I grind my teeth and turn my back at the audience, but I feel that Miguel and Marty's presence stays near even as I pace on my lawn. "I'll give you credit for not pretending that you had nothing to do with why I can't get into my own house, but that's it. I want an explanation right now."

"I figured this would be the only way you would call me." I can practically hear him shrugging nonchalantly.

Meanwhile, my jaw drops and I gasp hard enough to hurt my throat. With a raspy voice, I say, "I should call the cops. You're essentially trespassing on my private property."

"You could do that, yes," Dad muses in the most unconcerned way. "Or we could just have the conversation that you've been running away from right now."

I run a hand through my hair, pushing my bangs backward to give me minuscule relief from the humid evening heat. My mind races with all possible plans to escape from this moment —everything from feigning some mysterious pain, screaming about a sudden alligator sighting, pretending that I'm being mugged, or that my signal is weak and pressing on the red button with gusto.

But if my father's getting impatient enough to lock me out of my own damn house, it means he's willing to do anything at this point. That all my stalling tactics are up. Time to fess up.

"What do you want?" I grouch under my breath, my shoulders huddling as if I could make myself smaller.

"I know that you have done diddly squat to fulfill your end of the bargain," he casually says, "my lawyer confirmed that enough time has passed since we made our deal for you to have a new last name."

I plead the Fifth in my mind.

He continues, "So I just wanted to remind you of the consequences if you don't do your part."

Hope's and Rose's faces flash through my mind, first laughing during one of our margarita fueled girl's nights in our living room, then being all lovey dovey with their men. And then a new scenario, one that hasn't occurred. Them, crying and screaming because I ruined their lives.

I swallow hard enough that probably all Orlando can hear it.

Certainly my dad does. "Yes, there are consequences to your own actions. It's never too late to learn that lesson, right?"

"I'll file the application tomorrow first thing."

"That's not going to be enough now. How could it? I clearly can't trust you."

Now my brain's scrambling. "Let's make the announcement tomorrow as well. We can have an all employee meeting, or maybe do a press conference. Or what if we—"

"I want you to marry Henry Vos."

Silence.

Rather, crickets and frogs croaking in the background, and the rustling of light steps on grass somewhere behind me. Then a soft, little tug at my skirt. I glance over my shoulder at Marty and the concern etched in her face. She has no idea what this full conversation is about, but clearly she can sense that I'm screaming myself raw on the inside. I reach for her hand and face forward again, fixing my eyes on my car parked on the driveway.

"No," I say, with surprising steel in my voice. "That's not part of our deal. I just had to change my last name back to yours."

"I'm afraid it is," he counters back. "Allow me to jog your memory. In order for you to get your inheritance, as condition for revealing our kinship to the world, you were also to marry a man I approved of."

My lungs stop working.

With the little amount of oxygen left in my brain, I rifle through our conversation in late March and there it is.

This was allegedly his way of sweetening the pot. Bile rushes up my throat and I drop my phone, clamping my hand against my mouth so I don't barf churned ice cream all over the grass. My father's tinny voice comes out of the device but I can't make out what he's saying. I'm too busy swallowing hard and catching my breath.

"Audrey?"

So caught in my own tragedy I am, that I don't even realize my roommates have come back home until they appear in my field of vision. Rose is looking intently at me, as if that alone could pry the thoughts in my head for her to study them. Beside her, Hope looks at something behind me—Miguel. His voice echoes in my ears.

"Something's wrong," he says.

That's the understatement of the century. A sob escapes from my throat.

"Dad?" Marty mumbles, and a telepathic message must be shared between the Machados. Next thing I know, they're bundling me into their house, my roommates in tow.

Marty guides me to the couch and the second I sit is when I break down. Big, ugly sobs, and enough waterworks to drown myself.

"Oh, sugar. What's wrong?" Hope asks, rushing to sit on my right and wrapping her arm around my shoulders.

Rose follows suit on my left. "Talk to us, Audrey. You need to let it out for your own sake."

"I—I—" A wail interrupts me.

I hate that I'm making a scene but I can't help it. The dam has broken and no matter how hard I try to patch it up, the torrent of emotions is too violent. I fold over myself, straight up weeping into my cheerful skirt.

The girls rub my back. Marty's little hand brushes my hair. But when I finally lift up my head seeking oxygen, the one that's in front of me is Miguel, kneeling with a glass of water in his hand.

"Here." He offers it to me and I take it, at first drinking carefully until reflex kicks in and I chug the whole glass.

I collapse back against the cushions, leaning my head back to stare at the ceiling. Big, hot tears roll down my temples. A warm, calloused hand eases mine open and retrieves the empty glass. I wish he wouldn't have pulled his hand away. I feel so cold right now.

"I screwed up," I rasp out, sniffling. "Badly."

"What happened?" Hope prompts.

"I bargained with the worst person to do that with." All the air expels from my lungs. "My dad."

I don't even know how to explain this without sounding completely out of this world. Then again, Dad doesn't live in a normal society. He has the means to make his word law above the actual law if he wants.

Straightening out, and glancing from Hope to Rose, I explain, "Remember when Hope almost got fired for dating Cade, and Rose got put on probation for using the team's social media to help them?"

"How could we forget?" Hope grimaces.

"Best risk I've ever taken." Our other roommate folds her arms and lifts up her chin in defiance.

"Remember also how there were no real consequences?" I ask softly.

Hope bobs her head. "It was a really well executed plan."

I hug myself and duck my face. "It worked because I made a deal with Charlie Cox, who… is my father."

You could hear a pin drop after this.

Long enough passes in absolute quiet that I lift up my face. Hope is absolutely shocked, eyes and mouth wide in a way that would be funny in any other circumstance. Rose is glaring at Miguel for some reason.

"Why aren't you surprised?" she asks him.

"Er…" The guy squirms a little, rubbing his hands over his powerful thighs. "It happened by accident."

The journalist zeroes back in on me. "What did you promise?"

I fist my hands around the fabric of my skirt. "It—It's complicated."

Now Hope folds her arms as well, brow crashing. "We have all night if necessary."

They won't let me get away with just this much information, and I'm too tired to fight them. I take a deep breath.

"I proposed to reopen contact and show up at events with him and telling everyone I'm his heiress, but that wasn't enough for Dad. He wanted that, plus marrying someone he approves of"—I say this with air quotes—"as condition for me to inherit the team so I can do whatever I want with it and protect whoever I want in it. Somehow I didn't think he was serious, but now he wants to hitch me up with Henry Vos, who by the way is a complete slimeball and tried to hit on me at my brother's freaking funeral."

Something like a cross between a scream and a wail comes out of me, and my hands fly to my face to hide the horrible shame that's burning up my skin right now.

I hate that this is my life. I hate everything about it.

I never asked for it to be a low budget telenovela with no happy ending in sight. And even more, I hate that no matter what I try, I can't escape my tyrannical father.

"What the—" Rose catches herself. The couch tilts as she jumps to her feet. "Why did you never tell us any of this?"

"You had a brother?" Hope gasps next to me. "And your dad is the freaking team owner?"

"Does your father not know that this is the twenty first century?" Miguel shakes his head in utmost stupefaction.

"What does the word inherit mean?" Marty asks.

"To have wealth pass down from parent to child," her dad explains.

"Audrey!" Rose throws her hands in the air. "This is the kind of ish you have to tell us about with enough time to plan!"

"Is wealth a good thing?" Marty wonders.

"You had a brother?" Hope repeats, tilting her head in confusion. "Wait, you had broken contact with your dad? Even though he's the team owner?"

"It can be," Miguel tells his child. "When it's earned ethically and given willingly. Not like this."

Marty nods. "That makes sense."

Rose leans forward in front of me, hands on her knees. "How could you agree to something so ridiculous? Do you have no self preservation?"

Hope plucks one of my hands that had fallen back on my lap to hold it. "I'm so sorry for your loss, I had no idea."

My chin trembles. My vision grows blurry again.

"Dad, I think she needs more water," Marty whispers.

A little laugh comes out of my throat, and all eyes turn to me again. "Thank you, guys."

"Why are you smiling now? I'm still angry at you." Rose scowls.

"Would you really like more water?" Miguel asks, looking up at me with soft eyes that threaten to make mine spill over violently once more. "I'm afraid that I don't have something stronger, other than energy drinks and protein shakes."

Hope interjects. "Electrolytes might be a good idea. She's practically lost half of her weight in waterworks already."

The guy nods and smacks his thighs. "Right on."

As he marches back to the kitchen, I mumble, "What I really need is a locksmith and a way to escape an arranged marriage to a creep."

"A locksmith?"

Marty's the one who responds, "Her dad changed the lock."

"I will kill him," Rose mutters through gritted teeth.

"Okay." Hope squirms and produces her phone. "At least that part can be solved pretty quick. What do we do about the arranged marriage?"

Crickets. This time with no frogs.

Miguel comes back from the kitchen, circling around the coffee table to kneel back in front of me and offer me a new glass of water. As I'm taking it, his daughter breaks the silence.

"What if you marry my dad?"

My motor skills go to shit and I drop the glass. Cold water splashes like a fountain—yet that's the least of our concerns.

Even when absolutely every person gets wet, nobody has a single braincell to spend on the accident. We're all looking at Marty like she's a unicorn.

"What?" She glances back at all of us in turns. "You were

already going to fake being engaged. This is an even better plan. Carpet the diem and such."

Hope turns to me. "You what?"

"Audrey, are you Spider-Man?" Rose scrunches up her face. "Why do you have so many secret lives?"

I squirm. "It's complicated."

"If you say that one more time I'm going to smack you up the head."

I clamp my mouth shut, knowing that Rose does good on her threats.

"Let's do it."

The three words would normally be crystal clear in any other scenario, but when they spill out of Miguel's lips in a moment like this, they make every thought flee from my head.

He has the gall to shrug.

Shrug!

"What? We're both single, so this will be believable. And our next away series is in Las Vegas. We could do this as soon as in two days."

Rose is unable to hold herself up anymore, and she falls back to sit on the coffee table. "That's genius. If Logan and I faked being in a relationship to save my career, this is an even more noble deception than that. It's to save you from being miserable next to a man that clearly doesn't care about you and is probably just after your father's fortune."

I stumble upon attempts at speaking, but nothing coherent comes out.

"But they practically just met," Hope muses, "wouldn't it make more sense for her to marry someone like Lucky, who is also single and has been around longer? No offense, Miguel."

"None taken."

Rose snorts. "Who would believe that the unserious lady's man that Lucky Rivera is would seriously marry Audrey when they haven't been seen alone together once?"

"Hmm, that's a good point," our roommate agrees.

"Now Miguel…" Rose motions at him. "This is a serious guy—he's a responsible single dad, for goodness's sake. And he's also Miguel freaking Machado. It won't be hard for Audrey to pretend like she swooned over him very quickly."

The alluded clears his throat, one hand flying toward it to fiddle with the cross hanging from a chain around his neck.

"Yeah, I can see it."

I raise a hand. "Stop, you guys. I can't ask Miguel to do this in the middle of the season. He has enough on his plate in a new town, with the All-Star game coming soon, not to mention a *SPORTY* campaign and—"

"You don't have to ask me," he states clearly even with a soft voice, silencing me. "I'm volunteering."

"Why?" I blurt out.

"Because you need help," he says simply.

"That's it?" I blink hard, baring my teeth in a cringe. "You're willing to uproot your whole life to help a virtual stranger?"

"You're not a stranger, we're friends, remember?" Miguel shrugs those big shoulders of his once more. "Besides, there's no uprooting when we literally live next to each other and work at the same place everyday. I don't think there's anyone more equipped to help you than me."

"He's got a good point." Rose nudges me with her elbow.

Nonplussed, Hope looks at her phone screen and says, "The locksmith is on the way."

"You guys are wild." I shake my head slowly.

"So, are you in?" Rose asks me. "Because I literally don't see any other way out of this."

Me neither. That's the problem.

I don't have enough funds in my bank account to pack up and move to Australia or Mongolia, or farther if I could. Even if I did, I don't have enough funds to hide from my father forever. He has powerful contacts *everywhere*. No matter how long it might take, he will always get away with his.

Unless I ruin his plan before he can officially kick it off.

I allow myself to look into Miguel's steady eyes. There's determination in them, like he also understands that this is the literal only way to save my life.

But what's more important is that Dad won't lay a finger on Miguel and his family.

After all, he was willing to parade him around his acquaintances like a prize. Miguel is a baseball franchise on his own, with fans all over the world, and enough zeroes in his paycheck that he can at least lawyer up comfortably. I know this will be a pain in the ass for him one way or another, but it won't put him or Marty at real risk. They're safe. We could do this.

We have to.

Drawing in a deep breath, I say, "Las Vegas wedding, here we go."

CHAPTER 18
MIGUEL

Somehow my house has become a zoo.

"All right, folks. Here's the plan," Lucky Rivera says as he motions at the TV in the living room, where he has casted a note from his iPad. Chicken scratches adorn the screen in different colors, code for who is doing what. All of them are connected by red lines that look suspiciously like a certain meme. He explains, "We need to make this as believable as possible, which means scattering witnesses everywhere and posting proof on social media. For that we have our expert here."

He motions at Rosalina who raises her hand in a salute. "Aye, captain."

"I'm the captain," her boyfriend mumbles before taking a sip of lemon La Croix. My face twitches with a flash of amusement.

"You're the general of my heart, how about that?" She bats her eyes at him.

"Focus, people," Lucky says, as though he wasn't the most easily distracted person in this entire committee. "So as we have discussed, the first step is for the ladies to go shopping for wedding stuff—rings, dresses, and something blue."

My daughter pauses from munching on literal popcorn. "Who's bringing something borrowed?"

I take a deep breath and remain unmovable. I sit in the middle of my couch, Marty on my left and Audrey on my right, facing the screen. Cade and Hope sit on the armchair together, as in, she's on his lap. Inwardly I thank them for keeping it PG rated. Meanwhile, Logan—our captain, aye—and Rose sit on the carpet by the coffee table. No matter how many times I offered to bring them chairs, they refused. Clearly this is a comfortable setup for them. It also allows them prime access to the boxes of pizza on the coffee table that came straight from Cade's favorite joint.

The locksmith has come and gone, so in theory we don't have to be cramped in my modest living room, but this has become headquarters for the Marriage of Convenience Operation—name provided by a team captain who surprisingly reads romance books—and somehow Lucky has become the project lead. Dude has a glint in his eye that is almost scary, as if he'd waited his entire life for this very moment.

He gesticulates like an overhyped scientist as he continues speaking. "Listen, I can lend socks to the whole wedding party if I must."

"No," Logan fires back right away.

Cade shudders. "Hard pass, bruh."

Clearly there's some history here.

"I made friendship bracelets yesterday, how about those?" Marty offers from her generous, and also deeply amused heart.

"Way better options," Hope agrees.

Beside me, Audrey is as still as a statue. For the billionth time tonight, I check with a quick glance that she's still, in fact, breathing. Her eyes are so wide that the lamps brighten them a shade or two. Pretty sure she's scared of all these shenanigans, yet she's not putting a stop to them.

"You okay?" I whisper to her.

She turns slightly toward me. "Unsure."

"Should we stop?" Not just this strange pajama party, I mean, but everything. The whole plan. Call off the wedding, per se.

She just shakes her head as an answer.

"Now, the next crucial step is that we have to do Vegas rules." Lucky circles the air around the messy *Welcome to Las Vegas* sign he drew in a corner.

I reach over to my daughter and cover her ears. "Keep it child friendly, my guy."

"Of course." He nods theatrically and folds his arms. "All I'm proposing is group clubbing and some paparazzi type pics that we can accidentally leak."

Rose reaches for her phone on the carpet next to her. "Roger that. Creating a burner account as we speak."

"Dad?" Marty asks, "Can I hear the rest now?"

I don't remove my hands from her ears quite yet and ask Lucky, "Do we have specific situations that we want to, uh, capture on camera?"

I will yeet him into outer space if he proposes something I wouldn't let my kid see.

The smirk on his face tells me he can read my mind. "That's gonna be up to you two."

Audrey and I exchange a silent glance. She blinks a lot. I do my best for my eyes to not pop out of their damn sockets. A private conversation is definitely needed. I finally release my kid from the protective hold.

"Then," Lucky emphasizes, "We get drunk."

"Absolutely not," our physical therapist snaps, folding her arms tight enough to show muscle. "Not mid-season and certainly not on my watch."

"Boo, hiss," Lucky says, clearly enunciating the words. "Then how do we justify stumbling into a chapel for these two to get married?"

"We justify it by saying they're in love and couldn't wait any longer," she fires back.

Lucky turns to us on the couch. "Does that sound reasonable enough?"

No.

I nearly snort. None of this makes sense. I've never been part of anything more absurd in my life. Yet, I know that not so deep down it's not gonna be super hard to fake interest on the woman beside me. She's really freaking beautiful anyway, with those freckles over her nose and the pink lips. I'm not immune to her generous, very distracting curves either. And those gams...

Oof.

I squirm. What can I say? I didn't make a whole kid by osmosis.

Then Audrey finally speaks for the first time in at least an hour. "I can get drunk, at least." I turn to her like a whip and she asks, "What?"

"I'm not gonna marry a woman who is drunk and with impaired judgement."

"That's admirable and all," she returns, dripping in sarcasm. "But we're agreeing to the marriage days in advance already, and I'll need all the liquid courage I can get to make this happen."

Cade runs his hands up and down his girlfriend's arms. "Are you sure that at least Machado can't get drunk?"

She tosses a glare over her shoulder. "Miguel is in the lineup for the Vegas game, so no."

"What if he gets explosive diarrhea?" Lucky asks, calm as a cucumber even though he didn't just stun the entire room to silence. "Don't look at me like that, cabrones, I'm not saying

I'll cause it. What I mean is that a lil temporary inactive list never hurt nobody."

"And what if we lose the series because of that?" the Orlando Wild's first captain in franchise history asks in something like a growl.

Silence.

"I'll just pretend I'm drunk," I offer.

"Okay great. That's a solid idea."

"Whew, thought I was gonna die tonight."

"No more out of the box ideas, yeah?"

"Out of the box or out of the butt? Get it? *Get it?*"

I would laugh if I wasn't in the middle of this.

This is when I notice my hand fiddling with the crucifix at my neck, my knee bouncing, my palms sweating, my pulse hammering like I'm running home and a baseman is trying to tag me before I get there.

Last time I tried to get married the whole thing was dead on arrival. I'm not exactly prime husband material with being a single dad and on the road much of the year. But Marty's getting someone to role play Mom and daughter with at school, and Audrey's getting spared from an arranged marriage like this is still the 1800s.

All I have to do is… go along for the ride. My overthinking isn't welcome. This isn't real, no matter how much I look forward to the prospect of kissing this woman after we lie through our teeth with I do's.

I force both hands to hold my knees down.

"Anyway," the cowboy says, motioning with his hand so that his *bruh* continues outlining the plan.

"Then, once they get married we take pictures and move on to the hotel."

I smack my things. "All right, that's it. Marty, off to bed you go."

"But—"

"No buts. Let's get you upstairs."

"Talk about party poopers," she grouches, setting the popcorn bowl on top of an empty pizza box.

The others yap about this and that as I shepherd my wild daughter upstairs. She puts some resistance, dragging her feet at turns or stomping at others, but I manage to get her in her room.

She whirls on me and folds her arms, rising to her full 4 foot 11 height. "Dad, I know about the bees and the flowers."

I freeze.

"You don't have to treat me like I'm a baby."

I swear I'm quaking in my chanclas. My mouth flaps open and closed. Part of me doesn't want to ask, but the other part needs to understand if we're on the same page.

"Uhh, what do you mean?" My voice comes out like a squeak at the end.

Marty rolls her eyes. "I know I wasn't brought by the stork, so if you want to poke Audrey's flower—"

"Yeah, that's enough. Go wash your—"

"I don't mind because—"

"Marty, I *beg* you not to finish that sentence."

"Then she might stick around."

Once more, I lose all mobility function other than what it takes for my mouth to flap like a fish.

It really takes me a hot damn minute for my brain to form fully coherent sentences.

"Marty, there will be no flower poking because none of this is for real. Where did you even learn that? Did you bypass the parental controls somehow?"

Her eyes open really wide. "No, the teacher explained this when someone asked where babies come from. She said a bee pokes a flower and that's how babies start to grow." Now she huffs. "What I'm saying is that I wouldn't mind if I got a little sister or a brother. But I'd prefer a sister."

My shoulders deflate, but I'm not that much calmer than a second ago.

"Marty, Audrey and I aren't getting married for real, so we can't give you a sibling. This is all just temporary."

"So you say." She shrugs, and as she heads to her bathroom to wash up, she casually says, "But we'll see about that."

I can confidently say my beloved child has never scared me before—until this moment. A shiver rises up my spine and once I head back downstairs, I can't meet anyone's eyes for the rest of the night.

CHAPTER 19
AUDREY

Occasionally over the last few years, my roommates and I have joked about taking a day off together to do something fun, away from the testosterone fumes that permeate the air at work.

Never figured it would be to help me plan my wedding.

"What is my life?" I ask not for the first time today.

"Hmm." Rose taps her chin as we look at a store window at the outlets. Even though it's a weekday, the place is packed with tourists who speak all languages under the blue sky. "Honestly, your life is like the telenovelas my mom made me watch with her when I was a kid."

"What are we doing here?" Hope asks, and for a second I also think her question is as philosophical as mine. Then I catch her motioning at the wedding gowns on the other side of the glass in a literal way. "We can't carry that in our suitcases on the team charter flight."

I turn back to the creations. A row of elegant mannequins showcases dresses of all types, mermaid cuts, empire waists, and other things I can't really name but I objectively know are pretty. The gowns range from the purest white that hurts my eyes, to the smoothest cream. Across the store and at the opposite exhibit window are the bridesmaid dresses in all colors and patterns imaginable.

"I don't know," I respond frankly. "We said wedding dress and this is where my mind took me."

"Yes, but we need a casual dress. Like something you could wear for a night out clubbing in Vegas."

Rose then asks, "So then it doesn't necessarily have to be white, right? Like, who goes clubbing wearing white?"

"Nobody," Hope and I say in unison.

I turn my body away. "You're right, let's go find clubbing clothes. Besides, I don't think that anyone who gets drunk and married in Vegas is really thinking about what they're wearing."

"And probably most of the times the clothes end up on the floor." Rose and I turn to look at Hope, Rose with a smirk and I with a quirked brow. "What? Do we need to talk about how babies are made?"

Rose snorts.

I sigh and change the topic entirely, back to square one. "I just can't believe that this is what we're doing on our much awaited day off."

A hand falls over my shoulder, and the tallest of us says, "Don't worry, we'll also have brunch at a nice place. Then it'll feel like this was a normal girl date."

Except there's nothing normal about today.

On our list, we have to find dresses for tomorrow night, comfortable shoes that match or compliment, and wedding rings for Miguel and I. He couldn't get away from practice today, especially after already taking a day off yesterday to talk with Marty's school principal. Instead, he gave me both his measurement and an ornamental ring that I can use to ascertain whether the ring I'm buying—mind, with his credit card—will fit him.

I swear, his ring sample and his card weigh two tons in my purse. Pretty sure it's actually caused by my guilt for roping him into this.

"Let's check out that store. I usually love everything they have." Rose motions at us to follow her, and it takes some maneuvering through the throngs of people to finally make it.

The rush of cool air conditioner that greets us weakens my defenses just a tad, enough to not make me drag my feet as the former beauty pageant girl steers me toward a specific rack.

When I really pay attention, I discover that it's stuffed with miniskirt dresses. All of them. Not a single one would fully cover my things.

Once more, Hope and I voice the exact same thought. "No."

"Yes," Rose counters, calmly. She folds her arms. "Picture this. Our hot coworkers ask us to dance at a club. What's the one proven method that will keep their attention on us?"

"Our fantastic personalities?" I ask in my deepest sarcasm.

Hope adds, "Our gorgeous heads of hair?"

"That's a good one," I tell her, because honestly all three of us have spectacular hair—whether long and straight brown, or copious brown curls, or Alicia Silverstone type of blonde.

"Incorrect." Rose places her hands on her hips. "The one thing that will hold their attention is what they consume through their eyes. Men are simple that way."

I empty my lungs dramatically once more.

It's true. There's no denying this. However… "I'm not really planning to capture Miguel's attention or anyone else's."

"Sure, but a cute little dress will make the act more believable for when I take pics and videos to share online. Like if you dress in a potato sack I'll still think you're a knockout, but the internet is gonna wonder what Miguel saw in you enough to marry you on the spot."

I deadpan, "My stellar wit?"

"Well adjusted and non superficial people would agree, but they're in the minority." She offers me a cross between a smile and a cringe.

Hope narrows her eyes at her roommate. "That was a very nice way to diss the masses."

"Thank you." Rose grabs the sides of her skirt and does a little curtesy.

"Fine. We do have to lean on the physical angle to justify why we're getting married after knowing each other for like two months. But this?" I pull up a dress with more cutouts than fabric. "This isn't my style."

"Trust your friend." Rose points at herself. "I have great eye and also your very best interests in mind."

Fifteen minutes later, I'm in a changing room with five options, all of them in various shades of pink. Everyone knows that green is my thing, but we carefully looked at all the options in that color and let's just say, I wouldn't like to appear in my wedding pics looking like someone threw slime on me—they were that bad.

"I'm starting to hate my life," I mutter to myself as I pinch the fabric of one dress that looks like a Bavarian Dirndl. The blouse-like portion is made of see-through fabric, the low bodice consists of a webbing of lace that would probably not even let me sit comfortably, and the miniskirt is some kind of silky concoction that won't stand a breeze.

I slide it to the left of the hanger and look at the next option. This one has no shoulders and I immediately know it's not gonna work, even though the rest of it is cute. My chesticles are larger than average—on a significant scale—and I'm not looking forward to any wardrobe dysfunctions.

The third dress does have straps, but when I lift it up by the fabric it splays open by a thigh slit that probably makes it to my ribcage. Maybe this is supposed to be worn with another dress underneath?

"Rosalina," I say in my most commanding voice. "If you don't bring me something reasonable I'm going to give you the cold shoulder for three days straight."

"*Oh, no.* Not the cold shoulder," she repeats dramatically before sliding the curtain open and offering a handful more options. "Here, I found another rack at the back that has a bit pricier but better options."

I whine, "We should've gone to a thrift store instead." After all, I have too much mortgage left to pay.

"Absolutely not, the something borrowed is not going to be your wedding dress," Hope says from somewhere beyond the curtain. It really is a shame that she's been convinced by Rose that I should look… good, I guess.

Intrinsically there's nothing wrong with that. I also love how the pieces in my wardrobe make me feel when I wear them, especially when they flatter my top heavy proportions. But this? I grab the extra options and close the curtain again. Whatever dress I come out of this store with is going to feel like the garment I'll wear while I walk the plank. Not that marriage is the same as being killed by pirates. Not that this marriage is real anyway.

Ugh, my head hurts.

I pick one of the least obnoxious dresses in that it's a classic, strappy dress with decent coverage. The only defect is that it's so hot pink it would even offend Marty.

I walk out with my shoulders slumped. I find Hope wearing a yellow sheath number that looks stunning on her athletic frame, and Rose in a very feminine lilac dress that looks like it was made for a fairy, and shows her miles long legs.

"That's not fair," I grouch. "Why do you guys get to wear your favorite colors and I don't?"

Hope motions at herself. "These don't look like baby mucus."

Low in my throat, I mumble, "Fair point."

"What if we all wear pink?" Rose asks. "That way you won't feel weird on your own."

"Do I have to?" Hope frowns.

"Yes, join me in my pain," I respond firmly. "Anyway, what do you think about this one?"

They assess me quietly for all of three seconds each.

"Boring," one answers.

"Safe."

I look down at myself. "For whom? Because I'm really feeling the breeze in this one."

Rose raises her hand. "Let me rephrase. You look like an average woman in the '90s."

My brow tightens. "And that's a bad thing why?"

"Because," she enunciates with extra care, "you don't want to look average. You have to be the star of your own wedding."

I refrain from pointing out that the wedding isn't a real milestone in my life that I'll tell stories about to my kids. With how much I trust men in general, my kids are probably just going to be felines who won't pay attention to whatever I babble.

Stomping, I go back inside and close the curtain to try another option. I hear them do the same, and for a while there's only rustling and grunting.

Somehow, we manage to clock each other and come out at the same time. We take one peek at one another and—Burst out laughing like hyenas.

"What the—"

"Stop, I can't—"

"What is *that*?"

"You're not any better!"

"Stop, my stomach hurts."

We bend over, slam into each other, and I nearly fall into the curtain because I've completely lost my ability to compose myself.

Tears run down Rose's face. Hope's laughter has turned into pterodactyl screeches that send us into even more fits.

She's drowning in pink puffs like a porcelain doll from two centuries ago. Rose's dress is some kind of plastic thing that has rolled up into a complete wardrobe dysfunction. Mine has enough holes that it doesn't look sexy—it looks like mice ate entire parts of it.

"Stop, I'm gonna lose control of my bladder and it'll all be your fault," Hope screeches.

"I'm dying here. Positively dying," I confirm between aggressive hiccups.

Rose snort-laughs. "This is the most fun I've had in a while."

"Yeah, me too."

"Same."

We share wide grins, rosy cheeks, and I don't need to look myself in the mirror to know that my eyes are sparkling as much as theirs.

The third time's the charm. Nestled in my pile of options is a pale pastel pink dress that yes, is short, frothy, a bit risqué at the top, and has next to no fabric on the back aside from the skirt. But the fabric is layered properly and nothing will show accidentally, and it's long enough that I'll even be able to wear shorts. When I try it on, *I* feel like a fairy. I don't even mind that it matches the splotchy blush across my face and my chest. I do a little twirl and the skirt flows, but not enough to flash the figurative audience.

This is the one.

I step out of the changing room and gasps echo around me.

"Perfect." Rose claps slowly, shaking her head in awe. "I told you I have excellent taste."

"Then what were those other options?" I jerk my thumb behind me.

She full on smirks. "Those are called benign pranks, if you couldn't tell."

Hope bodily turns me around and whistles when she sees the back. "Va va boom, this is convincing enough."

"Yes, the internet will love this," Rose agrees.

"*Miguel* will love this." Hope wiggles her eyebrows at me.

I make a point of rolling my eyes as hard as I can manage. "Please, I'm not trying to seduce him."

Hope ignores me. "What do you think about this one on me?" She's in the same dress I tried on before, and the hot pink looks freaking gorgeous against her silky brown skin. It makes her blush pop in a way that I'm sure the Cowboy won't be able to resist.

"You know what?" I bob my head. "Yes, on you this is actually a whole heck yes."

"I agree." Rose calls our attention with, "And what about this one for me?"

We turn to study her outfit. It's a different one from the shoulder-less I had in my changing room, but closely related. The bodice is structured and cinched perfectly around Rose's shape, almost like she had it made instead of plucked off the rack. It's actually gonna be funny to see Logan's logical brain shut off at this sight.

"Bravo!" I exclaim.

Hope whistles again. "You look like a celebrity."

"Great," the pack leader of this expedition says. "Let's pay for our purchases and move onto the next leg of our journey. Is it gonna be shoes or rings?"

I sit in the awkward silence as they wait for me, in tune with how my heart picks up speed at the obvious option presented by my brain. The least desirable one—the one that is gonna feel like ripping off a wax strip.

"Rings," I finally mumble.

"All right."

We share nods, the girls go back in their changing rooms before me. It takes me a moment longer to activate my now trembling limbs.

"It's fine, everything's fine," I whisper softly to myself, my voice drowned under the rustling of clothes.

Yesterday, as we were brainstorming with the guys, Miguel and I concluded that simple gold bands will do. Not just because they're affordable, something that only I care about in this charade. But also because—get this—gold looks better on both of our skins than white or pink gold. We tested it with accessories that came straight from Rosalina's treasure chest.

I nearly died when Miguel and I put our hands together to compare the different golds. It almost felt real for a second, like we were really discussing what we were gonna wear for the rest of our lives.

Despite the good fun we ended up having in the store, which the large paper bag slamming against my thigh as I walk reminds me of, the feeling of trepidation I had earlier creeps back in with every step.

Am I doing the right thing? Couldn't I just book a flight to Lithuania on my credit card and change my name there?

The answers are no, but also no. If I run—and here my eyes lift from the ground to my friends walking in front of me, acting as icebreakers against the crowd—then they'll be at risk of my dad's whims. I will *never* do that to them. I love my friends too much to back down.

So, in we go into a jewelry store. This is less busy than the clothing stores, but still we wait for a solid while until a seller is able to greet us.

"Good morning and welcome. Can I help you find something specific?" the woman asks with the smile of someone who isn't implicating other people in the biggest screw-up of her life. Oh, to be her.

"Yes," Rose responds on behalf of the group, but she turns back to me. "My friend here is looking for wedding rings."

The sales woman, whose name tag reads Tonya, falters at that piece of information. Traditionally, people who are engaged would come together to do this. Here I am with two girl friends. By the way Tonya glances at us, I can tell that she's trying to figure out what the story is here. Before her brain explodes with creative possibilities, I speak.

"My fiancé unfortunately couldn't come, so my friends are providing moral support right now."

"That is so sweet." Tonya clasps her hands in a way that I can tell means, *glad I didn't step on a landmine there.* "Do your fiancé and you have a specific idea, or would you like to look at different options?"

I swallow hard enough that I'm sure the whole store can hear it. "We lean toward a classic gold band."

"Perfect, come with me."

We walk around the counter, following her to a different corner. The girls whisper in my ear, "you got this" and also, "it's gonna be great." Except I don't got this and it's gonna be a disaster.

Tonya pulls out two different cases full of rings in pairs, a larger one that is clearly supposed to be for a man, and a smaller one for a woman. My eyes get lost on all the shiny gold. What if a man is actually smaller than a woman? What if it's two people of the same gender? What if one wants yellow gold and the other pink? What if they're both the same size? What if they have different taste?

I figure these are all the things a regular couple that knows each other and truly wants to spend their lives together would discuss. Between them. Not with a group of friends. They'd be standing here in front of Tonya together, excited for what these rings symbolize.

I wanna barf. I don't even know what Miguel's favorite

color is—if he even has one. I don't know if he prefers a more modest ring or one that gets everybody's attention. I also don't know what we're gonna do with these after we legally divorce. Jewelry is like cars, where they start devaluating the second you take them out of the store. That means I'm making Miguel waste his hard earned money on me. Plus however much of his time will take to live this farce. And that's also not to mention the whole vacation day that Hope and Rosalina took to come here.

"I know this is a very exciting moment," Hope says, placing her hand on my back and rubbing circles. "But I'm gonna need you to breathe, okay?"

Rose asks, "Do you happen to have some water for the bride? I think she's simply so overcome with emotion that she's frozen."

Yeah, if *emotion* is the new name for *panic*.

"Of course!" Tonya says. "Would you two like some water as well?"

"Oh, yes."

"Thank you."

As she walks off to the back I glance at my friends. "Guys, what the hell am I doing?"

"The right thing," Hope answers with a determined set to her mouth.

Rose lifts her chin. "The only thing. And so help us, we're going to free you from your dad no matter what we do."

Tonya returns carrying three mini water bottles, chilled enough to freeze our brains. She walks us through the different shapes and finishes of the rings, adding some stories about what they mean in some cultures, and throwing some examples about past clients that are meant to build upon the concept of these being happily-ever-after rings and not the-one-to-rule-them-all rings.

There are matte, shiny, and etched rings in all sorts of

designs—straight lines, swirls, chevrons, and more. Some are flat, empty cylinders. Some have curves. Others are bulkier than their slimmer neighbors. Some are a standard band and some are wavier. I try to think about what makes the most sense for Miguel.

I'm sure he's not gonna wear it everyday, because it would be an obstacle for batting or lifting weights comfortably. It would even give him a new callus, and baseball players are very finicky about their hands in general. A slimmer profile might feel more manageable for him, and should definitely be cheaper than the chunkier rings.

He also strikes me as a pretty humble guy. For someone who sits on the slugger throne of the league right now, Miguel is so unassuming that if you don't know who he is, you'd think he's just an average Joe. That rules out all the etched options.

My eyes stop at a modest pair, classical shapes, but matte surface. Yes, I don't think Miguel cares for shiny things. Some guys wear branded bling bling around their necks during games, and this is a guy who has probably been wearing the same gold link chain and crucifix around his neck all his life, to the point that all shine is gone if there was ever any.

"These ones," I say, pointing at the two rings. "These are perfect."

"You have very good taste," Tonya offers with the sweetest sales woman smile. She carefully plucks out the two rings between gloved fingers, and offers me the smaller one. "Would you like to try it?"

"I, uh—yes." My hand shakes a little. As I slide it into my left ring finger, I realize that I forgot to wear my pretend-engagement ring. If Tonya notices, she doesn't say anything.

The ring is a touch tighter than I'd wear but I manage to slide it into place. The sight of it is a shock to the system, something like waking up one morning to a random tattoo on your skin.

In a reverent voice, Rose says, "That is absolutely beautiful."

"I agree." Hope covers her mouth, and her eyes look suspiciously shiny. "It's like this was made for you."

I don't twitch. There's no need to contradict them. It genuinely doesn't matter if I think the ring is pretty or not. It's just a tool for freedom, just like the marriage certificate will be.

"This is the one," I announce, all serious and sure of myself. "Do you have other sizes in stock?"

"As a matter of fact, we do," Tonya says, as if she wasn't sealing my fate with those words.

After getting the proper sizes for Miguel and I, and casually tapping his credit card on the payment machine, I walk out of the jewelry store with my friends like I'm in a pool—both floating and underwater, light and heavy at the same time.

I pat my purse absentmindedly, needing frequent reminders that I do carry a box with wedding rings in it. That my life is going to change in just over twenty-four hours.

CHAPTER 20
MIGUEL

My agent is the very best, no discussion. Not only she has helped me negotiate my way into a career I can be proud of, but she also has the patience of a saint. When I called her with the news that I'm getting married to help a friend, an average manager would've flipped out.

Think about your career! This is going to tank your image. Your fans will hate you and sponsors will leave you when the truth comes out.

Also, *have you lost your ever loving mind?*

Those are all the things I would've gotten from anyone but Amelia Herrera—but she's my cousin and she's seen my entire trajectory from pee wee little shit, to hormonal teenager with an eye toward the big leagues, to single dad major leaguer, to All-Star and top jersey seller of any team I'm in. She knows that I'm as stubborn as I am anxious, extremely awkward deep down, and that I never give up no matter what—even despite myself.

"I'll help you," was the first thing she said. "If only so that I can control how bad the fall is gonna be."

And that's my cousin. She will aid and abet without judgement, but she'll also make sure I don't destroy myself.

She's the one I'm texting as a limousine takes the group from the hotel to a night club. My thumbs fly across the screen in a hurry to get a full thought out.

ME

I haven't got confirmation yet about the flower arrangements

The bride needs a bouquet to really be a bride

The bridesmaids do too

And it would be nice if we have little flowers for our lapels too

We won't look like this is a hasty wedding that way

I did get confirmation from the photographer but I changed my mind and now want the VIP package

Can you also check with him? Pretty please?

"Hey dude, who you texting?" I feel Lucky shift closer to peep at my screen, and I angle it away from him. "And also, why is it a secret?"

"Have you ever heard of nunya?" I offer casually as I finish firing off one last text where I tell Amelia that I'll owe her big, big time.

"How sassy. This must be important then." He lowers his voice, which isn't really necessary with reggaeton playing at full blast, and the others chatting up a storm. "Is it your real girlfriend? Secret wife?"

"No, and no," I say, because I know him enough by now to realize he will never let go until he gets a satisfying enough answer. "The only girl I'm really attached to is my daughter."

Then a text comes in from my cousin.

SUPER AGENT

Last I checked with the florist they were turning over every stone to find you green flowers, you freak. But I'll check in again and I'll call the photographer too

I need you to get me the phone number of your friend who's gonna post this on SM. Need to approve what she posts before she does

What if she snaps a picture of you picking your nose and with a wedgie and blasts that to the internet??

ME

I don't pick my nose in public

SUPER AGENT

But you do get wedgies

You might forget sometimes, but you're only human

I know that... very well. My eyes lift to the back of the limo, where Audrey sits along with her roommates. She looks surprisingly calm, for someone who was freaking out this morning. Maybe they're making wise use of liquid courage, or she's come to terms with our ridiculous plan. And here I am, trying to make this wedding decent so that she doesn't spiral, because I care about what happens to her more than I'm ready to admit.

I run through the checklist in my mind again. Marriage license, check—filed online yesterday and secured today. Chapel check—the late notice caused me to do some bargaining with money involved, but it was worth it. Florist and photographer almost finalized. Audrey doesn't want to wear a traditional white dress, so no need to rent one. We'll go clubbing before the wedding, rather than doing a reception afterward, so that also took care of itself. Limo, check—we won't be without transportation all night. Dinner, already done —no one's starving under my watch. And hotel room, check.

My face twitches and I focus back down on the texts with my cousin. Players and staff stay together in the same hotel for every away series, and for this one we're two guys per room. I couldn't kick out my roomie—Lucky, funny enough—because then he'd have to book his own thing and that's just not fair. So I had to get a different room.

Here's the kicker, Audrey doesn't know about that yet. I'm not sure if she's planning to squeeze in with Rose and Hope, or if she already got a room for herself. But I got her an even better one so that she can decompress and bask in her newfound freedom after the ceremony.

SUPER AGENT

Are you sure you want to do this?

My thumbs hover in the air, and I really reflect on the gravity of the question.

This is gonna change things. Like, we're not gonna have a married life or anything, but we'll be more involved. Part of my flabbers are gasted that I'm doing this. But another part is actually looking forward to it, not even worried about the mess, a future fallout, or what anyone will say. I've even been practicing how to break the news to Charlie Cox after this is done, and it feels just the same as stepping up to the plate does.

Indeed, I've gone and lost my mind.

ME

Yeap

Amelia doesn't counter that. I bet she's even talking with the florist now. I really want those green carnations in Audrey's bouquet, they'll make her happy.

When I finally put my phone away, I find her attention on me across the limo. Audrey studies me like she has never seen someone stranger, with two whole heads and five eyes, green skin and steam coming out of his mouth.

That's all I glean from her because she turns back to the conversation with her besties, which is great because now I can linger. She's always gorgeous, but right now she looks like she could fool anyone into thinking that she's in love. Rosy cheeks and lips, flowing hair framing her face, a girly dress that really accentuates her, um, girl attributes, and legs for miles.

"Wipe your drool, man," Lucky suggests.

I close my mouth and do everything I can to not raise my hand and confirm whether said drool is really out.

I'm an adult.

But not around this woman. I become a fumbling teenager.

I wipe my face just in case.

"You didn't see that," I tell Lucky like it's a command.

There's no doubt that he's laughing on the inside as he says, "I have no idea what you're talking about."

I point at him, then at my eyes, and run my thumb in the air across my neck. He returns a thumb up.

The limo slows down and this time it's not due to traffic. A moment later the driver opens the door to usher everybody out to our next destination. This one is actually courtesy of Lucky, who found what apparently is the best Latin night club of Las Vegas for pregaming. I hang out at the back of the group, waiting to make sure that no one's getting left behind.

That's when, for the first time all night, the bride acknowledges my existence up close. We stare at each other in a full display of awkwardness.

"Hi," I manage to rasp out.

"Hey." Her eyes roam all over my face, like searching for something. I give her *nothing*. "Aren't you escorting me?"

The *nothing* is due to the fact that every braincell has fled from my skull, obviously. "Huh?"

"I mean…" She clears her throat and pushes her hair behind her ears. "This is when the show begins, you know? Once we step outside of this vehicle it's no longer just our friends and us."

"Mierda. You're right. We should've talked about this before. I don't know how you want me to act." My eyes widen to a painful degree. Somewhere between all the logistics I should've figured out that there was gonna be a certain amount of PDA involved in this deal.

Audrey takes a deep breath and offers her hand. "Just follow my lead."

Finally my wits boomerang back to me and I offer my arm instead. "I'll do you one better, I'm going to act like the perfect gentleman."

Lifting her chin almost in defiance, she slides her hand into the crook of my arm and I nearly see stars. Surely it's because I haven't been breathing properly and not because this is the best feeling in the world, right? I send a command to the rest of my body to be on my best damn behavior tonight, or else.

Or else I'm gonna have to find a quiet place to do some burpees until I drop.

We step off the limousine and I thank the driver. He's left us right at the club's door and is gonna wait around for about two hours until we have to head to the chapel. I'll tip him well enough to compensate for all this hassle and more.

"Welcome, Mr. Machado. Our hostess will show you to your VIP area," the bouncer says as we walk up to him, skipping the line.

"Thank you," I repeat, a little lightheaded without any alcohol in my system.

An explosion of sounds greets us the moment we walk in. It takes me a moment to readjust my brain and figure out that what's making the walls vibrate and hypes the people up is Cuban salsa. We follow behind our friends, herded by a hostess that takes us through hidden corridors.

I check in on my partner in crime. Audrey examines the dancing crowd until the corridor ensconces us away from the people who are actually here for a good time. She turns to me and says, "I don't know how to dance."

Right away, the image of her in my arms swaying to a waltz comes to my mind.

"You do," I counter. "You were really good at your dad's benefit."

"Trust me, I'm not. That was all you."

"Then I guess I'll have to teach you," I say with a shrug. This is what finally makes her lose her composure. Her jaw slackens and she trips on her own feet. Fortunately, I keep her standing.

"Okay, this is cool," the Cowboy says in appreciation as he takes in the private VIP section. "Good job, Lucky."

The Boricua throws his arm around the Texan's shoulders. "Thank you, I do anything for my amigos."

I stop for a second once we're inside the private area. It's larger than my living room, with furniture that gleams with expensive and new. Capped bottles of water, liquor and non-alcoholic beverages sit comfortable in a bed of ice in the middle of the low table—can't be called coffee table because there's none in sight. It opens up to a balcony from which we have perfect view of the crowd downstairs. Someone must've noticed us because Rose is waving down. There's a touchscreen against the wall that the hostess explains is the way to ask for further service. And we have our own private restroom.

This is something I can never say aloud because boo freaking hoo, but sometimes I forget that I'm rich now and that I can afford this.

Back when I was still in Venezuela, the clubs were rundown

and much smaller, packed with more people, with a DJ instead of a live band, and I couldn't buy a whole bottle of rum with everything I had in my bank.

I was much more relaxed, though—there for a good time with my friends. Bailar pegao, make out with someone, and get trashed on Cacique in that order.

I check my surroundings once more. I'll teach Audrey how to follow a few basic moves, but I won't stick to her like glue. We're definitely not kissing until we have to at the chapel. And I'm sticking to water no matter what. No way we're rehashing my previous night club escapades.

Our team captain immediately plops on the largest sofa, nearly swallowing it in its entirety, but his girlfriend grabs onto his hand and pulls. "Nuh-uh, we're gonna dance."

It's loud enough that I can't make out the literal meaning of his grumble, yet he stands up to tag along.

"No booze," Hope tells her man with a stern index finger.

The guy responds with "I don't need it," and grabs Hope's hips like this is their living room.

Lucky walks by me, saying, "Yeah, I'm gonna go find me a dancing partner. See ya laters, cabrones."

Audrey turns to me again. "I confess, I'm out of my depth here."

"Kinda same," I admit, running my free hand through my hair and down to the back of my neck. "The last time I did this I produced a kid."

She chokes. "Crap, don't scare me like that."

Weirdly enough, I find the nerve to laugh. "Don't worry, you're safe."

"What does that mean?" She cocks a defiant eyebrow at me, and it takes me a moment to figure out how she could take offense.

It's not that I don't want her.

It's that I know she doesn't want me, and I'll never impose myself on her.

I lean closer to her and whisper into her ear, "What I mean is that I'm a big boy and can control myself now."

Somehow. I don't know how. I'm certainly struggling from just having her hand on my forearm, and I keep clenching my muscles more than necessary. The sweet apple scent that clings to her skin is making my head spin, and my heart is beating to the same rhythm of the fast percussion of salsa.

She rises on her tip toes to say, "Good boy, good answer."

I'm overjoyed at my sartorial choices right now, because her hand falls right on my rolled up sleeve and she can't feel the goosebumps that have broken all over my body.

"So..." I drift off, searching for any neurons that are still functioning. "We have some time to kill, do you want to hang out here or mingle downstairs?"

One look at Hope and Cade line dancing across the expanse of the private area, and at the fact that our other friends have joined the masses, and she makes up her mind.

"Honestly, I don't want Hope to see how inept I am at Latin dancing, let's go downstairs."

I tease her back, "You do know that many more people will witness your two left feet on the floor, right?"

"I'm counting on them being too drunk to notice me." Audrey tugs at my arm and I'm happy to follow.

Her steps down the private corridor are strong and steady, no sign of the nerves that were fluttering inside of her. What a strange woman. I can't believe how no one has married her already.

The corridor veers on the right toward the entrance, and on the left toward the dance floor at the back of the establishment, close to the DJ and one of the bars. I switch us around so that she's behind me and I can break the ice. Her grip on my arm slides and I pause in between strangers, glancing back. After a pause, she grabs onto my hand—and I mean, fingers between mine, tight grip and no chill. Like we do this all the time. I turn back to the front and keep going, also like this is no big deal. But her hand is both soft and strong, also a bit too cool.

So she really is nervous, huh?

This is gonna distract her real good though.

I find us a good spot by the stage and whirl us around so that her back is against it, and the drunk strangers are behind me. "Ready?" I have to shout.

"No," she yells back and raises her hands like she's setting up for a waltz. "What do I do?"

I grab her hands and pull her closer, leaning into her ear. "Follow my lead," I paraphrase her.

She stiffens but still allows me to guide her hands. One goes to my shoulder, the other one stays nestled in my hand. My free hand goes to her waist, which is lower and more daring than a fancy European dance. And even though I'm sticking to my vow of keeping a decent distance, I still position her closer than when we danced the first time. Audrey watches me like a hawk, lowering her focus down to my feet.

I release her waist to tip her chin back up, and she blinks in confusion. "Don't look down, just go with the flow," I kinda shout into her ear.

In the same volume, she asks, "What if my flow is awful?"

"Then go with my flow."

She cringes like this is the scariest part of the night, and not the I do's that will follow. The good thing is that she's probably not thinking about that right now, though, and frankly neither am I.

I have enough Indigenous and Black blood to make me a percussion guy, and I find my rhythm with no effort. Audrey resists the motions at first, or maybe it's just that she doesn't know what to do. After a few easy steps back and forth in the classic 1-2-3–5-6-7, she starts to follow.

"This isn't so bad," she yells.

All I do is smirk a little.

The beat changes and I show her the classic Venezuelan style, which is probably the simplest of all. I alternate holding her hands as I swing to the side, moving away from her while my feet do their thing. She gets the hang of it, even if she can't yet add any swing to her steps. After a moment I return her to my arms, and the song starts to wind down.

A different beat leaks in slowly, and I don't need to have gone to college to know what's coming. El papá de los helados: a classic reggaeton jam by Daddy Yankee.

As the tune builds up, I speak into her ear again, "Are you ready for the big leagues?"

"What do you mean?" she asks.

Slowly, I slide my hands down to land at her hips—not her waist, lower. Where she's gonna have to move. We stand still. Me, waiting to see if she's not on board. Her, making a decision.

The response comes with her hands settling on my shoulders and her scream-saying, "Just don't let me fall."

I wouldn't. Never in this life. Especially not when I'm too busy falling myself.

Instead, I respond, "I got you."

Pressing my fingers subtly, I guide her hips to follow mine. Reggaeton is probably the easiest Latin dance, in that it doesn't require special footwork. It's all about the swing and the swag. We're as close as it can get without rubbing all up on each other, and she keeps blinking owlishly at me under the strobe lights. Someone bumps into my back but I couldn't care less, I have a handful of woman to focus on.

Daddy Yankee sings about a woman who is dura, which after playing with so many Puerto Ricans I learned is code for a hot woman. I fix my eyes at a blurry spot behind Audrey, trying to turn my brain off to the fact that she's hot. In my arms. Moving her hips along with mine. And that my skin is in flames, even when we're not close enough.

How the hell am I going to behave when I have to kiss her at the chapel?

CHAPTER 21
AUDREY

think I'm in shock.

The guys are trawling downstairs in search of a certain Lucky Rivera, who has been seen in so many different spots that no one knows who hallucinated him and who saw him for real.

Rose, Hope and I are in the private VIP area, sitting together on the couch and having tiny and very colorful cocktails that first hit you with sweetness and then with a punch to the solar plexus. It's exactly what I need, and yet it can't pacify me for reasons I don't understand.

Okay, I lie. I know exactly why.

The problem is that I'm super embarrassed. It's a damn shame that I can't bury my head in the sand and live like that the rest of my life.

The reason is because I'm today years old when I discovered that Miguel Machado is a man.

I know, I know. What else could he have possibly been all along? His pronouns have been clear, his testosterone levels seem pretty healthy going by his musculature, and he seems perfectly capable of growing a beard, even if he chooses not to.

But despite all of that I had put him in a very rare category of male friend, which has a tiny population. He registered more as a person than as a man. And before meeting him, he was in a mythical category reserved for baseball legends past and present, and for celebrities I have no chance of ever meeting in person.

Except that he dances very well. *Too* well.

I didn't say anything because I'm not sure if that's a stereotype, but when I told him I couldn't follow a tune to save my life I wasn't lying. I can't even do justice to my favorite songs. But he asked me to focus on him and *moved me* like it wasn't the first time we were doing this—the waltz doesn't count, because I wasn't close enough to see that he has spectacular eyelashes, and is really hot. Temperature wise.

Which in turn, made me notice that he's really freaking hot in the other sense.

Pretty sure he noticed that I was sweating bullets and probably attributed it to the exercise. In the meantime, I was losing my mind over the fact that I've treated this specimen of man like he was my bestie. I have been my most uncool openly in front of him. Heck, the first time he saw me I was in my fave pajamas and bunny slippers.

Bunny stinking slippers.

And now we're getting married.

How am I even going to be a convincing stepmom for Marty? The natural partner of someone like her dad would be a super accomplished, gorgeous woman who matches his calm and joyful energy. Not a neurotic mess who can't get out of problems on her own.

"Oh, Cade says they found Lucky," Hope informs us while reading from her phone screen. "Apparently he was just stuck in the men's bathroom because the door latch didn't work. So the search became a rescue too."

Rose laughs. "I love him, there's never a dull moment with him around."

See, that's also why Lucky wouldn't have been the right option for this absurd plan. Who could possibly believe that I'd capture his attention when I'm a dull English rose whose sense of humor consists of sarcasm to mask things I don't actually find funny?

I slump on the couch and cradle my frozen cocktail cup. It catches the girls's attention and Rose asks me, "Are you ready for the real show?"

"No," I spew out before I can make use of my stellar sarcastic skills.

It really quiets the room.

"I mean, is it too late to stop all of this?" I squirm and fix my dress to busy myself and pretend like I don't want to crawl out of my own skin.

Hope's expression turns very serious. "We can stop at any time."

"I agree but…" Rose bites her lips. "Then what's plan B?"
Nothing.

I've overthought this to death and nothing else is feasible. Dad would find me even if I become a sequestered nun. He bought a whole ass baseball team just to keep tabs on me, after all.

"Welp." I slap my thigh like I'm eighty seven years old and stand up. "Guess we're really doing this." Then I down the rest of my cocktail and set the cup down before letting out all the air in my lungs.

"Atta girl." Rose squeezes my shoulder. "I can't believe you're the first one who's gonna get married out of us."

I cringe. "Sorry for stealing you guys's thunder."

"Nah, please." She waves a hand.

Hope laces her arms with ours. "This is great, actually. I didn't want to be the first one because what if I screwed up somehow?" The two of us look at her. "Sorry, I didn't mean to make you more nervous."

"I'm gonna barf," I say in total deadpan.

"Hello, ladies!" Lucky bursts into the room, arms spread wide. "Miss me no more, I'm back and ready for the next leg of the party!"

"Good for you," I mumble under my breath. The girls shoot me amused glances.

Behind him, the other guys appear as well. Logan is the one who calls out, "The limo is here. Ready to go?"

I stay quiet.

No. Yes. Sorta?

I really want to see Dad's face when I tell him I'm married and to whom, and then see Henry's ego be yeeted into outer space forever.

But me? A wife? Oh my word.

Oh. My. Word.

"Ha ha, yes. Ha," I respond, clearly at my wit's end.

We file out of the club the same way we did, in pairs with our respective partners except for Lucky. It's a shame that I don't have another girl friend nearby for them to keep each other company, but my literal only other girl friend is a hotshot executive at *SPORTY* and lives up in Connecticut. She's visiting in the fall, and I couldn't in good conscience pull her away from her busy schedule for these absurd shenanigans.

Inevitably, this means that now I sit at the back of the limo alone with Miguel. He's texting again, just like he did all through the drive to the club.

I nudge him gently and ask, "Is that Marty?" His daughter is by far the best part of this bargain, and she was really pissed that she couldn't come to the wedding and had to stay home with Consuelo.

Miguel flinches a little as if I just asked the most surprising thing in the world. "No. It's my cousin."

Since when does he have a cousin? Or is that code for something else?

I don't actually know the guy, and this is the moment when that strikes me. We haven't talked much about our families beyond the immediate ones, or about our hopes and dreams, or about any boundaries during this arrangement.

Swallowing hard, I broach the more immediate one. "Miguel, can I ask you yet another favor?"

He's been watching my face all this time, and he remains calm and collected. "Of course." Nothing but sincerity behind his eyes, like he's cool if I ask him to steal a cruise boat together.

"Can we fake the kiss after the vows?" I grab at the hem of my dress. "I just think that should be kept for a real wedding with honest feelings, you know? I'm not, er, I don't want to mock something that is so important for other people."

He blinks exactly three times before opening his mouth. "Of course," he parrots again. "That's fine. We won't do anything you don't want to."

"Thank you."

He turns his attention back on texting his cousin. I try to fixate on the view outside the window. Lights of all colors streak by as we drive to the chapel. My stomach jumps, my whole body tingles, yet I feel exhausted already. Like an hour and change of dancing with the man next to me was the biggest test of endurance I've ever survived.

Well, I think as I peek at him from the corner of my eye, what can I expect from an elite athlete at the top of the pecking order? Even his fingers have muscles, for goodness's sake.

It's a good thing that I don't have to keep up with him for real, huh?

I turn back to the window so none of these hawk-eyes can catch the embarrassed cringe in my face.

I really need to put him back in the *person* category rather than in the *man* one. Just the same way I view Logan, Lucky, and Cade, and the rest of the team.

Too soon, the limo pulls into a gigantic parking lot and keeps going and going. One of my knees starts to bounce. Miguel finally puts his phone away. Lucky's giving some kind of speech that I can't focus on. The limo keeps rolling. I try to swallow but there's no saliva left, and I can practically hear the rush of my blood across my body. Why is the Cowboy getting up from his seat? Oh shit, the limo finally stopped. My heart trips on itself and I gasp.

Quietly, Miguel offers me his arm and for reasons I can't quite describe with my lizard brain, the gesture opens up my lungs again. I hold onto his steel-like arm and step off the vehicle with way more confidence than I really feel.

"Breathing is a good idea," Miguel whispers in a way I can only describe as kind. His eyes are molten chocolate and the corners of his lips are tipped upward.

I nod rapidly and force myself to take one deep breath after the next, until my head's no longer swimming and my eyes can focus.

Our friends walk in front of us into a reception area. It's large enough to play a full basketball game, with elegant chairs packed with couples and their witnesses. What surprises me the most isn't the screen with numbers like this is the DMV, but the fact that most people look pretty sober. I guess I did right by not drowning my sorrows with a bottle.

Instead of joining the people who are clearly waiting their turn, someone intercepts Lucky at the front of the group and after exchanging a quick word, they guide us to keep going.

"What's happening?" I ask Miguel.

"We're a couple of minutes late, so it's our turn already," he explains, and all I can do is let out a tiny mewl. His other hand comes on top of mine, large, hot, and calloused. Very man, mucho macho.

We keep to what would otherwise seem like a grim silence. But in my case I'm just freaking out, and maybe Miguel is too. I guarantee he didn't have getting married in his bingo card when he moved to Orlando, or that Elvis was gonna be the officiant.

But on that I'm wrong, because the chapel coordinator shuffles us all around so that the men go in first and I can't get a clear look, but the one at the altar looks like an older woman in a normal outfit. The door closes and the coordinator extends her arm in a different direction, "Please follow me."

My roomies turn to me. I fill up my lungs, straighten my back, and say, "Let's do this."

We follow the stranger woman to a hidden alcove where another employee awaits. This one's a guy and he starts passing stuff to the three of us—flowers.

Wait, what? I forgot that I needed to get a bouquet!

And right then, the most perfect arrangement appears in my hands like magic.

My jaw drops as I take it in, the sweet fragrance of fresh flowers and eucalyptus. I'm not very savvy about this but the palette is green and white, which instantly makes my belly feel warm, and the main flowers seem to be carnations. I didn't know green ones existed.

The girls also have similar bouquets, only smaller. They look absolutely adorable in their pink dresses and with the flowers, and they're smiling like nothing about this is a sham. Or like it's gonna keep them entertained for the next five years. Maybe both.

The warmth in my stomach dissipates, giving room to nerves again. The words *oh my word* keep repeating in my head as I'm asked to remain alone in the alcove.

Right, the bride enters last and all that.

"Excuse me, miss," a third employee says as he walks in dragging a rack with a ton of fabric hanging off it. "Which veil would you like to wear for your special night?"

A veil! I also forgot about that.

There must be at least fifty choices. I'm sure time is precious both in terms of money and also on account of all the people waiting outside to tie the knot. I roam my eyes across the selection once and a ruffle catches my attention. Clutching the bouquet against my chest, I reach for it and fan it out. It's one of the simplest ones, intricate lacework in the shape of… carnations? Seems like serendipity.

"This one," I declare.

"Excellent choice, please allow me to fit it."

Dude's near my height, so I take a seat as he works on pinning the veil to my hair at the top of my head.

Suddenly, the veil comes over my face and oh, shit. This is really happening.

My legs are lead as I get back up. My head is also just as heavy. Veil guy ushers me toward the door and he says something. Going by his smile, it's a good thing. I return the gesture and walk in. And freeze.

The wedding march plays from a piano delicately. The inside of the chapel is cozy—no basketball will be played here—and there are lovely green touches everywhere. In ribbons, flowers, even crystals. Nothing looks cheap, like actual effort was put into this. There's only one problem, though.

I didn't put any.

My eyes snap to Miguel and I really look at him.

He's in a pristine white button shirt that without a doubt was tailor made. No off the shelves clothes would ever fit those massive shoulders and arms, and a tapered waist like that. Same for his blue slacks. His thighs and calves would rip normal pants off.

Also, how are his legs so freaking straight? Most people

with his height have some bow to them. I look down at my legs. Even mine are a bit curved.

And there, pinned to his shirt pocket, is a tiny arrangement with one carnation that matches my bouquet.

Someone slides next to me and I jump. It's Lucky. He offers me his arm and throws a smirk as a freebie. "Normally dads do this, but none of us are big fans of him, so I'll be usurping him gladly."

I shake my head in awe. "Never change, Lucky."

"Definitely not planning to," he says casually, and with no further warning he starts walking me down the aisle.

The wedding march continues uninterrupted. Flashes go off from the sides—someone's taking pictures. Behind Miguel, Cade and Logan stand with matching green carnations pinned to their shirts. Also white. And they also wear blue slacks of different shades.

My eyes ping back to my bridesmaids in their varying pink shades. There's no way this is a coincidence. These adorable jerks must've planned this behind the scenes so that we look like we meant to be here on purpose.

And the flowers too. And the decoration. And absolutely everything else I didn't even imagine was necessary.

Well, that explains why Miguel has been busy texting the whole night. He was busy planning everything with whoever his cousin is.

My eyes narrow at him as Lucky and I approach, and Miguel tilts his head with some confusion.

Lucky deposits me right in front of Miguel, and the officiant between us starts talking. I can't focus for shit, especially when Miguel's lips are moving without making any sound.

You okay?

I return a tiny nod.

Miguel offers a hand and I take it. I need all the anchoring I can get. This freaking guy starts to guide me through breathing exercises as the officiant keeps delivering the ceremonial speech. My, er, groom's attention goes to our joined hands and I realize that I'm squeezing his to death. He runs his thumb across my knuckles and the most curious thing happens.

I actually calm down.

"And now, the vows," the officiant says.

A long pause happens.

I also forgot that vows are a thing at weddings.

Miguel does the thumb-knuckle thing again, and his full lips stretch into an amused smile. "I'll be your rock," he says, all confident and relaxed. And adds nothing else.

The officiant blinks owlishly at him, and then turns to me in expectation.

Doubt flashes through my mind just one time. What I'm about to say is probably the most absurd vow this woman has heard, even accounting for the drunk marriages.

"And I'll be your hard place," I return.

Miguel chokes back a laugh. My lips twitch, and our composure shatters into unhinged giggles. It makes sense that a sham wedding should have crappy vows. Neither of us will forget that.

The officiant clears her throat and continues onto the last part of the ceremony. Meanwhile, Miguel and I are still fighting to stay serious, and for the first time all night I'm not freaking out. The fog in my head clears. I'm no longer strangling his hand.

"You may kiss the bride now."

Never mind, my heart leaps in my throat.

Someone taps my arm and I half turn. Hope takes my bouquet and I automatically move back to the front. More flashes go off, and they're almost blinding.

Miguel takes a step closer and gently holds the ends of my veil. I watch transfixed, as if this was a very interesting movie that's happening behind a screen.

And then the veil is off. The cameras flash even faster. I blink almost violently between the lights and the fact that Miguel is bringing me closer, just like he did at the nightclub.

One of his hands circles my waist until his arm is around me, and I'm flush against him. It's a jolt to the system—I can't remember the last time I was held by a guy. I don't think any of them ever did it so tenderly.

Wait, his other hand is cradling my jaw.

How? *Why?*

We're not supposed to kiss.

I can't unglue my lips to speak. Not when Miguel is looking at them like they're the most interesting thing in the entire world.

Oh, gosh. Are they chapped? I didn't think of fixing my lip oil. Is it gonna smear all over him? Argh, where's the pause button?

Then he twirls me gingerly, putting his back between the cameras and I. He comes closer still and I swallow hard. His breath fans my face, revealing that he popped some mints before this. How kind. How nerve wracking.

I start lowering my eyelids and then he touches my lips—

With his thumb.

The same one that soothed my knuckles earlier.

My eyes pop open. Miguel's looking at me calmly, all hooded eyes but serious. His own mouth is pressed against the other side of his thumb, and the officiant announces us officially husband and wife.

Of course. Miguel would never betray my trust. I asked for a favor and true to him, he followed through. He even goes as far as shifting his head just a tad so that everyone else thinks the kiss is real. Our friends break into loud cheering, completely fooled by our act.

He might've been keeping track of the time because Miguel finally deems it reasonable enough, and carefully straightens me back up. Everything feels like I'm underwater and my whole body burns. Without looking at myself in the mirror, I know for a fact that my splotchy blush covers me from head to toe.

The officiant gets our attention again and presents the documents. This is the real marriage—the one I need to defeat my male progenitor with. Miguel is the first one who signs and when it's my turn, I stare at his handwriting in fascination. The signature is a handsome scribble, and his print name is large, easy to read, and friendly. It strikes me as so him.

Miguel Machado.

Machado.

Before I can overthink myself out of it, I sign my name as Audrey Machado.

Screw it. I'll never be Audrey Cox again. The second I get home I'm shredding my previous name change application and throwing it like confetti in my living room.

When Miguel walks me down the aisle as my husband, and me as his wife, I'm free at last.

CHAPTER 22
MIGUEL

Lights dance in my vision as the limo takes us back to the hotel, after an hour of pictures in all angles and poses. At least half of the pictures alone are between Audrey and I, which is awkward enough, but then we get the others in on the play and it adds an extra layer of what-the-hell-are-we-doing.

But what's done is done. I hold in my hands a fancy folio with the marriage certificate, and in it, she signed using my last name.

The folio nearly slips from my sweaty palms and I catch it mid air before it crashes on the floor.

"So what's the plan after this?" Rose asks her newly married friend from her seat on the right side. "Are you going back home to tell your father that you just nuked his plans, or are you sticking around a bit?"

Audrey sounds like she's about to drop asleep when she responds, "I travel back tomorrow afternoon, but I'm not planning on breaking the news to him right away. I need to buy myself as much time as possible."

"Yeah, that makes sense."

Nothing makes sense anymore. I'm just along for the ride.

However, my brain spews out a single thought. "By the way, I got a hotel room."

Every conversation dies off and all eyes settle on me.

"What?" Then it clicks in my tired and overwhelmed brain. The folio's destiny really was to fall on the floor of the limousine after all, and I raise my hands in defense. "I mean, for her! Not for both of us, you creeps."

"Oh."

"Whew."

"I knew you were a good guy all along."

My chest is on fire. Luckily for me, that's where my embarrassment concentrates and not on my face. Since I'm fully dressed, only I know that I'm dying on the inside.

"Actually…" Lucky taps his chin, eyes narrowed in thought. "Wouldn't sleeping in separate rooms after just marrying look weird?"

I blink hard at him. That's not a thought that had crossed my mind until this moment. Audrey's expression tells me that this is also breaking news to her.

All Hope can say is exactly what I'm thinking, which is "but…"

Then Audrey waves a hand. "Guys, we don't have paparazzi chasing us."

"Oh." Rose raises her hand. "Didn't we agree that I was going to take some paparazzi type of shots? Because I've been doing that all night and I was planning on distributing them."

"Right." Lucky snaps his fingers. "This was part of the master plan all along, so you two are gonna have to suck it up and get captured going into the same room together. Otherwise this will all have seemed for show."

"As it is, you mean?" Audrey mumbles low enough that only I can hear. I busy myself with bending forward to collect the scattered documents and put them back in order. "Fine, I guess. Let's do this right," she adds.

Amid the new heavy silence, I catch both Cade and Logan staring at Lucky, who is just sitting peacefully while drinking a bottle of water like he didn't just cause a seismic change.

That's how, after thanking the limo driver with a few Benjamins, we get to the hotel where the team is staying, and sneak into our respective rooms to pack.

"Don't mess this up," Lucky says from his bed as I pack up all my shit, scattered around the room we were supposed to share for four nights straight.

I zip my duffel bag and lift up my head. "I don't plan to."

"Good."

With that strange blessing, I grab my bag and make my way downstairs. The elevator takes five centuries, all through which I tumble from one crisis to the next. I fumble with my phone to check what kind of room I booked, and a mix of contradicting emotions flushes over me when I notice that it's for two queen beds. Past Miguel knew something that current Miguel isn't sure should be making him feel this way.

But it doesn't matter. I may want the woman but more than that, I will *protect* the woman. Also from myself.

So I transition to the next phase, which is stoicism. Even though I forgot about vows, I did mean what I said. I plan to be a support system for Audrey, and that means that I can't inconvenience her.

A massive yawn becomes phase three. More than sleep, I think this is an adrenaline crash. The second we were declared married, my legs started to feel heavy, and it started to become harder to keep my spine straight.

Finally, the elevator reaches the lobby and pings as the doors start to open. I have clear view of Audrey and Rose waiting at the front, and everything I feel is reflected on Audrey's face as well. Or most of it—certainly the exhaustion.

Rose takes over. "Here's the plan, I'll stay at the back and will start taking pictures of you as you walk into the other hotel and check in. Then I'll follow you in the elevator and capture the moment you walk in together into the room. Before either of you sets a foot outside of the room tomorrow morning, I need you to text me so I can rush over and also capture the moment the lovebirds come out together looking glowing and happy. Do we have a plan?"

"Sure," Audrey says without much interest. All I'm capable of is showing a thumbs up.

I grab Audrey's suitcase in my free hand and veer for the exit. The lobby's busy enough with people coming and going, that I only notice the girls aren't following when I'm at the doors. In their crystal reflections, they're both staring at me from the original spot. I turn, blinking at them with the effort it takes me to stay awake.

That prompts them to reactivate their feet, and all is quiet for the smoment it takes to go from the entrance of one hotel, to the one next door.

"Wait," Rose commands, and Audrey and I stop. "I need you to at least hold hands as you go walk in."

Shifting, I drop my duffel on top of Audrey's suitcase, and grab the handles of both luggage pieces with my left hand. Then I offer my free hand to Audrey.

She stares at it like it's the first time she realizes I have these appendages. Her friend prompts, "Blondie?" And finally she grabs on.

Not on to my hand. My whole arm.

"This is probably more newlyweds-like," she explains.

Rose is the only one who can reason. "Perfect, this definitely looks more natural."

Checking in goes quickly, and it would even be pleasant if it wasn't for the Orlando Wild's social media manager capturing every single second with her professional camera. I manage to note some relief on Audrey's face as she hears that the room has two beds, and I'm too tired to have any feelings about it.

In the elevator, we follow Rose's prompts of looking at each other like we care, holding each other close. My mouth is dry as a desert and Audrey's looks very moisturized. That's gonna haunt me for a long time for reasons I can't admit.

Finally, we reach our door and perform some final acting for Rose's camera. "Excellent," she confirms as she quickly checks out the shots. "Miguel, I'll get in touch with your agent like she requested, and then I'm posting them."

"Thank you," I mumble without much power. After clearing my throat, I add with a bit more confidence, "For everything."

She nods in all seriousness. "Everything for Audrey."

I nod back. She's who we're all doing this for.

She's also staying suspiciously quiet. I touch the room card on the pad and open the door for her. "After you."

Audrey glances back at her friend, at me, and back again. "Good night, Rose. See you tomorrow morning."

"Sleep tight, wifey." Her friend breaks into a twinkling giggle that fades away as she heads back to the elevator.

I turn. "Wait, Rose. Let me walk you back."

"No need." She waves me to go in. "Logan should be waiting for me downstairs. We're going on a little solo date after this."

At midnight? With a game tomorrow?

Well, when real feelings are there, it makes you ignore time or exhaustion. Good for them.

"Then, have a good night," I say and finally walk into the room after Audrey.

I find her in the middle of the two beds, staring at me with tired eyes but arms crossed.

"Okay, let's establish some ground rules," I say, anticipating what's coming. I rest our luggage against a mirrored wall. "Bathroom is yours first. I promise to stay on my bed all night —unless I need to use said bathroom, I guess, but you know what I mean. You can change in there or out here if it's more comfortable, and I can either wait in the bathroom or outside. Also, Marty says that I snore. If I'm bothering you, feel free to shove me until I stop snoring—I sleep pretty heavy so it won't bother me. What else?" I look at the ceiling for inspiration. "Oh, and we can get all the room service you need."

She stares at me some more. I almost wonder if she's fallen asleep with her eyes open until she shakes her head slightly.

"You don't need to go outside, I'll just change in the bath-room," Audrey says. "And I don't know if I snore, but I also sleep pretty heavy so it should be fine."

"Great."

"Great."

The air conditioner fills the quiet for a long moment. She's still looking at me like there's something more she wants to say but doesn't dare to. It makes me wonder if I've screwed some-thing up along the way. I use my last braincell to run inventory of what we've done so far and what could be missing.

"Coño!" I jump in my skin and pat my pockets. "I forgot the rings. We need to wear rings for the whole world to believe this."

"It's okay, the rings are in my suitcase. Let's just..." She motions vaguely around. "Let's just go to sleep, please? I could collapse at any moment."

"Right." I turn this way and that, until I remember the luggage. "Here you go. I'll uh, change out here."

"Thank you." She receives the suitcase from me, careful not to make contact, and locks herself up in the bathroom.

I send a prayer to the heavens to give me strength not just for this night, for what this new life is going to be.

I make very quick work of changing into my pajamas and

get my bed ready for sleep. When she comes out, I'm too tired to even lift my head. We just exchange places and I brush my teeth quickly. Once I come out, I can't even muster the willpower to pull up the bedsheets. I fall face down and turn off like a light.

CHAPTER 23
AUDREY

When Miguel comes out of the bathroom, I'm in the middle of tying up my hair in a loose bun on the top of my head. Once I'm done, I lean forward to pull the sheets up and freeze.

This man seems even more tired than I am, going by how he drags himself. But that's not the problem. I'm not going to say anything about it—even if I did, he wouldn't hear it because he's on autopilot.

The problem is that he's shirtless and in gray sweatpants.

Does he *not know*?

In fairness, other than earlier tonight I haven't seen him glued to his phone before. Everyone on the staff side of the team knows that he has no personal social media presence. If he ever did, he must've deleted the accounts at some point. It's safe to say that he's not chronically online and probably has no idea that this, er, outfit, is essentially a bat signal for thirsty women.

I check the windows and thankfully the curtains are down. Pretty sure he would've stopped traffic otherwise and incited many couples to fight.

Using all my willpower, I focus on the bed sheets and tuck myself in. At the same time, he flops down on his bed, face turned my way and smushed against the fluffy pillow, his giant frame absorbing the entire queen bed to the point that his feet hang out the edge. And just like that, a tiny snore escapes from his mouth.

This is when finally my jaw drops and my eyes widen. His hair got messy somewhere along the way and a strand falls over his forehead. Being collapsed on the bed accentuates things I didn't register before, like the incredibly shaped shoulders, arms that any other guy would kill for, the line of his spine as it narrows the lower my eyes go, and then…

The butt.

I blink hard and pull up the soft sheets around my chin. They stay there, because I'm a red blooded heterosexual woman and I can't help staring. Especially because it's the first time I've allowed it.

Is that dump in his trunk genetic or did he gain it with years and years of exercise? Probably some combination of both. No matter how much I worked out in my early twenties, I couldn't develop cakes anywhere close to Miguel's.

Poor guy, he should've put rules against me checking him out.

That's the thing, though. In the course of tonight I realized how absolutely selfless he is.

Of course, seeing him interact with his daughter, her nanny, other teammates, and our friends, I already had a clear understanding that he's a genuinely good person. But everything he's done for me in the past three days is next level. Not only he agreed to this wild scheme with me, but he's also thought about my needs every step of the way.

No one's had to say it, but I know he's the one who made sure the whole wedding went smoothly. And something broke inside of me when, even though he was absolutely destroyed by the day, he still grabbed my suitcase so I didn't have to make any effort. When he asked Rose if he could escort her back?

Ugh, where do I nominate him for best guy award? Up there with golden retrievers, to be honest.

Here's a big difference, though. Golden retrievers are cute. This guy is freaking hot. A stab pierces my chest—hard enough to make me gasp—made of sharp guilt. I suddenly feel terrible for the woman who is supposed to be by his side, whose role I'm usurping for my own gain.

I press my lips, but that does nothing to slow down the hot tears the pool in my eyes. Pushing the sheets away, I sit up to wipe at my face with the sleeves of my comfy sweatshirt.

I better treat him nicely too. The least I can do right now is to cover him up so he doesn't catch a cold.

Sniffling, I hover near his bed and take in the challenge. Fortunately, he's not fully on top of the sheets because there's no way I can move the incredible mass of muscle that he is. Even shifting one of his legs so I can reach the sheets is a work-out. My grunting doesn't wake him up, so I guess it was true that he's a heavy sleeper. The other leg kinda hangs out, and all the effort I have to do there is to push it over the mattress.

Finally, I bring the sheets over him and whisper, "Good night, Miguel."

There's no response, only a soft exhalation.

I run my sleeve over a stray tear, get back in bed, and turn off the light.

*

An alarm goes off.

I flinch but other than wishing it away, I can't do much else about it. A string of deep words in a foreign language makes me think of a cursing man. But why would one of those be in my bedroom?

Oh.

My whole body grows stiff as a plank. The alarm finally quiets and I force my eyes to stay closed for a moment longer. I recall saying that I also don't sleep like a feather, so it should seem believable that I can sleep through an alarm, right? It also didn't ring for a long time. It should be fine.

Miguel yawns and slowly, I crack one eye open, the one that's closest to my pillow as I lay on my side.

Oh, *no.* I shouldn't have done that. I slam it shut.

Then a hidden part of me comes out from a corner and asks a very simple question: why not?

If I wanted to, I could plug his name on a search bar at any browser and get all sorts of pictures. Miguel in the middle of games, on ads, pictorials, and with varying degrees of dressing.

So I peek the same eye open again. He kneels on his bed, half turned away from me as he yawns into the sun that filters through the window curtains. He stretches his arms wide, purely to relieve his shoulders and not because he's trying to show off his absurd wing span, or the way his shoulder and back muscles play with the motion.

I tuck my hand against my mouth to allow not a peep to escape. I knew he had good shoulders, I even felt them under my hands last night while we danced again. But seeing this? Leonardo DaVinci and Michelangelo would've killed to have such a perfect study subject. He must've moved enough during sleep that the sweatpants slid down, revealing the waistband of his *SPORTY* underwear that has also betrayed him a little— enough that I can see the exact point where his tiny waist ends and his pancakes begin.

That's when I squeeze my eyes shut. I have no right to look any further, especially the moment he turns around. What if his clothes have also slid down at the front? I would die. And then he'd notice that, and he would also die.

Shifting that big body causes inevitable noise, and I pretend like that's what's stirring me from sleep. I make a big show of rubbing my eyes, and he takes it as his cue to rasp out, "G'morning, Audrey. Would you like to use the bathroom first?"

That rasp also does something to me. It's an almost physical experience.

In turn, I squeak out, "G'morning. You go ahead."

"Okay, thanks." He yawns again and rustling tells me he's getting out of bed.

Continuing with my pretense, I sit up in my bed and ignore his existence entirely as I feel around my pillows for my phone. I find it just as Miguel's closing the bathroom door.

I collapse against the headboard. "What the hell am I doing?" I ask myself.

A sign from the heavens appears right that second, in the form of my phone buzzing in my hand. When I see the name on the screen, everything makes sense again.

I pick up, not wanting to put this off and cause him to call me again. "I told you to only call me for work reasons," is my greeting.

"Good thing that this is work related, huh?" Henry Vos laughs into my ear and I have to pull my phone away so that I don't audibly gag. "I saw your out of office notice, and it left me with no choice but to call you. Did you forget that we were supposed to have a meeting this morning?"

Why does he say it like it's midday already? I check the clock and it's only eight thirty.

"I didn't forget," I retort nasally because I need to blow my nose. Ugh, is this how I sounded to Miguel a moment ago? Gross. "That's why I sent you a new time proposal, and I'm going to finish this call because I'm off the clock right now."

"Wait a second, please." It's the *please* what makes me pause. My brain short circuits because the guys in my dad's world never use that word, or any other expression of politeness, so I trained myself to welcome it from normal people. But then he opens his mouth to say, "We can talk about that later, but there's one more thing. Your dad asked me to escort you on the cocktail party we're hosting this weekend to celebrate our new partnership. I said yes, of course. Can you wear a red dress and some makeup?"

The hell I can. I grit my teeth hard enough to hurt.

Before I can formulate a response that is even more cutting than that fleeting thought, Miguel comes out of the bathroom —now with his sweatpants pulled up properly—and freezes when he sees that I'm on the phone.

Staring at him, I raise a finger to my mouth. Then say to the guy on the other end of the line, "I'm going to hang up and you're not going to call me again until I'm back to work."

"But—"

I take great pleasure in tapping the red button, and then I navigate in his contact info to block him. I may leave him in that status forever from now on. He can reach me on Teams and I'll answer when I can.

"Everything okay?" Miguel asks.

I lift my face and get a frontal view of a heck of a lot of man. A gold chain with a crucifix hangs from the thick column of his long neck, nestling between the tight masses of his pecs. They look like dreamwork, not big enough to look like boobs but defined enough to make my hands itch. He doesn't have clear abs like some of the other guys do, but there's enough muscle to reinforce the knowledge that he's not a run of the mill type of guy.

But his shoulders, oh, his shoulders.

Parting from that thick neck, the tight muscle tapers in the perfect way to dip at his clavicle before giving spotlight to his arms. *That* has to be genetic. Only the Big Guy in heaven can create something so perfect.

I shut my mouth and force my mind back to more reasonable, and definitely unpleasant matters. "Henry Vos just called. He asked me out to a silly cocktail party in the most condescending way."

Miguel grunts and puts his hands on his hips, in an annoyed-dad pose. "I guess that's our first assignment."

"I guess," I repeat, for lack of anything better to say.

He nods, and with that he continues his journey to rummage for something in his duffel bag. That triggers something in my addled brain, and I jump from my bed.

"The rings!" I scramble to my suitcase and splay it open in the middle of the room. My intimates are hidden by the side of the suitcase that has a full zippered cover, and the rings are on the other side, the box bundled in the sweatshirt I'll wear to travel back to Orlando. I take the box and straighten out. "Voila."

Miguel approaches with a clothing bundle tucked against his ribs, and he stares at the box. "Right." He motions with his lips in a way I've seen all my Venezuelan friends do before. It can have all meanings under the sun—there it is, pass me that, look at that, etc.—but in this case I interpret to mean, *open it*.

And so I do, and we both stand still for a long moment, admiring the rings that look very much real.

"Can I?" he asks in a whisper. I nod, even though I don't know what he's asking.

Then Miguel plucks the smaller right from its nest, and raises his other hand, palm facing up.

"Oh." I hasten to put my left hand on his.

And then the wildest thing that's ever happened in my life *happens*. A man slides a ring into my finger, until it meets the engagement ring look-alike I've been wearing the past few days.

My heart slams hard against my ribcage and my stomach is doing something confusing, like it wants food but also to empty itself.

With slightly trembly hands, I grab the other ring and mirror the motions. Miguel's hand feels so warm and heavy, but those big muscles of his keep it in place so there's no effort for me. We both know I had a sample to measure his ring against, and so it fits perfectly. The contrast of the gold against his velvety brown skin, versus mine against my white and pink finger is a shock.

I look up and find his eyes on me, a sun beam hitting them in a way that makes them look like translucent amber. I swallow hard.

A corner of his lips rises. "Hello, wife."

I almost choke in my own saliva.

"Husband?" I rasp out.

Miguel nods. "Good girl."

And I nearly expire.

CHAPTER 24
MIGUEL

I march from the on-deck circle toward the batter's box, ready to make my daughter proud. Noise from the crowd rises to decibels that would be dangerous for someone whose eardrums aren't used to this. Twirling the bat a couple of times, I cast a sweeping glance across the diamond and outfield. Then I make a big production of getting ready while I observe the position of the players in both teams.

I've been asked by the press about my jinxes, if adjusting my hat, then pulling my pants up, tapping my shoes with the bat to get the sand out, pulling up my left arm sleeve, swinging the bat three times, and then holding my bat upright in the same non-aggressive position all the time is the recipe for my success at bat.

First of all, no. The only reason I do all this shit is because it buys me exactly two minutes.

During that time, I make a mental map of the game. I know that the outfielders have pushed back as much as they can, expecting either a long hit or a home run, which makes them very unprepared for a simple hit or even a bunt. Those are also tools I employ occasionally, when they best suit me. For example, right now I'd really like to work on my base stealing record, so a home run isn't convenient.

However, Lucky's on second and our captain on third. We're scoring no matter what happens.

Lucky's lead is bold—dude's nearly half of the way to third base. Meanwhile, Logan's conservative. Not because he's a chickenshit but because he knows the exact same thing I do. He runs his hand across the peak of his helmet—our code for going wild.

Has anyone realized how many incredible puns can be made with the name of the team?

Anyway, the pitcher has a certain gleam in his eyes that gives some red flags.

What would a normal person do? Be careful, stand back.

What do I do? Stand as close to the catcher as the batting box allows.

"Dude, are you sure?" the catcher asks me.

I don't respond. I've studied enough film of this team to know that their first baseman runs very well, but can't jump high enough. Their second baseman is mid, and the real challenge is the shortstop. That's gonna be Lucky's problem first, so I'm gonna target the first base.

And here's my real jinx: I cross my self and touch my crucifix. Then the music stops playing.

Ah, yes. This is actually my fave kind of pitcher. The ones who are young and don't know any better.

Sure enough, the first pitch spins the ball into a pink dot. Quite easy to predict. It whiffs by close enough that I get a nice breeze, scented like leather and all.

"Ball!"

The sweet frustration on the kid's face… I manage to keep my expression immutable out of sheer practice but if I could, I'd have the biggest shit-eating grin in the world.

I stay put exactly just inside the line of the batter's box.

The catcher mumbles something that sounds close to concern for my wellbeing. How mindful of him.

Enough bravado has slipped from the pitcher that the next pitch slips early. My body moves by itself. I lean back from my waist, enough to change my center of gravity. My tree trunk legs pick up the slack and keep me put even as I swing the bat like a hurricane. Sound comes like an explosion—probably because my bat just disintegrated in my hands from the hit.

I take off.

I'm almost halfway through first base when the ball appears in the corner of my eye, flying at the first baseman. It rockets right over him. My legs pump full force, balls of my feet digging into the dirt as I go. His glove falls short by maybe an inch. The ball lands inside bounds as the poor sucker runs after it. I step on first base. There's roaring in my ears. My legs keep going. I make a bet that they'll target tagging Lucky out. Play keeps going. It's chaos ahead of me. Lucky's chased by the ball. Third baseman's afraid and stays put on base, reaching to catch. Lucky honors his name as the ball passes him by—*and* the third baseman.

I run faster. Harder. Stronger. The roaring's louder. Base coach windmills his arm. I press even harder. Tunnel vision takes over. Catcher's too far from home. I don't slow. He's preparing to catch. I tilt back and slide. The momentum is so strong that it pulls me up on my feet like I'm a spring, and I walk away from home after wiping the floor with the opponent.

Only know do I notice the stadium exploding in noise.

"Hot! Damn!"

"Are you—What *are* you?"

"Can you give me your autograph?"

That one makes me snort while I'm in the middle of bumping someone else's chest. Then two high fives. A low one. Bumping forearms. Getting my helmet tapped and then tapping back. A hug. Getting my ass slapped. Baseball boys be like this.

When the manager says "that was savage," to you and pats your shoulder, you know you did a good job.

If so, why is something bothering me?

The nearest person now is Logan Kim as he's putting on the easy catcher pads first. I tell him, "Hey, I'm heading inside real quick."

He gives me a side glance and zero words, and yet a whole conversation passes.

You okay?

Yeah. Just need to check something.

You better not be hurt, you jackass.

I'm sure it's nothing.

One minute. Then I'm coming for you.

Thank you, Grandpa.

Shaking my head, I head into the tunnel and when I'm far away enough from cameras, I remove my batting gloves and flex my fingers.

"Ohhh," I say, finding the issue right away.

"Miguel Lucas Machado," a feminine voice says all of a sudden.

My eyes snap up and there she is, goldilocks herself descended from her throne to this humble away-clubhouse. "Hmm, my middle name isn't Lucas."

"Jose?" she guesses a second time.

I don't confirm it but that is, in fact, my middle name.

Instead, my eyebrows rise. "What brings you to this sweaty place?"

She leans forward, hands on her hips and expression as furious as it probably gets. "Are you hurt?"

I look backward. Did Logan say anything? But the way behind me is clear of any snitches.

"No," I respond as I turn back. "It's not a big deal."

"Then why are you doing that with your hand?"

I glance down. I'm still flexing my fingers. I turn my hand around again, palm facing up. The impact that blew up the wooden bat in my hand made my new wedding ring dig into my finger, and a blister's already forming.

That's it. That's the big injury. Boo hoo.

A shadow falls over me and then her hand is on mine. She spreads my palm wider and gently taps at the annoying little blister.

"Oof, that looks bad." She's frowning like she just got really bad financial news. Then, just as tragically, she meets my eyes and says, "Take it off."

I splutter.

Her eyes narrow. "The ring, you perv."

"Right." She has no idea that sometimes—often—she makes my brain short circuit. I grab the ring and start twisting and twisting.

"Don't tell me…" She gasps softly, enough that I feel it everywhere I have bare skin. "Is your finger swollen?"

The question comes out in horror. It takes me a moment to understand that this is coming from concern, that she may be wondering if I hurt my finger or something.

I clear my throat. My voice is a bit too thick when I explain, "Well, yeah. But so is everything else."

Silence hangs heavy as her eyes widen.

"I mean!" Now my voice is but a squeak. "Blood flow! When you work out hard. It just goes up—gets faster, I mean. Uh…" I clear my throat again, nearly hacking out a lung in the process.

"What's going on?" A dude's voice comes from behind me as my coughing fit starts to ebb away.

Audrey turns a very red, yet serious face toward the team captain. "Hey, Logan. Miguel's hurt."

"No, I'm not," I choke out, thumping my chest.

"Where?"

The pretty snitch points at my hand. "Finger."

I voluntarily raise my hand up so he can assess the damage. "It's just a damn blister. Everything's fine." My lungs aren't. Neither is my heart rate. Blood flow is excellent, though.

Logan clicks his tongue several times in a row. "This is why guys take them off entirely or replace them for silicone rings."

I refrain from pointing out that Audrey had the same immediate solution. However, my mind, ever so useful, decides to run away with a dream scenario—one where my fake wife and I are taking off our very real clothes off. That'd be nice.

More than nice.

"Anyway, I have it under control." Barely. I keep twisting the ring though, until it finally comes off my very uninjured finger. I keep it nestled in my palm as I raise my hands and find the clasp of my chain and pop it open.

Audrey's voice sounds more relaxed. "That's a good idea, too."

I slide the ring into the necklace until it bumps with the crucifix.

"Pop the blister and come out, the next inning's about to start," Logan commands.

"Aye, captain," I say as I'm clasping the chain back in place.

"What do you mean pop the blister?" And now blondie sounds horrified.

Chuckling, I follow after Logan, tossing over my shoulder a very poetic "it's cool, sugar. A little blood never hurt anybody."

*

The embarrassment of that phrase is still haunting me as I sit with Beau and a couple other players for the press junket after the game. We won with a whopping 13-2 and five different team records were broken.

Turns out I got one of them. The speed of my bat for the blister-hit is the fastest in the team's history. And also of the league—in all its history. A whopping 123.1mph.

"Machado," one of the journos calls out. "Why do you think the hit that clocked the fastest swing speed in the league's history wasn't a home run? Are you entering a slump?"

Once again, I employ my best acting skills and give him nothing with my body language. My hands are laced over the table, and no one can see how I'm fingering the Band-Aid over the hole left by the popped blister.

I have a couple options here. One, I could tell him where to shove it for his sensationalist take, but that works exactly zero percent of the times. Two, I could be honest and piss a lot of people off even while saying things gently.

The choice is clear.

"Well, Mike," I say, leaning closer to the microphone. "There are two reasons for that and neither are called slump. One, I really wanted to practice my base stealing, although that didn't exactly go according to plan." As a round of chuckles goes around the room, I reach behind the neck of my T-shirt and pull up the chain. "And also, because I'm not used to my new wedding ring yet."

The press room sounds like a tomb at the strong whiff of even juicier stories than a slump.

"Thank you for your questions." I pat the table in that *welp, gotta go way* that is unique to dads, and make my way out of the press room wearing the shit-eating grin I contained during the game.

And now for people to start cussing me out.

CHAPTER 25
AUDREY

Nothing like working in PR and being the one to set off a PR storm for the team.

Technically, the author of the disaster was Miguel with his press comment about a sudden wife. But then Rose worked her social media magic and released the paparazzi-like pictures of us getting married and walking into a hotel room together, and now the baseball and sports internet is buzzing.

The best part is how my clever friend didn't get my face captured on camera, only Miguel's. My blonde hair is unmistakable, though, and I have no idea how no one at work has put two and two together.

Okay, maybe there's one exception. And it's not really the one I expected.

Instead of my father bursting into the PR team area and demanding answers from me, or even his latest minion doing the same, it's my boss, Karen, the one who has spent the last two days giving me funny looks.

I haven't heard any rumors, so I guess she hasn't dared to talk smack with anyone. The way she looks at me, with the clear desire that she wishes I was anywhere else but in front of her, and also how she made me do most of the work the past two days to put out the flames, give me a feeling that she's really going to be pissed off when she confirms that I did, indeed, marry Miguel Machado.

Currently that doesn't concern me though. I'm getting ready for the cocktail party where Miguel and I will reveal the identity of the slugger's new wife to the public, including my male progenitor.

Meanwhile, Marty's on her bed, head propped up by her hands as she watches me apply my makeup, feet swinging back and forth in the air with the innocence of someone who doesn't fear for her life.

"Did your mom teach you to put on makeup?" she asks.

"No," I respond truthfully but withholding the part about how my mother's professional makeup artist is the one who taught me everything I know. Also TikTok, I guess.

"Why not? Isn't that how most girls learn?"

I finish darkening my near transparent eyebrows with a pencil that makes them look properly blonde and full, and as I tuck it away in my makeup bag, I say, "Believe it or not, my mother cares about me even less than my dad does."

"What?" Rustling comes as she shifts to sit at the edge of the bed, leaning forward for the tea. "Why's that?"

I don't know if speaking candidly to a child is a good thing, but from experience—and by that I mean the fact that my parents barely ever spoke to me when I was a kid—it's probably not the worst thing in the world.

"She moved to Paris a long time ago and has basically stayed out of my life since."

Right after Adam passed out, to be precise, leaving me alone with the same father who drove my brother to self-medicate with alcohol. This part even I know is too much for a ten-year-old girl.

Marty gasps. "We're the same!" That tears my attention away from putting on blush. "My mom also abandoned me."

I do a double take. Why does she seem excited about this?

"Is that so?" I ask to buy myself some time to rifle through my memories.

I don't recall Miguel putting it in such harsh terms, but then again I can also see why Marty would take it this way. Not having your mom around, knowing she's alive and caring about other things or people much more than you, frankly sucks.

"Well, she visits once a year but my classmates's moms live with them, so isn't that the same?"

Put that way, the truth is evident. And even though she appears to be fine with these facts, I'm not. My heart twists painfully for this sweet and grumpy child who has been hurt so early in her life. I want to squish her, but she would probably go angry kitten on me.

Instead, I scoot to one end of my seat and pat the minuscule open space. "Want me to teach you?"

"Let's do it." She jumps from the edge of the bed, all serious and determined, as though this was more a chore than something she's obviously been wanting for who knows how long.

I'm supposed to finish getting ready in the next fifteen minutes, but who cares if I'm late for Dad's party? That's just buying myself a moment longer of peace.

Shifting a little toward her, I explain, "First of all, I want to share with you the reason I wear makeup sometimes."

"Okay." She nods like we're in a classroom.

"It's not because I look prettier with it or to impress other people," I continue, adopting her air of solemnity. "It's because I like to look at myself in the mirror and not appear so pale. That is all."

"Am I pale?"

Taking in the beautiful brown golden skin that she got from her dad, and the wavy brown hair that probably came from her mom, I answer, "Not at all."

"Then why should I wear makeup?"

"You don't have to." I reach for the blush brush and dab it on the color a bit. "And if you do, it can only be because you want to and not because anyone else says so."

"Got it." She nods. "I'm good at that."

She is, the little spitfire.

Chuckling, I show her where to put blush. The color is off for her, and I make a mental note to find her something that really makes her glow. I'm sorting through different lip tints and glosses when there's a knock on the door.

We both turn to Marty's bedroom door, where Consuelo is peeking in. "Excuse me, ladies," she says in her lilting accent. "But Marty really should start her homework before it gets any later."

"Ugh."

Even I'm bummed. But I start putting everything away into my makeup kit, and remove the giant rollers I put on to give my hair a semblance of volume. By the time the night ends, it's going to be flat like an arrow again—bleh.

"C'mon, let's grab our things and head downstairs," I tell Marty with a little pat to her back.

"Fine." She stomps her feet on the way back to the bed, where her study materials lay scattered. I do the same with all the paraphernalia I brought over to get ready with her.

Last night, when Miguel sent the request over via text, he added an apology like this was the biggest favor ever exchanged in our strange friendship. I answered that it was absolutely no problem and that I love hanging out with Marty. Both are true. His daughter is how I wish I had been like when I was her age.

The three of us are chatting up a storm about Marty's

history homework and how mush she'd rather work on the arts one, as we walk down the stairs together. I spot Miguel in the middle of the living room, wearing an impeccably tailored green suit that matches my dress very well—his idea, by the way. Although his is a deeper hue than my silky emerald dress.

His back is toward us, head bent forward like he's reading something. Sure enough, he slowly turns as our racket approaches and he finishes texting whoever is on the other side of his phone, putting it away before he looks up.

Miguel's jaw tightens so hard that I can see a muscle jump.

"—Bring me ice cream and we have a deal," Marty's saying as we reach the landing.

Without tearing my eyes from her dad, I say, "We may come back pretty late, so does a trip to the parlor count?"

"It *so* does!"

Consuelo leans to me and whispers, "I just want to know if something juicy happens between you two tonight."

I inhale deeply and turn to her, but she's already grabbing Marty's hand and steering her toward the kitchen counter. That's where Marty does her homework while Consuelo works in the kitchen. Meanwhile, it means that I've been left abandoned to the wolves.

Or wolf. There's something sharp about Miguel's eyes right now that is unsettling. I've never seen that look on his face.

Clearing his throat helps him relax a tad. He walks by me, leaving a stunning male scent behind him—something like cedar and spice—and places a big kiss on top of his daughter's head.

They're so friggin' cute, and Marty's so fortunate to have a dad like Miguel who is a complete simp for her. I bet he cried on her first day at kindergarten.

A moment later, as we walk toward the Maserati we borrowed from Logan Kim, I genuinely ask Miguel precisely that. "Did you cry the first time you had to drop Marty off at the kindergarten?"

He comes to a full stop, and I do too since my hand is on his arm. Miguel blinks up at the darkening sky, as if doing math in his head. "Maybe?"

That sets me off into a barrage of chuckles. "You *so* did."

He helps me get into the uncomfortably low car, even going as far as picking up my skirt where it would've gotten jammed by the door, and closes it for me. I watch as he walks around the vehicle, rubbing his chin like he's maybe contemplating his life choices. His left hand is on his hip, and I catch the glint of the wedding ring back on it. Seeing it is jolts me.

Miguel gets in with far more ease than I did, for someone who isn't getting any help at all, and the one thing that throws him off is the dashboard of the fancy ass ride. I've also never seen as many sleek buttons and lights in my life, and that's saying something. Dad's always been keen on the Bentleys.

Drily, I point toward the bigger one. "I think that one starts the engine."

Miguel snorts through his nose, lips stretching into a big, amused smile. He presses the big button though, and the engine roars to life in a way that screams power.

Not gonna lie, it makes me nervous. I've never had a great relationship with cars. When I was a kid, Dad drove like he didn't care about his life, ours, or anyone else's. And in the end, it was a car what took my brother from me.

I clench my hands at my lap as Miguel pulls away from the curb, and then something odd clocks with me. The houses and the trees outside are passing by fairly slow for how hard the engine's purring.

I whip my head toward Miguel. So, he's a slow driver, huh?

Why's he so intent in not looking at me though?

"Miguel?"

"Hmm?" he hums from deep in his throat, almost as rumbly as the Maserati engine.

"Are you okay?"

"What?" He finally glances at me. "Why do you ask?"

"You've basically been quiet this whole time. That's unlike you, you know?" We're close enough that I can nudge his rock solid arm just a bit.

His response is to stay quiet even more, and I'm starting to worry.

Surely this can't be about the blister in his hand, so does that mean he's hurt somewhere else? Sick? Should we turn back around? I'd much prefer that, actually. But this isn't about me. I already feel like garbage about roping him into all of this, the last thing I want is for the best baseball player in the world —and probably the best dad in history—to get hurt under my watch.

Before I suggest we cancel the outing, Miguel finally speaks. "I'm okay. I was just kicking myself for not telling you how beautiful you look earlier, but then I was wondering if it would make you feel uncomfortable."

I'm stunned to silence, my mouth slightly open.

We're at a red light, and Miguel turns to me with a little frown. "There, that's what I was trying to avoid. Looks like overthinking it made it worse, huh?"

An ugly cackle tears out of my throat. It takes enough to calm down that the light changes and off we go. "Wow." I cough a little and thump my chest. "Is this the real Miguel? An awkward turtle?"

"Yep." He shrugs. "Don't let the action shots fool you."

Rather, this puts me at such ease that I don't think I've ever felt so relaxed before in my life.

A certainty washes over me that there's no one better I could've found to pretend to be my husband in front of my dad. Tonight won't be a complete disaster after all.

<h1 style="text-align:center">CHAPTER 26
MIGUEL</h1>

've never been more annoyed in my whole damn life than at this moment, as I walk into some bougie place with Audrey holding my arm. That's not the problem, though. I'm fully decked in a form fitting suit that won't let me find a quiet corner to do a thousand quick pushups so I can get rid of all this energy coursing through my veins like hot lava.

Audrey looks absolutely mouthwatering. Enough that when she climbed down the stairs with my daughter, I felt something sharp, visceral, and primal that I've never felt before.

The need to make her mine—ours.

I could picture it so clearly, Audrey helping Marty with math on the kitchen counter, while I make us a quick breakfast before Consuelo arrives and we have to go to work. The three of us sitting under a tree at a pretty park, having a picnic and chatting about our plans. Marty walking to her school event with a real new mom, and not a fake one. Audrey waking up in my arms, eyes sleepy but smiling. And naked, because why not?

I'm going to have such a miserable night if I let my head keep running rampant.

"Are you ready?" she asks softly beside me.

For all that? Hell yeah. More than ready. I *need* it.

Eso no, pendejo, a voice that sounds suspiciously like my dad says in my head.

"Yes," I respond, hanging by the last thread of civility in me. "And you?"

"I'm having a real life case of the sunk cost fallacy."

"The what?" I do a double take at her.

Her glassy eyes stay scanning the attendees ahead of us as she explains, "You know when you've invested too much into something that you know is a complete mess, and you convince yourself to not give up when you probably should?"

"Yeah…" In fact, the one case that comes to mind about that was a year of trying to make a family with a newborn baby, and a biological mother who knew that wasn't her calling. How does that relate to this situation, though?

Maybe this clever woman can clearly see the question in my face, because she stops to face me. "This thing we're doing? Wild. Telenovela like. Very K-Drama."

"What's a K-Drama?"

"A South Korean telenovela," she says without missing a beat.

"Ahh."

"But we're still forging ahead, aren't we?"

I bob my head. "Sure are. Unless you're having cold feet."

"Surprisingly, I'm not." Her eyebrows rise. "What about you? We can put a stop to this the second you're uncomfortable."

Me, uncomfortable next to her? Nah. Enjoying it a bit too much to be considered proper, actually.

"I'm good," I say. But I'm not. I'll force myself to be, though.

Blondie nods like we're about to walk into battle, and steers me by the arm to the middle of the fray.

My lips can't stop twitching. I want to laugh. Her pretty

hair swings the opposite way her hips go, and it's a shame that the skirt opens up from her waist and doesn't let me catch the contour of her body. Her legs look absolutely incredible, though, and I bet they'd look even better wrapped around my—

"Hi, Dad," she says in a shockingly cutting tone that snaps me out of my dangerous fantasies.

I kinda wish I'd been paying more attention to my surroundings so I could prepare myself psychologically for what I'm about to do, but here goes nothing. I slide my arm around Audrey's waist, nestling her against my side in an unmistakably possessive way.

The world doesn't stop spinning. No one stops and stares. Charlie Cox sure takes notice, though.

He turns away from a conversation mid sentence, and scans us from the top of our heads to our feet. On the return, his eyes stop at his daughter's hands, which she has elegantly clasped in front of her.

Even I can see the glint of her rings from the corner of my eye.

Showtime, huh?

"What is this?" The team owner faces us, holding very tight to a glass of something that looks like whiskey. His eyes, same color as his daughter's but completely cold and distant, zero in on my face. "Don't tell me that this is what I'm thinking it is."

Audrey and I exchange a glance. It's interesting to see a glimmer of amusement in her eyes, when I also feel it on the inside.

This really *is* like a telenovela, after all.

Finally, I get into character and announce in the most obnoxious way, "Mr. Cox, may I present to you my wife, Audrey Machado?"

Okay, someone's gasping nearby now. Thank you for being such an excellent unpaid extra.

Wait, why is Audrey staring at me like this is the most shocking thing I've ever done, and not breaking a swing speed record or something like that?

But then she gets with the program. Her expression softens into a smile that hits me in the chest like a donkey's kick, and she leans her head on my right peck like it belongs there. The scent of something sweet—apple, maybe—drifts to my nostrils, and I drag in as much as it takes to commit it to memory.

Her father spears me with flinty eyes. "You did not."

Me, a top notch specimen of maturity, volley back a "did too."

Audrey snorts hard into her hand. She recovers quickly, though. "Dad, I have to thank you for introducing me to Miguel. I know it's been really fast but he really is the love of my life, and I know that you approve of him or you wouldn't have introduced us, right?"

I haven't dealt with this mogul a very long time, but I'd hazard a guess that the fact that he's used to controlling the world around him with money or sheer presence, makes this moment more significant. Because he turns into a statue that has lost the ability to use words, even though it's clear he wants to use many vile ones.

Meanwhile, I'm staring at the top of Audrey's head in awe. I mean, shit, I already knew that she's smart. She can math and philosophize, a conversation with her is full of fun twists and turns, and I once heard that sarcasm is a marker of smart people—and she exercises it at a master level.

But to use her father's own manipulative and threatening words from months ago against him?

This is some 3D chess shit. I feel both inadequate and turned on, and I can't explain it.

Still taking advantage of the older man's silence, she adds, "I'll work with Karen on Monday to put out a statement that will include our kinship, which I believe will fulfill all of your conditions."

Charlie Cox flaps his mouth open and closed. My body moves by instinct and I catch the glass slipping from his hand. After making sure he's holding it again, I turn back to his daughter.

"Look, mi vida. That's our song," I bullshit about some random waltz that's starting. I offer my hand to her. "Shall we?"

"Of course." She sounds chipper than ever. When we're away from her father, she asks, "What does mi vida mean?"

"Ehh, it's just an endearment." I'm sure she'll find out sooner or later what it means, but I've already put my foot in my mouth enough times today. As we start dancing, I direct our conversation to the most important thing. "How do you feel after all that?"

"Electric." Her eyes are wide enough that she could've been zapped, actually. "Deep down, I know there will be consequences, but I'm trying to ignore all that and focus on the present."

"Good call." There won't be any consequences under my watch, though.

Something snags my attention over her head. Charlie Cox and the jackass who was his first choice for Audrey's husband are watching us with zero reservation. In fact, people near them are starting to do the same.

Pulling her against me, I gently turn us around and whisper in her ear, "My six o'clock."

Of course she knows what I'm talking about right away. Audrey leans to peek around and the way her expression hardens tells me she spotted the same thing I did. "Ugh," she mutters.

"Ready?"

She looks back up at me, not getting it this time. "What for?"

"A big show." I slide my hands down her bare arms slowly, like I have all the time in the world to explore her skin. She only glances down once I've reached her hands. "Remember our wedding night?" The corners of my mouth rise.

"Which part specifically?"

"The one where we danced real close," I answer in a measured tone, more so for my own benefit. I'm working really hard at keeping it together. "I'm thinking it would be a quite scandalous thing to do around here."

The same sort of mischievous smile comes to her face, and with that she's waved off the dark cloud that briefly fell over her upon seeing the jackass. "But with a waltz? Really?"

"Oh yeah. Watch this."

"Boy, those are famous last words—eek!"

I twirl her around and bring her back flush against me like I'm not afraid of dying tonight, and wrap my arms around her while still holding her hands. A couple of dancing pairs nearby give us nasty looks, like how dare we disrespect their waltz culture. What's up with rich people and boring music, though?

Guess I should be glad, though. If this was reggaeton I'd be in serious trouble.

Audrey dances along, trusting me to twirl her around dramatically, and even through a theatrical dip. She's all laughter, like freedom and irony have collided in her and she can't contain the shrapnel. I'm happy to let it land on me, infecting me with laughter.

And maybe our antics inspire the live band to play something of this century, because suddenly it's way less difficult to dance close and personal at the sound of a jolly classical rendition of Twist and Shout. Heck, even the stiff rich people are starting to liven up.

Maybe that's why I don't realize that this isn't the happy ending moment, but the beginning of a fight that neither of us is really safe from.

CHAPTER 27
AUDREY

debate whether to leave her on read, but that won't pass my journalist roommate's sniff test.

The truth is that Miguel has me drenched in sweat all over, and that I really will have to do something so I can keep up with him. Not that I'm a fan of working out, but he's an incredible dancer, to the point where he makes me forget that my body's composed of only left feet, and I even have fun being twirled around.

Like, who is this Audrey that watches me on the mirror with a full body blush, gleaming skin, flat and messy hair, shining eyes, and the toothiest grin in the world? Anyone who takes one glance at me will really think I'm a real newlywed wife.

But Rose and Hope—since the conversation's happening on the group chat—don't need to know all that. No one needs to know that I'm feeling like I'm on the senior prom right now.

ME

The news have been dropped

Landed like a bomb

Dad hasn't talked to me since

These are factors that sure as hell are contributing to the wide smile on my face. I believe that what really sold the news was when I said that I had fulfilled the terms of the bargain by marrying a guy he approved of. That was a stroke of genius that came to me in the moment. I've really spent all night dancing with a hot guy to celebrate my freedom.

Our freedom.

ME

This is it, girls

We're free from my tyrannical father

DARLING HOPE

Ugh forget about us

What's important here is YOU being safe

PRINCESS ROSE

And also having some fun with a certain hubby

ME

Good talk, bye

A cascade of laughing emoji and stickers follows after that. I wish I could muster my usual disdain for a big eye roll, but the truth is that I wouldn't mind staying a bit longer and having another turn at the dance floor with the hubby. Er, I mean, with Miguel—my neighbor, coworker, and friend. Nothing else.

I snatch a few more paper towels and pat my face dry, my

neck, and even my pits just in case I'm starting to stink up like a swamp monster. I brush my bangs to the side, because they don't look super great when they stick to my forehead. My dress has pockets—of course—and I fish in one of them for my lipstick. I've snacked on fancy finger food enough that it's virtually gone.

After smacking my lips and waiting for the product to dry, I straighten out my silky dress and head out of the ladies restroom in search for my partner in petty crime.

The one I find waiting for me outside is Henry Vos, though.

He tucks his hands in the pockets of his slacks. "Finally, we can talk," he says, as if I'd been waiting for this moment the whole night.

Two women have to walk around us to enter the restroom. One of them is kind enough to make eye contact in a way that's reassuring. I nod my head at her because sadly I know this jerk, and we're still in a very public place. I'm sure this little lobby that exists as a buffer between the restrooms and the side entrance of the main venue must have cameras and all.

I fold my arms tight and lean my weight on a single leg in the universal body language speak for *make this quick, you walking piece of garbage.* Or at least that's what I'm trying to convey. "What do you want?"

"Your father told me." There's a half smirk on his face, even though his eyes are like shards of ice. "You can't possibly expect me to believe that your sudden marriage is real."

The warm and fuzzy feelings I was enjoying part, allowing a block of ice to slide down my spine.

On the outside, I keep my composure by shrugging. "Think whatever you want." I sidestep him and all is well for one second.

The next, I'm seriously regretting having told Miguel that I was fine with going to the restroom by myself. Henry grabs me by the elbow and pulls at me so hard, I nearly lose my footing. He throws me against a wall in a nook I hadn't realized was here. A staff door is across from me, if I can reach it I can get rid of this pest.

But of course, Henry blocks my path with his wiry body like he once did by the coffee machine at work.

I'm sweating again but for a completely different reason. How could I remember that this asshole isn't above cornering me and making me extremely uncomfortable?

I hope Miguel realizes I've been gone a tad too long. And that he doesn't think it's just because I'm pooping.

Lifting my chin, I try for my usual bravado, but I'm betrayed by a heavy swallow. "What the hell do you think you're doing?" I try to free myself but he grabs even tighter onto my arm. "Let me go or I'll scream bloody murder in your ear."

"Have fun with that, I'll just pretend like you're the one having a mental breakdown for no damn reason."

Oh, so he admits he's actually acting unhinged, huh? Self preservation allows me to keep my mouth shut, though. Also because my arm is starting to hurt and he's way too close. The nook is significantly darker than the lobby, and on top of that he casts a shadow on me.

"I knew you were kind of slippery, Audrey," he whispers, like he's not being a serpent right now. "But I didn't know you'd go as far as doing something like this."

"What? Falling in love and marrying the love of my life?" I ask through gritted teeth. The lie sits heavy in my stomach, or that could just be the fear that's churning my guts.

He snorts. "Maybe Charlie believes that bullshit, but I don't. You haven't even kissed him once all night."

Shit.

I'd never thought about it like that. It's true that lovey

dovey newlyweds would be all over each other, no matter where they may be.

"What's that to you?" I grunt, trying to pry him off with my free hand. I hate that he's so much stronger than me. "Let go of me, you brute."

"I won't. Not until you reveal the truth and end this sham marriage," he threatens.

It's a good thing, really. It allows anger to kick self preservation to the curb.

"Or else?" I demand, wondering just what power he thinks he has over my decisions. Even if Dad supports Henry, I now have enough friends that I don't feel so helpless anymore.

But then a really ugly smile forms on Henry's face, something out of the book of serial killers. "Or else I'm going to ruin your marriage myself."

Then something horrible happens. He swoops down to kiss me.

I scream. I beg in my mind. I call for one name from the bottom of my soul.

And *he* appears.

My arm is free, and a violent thud echoes in the quiet nook. Slowly, I peek one eye open and all I see is an expanse of dark.

I open both eyes wide and my breath hitches. Right in front of me is the person I most wanted to see right now—Miguel, his gigantic back to me, and the dark was the deep green of his suit jacket. My eyes fix on the thick column of his neck, and the second I feel his hand near mine I latch on for dear life.

"Stay away from my wife."

Miguel's voice comes out like a feral growl, something I've never heard before.

And a flash of heat chases away the fear from my spine. My skin breaks into goosebumps. My knees threaten to buckle.

Some rustling follows after Henry's creepy laugh. "Your

wife? You want me to believe that you care about Audrey when you just married her for her inheritance?"

"Is that a self projection?" Miguel asks with that growly voice, sharp as a knife.

"Look at you, using big words when you're just a trained circus monkey." Henry's condescending little speech makes Miguel's back tighten even more. "But it doesn't matter. You may think you won, but in the end Audrey will end up with me."

"The hell she will," Miguel snaps, his free hand balling into a tight fist. "Touch her and you die, asshole."

Henry gasps. "What would your fans say if they heard you talking like that? And what about your daughter?"

I take a sharp breath.

Next thing I know, Miguel's fist is coiling back.

"No!" I scream, throwing myself at him. I wrap my arms like velcro around his torso, hands digging into his body with all my force. "Stop, he's trying to make you throw your career away!"

But Henry's not done. He throws another mocking laugh. "See? She's too smart for you, man. Why would she ever give you the time of the day when you're so beneath her? The sooner you end this, the more embarrassment you'll spare when I go to the press with the news."

"Shut the hell up, Henry," I shout into Miguel's back, squeezing him tighter. "Shut up and disappear, will you?"

"Divorce him and I will," he sing-songs back.

"Never." I drag the r in a way that my roommates would be proud of. "Miguel is my husband. Suck it up."

And then, I don't know, I glitch—I guess.

In the grand scheme of events, this is absolutely not the wildest thing I've ever done. But I can only think of one way to put an end to this nightmare. I release Miguel, and just as he's turning to check on me, I grab his face and bring it down for a kiss.

He draws in air and for a moment that feels eternal, Miguel doesn't move. My fingers slide into his hair, grabbing tighter onto his powerful jaws, and it works. He's finally playing along.

A tiny peep dies in my throat as his arms come around me, one hand holding the back of my head and the other at the small of my back as he tilts me back slightly. Our lips desperately latch onto each other, seeking taste and heat and closeness. More of each other—*please*.

He reads my mind again, and next thing he's opening my mouth with his, and I let him, and our tongues meet in a silky brush that I feel all the way down to my toes. His jaw works hard under my hands, and the reminder of how big Miguel is, how coiled is the strength of his finely honed body, puts into starker contrast how tenderly he's holding me. Like I'm delicate.

I would swoon in his arms if it wasn't for Henry cursing and mumbling some garbage that I can't make out while I'm busy, well, making out.

It takes herculean effort to come back down to earth. I don't know what I'll find when I open my eyes. When our lips part with a smacking sound, I bury my face in Miguel's chest and hope for the best.

He's breathing harshly, chest going up and down fast, heart beating violently. I'm not doing any better—actually, I'm completely out of breath. Miguel's arms are still around me and I don't feel cold at all, not one bit.

I feel him shift slightly, and then his voice wraps around me. "He's gone. You're safe now."

I squeeze the lapels of his suit jacket and stay still, knowing full well that I'm safe because Miguel was here.

CHAPTER 28
MIGUEL

For a wild second that stretches into forever, I can't tell where Audrey and I end and begin. I just know that this is what's right and everything else is a half truth.

Then she's pulling away, tucking her face against my chest while I just stand there, cold and broken when I have to face reality again. My eyes stay glued shut, a tiny rebellion against the facts.

She's not really mine. That kiss wasn't real, even though it sure as hell felt like it.

Slowly my mind reaches out to my senses. My skin is running on overdrive, tingling in an almost painful way every-where, especially where she's pressed up against me. My chest is working around the clock to catch some air, and my heart is competing for attention. I swallow hard when I find that my arms are still wrapped around her—tight.

As I begin to loosen them, Audrey takes it as her cue to begin slipping away. Everything I'm made of rejects that concept, but I let her. The lucid part of me unfortunately prevails.

Her hands stay on my chest as she takes a look around. A

curtain of her hair obscures her face from my eyes, and I'll stay forever curious about the expression she's making.

"He's really gone," she says in a sigh, and it takes me far too long to clock why those words matter. After a step back, keeping her head down, she adds, "Be right back, okay?" With that, she turns around and disappears into the women's restroom.

I backtrack until I slam against the wall behind me, and my entire frame slackens. I run a hand down my face until it stops at my mouth. A groan escapes from my throat.

I'm never gonna forget that kiss, am I?

Now I mess up my hair, waxed as it was. I'm gonna have to get real acquainted with being frustrated with want for this woman.

Light steps echo nearby, and I hide my hands in my pockets like they're guilty of a crime—which I guess they are, it's a crime for me to be starving for more of her.

Audrey returns with two tissue bundles in her hands. "Let me?" she asks, like I would ever say no to her. Reaching up, she starts wiping my mouth with the damp bundle. All I can do is blink like an owl. "I, uh, smeared lipstick all over you."

"Huh," is all I manage to vocalize.

Her startlingly green eyes are focused only on the task, face drawn into determined lines that give me nothing about what she's thinking or feeling, and I know for a fact that I'm going to overthink myself to death about this later tonight when I'm trying to sleep. I hope she doesn't. I hope she sleeps sound and safe.

"There." She nods, balling up the tissues. Our eyes meet for all of one second until she turns away to glance at the corner. "The coast is clear, shall we bounce?"

I bob my head in all directions. Luckily she takes it as a yes, and I follow her around the edges of the party on our way out. The noise of scattered conversations, laughter, glasses clinking, and dissonant music assault my senses, bringing me back to a very rude reality. I manage to tear my eyes away from the patch of skin at Audrey's back that her hair lets me glimpse at, and take in our surroundings.

I spot Audrey's father watching us like a hawk from across the room, with the same kind of hawk-like precision back from me. He's surrounded by other old men—one I even recognize from the politics section of the news. Not pictured among them is the asshat that harassed Audrey just minutes ago.

He's nowhere to be found, yet I know just as I know that my full name is Miguel Jose Machado Jimenez that tonight won't be the last we see of that piece of shit.

We emerge from the crowd uninterrupted, and with Audrey leading the charge she's the one who reaches the elevators first and presses the button. I hang back, doing my best to keep my eyes forward so they don't lower back down to her legs.

Nope, heaven forgive me but my eyes stray. Her legs look soft enough to make my hands tingle.

The elevator dings. A few people come out once the doors open, and one of the hotel employees remains inside as Audrey and I step in. Polite greetings are exchanged, and that would be it if not because the cleaning lady does a double take at me. Something like an eureka flashes on her face, then she peeks at Audrey, and back to the front.

Audrey nudges me. I return a little shrug and shake my head. I can't presume that this lady really knows who I am. Unlike the prick who traded from the Wild to the Riders to become the team's flagship pitcher, I don't go around offering autographs before they're requested to stroke my ego. Somehow Audrey seems to understand because she nods, and that's that.

"Umm, I'm sorry to bother but..." We both turn to the other lady. She's wringing her hands. "Are you Miguel

Machado? My husband is a big fan but I don't have anything on me to get your autograph."

Audrey flashes me a smirk before addressing the lady. "That's not a problem, could I take a picture of you two instead?"

The woman's face lights up for a second. "Oh, but I shouldn't impose, I'm so sorry—"

"It's okay, carpet the diem!" Audrey exclaims like my daughter once did.

At the lobby, we find a clear background for Audrey to take a picture of the cleaning lady and I. I do my best to smile in a happy way, even though my head is swimming.

Do I have a chance with Audrey? Or is it going to be super creepy to come out and say *hey, I said we were friends but actually I want more?*

In contrast, she's unbothered as she grabs my by the crook of my arm and bids our combined farewell to the nice elevator lady. We walk together in awkward silence again, stopping at the valet to request our car. The air outside is hot and humid, fat drops falling all around. The sky rumbles with a threat, setting up the perfect stage for me to have an existential crisis when I get home. I just have to keep it together until then.

The sound of the Maserati's engine alerts me. I blink awake and notice that the rain is starting to pick up. Neither of us brought an umbrella, so my jacket will have to do. Audrey watches me remove it with clear confusion on her face, but then the car is in front of us and I hold the suit jacket over her.

"Shall we?" I ask.

"Ah, yes."

We shuffle toward the passenger door off tune, bumping into each other a couple of times. I prompt her to hold the jacket as I open the door for her, cold drops slamming on my head and the back of my neck, helping to cool down the raging volcano heat of my skin. When she tries to offer the jacket in return, I lay it across her lap and close the door.

I take just a second to look up and close my eyes against the rain. By the time I get into the small enclosure of this sports car, I better be acting like my normal damn self, or else.

Or else I'm gonna be in serious trouble.

I walk around the car at a leisurely pace, receiving the keys from the valet driver and getting in without much ceremony.

"Miguel Jose," Audrey says in a serious voice and armed with the new ammo of my middle name. "I won't be responsible for you catching a cold."

When my lips stretch, I know that the trick worked and I'm back to normal. "You do know that I train and play in the rain too, right?"

She ignores me. "Let's turn down the A/C, at least."

I let her fuss with it for a moment. We fasten our seatbelts and I pull out of the hotel parking lot like the night has been completely unremarkable. From the corner of my eye, I notice that she's still fussing—now with the sound system. She stops at a radio station that's playing some early 2000s classics and leans back.

Right as I'm starting to hum to As Long As You Love Me, Audrey says, "I'm sorry about all that. I shouldn't have kissed you all of a sudden."

And just like that, my veneer of normalcy falls off in one swoop.

My hands tighten around the steering wheel. "It's okay."

"No, it isn't," she whispers. "It's just, he suspects that we're not married for love and started throwing accusations, and it was all I could think about to shut him up."

"I understand," I say somewhat robotically, even as my chest squeezes uncomfortably. I focus on the road, the wipers working hard to clear the rain.

"I know you do. You're the most understanding person I've

ever met." Audrey lets out a dry chuckle. "That's what makes me feel worse about this whole thing. I'm using you, Miguel, plain and simple."

I have no problem with that, I nearly spew out, but even when I'm still turned on like a torch I know better than to say that. Just because I don't mind being her cover with kisses worth of a telenovela, it doesn't mean it will lead to something real.

However, she's wrong about something. "You're not using me when I'm collaborating, you know?"

"Even then." Sighing, she turns toward the window as we roll to a stop at a red light. "I... I—"

She gets interrupted by a streak of light in the sky. An explosion-like thunder booms all around us, the kind that makes every hair in your body stand up. And then it's not raining anymore—rather, buckets of water are pouring over the whole area and it's near impossible to see.

"Er, is it okay if I park somewhere to wait this out?"

"I—yes, of course," she responds.

I'd never been more thankful for franchises being so uniform across the board, because even with the diminished visibility I know that what I'm pulling into is a McDonald's parking lot. I find an empty corner and park us there to wait out the worst of the storm. I turn the A/C vents toward her and lean back on my seat.

"What now?" Audrey asks.

I rest my hands across my stomach. "There are a few options. We can just listen to the radio or a playlist. We can chat about everything and nothing, or even take a nap. If you're hungry, we can actually use the drive through to get something. Up to you."

"Up to me, huh?" she repeats, humming a little bit from her throat.

Glad that she can't see how that little sound makes me break into goosebumps. Ironically, You Belong With Me starts playing and I have to just sit here, quiet and normal, unable to do pull ups or burpees to trick my body out of this state.

Rustling, and then Audrey's voice is clearer. I turn to find her facing me. "Or we could do something else."

My brain whirs. What else would she want to do while trapped in the rain in a McDonald's parking lot?

"Dance in the rain?" I ask, my face scrunching in thought. "I think these seats are real leather, though. I'd rather that Logan doesn't kill us."

"Not that." She waves a hand. "It's just, I was thinking…"

I blink. Surprisingly, I'm unable to read her mind. "About what?"

"The kiss."

I swallow hard.

Yeah, me too.

Non stop.

With every cell of my being.

I stay silent, though, unwilling to put my seventeen size foot in my mouth.

Audrey shifts a little. "It's just—yes, I'm very sorry for how that came about. I know for a fact that it was very unfair to you, and I'll be apologizing for it the rest of my life. But…"

Another roll of thunder. The wipers seem to make even more noise than normal.

"But?" I press.

Finally, she lifts her eyes to me and as serious as a doctor delivering bad news, she says, "I haven't been kissed like that in a very long time."

At first, I'm just a statue of Miguel Machado, father of one and All-Star slugger.

But then my eye twitches a little.

Wow, okay. So the kiss was not the best in her life. Maybe if I'd had time to prepare… No, the point is that I'm just one in the list of guys she's played tonsil hockey with. Not the best, not the worst. My competitive spirit cannot freaking take it.

"Like what?" I prod for a hint that will let me rank myself in her roster.

The look on her face, as lit up by more lightning, is like she can't believe I'm asking. "Like the guy knows what he's doing, you know?"

Hmm. So better than her average, but not enough information to know if I was the best. And I *want* to be her best.

"The thing is…" She tucks her hair behind her ears, hands falling back down to clutch at my jacket. "It reminded me that it's not too bad to kiss a guy."

"Not too bad?" I blurt out, offended.

She catches on right away and bursts into chuckles. "What I mean is that I forgot how good it can feel to forget about the world in a kiss."

Oh.

Yeah, I did that too. I forgot what year we were in the second her lips crashed on mine.

"So I was wondering…" Her amusement ebbs away and she no longer keeps eye contact with me. "Could we… do it again?"

Pretty sure this time the thunder is in my head alone.

"Do what?" I ask, unable to process whatever the hell is happening right now.

"Kiss," she answers very calmly. "Without duress, that is. Like a good, proper kiss where we give it our best but it means nothing. Just out of curiosity, while we wait out the rain."

I don't think, therefore I don't exist.

She turns back to me and studies my face. "Erm, you know what? Forget about it. That was way too unhinged even for my standards, especially after—"

"Bueno." I shake the glitch off my head and say, "Okay."

"Okay?" She jolts a little.

"Sure." I sound way calmer than I really feel on the inside, the normal life version of speaking into a glove so no one else can tell what you're really saying. "That's another way to pass the time."

"You don't think it's weird?" Her eyes widen to the maximum possible.

"Weird how?" I shrug one shoulder. "We're two single, consenting adults."

"But, I mean. One thing is faking in front of Henry Vos, another is making out alone in a car like we're in high school."

I use all my willpower reserves to not point out how she changed a kiss into making out. The latter option would be even better.

I'm glad I didn't wag my tail from the get go, because I'm not going to pressure her into doing something she's now talking herself out of.

I reach for the volume dial. "Then we can just listen to some music and—"

"No."

Her hands grab my forearm. I look up at her. "No?"

Audrey's mouth opens and closes, and my attention gets sucked in by her lips. Even in the dim lighting from outside, they look plump and glossy, and my mouth starts watering like the perv I am deep down.

Her hands cinch tighter around my forearm. "I—I want to try again. To feel feminine and careless and fun. And I know it's going to be safe with you."

I nearly mewl because if she knew how spicy my thoughts were getting, she may start to doubt that. Tearing my eyes away from her lips, I find earnest green eyes that skewer through me.

Gently, I pry her hands off my arm and lean away. Audrey wilts a little, but I keep watching her as I push my seat away from the steering wheel—which is slow enough to get a tad awkward—and then unfasten my seatbelt.

"Come here."

It doesn't matter that my voice is the thickest it's ever been, or that maybe I should've added a please at the end of the sentence. The embarrassment in Audrey's demeanor evaporates and next thing, she's also unfastening her seatbelt and shoving my jacket off.

Somehow I'm not nervous as I watch her lift up her dress skirts to maneuver. I feel just the same as if I was standing in the batter's box, ready for a ball to fly at me. Just the same, I reach for my crucifix, almost confused that I don't find the wedding ring next to it until I remember that it's proudly on my finger.

That's right, none of this is real. But it doesn't mean I can't enjoy it.

I reach for Audrey's waist and lift her carefully unto my lap. The height puts her neck at an uncomfortable angle, and I find the controls again to lean my seat back until she has to make no further effort.

Even better, it makes her collapse on my chest.

Our noses bump, but instead of meeting me halfway for a kiss, Audrey pulls slightly away. "Some ground rules."

"Okay," I say, swallowing hard.

"Hands above the waist," is her first one.

"I kinda like your legs though," I admit.

"You do?" Her eyebrows rise. "Okay, you can touch my legs, but that's it."

My lips stretch a little, and this time she's the one staring at them. After running my tongue across them, I ask, "What else?"

"Um…" She focuses on my eyes again and shifts a little. "Right, kissing only. And Vegas rules—"

I splay my hands more possessively around her waist. "What happens in this car stays in this car."

"Exactly." Audrey nods solemnly. "And also, only this once."

I take in a deep breath.

She's right, it can only be one more time. If we kiss again —and again—it's going to be so much harder for me to contain how much I want her.

However, I'm not a complete fool. "Does that mean one kiss only or one make out session?"

The question catches her off guard, and she has to meditate it for a second. "Make out session. Just until the rain stops."

That's a good deal. In Central Florida it can last all night long. I don't say that, though. Instead, I just say, "Then kiss me, woman."

CHAPTER 29
AUDREY

gasp a little.

And yet… *yes*. This is exactly what I want.

I lean one arm against the headrest, placing my free hand against his jaw again. Gosh, does he know how perfect it is? His whole face, even. The Roman-like nose, his shockingly soft lips, and the half mast eyes that are doing things to me.

He is doing things to me. I forgot that I could feel this way entirely.

Finally, I lean down and close my eyes. A girlish sigh comes out of me once our lips meet again.

I'm going to take it slowly this time around. The rain beats at the car violently, and there's nowhere better to be than right here, right now. Miguel grabs my waist in handfuls and finally my brain turns off.

I breathe him in deep, the cedar and the man, and his own breath as it mingles with mine. Miguel matches my pace, his lips caressing mine softly, mapping every contour like he wants to preserve it in his memory. He's so hot, so tender, that I'm melting on top of him. And then the itch for more starts, first in my belly, gradually expanding until every cell in my body's vibrating. Until I need him more than air. Until I can't take sweet anymore.

I need hot.

My tongue comes out to savor his lips, and I can't hold back after that. Miguel draws in a harsh breath and opens his mouth, and since I'm on top of him I make the big effort of tilting my head for better access. And he gives me all of it.

It's like an explosion when our open mouths let our tongues meet. Fireworks and lightning, a volcano's eruption, a car crash that spreads flowers all around. I smile into Miguel's mouth because I didn't know I had it in me to be so melodramatic.

One of his hands makes a bold journey from my waist, down to my hip and outer thigh, finding the end of my skirt and sneaking underneath. A moan tears out of him the second he finds skin, and I suck in air.

"Too much?" he rasps out against my mouth.

Yes. No. Not enough. Definitely too much.

I respond with a thick, "I did give you permission to touch my legs."

"Hmm, thank you for that," Miguel whispers, his hand rising above my knee and awakening every pore in my skin. "Now, kiss me again."

I comply. Swiftly. Happily.

We both moan in a way that is so not safe for work. Oops, I Did It Again is playing in the background and I wish I could tell Britney that yes, indeed, I'm kissing Miguel a third time. Thank goodness for the storm that keeps raging outside. My back arches unbidden, pressing me even closer to the man burning up under me. He mumbles something in Spanish that I can't understand consciously.

Subconsciously I do. It means *more*.

My hand palms the powerful column of his neck, muscles working as we eat each other's mouths like dessert. His hand under my skirt grabs tighter onto my outer thigh, like it's his. Like it's a truth universally acknowledged.

Me too, I scream desperately from the bottom of my soul. My hand meets the neck of his dress shirt and tries to slide underneath, but there's too much resistance. I find the evil button that's getting in my way, but my fingers are clumsy and too stiff.

Our lips make an embarrassing smacking noise as I pull away. "Help me," I demand with the same attitude as him when he commanded me to kiss him.

The sneaky man leaves his hand on my thigh, releasing my waist to reach for his button. We're both breathing like horses as I brace myself against the seat so he can access the button, and he undoes it without an issue.

Then another.

I glance at his face, and the tiny smirk stretching his lips almost makes me faint on top of him. "Should I keep going?" Miguel asks with the deepest, raspiest voice that wraps around my sensitive skin like velvet.

I can't suppress a shiver.

"Sure," I respond, with far more bravado than I feel.

My eyes have a difficult time moving away from his lips, especially when he gives the full bottom one a little bite. I grip the seat even harder and force my attention lower, first at the delectable chin I now want to bite, at the Adam's apple at his throat that bobs with a swallow, the dip at the base of his throat, the dusting of hair at his chest. His hand keeps working, now at the third button. There's a deep ridge where his pecks meet and I snap my mouth shut a second before drooling.

"This good enough?" he asks.

I draw in a sharp breath. "Keep going."

His pauses just for a second, and then resumes the work.

His stomach starts coming into view. I should probably say that's enough, but for some reason I can't—a reason that has nothing to do with my brain and everything to do with my hormones. I stay very quiet as Miguel reaches the last button before his pants begin, and I almost regret that they're in the way.

Oh my word, he has a happy trail.

I swallow hard. Of course he does. He's a man—one with impressive testosterone, and a body sculpted by the heavens. His muscles tighten to the point where his abs become prominent.

"Wow, so you have a sleeper build," I whisper in awe, not even registering the fact that one of my hands is on his skin.

"Uh…" Miguel tries to clear his throat, and it doesn't work by how his voice comes out next, "Trust me, I'm very much awake."

"Does this bother you?" I sound a little shy for the first time tonight, even as my hand is splayed right in the middle of his chest.

After a pause, Miguel responds, "Not one bit."

Somehow I manage to murder a squeal just as it starts to form. I can't believe I'm doing this, touching a man—and not just anyone, but Miguel. The single dad next door. The new star of my baseball team. Someone who gets recognized in elevators, who other women would kill to be in this position with.

Moreover, I can't believe he's letting me.

But here we are, my hand slowly feeling his chest, the velvet of his skin, the dusting of hair, the steel of the muscles beneath. His breath comes out harsher as I find his abs, like he's definitely sensitive around here. And as proof, his hand under my skirt rises some more.

There's nothing soft about how I kiss him now.

Years of pent up need to feel desired finally rush out of hiding. There's no way after this that I can go back to lying to myself that I'm fine. That I'm better off without this closeness.

Miguel's other hand finds the skin at my upper back, blazing a trail of fire to hold the back of my neck as I devour his mouth. With his other hand, he pushes me closer against him and for a wild moment I hope that it keeps climbing up, but it doesn't. In fact, it makes a slow descent toward my knee, and surprisingly I find myself not disappointed at all. Not one damn bit.

His mouth is so hot, his larger lips so perfect against mine. His hair is so soft, his chest so hard. What a perfect man. I'm going to dream about this moment for the rest of my life.

Violent thunder goes off, breaking the fantasy just a little bit. My jaw hurts and I'm struggling for breath, so I slow down a little—a lot—but I can't pull away. Not yet.

"It's still raining," I whisper, a clear plea to keep going.

"It sure is," he volleys back, all serious.

A little laugh tears from my soul. Who cares if my jaw is tired? I'm never going to have another chance like this.

I slide my hand up, under his shirt until I find his sculpted shoulder. Miguel's watching me with almost sleepy eyes, if it wasn't for the fact that there's very clear hunger behind them. I'm sure mine aren't any better.

He caresses my calf, slowly going up and down, his touch firm and uncompromising. Like he's also enjoying the moment.

"What if it rains all night?" Miguel asks in a murmur.

My other hand returns to his jaw, sliding slightly forward toward his chin, until my thumb finds his swollen lip. "Then we kiss all night," I respond like that makes sense and should be obvious. As if that wasn't dangerous at all for either of us.

Miguel bobs his head a little. "Sounds good," he says against my thumb and next thing, he's biting it softly. The gentle scrape of his teeth against the pad of my finger nearly undoes me.

"M-Miguel!" His name trembles in my slip.

The little jerk smirks again, my thumb still captive. When he flicks his tongue against my finger I see…

Not red. I just see him. Pinned under my weight willingly, touching me. Tasting me.

I claim his lips again—or so I tell myself, and not that he's the one doing the claiming with both of his hands on visible bare skin, with his heat surrounding me, the steel of his body against my much softer one, our breaths becoming one, hearts beating against each other's chests.

I will the rain to keep pouring, thunder to keep cracking, for this night to never end so I don't have to wake up from this dream. So I can stay in the embrace of a sweet and delicious man.

So I can keep kissing Miguel.

CHAPTER 30
MIGUEL

My favorite part of the All-Star game is before it even starts, when the players get to meet some of the little fans. It's a shame that it can't be open to every single family that purchases tickets to the game, but I think rather than this being a safety concern, it's more an issue that there's way less players than fans. A very good first world problem to have.

I'm crouched down between two siblings, a girl and a boy, and we're smiling for the camera. As we cheese it out, I wonder if Marty still finds all of this too cringe or if she'd be up to taking a picture with her dad.

Eh, probably the former, but I wouldn't be where I am if I wasn't a try-hard.

ME

Can we take some pics after this?

MI NIÑA BONITA

Like this?

A moment later comes an attachment of her sitting on

the stands reserved for the players's families. To her left is Consuelo with an enormous bucket of popcorn that almost obscures her entirely. On Marty's right is a mountain of women—I think that would be a good plural for them, since they're all larger than life. Audrey's squished next to my daughter, and she appears grumpy about the fact that her two roommates are basically on top of her, matching Marty's grin.

Well, thanks. Now I'm bummed that I'm not there.

"Can we have your autograph?" the kids ask, looking up at me like I still have hero-shine even though I already warmed up and I kind of stink.

"Of course." Like magic, one of the organizing staff passes me a stack of papers with the logo's event and a marker. "What are your names?"

"I'm Aaliyah!"

Then her little brother adds, "And Elijah!"

Their smiles are so contagious that I can't help but mirror them as I work on the autograph. The two are in pee wees together, but it's actually Aaliyah the one who wishes to be a professional baseball player—that was actually their introduction earlier. Breaks my damn freaking heart that it doesn't seem possible the way things are set up. As a girl dad, I want Marty to have whatever she wants.

"Here you go, champs. Stay safe, okay?" As I offer them the autographs, and since it looks like their hair took a lot of effort, rather than patting them on the head I offer my fist for them to bump it.

As they wave me off, new kids start on the *me me me* chants. I check the players nearby. The guy from Philly's team is still still occupied with a tween boy who's asking for pitching tips. On my other side, Ben Williams is just sending off a girl. The problem is that the kids in the waiting line aren't looking at him for their next turn.

This grown ass man rolls his eyes at me. "Look at you, Mr. Popular."

As I did while I was still a Rider, I ignore him.

"I hate that about you, man. Acting like you're more important than everyone else."

I mention to the staff member, "I'm ready for the next kid."

"Great!" she chirps. It takes some finagling with the line to find who has the next ticket to meet me.

Meanwhile, Williams takes that as an invitation to keep yapping. "I still can't believe you left us for a subpar team like the Wild."

That's not enough to goad me into conversation. Not only was the Wild a legit contender for the championship before I came along, but *he* is the second reason why I left Denver. This guy has the touch of the stomach—everything he touches turns to shit. The Wild was a better team before him, and it's drastically better after him. And the second he arrived to the Riders, the environment started turning into Chernobyl levels of toxic.

I prepare for whatever's coming next when he turns around so no one can read his lips. "Are you getting some good tail, though? Orlando has a surprisingly juicy crop of women." He fake gasps. "Wait. You married my ex's friend right? Then the tail must not really be good."

That does it.

Not because he's getting under my skin—and Audrey would have an even better takedown for him if she was here—but the staff member is wheeling in the next kid and I'd like to preserve his innocence.

"Did you forget that the last time you said something like this, you got your nose broken?" I point at the new curve of his nose. "I guess it's possible since you can't see it, but it's there, trust me."

His hackles rise. "Are you threatening me?"

I go back to ignoring him and crouch for the next kid. "Hey, buddy. Are you having a good time today?"

"Yeah!" The boy's face, already open and happy, all but explodes from excitement. "I got a picture with two Hall of Famers already, *two!* Can you believe that?"

"Wow, that's so cool. Who were the lucky guys?"

He uses his fingers to count them. "First it was Derek Jeter, and then Pedro Martinez. But I also met Andres Gal—Galg..."

"Galarraga?" I ask, my Venezuelan accent coming out in full force.

"Yeah, my dad was his fan!"

"So was I." I start working on an autograph for him, using my thigh as a table. "He's one of the players I looked up to when I was a kid in my home country, dreaming of being pro one day."

Andres Galarraga, Omar Vizquel, the legendary hero Luis Aparicio from my hometown. These are some of the guys that make me believe in myself when I was a kid. That I could go somewhere with this sport.

"Whoa!" he exclaims.

"What's your name, buddy?"

"I'm Jimmy! It's so cool to meet you." Then he leans a little bit toward me, hands gripping the armrests of his wheelchair. "Wanna know the truth?"

I look up with interest. I'm not against being trusted with a secret. "Of course, what's that?"

"You're actually my favorite player of all," he says in the loudest whisper I've ever heard. That, and the fact that he looks like he just won the lottery, make my chest bubble with joy.

I pretend like I'm very serious, though, and I also lean forward to share a big secret. "Well, don't tell anyone, Jimmy, but you're my favorite fan."

"Yes!" He pumps a fist in the air and we pose for a picture with him holding the autograph.

I'm grinning from ear to ear when I make the mistake of straightening up and making eye contact with Williams. "You're my favorite player," he mocks with a high pitched voice.

From the corner of my eye, I confirm that Jimmy's far enough, surrounded by other kids, and shows no signs of having heard the mockery.

Unfortunately, I'm only human. All the happy go lucky feels I had part like the ocean to give room for anger. Slowly, making full use of the nine inches I have on him, I say, "Another rhinoplasty's in your damn future if I catch you making fun of a child again."

Williams snaps his mouth shut.

There, there.

When I turn back to find the coordinator, I instead meet a different one approaching me. This one's a fairly young guy and he looks like he just went through something traumatic. "Um, excuse me, Mr. Machado, but Mr. Cox is looking for you."

Audrey's dad? Whatever for, I think sarcastically. I think she's starting to rub off on me.

A flashback of her rubbing up on me in my team captain's car goes through my head. I shake it to clear the incredible memory away.

I clear my throat. "Let's check with the event coordinator first."

"Of course." The guy nods rapidly.

I glance back at Williams, who is still glaring a me with unmatched fury. It makes my lips quirk. "Turns out your nose lives to see another day."

"You—"

Whatever he says next is drowned by the kids, because the

coordinator gives the other staff member a thumbs up that I'm good to go, and starts guiding me away.

"I'll be back," I say in my best Terminator voice to the kiddies, and they react entirely the opposite way my own child would. Like they're excited about the idea. No one is a prophet in their own land, after all.

The behind the scenes of an All-Star game is even more of a circus than a normal one, and sometimes even more than a World Series, depending on the egos and the grudges that get intermingled here. Williams isn't the only guy who wishes for me to trip on my shoelaces. One of the guys I'll duke it out against in the home run derby later is giving me some lip as we pass him by. Most of the players are respectful of each other but some—like this dude, who is actually older than me—have the mentality of an elementary school bully.

What's funny, though, is that in front of the cameras they look like the picture of wholesomeness. But since I ignore them, they like to circulate rumors that I'm the bad apple. That I'm rude and cocky.

And yeah, I kinda am. I don't clock people who have no say in my life. Let's see if Charlie Cox is gonna learn that lesson today.

This show of course also includes executives, managers, and some of the owners from the teams that are represented. Just as I'd like to be able to join Marty and Audrey in the stands, or to still be meeting the future players and fans in line, I'm forced to be a professional and follow the staff guy to the area with the powers that be, where the cheapest snack is caviar.

Which by the way, is incredibly gross and I'll take no questions about it.

Of course the owners are hanging out by themselves behind closed doors. Many of them stop and stare at my arrival, and the kid guiding me through the maze visibly grows smaller. My bet is that this is why he's so nervous, because dealing with the ultra rich isn't for the faint of heart.

Of course, Charlie Cox isn't even mingling among them. He's in an even more private room, drinking from a glass, staring out at the stadium as it continues to fill up before the game, and brushing his twirly mustache like the villain of a cartoon from the 1940s.

"There you are," he says in what frankly is an ominous voice. He looks at the young staffer and waves him off, like this is happening in a movie. Once we're alone in the private balcony, he says, "We need to talk."

I wish I could ignore him too. Alas.

Folding my arms, I offer no further sign of interest in what he has to say.

I don't know him very well, and I don't need to. What he's done and also attempted to do to his own daughter already put him in a specific category for me. The no bueno kind.

He sets the glass down on the bar by the window with the great view, leaning against it to face me. "This conversation has been long overdue. However, I've been occupied with other matters, so I will get to the point."

I stare. Does he realize that that was quite a long preamble already?

"What you did to my daughter raises suspicions."

Luckily for the both of us, I'm pretty good at not giving away what I'm really thinking or feeling. It's a job hazard of being a baseball player. I do itch to grab onto the crucifix and the married ring at my neck, though.

"So, tell me the truth. Even if I don't like it, I will prefer it than discovering you lied. And trust me, I'm not above suspending you the rest of the season for it."

The threat is there, clear as the bright sky of A-Town where this All-Star game is happening. I would not enjoy having to lawyer up to fight an unjust suspension. But no one who has developed the skill of hitting a hard ball flying at your face at a hundred miles per hour, and making it fly off even faster, is ever a coward.

Since I give him nothing, he finally gets to the point, "Did you marry my daughter for her inheritance?"

I fully crack with a "huh?"

The old man's forehead wrinkles in something that is either anger, or confusion, or a child of the two. "You and I know that Audrey's getting the team in her trust fund, and I would have never—and let's make that very clear—*ever* chosen you to manage it for her. That honor was to be for Henry Vos, who is a true and tried businessman. Not to someone who only knows how to swing a big stick and already has a child from another woman."

Consider my hackles raised now.

"First of all, no. I had no idea." I wrinkle my face in disgust. "Second, why would you think Audrey's fortune should be managed by a guy?"

Silence.

Pure, complete silence that I break with a snort.

"I suppose since you're one and you've been managing her inheritance until now, you may think that's the way of the world and that she has no say in it. But trust me, she's more than capable—my daughter's now good at division because of Audrey. And guess what too?"

Charlie Cox frowns. "What?"

"Audrey would be way better focused to manage her assets brilliantly if you treating her like a puppet didn't take up so much room in her brain."

I loosen up and take one step closer that makes him visibly uncomfortable. I guess it's also because I'm a head taller and a few pounds of muscle bigger.

"I'm speaking as a girl dad to another girl dad." I jab him in the chest moderately, but he stiffens in a way you'd think I almost punched him. "Unless you don't want them to become their best selves, you don't raise them by manipulating them."

That makes him inhale a sharp breath. Like maybe I just hit a nerve. Like maybe this is the first time someone has presented this concept to this rich, powerful, and selfish man.

A truly toxic one wouldn't care, though. So does he?

I pull away enough to give him a false sense of relief. "So threaten me all you want, but if you come for my wife or my daughter, you'll find out that I don't threaten back because I don't have brains for it. I sure have brawn, though, and I have *a lot* of big sticks."

CHAPTER 31
AUDREY

like that the armrests at this stadium can be tucked away. Thanks to this, Marty has her head on Consuelo's lap, and her legs on mine as she takes a nap. It's a mutually beneficial arrangement too, because Marty isn't bothered about me propping up my popcorn tub on her calves.

"You guys look so at ease with each other," Hope points out —with her lips—at the scene next to her.

She catches me in the middle of lifting a handful of popcorn toward my gullet. I pause to say, "I have terrible news for you two. Marty's my best friend now. Not sorry." Then I stuff my face with popcorn. The caramel kind, because I'm a monster.

Hope releases an exaggerated gasp. Rose leans forward for visibility and says, "How dare you betray us this way." Even someone who doesn't know us would see our silly grins and know we're having a blast.

I lean a bit toward them, hoping that the stadium noise is enough to drown my voice. "Actually, she reminds me a lot of me when I was a kid. But she doesn't have a cool older brother to amuse her, you know?"

"Not all older brothers are cool, trust me." Hope shakes her head, but then she pats my shoulder. "But I get it, you're trying to fulfill the role."

"A little bit, I guess," I admit as I chew, with an elegance previously unseen in these here WAG stands.

"Do you miss him?" Hope asks. The problem is that Miguel's walk up song is starting to play, but his daughter is passed out, drooling on her nanny's lap.

"Who?" I shout back.

It's hard to understand when everyone around is yelling like they're seeing Babe Ruth in the flesh, but also I get it. Every time Miguel Machado steps up to the plate, there's a collective understanding that magic's about to happen.

And if you're in the opposing team, it jiggles your bones in fear. It's fun. My brother would've loved to watch him play.

That's when it clicks who Hope was referring to. I tear my eyes away from Miguel performing his jinx ritual. "I do," I say at last. "Every single day. But it's been so long that now I just miss him in the back of my mind. Is that bad?"

Instead of cringing, Hope bobs her head. "No, I get it. I feel similar about my mom, and I didn't even get to meet her."

"Ugh." Rose leans forward again. "I can only hear bits of your conversation but it's so freaking—"

Whatever descriptor she was gonna use completely fizzles in the air as basically the whole stadium jumps to their feet. The most impressive part is how they still had even more gas in the tank to produce more noise. Marty jerks awake and honestly, I'm glad because I was gonna worry. Consuelo tosses me a wink, like she finds the whole thing amusing.

Marty swipes at her chin as she shifts to sit up, glancing around with one eye more open than the other. I can't hear her but I know her mouth just formed the word *what?*

Your dad, I voice back, not even sure if I tried to use my voice box at all.

She makes a face and goes back to laying down. I can't help but howling at this kid. I have a feeling that even if she knew about all the other kids of all ages that line up to meet her dad, she'd still be bored about the whole thing.

And that sets off an unexpected eureka in my brain. They have such a good relationship. Marty's not compelled by fear of her dad to fawn over him. He doesn't demand anything of her other than doing her homework and being a good kid. Everything he does is in one way or another for his daughter, from ice cream to moving across the country so she stops getting bullied, including something wild like marrying a virtual stranger for her sake.

Marty's not like me. She's a blessed child, with a dad who deserves awards outside of baseball.

I notice that I'm smiling from ear to ear only when I take the next handful of popcorn to my mouth.

People start sitting down at last. Even when we're so far, Miguel is so larger than life that he takes all the focus as he rounds the bases. His hand is raised, pointing upward. So that was a home run, then.

From two seats away, Rose asks, "Are you thinking what I'm thinking?"

"I am." Hope shrinks a little. "But I'm worried that even thinking it is gonna jinx us."

I need no explanations. I'm thinking the exact same. How incredible is it that someone like Miguel Machado came into our lives, into our team? It makes anyone start to dream big.

It makes even a girl like me start to dream about things she had forbidden from her life. Things like dancing in the rain and being held by strong arms that won't ever let you fall.

In fact, I bet Miguel would never smash cake in his bride's face.

Damn, whoever he marries for real is going to be such a

lucky woman. He also kisses better than he bats, and that's saying something.

I sigh.

"Speaking of Miguel," Rose says, and I jump in my skin. Did I have that whole monologue aloud? "What's the next step in your marriage?"

Of course, this is the moment when the women sitting at the row below us decide to pay attention to our conversation. "Oh, are you planning on having a baby with Miguel?" this weird woman called Amber says, her eyes shining in something that isn't happiness. More like she thinks she just got the century's juiciest piece of gossip.

This is also when Marty decides to jerk to attention. "You are?" And unlike the weirdo sitting in front of me, Marty's eyes are full of hope.

Welp.

"Chill, Amber," Rose says in a direct tone. "We'll know exactly who spread rumors about this if they start going around, you know?"

The woman's smile dims and funny enough, her eyes stay the exact way they were before. Sharp but absolutely flat. Like a robot lives behind them.

She reminds me of the rich daughters who used to bully me in school. One time, it got so bad that when Adam found out, he burst into my classroom in the middle of an exam to put them in their place. He got suspended and the bullying didn't stop, but it did get less loud.

People like this… they just can't stand being shown up. Also like the Henry Voses of the world.

I lean forward. "So, Amber. What are your next plans with Mike? And is one of them exiting my personal bubble?"

"Nice," Hope whispers and from the corner of my eye I see her offer me her fist. I bump it, and then way less discreet, Rose reaches out to do the same.

Amber's thin façade of friendliness vanishes. "Ugh, just who do you all think you are? I was just trying to make polite conversation, since you're all new WAGs and have no friends."

"We have friends," Rose chirps immediately.

"Yeah." I motion at our row, from Consuelo to Rose. "Plural."

"Guys." Hope motions at Rose and I with her hands. "We don't owe any explanations."

"Damn right," Consuelo says all of a sudden. We all look at each other and burst out laughing.

We're so unserious that it bores the head honcho of the WAGs, and we all—except for Marty—return to watch the last of the game. The team our boys are in is winning by a mile, so there's not gonna be a home run derby at the end. Probably a good thing, since Marty legit seems to be in need of a bed. I stretch to look at the field and spot her dad not too far from us. The number three emblazoned on his back is turned toward us. Well below it are the most perfectly rounded beef cakes anyone's ever grown.

I rest back against my seat. Bad Audrey. That's not what you should be paying attention to.

But then the game ends and everyone starts getting up, and the beef cakes are wholly inaccessible to view now.

I try not to think about it too much as we slowly make our way back to the family lounge, but it's hard to erase the memory of Miguel and I making out in a car like teens after prom with a strict curfew.

What's next in our marriage?

Sheesh, I don't know, but it sure isn't going to be another make out session that fogs up the car windows—although that was partially because of the storm. And the fact that that's a big bummer worries me. It's not like this whole arrangement is forever.

"Martina!" the star of The Show exclaims upon sighting

his daughter, even elongating the last letter. And in his hands is the glass bat that is awarded to the MVP of the All-Star game. I shouldn't be surprised, yet I am.

Rather, it's more like he keeps surprising me every time.

Marty's nowhere near as impressed. "Dad, we don't have enough room in the house for another glass bat."

My laughter transforms into a snort. It distracts the poor guy and when his attention sets on me, his smile widens even more.

Calm down, heart. No tripping on yourself.

It's hard not to, though, when the man looks like that and he has a mouth that knows how to tease, smile, defend, and make one's prudence fog up a car's window.

"There you all are," an unexpected voice cuts into my thoughts. I wipe every emotion off my system and turn to my dad. He's motioning at some woman with a gigantic professional camera. "Let's take a picture with the whole family."

"Ugh," I mutter under my breath. But I guess this is the price of freedom. We did agree that I was coming out of the figurative closet.

And then the first one to move is Miguel. He slings the bat over his shoulder like it's a normal wooden one, and marches over to my Robber Baron father. He even wraps my dad in a one armed hug that ends with his big hand squeezing my dad's shoulder.

What's that all about?

"Go," Rose whispers in my ear. "The quicker you're done, the less pain you'll suffer."

True. I drag my feet, Marty-style, and then I find said little grump tagging along and dragging her nanny by the hand. My dad's expression screams that this wasn't what he had in mind, but even he knows better than to make a scene in public.

That makes me feel way better and I sidle up to my so

called husband. Before the camera starts going off, though, he swings the bat and offers it to me.

"What?" my last neuron asks.

"It's for you, my beloved wife." Then he follows in the Consuelo books with a wink. The difference is that, mischievous as the gesture is, it also lands in my belly with an explosion of warmth.

With his free hand, he brings me against his hard side. He's still hot and sweaty from the game, yet somehow the guy managers to still smell spectacular.

Marty and Consuelo get close, and as the photographer starts snapping pictures, something moves across my vision that catches my attention. It's none other than Amber, the mean girl WAG, and she's staring jaw dropped at us taking a picture with Charlie Cox, the untouchable team owner.

Guess what? She won't even have the chance to gossip, because this is gonna be all over the news tomorrow. Let the social media games begin.

CHAPTER 32
MIGUEL

don't know what I've done to deserve this but I also won't question it because I'm having a blast.

My kid, blood of my blood, who refuses to do things the way others want her to, has found someone who matches her energy in the form of my fake wife.

The two are currently engaged in a singing contest of sorts, to the tune of BTS. Turns out that Audrey's also a fan of the South Korean boyband, and she knows as many of the hits as Marty.

And by that, I mean they sing the parts they understand in English and Korean, and loudly hum or *nanana* the parts that they don't. It's kind of beautiful even when they go a completely different way from the music.

The current bop is about being an idol, and that's as much as I catch while still keeping my attention on the road. Every chance she gets, Audrey turns back to pass an invisible mic to Marty at the back. We're at a long red light, so I focus the rearview mirror on my kid, who for the first time in what feels like forever is being a free, careless little girl. She wiggles her torso and plays a cross between an air guitar and air drums as she shouts music, eyes closed and hair all over the place.

I could cry right damn now. My kid is happy. It wasn't my own doing so I don't know how to replicate this, but it doesn't matter. I just wish this moment would last forever.

Audrey's happy too. Her cheeks are red as apples. Strands of hair fly off the bun at the top of her head. Her bangs are spread out like a fan over her forehead. She half sings and half laughs. Right now, she tries to pass me the microphone but I can only hum—Marty's made sure I listen to all the songs, but I don't know them by heart. I'm not smart like they are. Too busy being a fool in love.

Oh.

The car behind us starts honking. I do a double take and find that the light is green. Maybe has been for a while.

Swallowing hard, I set us in motion again. We're close to home, where I'm gonna go into my room to have a thinking session that will consist on hanging upside down from my pull ups bar. Maybe then I'll have enough blood flow in my brain to figure out if... if I'm really...

Mierda, y más mierda. I think I am. I think I've gone and caught real feelings.

The song changes to something that sounds a lot more dramatic, and then the singers are screaming about a fake love. My eye twitches.

There's still a chance that they're not really real feelings. Obviously I care about Audrey as a person. I wasn't lying when I asked her to be friends once upon a time. And I'd be lying if I said that I don't find her the most attractive woman I've ever met, with her green eyes, the sassy curve of her lips, the taste of them, the feeling of her pressed against me—

I squirm. This is probably it. I'm starting to confuse attraction for something bigger.

"Hey, Audrey?" My kid scoots toward the middle of the

backseat as far as the seatbelt lets her. "Wanna come over to sing more?"

This catches my neighbor in the middle of a solo. She clears her throat and turns back a little. "I'd love to, but I'm sure your dad will want some peace and quiet for a bit."

Actually, this *is* peace—okay, not quiet, but I'm walking on sunshine right now. Even more than after having won another glass bat. I don't want this to end. I also don't think it's right to act like clingy lint to Audrey's T-shirt.

I'm still debating how to navigate that after we're parked by the curb, and all three of us are getting out of the car. My genius strategy is to stall some more by stretching, which also isn't entirely an act. We got stuck on some really bad traffic coming up Semoran after taking Consuelo home, and I was about to become welded to the car seat. The sound of the back door opening spurs me to action.

"I got it, I got it," I chant as I hurry. My suitcase is pretty heavy between Marty's stuff, mine, and All-Star paraphernalia. Audrey's looked about similar size, so maybe it's heavy too.

And then something catches my attention. Between evening cicadas and a hot breeze, I hear something like a click. It wouldn't register if I didn't hear it again. And again.

I glance around and there it is, a dark figure in a neighbor's bushes. The thing making the sound? It's a camera with a very long lens, aimed right at Audrey and my daughter.

I don't know what happens, one moment I'm about to take care of my family's luggage. The next I'm sprinting across the residence.

There's some scrambling. Someone yells. My legs pound the ground with violence. I don't know if I'm breathing. My entire focus is on catching the paparazzi. No one takes secret pictures of my kid—*no one*. I hear my name in my brain. I shout back at it—*not my family!*

The man tries to run. Luck strikes for me, and the bushes

tangle him up. I catch him by an ankle and yank him like a rag doll. I land one knee on his back, pinning him with no chance of escape. I'm breathing like a race horse as I reach for his arms. He tries to squirm free, but there is no way in hot hell that I'm letting him loose. I pin his arms with my legs and lean over him.

"Who the hell are you?" I bark in his ear. "Why are you taking pictures of my family?"

Dude tries to spit some venom at me and I have minus patience for this bullshit.

I free one hand to dig his head deeper in the grass, and speak very low. "Answer or this is gonna get damn uglier."

"I'll—I'll press assault charges," he squeaks out.

"I'll keep pressing your face into the dirt *and* also press charges for stalking a woman and a minor, how about that?"

"Screw you!"

Tip taps echo until two sets of legs appear before me. One is from my daughter, and she's holding one of my signed wooden bats. The other one is my wife—Audrey, I mean. She's waving a… spatula?

"I called nine-one-one," the woman says out of breath, her eyes volleying between the intruder and me, back and forth. "Who is he?"

I lean forward to whisper at the man. "Answer the lady." The order goes with a bit more force from my hand.

"I'm a PI! I was hired for this job!" he finally spills out, completely catching me off guard.

A private investigator? And not a paparazzi?

Thankfully, Audrey has kept her marbles. "Who sent you?"

"Your momma," the asshole tries, spitting out some grass blades.

"That's funny," Audrey says in a flat voice. "Try again before the cops arrive, and maybe we'll see if the charges can be lighter."

The pause indicates that the guy is giving it a thought. But then he says, "I can't reveal that."

"Audrey," I say with some difficulty, not from keeping the guy prisoner, but from keeping my anger and fear in check. "Ch-Check the camera," I stutter through a tight jaw.

She drops the spatula and scrambles to grab the thing. When the PI jerk crashed, his equipment went flying off and is possibly broken. Audrey picks up the camera and the lens stays on the grass. Even though her expression is confident, bordering on annoyed, I can see the way her hands shake as she fiddles with buttons.

"No! You're going to break it!" the jackass has the nerve to say.

I lean down again and speak with my lowest voice, so my daughter doesn't hear. "I'm going to break something else if you don't tell me who sent you."

"That—That's assault!"

"It might become murder depending on what's in that camera," I add almost conversationally.

Guy spits out more grass and finally wheezes it out. "Henry Vos hired me."

Audrey hears the name. She tears her eyes off the camera and lands them on me. There's real fear in her face now.

Something twists in my gut, visceral and burning rage. I hate that a moment ago she was happy and now this.

"Audrey, Marty." I swallow down the hot lump in my throat. "Can you wait for me at home?"

"But—" Audrey starts.

"I can hear the sirens already," I explain, calmer than I really feel. It's not a lie, either. But I don't want them to have to deal with the rest of this mess. "Go, please."

My daughter's the one who grabs onto Audrey's hand and pulls her toward the house—our house.

*

It takes a couple of hours to deal with the mess. Of course the piece of dung tries to convince the cops that I'm the one who assaulted him. Fortunately, not only Audrey and Marty witnessed the thing, a couple of different neighbors stepped forward as witnesses backing up my account. I get my cousin involved, anyway. If we have to get legal involved, my agent is the best person to manage that.

What's stored in his camera also paints the picture. He'd captured all angles of the house, entrances, where the security cameras were, and even Audrey's car that's still parked in her driveway. It takes no rocket scientist to deduce that he was gonna park around here, capture every moment of our lives, and feed the information to Henry what-the-hell-is-his-problem Vos.

I didn't share with the cops that the reason the rich man baby is doing this is because he believes my marriage with Audrey is fake. That's what he was trying to find proof of, and maybe also something that could ruin my reputation as a standup pro baseball player.

Joke's on him because the marriage is very real—on paper —and the most scandalous thing I do is drink orange juice straight out of the carton. I always keep a separate carton for Marty, anyway, so why dirty any cups?

"Ugh." I drag my feet home once law enforcement finally drives off.

By this point, even the fortunately nosy neighbors have given up and gone back home. I'm going to make sure Marty and Audrey are okay, and then I'm laying facedown on the nearest surface.

I'll proceed to wallow in shame the rest of the night. Something went off in me and I was just trying to protect, but I got pretty intense out there. Or put plainly, I was a neanderthal. I don't know how to make that up to my kid and Audrey.

So much for being a calm force, for being able to talk someone down from an anxiety attack. I wouldn't be surprised if instead I'm the reason Marty and Audrey freaked out.

Slowly, I open the door into my house, and I force myself to lift my eyes and face whatever awaits.

A boulder slams into me. I stumble back against the door, slamming it shut with my body. Barnacles squeeze around me with shocking strength. In front of me, Audrey's watching the whole thing with wide eyes and a pale face. The barnacles start wailing.

"Marty?" I ask, struggling to understand what's happening.

All that comes out of her is muffled wailing against my stomach. Her arms are so tight around me that she probably could've kept the intruder pinned against the ground.

"I—Uh…" My mouth flaps open and shut, but instinct kicks in and I wrap my arms around the trembling twig that is my daughter. "It's okay, Marty. You're safe now."

"Not me!" she yells, finally looking up. Rivers of tears and snot run down her angry little face. "You! I was afraid something would happen to my dad!"

A sob comes out of her and she buries her face in my T-shirt again.

I look up at the stoic older woman, wondering what the hell happened in the course of these past hours. But her chin is trembling too, and her pretty eyes are starting to turn into puddles.

"What am I doing?" she whispers, her voice cracking. "I can't believe I put you two in danger."

My lungs cease to function for a moment. I free one hand and reach of Audrey, drawing her closer. She comes willingly as the first tears start to fall. I swipe them away with my calloused thumb, but more of them keep spilling out.

"That's not true," I explain, still missing air in my lungs. "Henry Vos is the one who did."

"But…" Audrey looks away, biting her trembling lower lip. "It's still my fault."

Sighing, I say, "come here." I spread my arm open and she takes the invitation, snuggling into Marty and I. My daughter shifts to wrap one barnacle around the unsuspecting woman, who is now going nowhere no matter what she tries.

I guide her head to rest against my chest, and soon she's grabbing fistfuls of my T-shirt and also letting it all out on it. Two hot and wet patches compete for attention, but I do happen to have two hands. I stroke the backs of both of their heads, surprised at the difference in texture and still the similar softness.

They were both so damn happy, singing along with the Korean pretty boys like it was the only important thing in the world.

Damn Henry Vos for doing this.

Damn Charlie Cox for getting a weasel like that in his daughter's life, and now in my daughter's too.

I don't know how, but I'm going to protect them. With whatever it takes. Somehow I'll figure it out.

*

I think I'm fueled by spite because later, I'm fully awake, sitting on the couch between the two ladies as they calm down with some chamomile tea. For some reason, just the smell of it makes me angrier and my cup lays untouched on the coffee table.

"I'm going to sue," I declare.

Audrey sighs a little into her mug. "It's not worth it. He'll just drag all your private stuff out into the open."

I don't have anything to hide, but I do have to safeguard Marty's privacy.

Running my sweaty hands up and down my thighs, I say, "Then we have to talk with your dad. I'm sure even something like this is gonna snap him awake."

"I don't want to tell him." She sets her mug down as if she hadn't just dropped a bomb.

Even Marty agrees when she demands, "Why not?"

Audrey takes in a deep breath and lets it all out at once. "Because I don't want to know if he's also not going to care about this."

I squeeze my eyes shut.

Right. I'm a jerk. It's not like they have a normal relationship.

"I'm sorry—" I start to say, but then a smaller, cold hand falls over mine and I open my eyes. The gold band and the glimmering rock on Audrey's finger taunt me. Gently, I turn my hand around and she lets me. She grabs on tight.

"You don't have anything to apologize for, Miguel." She turns to face me, her puffy eyes scanning my face for something. They stop briefly on my lips, enough that it almost feels like a touch, but then she continues. "I think it's time for us to divorce."

Marty gasps from my left.

I stay quiet, thinking a million thoughts that make no sense, trying to survive through the needles stabbing my chest in all directions. I stay quiet, because what I really want to say is *no*. That I don't want to. That I want her here with me. That I want to be the one who keeps her safe.

And then—then two neurons rub and finally make a worthwhile spark. Without filtering, I blurt out the whole idea. "I think you should move in with us instead."

"What?"

"Yes!" My daughter jolts.

"Miguel—" Audrey looks from Marty to me. "That's not the solution."

"Divorcing isn't, either," I respond with ease, like there isn't a riot in my gut. "That's just gonna open you up to that vulture swooping in for you. What we have to do is the opposite, keep you safe and cozy away from him."

"Exactly," Marty agrees, even though I can't tell how much of that she actually understands.

Meanwhile, Audrey's looking at me like I've grown another head. Her hand is still squeezing mine, though. Maybe that counts for something.

Or I wish it does.

"What if something like this happens again? Or worse?" She shakes her head. At some point she gave up on the updo and her hair is a mess all around her face. She's never looked more beautiful than this moment. "I can't—Miguel, I refuse to put you two in danger again."

"We want to defend you," my daughter quips in, leaning forward so she can watch her intended's reaction. "And you saw me, I also know how to use a bat."

"Quite well," I add. A couple of years ago before the bullying at school really started, Marty and I used to hit the batting cages at an arcade center, and her record was nearly as good as mine.

This succeeds in getting a little laugh out of Audrey. "Guys, I'm serious."

"So are we. Right, Dad?" Marty looks up at me like I better say yes or else she might test her swing on my car next time.

I just smile at her like, *of course. No way I'm skipping out on this woman when she needs help.*

When I want to be there for her.

Turning back to Audrey, I answer, "We're both serious. We want you safe, Audrey. So… will you move in with us?"

CHAPTER 33
AUDREY

The worst part is that after all that, I had to come in to work the next day to help put out the PR fires that I caused.

They're not so bad, though. We're not losing any sponsorships—which is a bummer, because I'd really love to shred the contract between us and Henry's company. We're also trending on social media as the baseball team of love, which for some fans it's cute, for others it's a crime against the players's focus, and for the haters it's a great source of fiber for their diets as hatred organisms.

The players? They couldn't care less. A couple that I ran into this morning greeted me with *hey, boss* before they kept walking toward the gym. And that was it. I don't believe their focus of getting into the postseason has been impaired.

It has caused more work for everyone in the communications, marketing, and PR teams though. I get that an advanced warning would've been nice, but I'm also not in the mood to explain why everything had to be done so hastily.

However, my boss seems to think otherwise.

Knocking on the glass door of the meeting room, I wait

until Karen looks up from her phone to acknowledge my existence. There's no way that this is gonna be a nice little chat, so the last thing I want to do is start it early by barging in. Sadly, she motions me in.

I drag my feet but there's only so many seconds one can waste between a meeting room door and a chair. "Hi, Karen," I greet noncommittally once we're sitting face to face across a table, without the buffer of anyone else's presence.

For the last few days we've survived pretty well by communication via email or Teams only. She commands in a rude way, I respond with thumbs up emoji, deliver the thing, and don't hear back from her. It's been a great deal.

Until now.

Maybe communications posting a family picture from the All-Star game where I'm described both as Miguel Machado's wife *and* the team owner's daughter was really too much.

While the players haven't been interested in the news at all, the staff members have been. If stares could bore holes, I'd be a colander by now.

Karen's proving my point by studying every one of my features like she has never really looked at me before. "Hmph, I guess you do have some resemblance." She leans back and folds her arms.

Silence.

I wouldn't say I'm uncomfortable, but I definitely want to go back to my cubicle covered in cozy little green plants. I regret not bringing over my apple green emotional support water bottle, so I can at least hydrate myself while I waste my time.

Finally, she can't take the quiet any longer. "Why didn't you tell me?"

This is probably where the myth of blonde women not being smart came from, because I'm going to pretend like I don't understand her. I just wanna hear her spell it out.

"Sorry, tell you what?" I tilt my head and widen my eyes a little.

Karen bites. "That Charlie Cox was your father. I would've never guessed it because you used the last name Winters for so long."

Look at the point flying well over her head.

But also, since when does she talk to me in this sugary and calm way?

I wish I could find this funny, but it's one of the smaller reasons why I didn't want everyone to know. There will be mass amnesia about the fact that I applied to my job, interviewed for it, and was selected by a panel of people who were not yet in Dad's payroll. I'll never pretend like my great—and expensive—education didn't give me an advantage, or that the way I look also buys me a lot more leniency than I deserve. But I also could've been just one more rich bum who graduates from an ivy league college without any effort, and then straight up inherits the family's business.

None of that is gonna matter now, though. I knew it the second Dad swooped in and bought the team. It was just a matter of time before it all came out.

However, the obvious attempt at tact in her comment, and the nosy nature of it, are a great opportunity to get some justice for years of Karen's corporate bullying. And I'm not above carpeting the diem, like Marty said.

"How would that have changed things, though?" I let that dangle uncomfortably in the air.

Karen clears her throat. Rearranges her stuff on the table. Even brushes her hair back—all without meeting my eye. I press my lips not to burst out laughing.

Everything. Every request, every meeting, every little interaction. Everything would've been different. She would've been sucking up to me all the time, treating me better than any other employee.

And also *nothing*, because all that would've accomplished would've been driving the perceived chasm even deeper between my coworkers and I. She would've made me a pariah in a different way than she did in reality, in both cases for her benefit.

"I've been a fair manager." She lifts her chin. "I hope you recognize that I was just guiding you into being the best PR professional in the organization."

Amazing. Now she's found a way to take credit for all the extra work I succeeded at that she didn't give to anyone else because she liked them better. She must still think that the *SPORTY* sponsorship belongs in her resume.

I don't acknowledge her sorry excuse. "Is there anything else we should discuss today?" I make a show of checking my watch—and no, it's not an exclusive edition one or anything. I got it from a thrift store. "I actually need to go home to my family soon."

Laying it a bit thick, the whole family thing. But eh, it's a great reason to not continue swapping air with this weirdo.

"Nothing further, you may go," she says, trying her best to maintain her previous sense of dignity in front of me. Without further ado, I push away from the table and am about to bounce when she speaks again. "Actually, there's one more thing."

I plop back on the chair. "Yes?"

She laces her fingers, then stacks her hands, then spreads them over the table, and finally pulls them away to hide under the table. She does the chin thing again. "What are you planning to do now?"

I point at myself and the door. "Go home...?" This time I don't really get her meaning.

"Are you going to fire me?"

There it is.

I see why this conversation couldn't have been an email but

geez, it sure could've been so much shorter if she wasn't trying to gaslight me the whole time.

"You're my boss, Karen. How could I fire *you*?" I cock an eyebrow for funsies.

She waves a hand. "That is irrelevant now that we know whose daughter you are. And we both know we don't have the best relationship, unlike you and those two girls who are always around you."

The way she says it is so snotty that I snap.

"You mean my friends? The ones who have always had my back and were my maids of honor?" I ask, barely containing my annoyance that she dares to imply Hope and Rose have been interested in my father's privileges from the beginning.

"You know what I mean," she grouches, the thin mask of politeness finally wearing off.

Humming as if in thought, I stand up and lean over the table, looking her dead in the eye. "No, I'm not going to fire you for having bullied me." Relief flashes through her beady eyes until I add, "But I'll keep you in observation. That answer may change if I find proof that I'm not your only victim."

Gah, I'm so annoyed that this incredible high is being sponsored by my dad indirectly. I wish I could've shown her up all on my own.

Karen isn't the type of person who changes her mind upon receiving excellent work, though, or she would've started treating me decently before. The fact of the matter is that she's never liked me from the beginning, and it's killing her to have to pretend like she does now. That's enough revenge, even if it's not super satisfying for me.

It feels bitter to wish her a good evening and leave, but I copy her chin thing and hold my head high as I make my way out of the facilities, even with dozens of eyes poking holes on my face.

*

After dreaming about nosediving into my bed during rush hour traffic, I get home and find a bunch of packed bags on the foyer. I blink at them slowly, riffling through memories until I land on the one where I agreed to move in with the Machados.

"Right, I did this in the morning," I mumble, looking down at them.

Instead of getting the immediate rest I wished for, I make several trips between my house and next door, carrying all the bags, pillows, suitcases of things that I want immediate access to, to feel somewhat normal in Miguel's home. His car isn't parked out front, but Consuelo's is so I ring the doorbell.

Bumps come from behind the door until it opens to Marty beaming up at me. "Welcome home, Audrey!"

I feel it like an earthquake, the cute aggression that rises up my spine and threatens to make me lose reason. If I did, I'd be squeezing her against me until I deserve to be kicked.

"Stop being so freaking adorable, child," I frown at her but we have a similar sense of humor, and all she does is chuckle.

"Come on in!" Consuelo calls out from the kitchen.

I obey, dragging the first couple of things I could reach. Marty starts working on a third one—a suitcase with operating wheels, like the smart cookie she is.

"Great timing," the older woman says, wiping her hands dry with a kitchen towel. "I was just about to leave, but I really wanted to leave you all settled."

"Thank you, you don't have to bother—"

She says something in Spanish that clearly means I should zip my mouth, and I do. "Miguel asked me to help the family, and so that's what I'm doing."

A true smile forms in my face. I love these people, not because of all the extraordinary things they've done and continue to do for me. But for the fact that they even did. That they have the heart to help a virtual stranger.

These are the people I want in my life, not the Karens of the world.

Between the three of us, we make pretty quick work of bringing everything into what's going to be my room. It's on the first floor, the equivalent one that Rose uses next door, and it's fully decked for comfort. A large, plush bed sits in the middle, flanked by night tables. There's a dresser on the opposite wall, and enough floater shelves that this could be a very livable place.

And more notably, there's a lot of greens.

In the bedding, the cushions, the carpet, and even plants that look pretty real. Everything is soft, pastel, and beautifully coordinated. Like something out of a catalogue.

"You like it?" Marty asks, her eyes the shiniest I've ever seen them.

"I *love* it," I respond sincerely, with the remnants of cute aggression coursing through my veins. "Did you do all this?" I glance at her and Consuelo.

The latter responds, "Miguel told us what to get, so Marty and I went to a store in the morning, came home to wash everything and set it up."

My mouth does a lot of flapping and none of the yapping. I throw myself at Consuelo and give her a bone-crushing hug. No matter what she says, her job is to take care of Marty, not to do things for me.

Patting my back, she whispers into my ear, "Save this for Mr. Machado." When she pulls away, she's laughing like a fairy godmother.

She leaves us settled in the living room with some background music for focus, snacks, and lemonade because—as I learn along the way—Miguel excused his daughter from summer school again for the sake of the shopping trip. So now I'm in charge of making sure that she finishes her homework.

And Marty doesn't wanna.

"Let's try to dance to ON instead," she suggests, as if I didn't know about the difficulty level of that particular choreography.

"Excuse me, Miss Martina," I say with great affect, lowering my brow. "You might not have realized it but I have two left feet."

"But Dad says you dance very well."

I would trip on my two left feet if I wasn't already sitting by the coffee table with her.

"Uhh, he was being very generous. Trust me, I wouldn't even manage the first thirty seconds of Just One Day, and that choreography uses a chair."

She taps her chin. "What if we freestyle it then?"

I point at her homework spread out in front of her with my lips, like her dad would. "Why don't you freestyle your assignment instead?"

"Ugh." Marty drops her head back on the couch seat.

"Tell you what," I offer, shaking my head a little. "I'll do some work too. For every task we finish, we eat one of those." I point at the colorful bowl of chewy candies that is in- *and* conveniently placed between us.

"And then we dance?" she presses.

I guess there's no avoiding making a fool of myself. But honestly after the day I've had this will be fun.

"Deal." I offer my hand and she shakes it solemnly.

Now that this is a binding contract, we get serious and fire up our iPads. Hers is loaded with more math questions. Mine with my little investment account that I've been trying to grow all these years, to see if it was enough to escape my controlling father. It still isn't, even after all that's transpired, but I check it every night out of rote.

Marty grabs a candy and unwraps it. I peek at her note-book and confirm that she did, indeed, just finish a problem. And I confirmed that I'm still not rich all on my own, so I also take one candy.

The ten-year-old spitfire gives me a look like she can't believe I'm matching her pace, and I click on something random on my iPad, pretending like I just completed another task. Grabbing another candy lights up a fire under her, and next thing we know, we're competing for the prizes in the bowl, and chugging lemonade to make space for more. She works, I work, and it all seems like harmless fun…

Until it isn't.

CHAPTER 34
MIGUEL

'm singing on the way home. It's one of those songs that produce the deepest cringe in my daughter—heck, probably even in my parents. It seems like no one listens to joropo anymore, but occasionally I like to remind myself that so far, I've still spent the larger portion of my life in Venezuela.

Today's jam is Toy Contento by Mario Suarez. Hummingbirds kissing flowers feels apropos when today is day one of Audrey rooming with us.

Am I—the hummingbird—going to kiss her—the flower? Who knows. Probably not. But am I going to wish I could? Hell yeah, every freaking moment.

"Calm down, dog," I tell myself.

The music stops, replaced by the amplified sound of my phone ringing. I take it as a sign that I was about to go down the path of misbehaving in my thoughts. After checking the caller ID, I answer using the steering wheel controls.

"What's up, prima?"

Amelia makes a sound of pure disgust. "Ugh, why do you sound so happy after giving me so much work?"

"If it makes you feel any better, I was planning on giving you a generous bonus to express my gratitude."

"In that case." She clears her throat and flips the script. "I was calling to tell you that the legal team's on the case and you have nothing to worry about. The one who should be sweating it out is the maladjusted jerk who put a snitch on you."

Sadly, I doubt it. No interaction I've had with that Vos guy has led me to believe that he's capable of regret.

"That's good," I say, all things considered.

"However…" My cousin drags the word enough that I almost drive a mile in the silence.

"If you're not gonna talk I'd rather go back to listening to joropo while I drive."

She sighs. "It's just, I don't know how to say it because I already know what your reaction will be. But you really should start considering some extra security."

Ah, yes. This isn't the first time we've had this conversation.

Ever since my career hitting a ball with a big stick really took off, and the associated fame and salary started catching public interest, Amelia has been suggesting that I get some bodyguards or something like her clients who are soccer players or celebrities. They've been all over the world, and that brings a heavier layer of scrutiny than I can imagine.

The thing though, is that even though baseball is still 'Murica's sport, I don't get accosted by people when I go to Trader Joe's. The risky moments are before and after games, when tipsy fans are closer to us than ever. And the team and stadium staff have that fine tuned to an art.

"No." Before she protests, I add, "Not for me, at least. Can you get someone to watch my girls from a distance? They'll panic if they know another dude is following them, even if it's someone looking out for them."

"Your girls?"

"Look at that, I'm arriving home already," I mention in my

most innocent tone, but there's no hiding that little blooper there. My agent just caught onto something I'm not even willing to admit to myself—shit.

"Hmm. Fine, I'll get two guys on the case. Let me know if you change your mind for yourself."

Not gonna happen.

"Bye, Amelia."

"Bye, you insufferable goodie-goodie two shoes."

With that, she ends the call and the music returns. It's a shame because I'm already pulling into the driveway, and I can see that Audrey's car is parked out front. I turn off the engine and take a few deep breaths, one after the other.

Finally, I smack my cheeks and say, "no te hagas ilusiones, papá," as if I was talking to some other dude and not myself.

My heart drums as I get out of the car, forcing myself to move at a normal speed that won't betray my excitement and nerves. I grab my duffel bag from the back, stuffed with dirty clothes I wore for practice earlier, and more empty food and drink containers than a regular person would believe. The Mario Suarez tune escapes from my lips as a jolly whistle, and I manage to key in the door code without fat fingering.

A blast of entirely different music hits me as I walk in.

My—er, the two girls who currently use my last name are in the middle of the living room. They've cleared out the coffee table and are jumping around the carpet… dancing? And doing some more of that singing that is a mix of words and sounds. The TV screen behind them shows a music video from the South Korean boy band they don't get tired of. Glad that the events that happened yesterday didn't ruin the band for them.

I close the door behind me with my butt, standing here, wondering if they'll notice me or if I should say *honey, I'm home*. That would probably make them both grimace in secondhand embarrassment, so I stay mum. And they still don't notice me.

That's great, because I'm gathering fodder for teasing them in the future.

Amusement spreads across my face as the two of them, their backs turned to me, keep shaking everything they got to an upbeat rhythm. They're still doing the air microphone thing, pointing it at each other in turns. Then, while shaking her bootie, Audrey finally turns and spots me.

She chokes on her spit.

That gets Marty's attention who peeks over her shoulder. "Oh." She slows down. But even while she tries to act cool, I'm her father. I know what the hotter cheeks mean.

I'm full on grinning now. "Don't stop on my account."

Marty nudges her grown friend. After a few more coughs, Audrey finds enough strength to say, "Welcome home, Miguel."

The duffel bag slides off my grip. The pretty boys singing in the background dampen the sound of it landing on the floor.

Heat explodes within my chest, spreading to every corner of my body and even deeper, finding a hole that I didn't know I had. A hole in the shape of someone I can love.

"H-Hi." Now I'm the one struggling for words.

Meanwhile, Marty bends down to pick up the remote and bring down the volume. As she rises back up, she opens her mouth to talk when something unexpected—and horrible—happens.

Whatever's in her stomach rises back up.

She barely manages to hold it in with both hands.

Now no one's amused. Everybody's eyes are wide like saucers. Another wave hits her and Dad instinct kicks in. I rush toward her and lift her up. "Hold on, Marty! Keep it in!"

She makes muffled sounds but her little body makes another attempt to empty itself, this time on me. Audrey's steps follow closely behind. I make the decision in a split second—

this is gonna be a very stinky welcome, but we won't make it if I try to get us upstairs to Marty's bathroom. Audrey's it is.

Bless the heavens, for the doors are all open. My sneakers screech to a halt in the pristine bathroom floor tile, and I manage to set Marty down. I press my hand against hers on her mouth as I turn her to aim, and thankfully Audrey has already lifted the toilet lid.

Rainbows explode out of my daughter's mouth.

I blink a couple of times to clear my vision, just in case I'm hallucinating the whole thing. But nope. All sorts of colors keep coming up. My poor kid's about to fall into the toilet, so I wrap an arm around her and with my other hand I clumsily gather her hair.

"Erm, there, there. Let it all out," I mumble, not knowing what else to do. I glance up at Audrey but the confusion, even the worry I expected in her face, isn't there.

Instead, she looks like she's about to throw up too.

I know she loves green, but I'll never tell her she looks kinda like it right now.

I swallow hard, which is a feat when the air is permeated by regurgitated rainbow. "Um…" My voice trembles. I'm hoping that she doesn't projectile vomit on us, but if that's how it's gonna be, then I guess my fate is sealed. Miguel Machado, record-breaking All-Star hitter, dead by drowning in puke.

Somehow, I manage to jerk my head at the shower. "Maybe try going in there?"

The poor woman has tears in the corners of her eyes as she nods. She squeezes in by me, pushes the curtain aside, and off she goes. I lean for a peek and, sure enough—more rainbows.

"What the hell did you two do?" I ask, half scared and half intrigued. The only response I get for a long while is the sound of more arching, barfing, and groans of pain and suffering.

Yep, this is officially a family, a'ight. Nothing like being sick together to real bond.

CHAPTER 35
AUDREY

I would really like it if a hole opened up right under me and swallowed me whole, please and thank you.

There is no moment in my life where I recall feeling more embarrassment than I do right now. Not even when my brother burst into class to defend me from mean girl bullies because I wasn't able to do it myself.

But this? It's a million times worse. And it's not about the part where I emptied my guts on the shower floor of the place I'm staying temporarily at, and in front of the owner—who will never want to kiss me again now that he knows what kind of art piece my mouth is capable of.

No, it's because I made his daughter barf half of her body weight.

We're all sitting on the bathroom floor, probably sharing in the same wish I have of just disappearing forever after this.

Marty leans back on her dad, limp as a wet noodle and letting out a continuous little groan. Miguel provisioned himself with an entire roll of toilet paper, and he's currently using a wad of it to clean his daughter's face. His head is tilted down to watch what he's doing, and his shoulders shake with absolute rage.

Well, I guess I'm glad I didn't unpack already. I hug my legs against me. I can just go back home next door, hide under a blanket, and never be seen or heard of—

Miguel lifts his head and it's worse than I expected because he's *laughing*.

The spams all over his body aren't from an effort to contain the volcanic rage of a father whose beloved daughter got intoxicated with candy and dancing. No. It's because he's struggling to contain what would appear to be great guffaws that would decimate our delicate eardrums and what's left of our egos.

I groan and bury my face between my knees. "Kill me now." My own breath makes me wanna barf again.

"Me too," mumbles Marty.

Meanwhile, Miguel sounds like he's choking. "C'mon, party girl. Let's get you washed up and in bed, okay?"

His daughter dramatically throws herself at him and Miguel settles her against his shoulder, as if she was but a puppy and not a ten-year-old who's going to pass me in height in two years or so. This mountain of a man gets up without any effort, his black joggers straining against the incredible power of his thighs.

He catches me staring and I blurt out, "Can I help? Even though I'm technically the one who caused this mess?"

Miguel's still biting his lips to contain his amusement, and barely manages a "sure."

My old lady bones creak as I unfurl myself from the tight ball I was in, and get up to follow. We make a very slow trek upstairs, me clinging to the banister and dragging myself in turns. Miguel leaps like friggin' Legolas in the snow and waits for me to make it upstairs.

"Maybe I should've carried you too?" he says under his breath once I'm next to him.

I just give him a look. I have no doubt he could, but whether he should is a different matter entirely. Because I may barely be taller than Marty but I sure am several times heavier, and the thought of this man tumbling down those stairs because of me makes me want to puke my legitimate guts out, not just the content in them.

Finally, he sets the poor kid on her two feet in her bathroom. It's all black and white but I see pink towels and a matching shower curtain. It gives the same grumpy and cute energy that she does.

"Here." Miguel reaches for her toothbrush and hands it over to her. Then he turns his focus on me. "Can you please help her out? I need a quick second."

Probably to laugh at us against a pillow or something.

"Of course," I croak out. Luckily, he leaves before he can see that I'm shaking like a leaf. "Marty, I know you won't trust me with anything after this because I suck, but where can I get your pajamas?"

Sass has left her body and she points feebly toward the door. "In the dresser with the cats."

That sounds like something I'll be able to find even in my addled state. I grab onto the doorframe, a chair, and even the wall to keep my balance on the way to the dresser. The cats are stuffed toys of all sizes and colors, some more realistic and others adorably cartoonish. Now I know what to get for her birthday if the Machados give me the time of day after this.

"Ugh." She's finished washing up and dragging herself out of the bathroom. "Next time less candy and more dancing."

Somehow I find it in myself to laugh a little. "I don't know that there'll be a next time. Your dad's gonna toss me out to the curb."

"He wouldn't dare to do that to my best friend," she says in a very casual way as she takes the pajama top from my hands.

Kids, man. They can just casually say the best thing you've

ever heard in your life, injecting a rush of pure warmth and tenderness into your shriveled heart, bringing it back to life and causing your eyes to tingle, all without missing a beat.

That's when Miguel strolls into the room, carrying two bottles that everyone on earth probably recognizes.

"No," I whisper in horror, staring at the electrolyte drink bottles for kids. One is pink and the other one transparent.

"Do I have to?" Marty asks, voice muffled as she puts on her pajama top.

"Yes, the two of you have to." He raises both options. "Who wants which one?"

There is something incredibly restorative about these drinks—not only in the electrolyte sense, but also in that it restores every memory of feeling sick as a kid. The staff were always the ones who fed me these, not my parents. But here's Miguel, probably tired and hungry after all the work this week, and making sure to take care of both of us.

Marty turns to me. "I'm fine with either," she mumbles.

"Um, same."

"All right." Miguel sets one down on the night table, and works on opening the other one. He does it easily and without needing pliers too, hmph. "Marty, you get the berries and Audrey, you're getting the tutti frutti."

Various noises of reluctant agreement.

He waits until Marty's done changing to give her the bottle, which looks massive in her hands. Then he motions at me. "Come with me."

I guess there isn't a molecule of sass left in my body, either, because I just get up slowly and follow after the man who carries a the bottle meant for me. "Where are we going?"

"To brush your teeth."

"I can—" Turns out that's a lie because my legs wobble.

I don't know how Miguel catches me in time before I melt

into the carpet, and I also don't know why my body melds against his side so perfectly. Like lock and key.

Slowly, I raise my eyes to his face, and this time there's no laughter there. Miguel is serious—intense even. He's studying my eyes like they're an open book and I want to look away, hide, but I also don't know why I don't. I stay frozen just like that, fully exposed in a way that should be uncomfortable, but isn't.

Everything about this—and not just tonight, but the whole arrangement—is the kind of thing that would normally send me running for the hills. The lesson I learned after growing up in my twisted, gilded world is to never trust men. That even the ones who do love you will leave you when you most need them. And even when my brain screams that reminder to the rest of my body, it's my soul the one who says *not this time.*

Not *this* man.

I wonder if it's because he just caught me easier than a tiny white ball rocketing into the outfield. Or if maybe this moment is just a metaphor of everything he's done these past few months. Or simply, of who he is.

He really is the rock and I really am the hard place, huh?

"Why do you have so much trouble accepting help?" Miguel asks softly, not realizing that he's getting so close to the core of the issue.

"I—Well, I caused all this, so I don't deserve help."

For the first time since I've known him, his eyebrows come together into a little wrinkle. He doesn't comment anything on that and instead tugs me forward, his grip around me firm and speed gentle for my jelly legs. I don't even pay attention to his room, all I know is that his scent does good things for my stomach, and that the room is too cold.

He also deposits me in front of his bathroom sink, and sadly I have to lean against it now that he's stepped away. After rummaging in a drawer, he produces a new toothbrush and this one's a struggle to open up. His hands are too big for the packaging, and he foregoes the pull tab and just rips the thing apart, offering me the brush like it's sacred.

His eyes widen. "Wait, why are you crying? Do you feel worse? Should we go to the ER?"

"I'm crying?"

I have to look at myself in the mirror to confirm that I am, in fact, raining out of my eyes. Red splotches adorn my skin everywhere it can be seen, my hair is an absolute disaster, my blouse askew and sweaty, and my lips are pale.

"How are you not crying after this mess?" I ask in a completely level headed tone. Not.

"Frankly, I thought the whole thing was really funny until about now." He sets the other drink bottle on the counter, his hands raising as if to touch me. But they hold themselves back. "Seriously, I'm worried now. Does something hurt?"

Yes, my heart.

My soul.

Everything.

I can't believe he was walking around in this planet with all that goodness in him, and I never caught a glimpse until I was broken and jaded. And now I don't know what to do, if run, hide, cling, or beg. I don't know if I can burden him with *me*. He deserves better.

And then I'm sobbing, and his arms and his warmth and his scent are all around me, his strength keeping me upright, his breath fanning over my head, his heart beating fast against my face, tucked into his chest. "Hey, Audrey. Tell me what's wrong, please. I'm freaking out here."

I squeeze handfuls of his purple Orlando Wild T-shirt. "I'm sorry. I'm so sorry."

He sighs as if relieved.

"Shh." One of his hands rubs my spine softly, up and

down. "It wasn't your fault. You two were just having fun in a homemade rollercoaster."

"It *was* my fault. I am the adult." I struggle to push him away, not because he won't allow it, but because my own muscles fail me. I force myself to meet his eyes. "If I was you, I'd toss me out and end this whole thing at once."

"Luckily, I'm not you, huh?" The corners of his lips rise a little. "I know that we all make mistakes but we *aren't* our mistakes. And I also know that this didn't happen on purpose and that you're really, *really* sorry about it."

"But—"

"And," he cuts me off and chuckles a little as he continues. "I also know that feeling yucky is all the punishment you two deserve."

I drop my head. Right on his chest. He strokes the back of my head, which feels amazing physically but adds to my guilt. "But all I do is cause you trouble, Miguel. You shouldn't keep putting up with me."

"That's not true." Then he holds my head gingerly, lifting my face from his chest—and presses his lips on my forehead. Intentionally. Patiently. Unashamedly. When he pulls back, those same lips are smiling. "You only bring joy to Marty's and my life, you know? Somehow, you've made me realize that I can't control what happens to my family, but I sure can do my best to protect it." He glances up as if in thought. "My anxiety has got a lot better since I met you, actually."

My teeth make a clacking sound as I snap my mouth shut.

Miguel takes a step back and slides his hands into the pockets of his joggers. Clearing his throat, he says, "Anyway, I'll go check up on Marty and then clean your bathroom. So, uh, take your time. Holla if you need me."

"Okay," I reply with a thread of voice, watching him rush away.

My knees buckle and I prop myself up on the vanity, my

heart racing like a horse. I raise my hand to touch the hot spot where his lips branded my skin. "What… what just happened?"

What he said just now, why did it make me want to cry even harder?

CHAPTER 36
MIGUEL

A couple of peaceful weeks have passed after the colorful and chaotic first night of Audrey living with us, and since the last time Henry Big Asshole Vos reared his entitled head. Part of it is because I'm suing him, and the other part is because allegedly he's been on a business trip. Who the hell knows if that's true—after all, I'm not gonna hire someone to follow him back like a stinking creep.

Or at least, that's how the passage of this time seems to have developed for my kid and Audrey. They're pleased as punch in each other's company, working side by side, or playing in a more civilized way—such as baking cookies together with Consuelo—or watching movies together. They both pretty much ignore me every time I'm home.

It's great. Pure bliss.

Not.

I am *dying* inside. This is how dogs must feel like when their humans aren't paying attention to them. Thankfully I don't have a tail to wag, and I somehow manage to keep my tongue inside my mouth.

Sometimes I forget that this is only a convenient arrangement and nearly make a fool of myself. For example, a few mornings ago before flying out for an away series, I was mixing a protein shake to chug on the way when Audrey joined me in silence, brewed a pot of coffee, and poured two mugs—one for herself and one for me—still without saying a word. As if we'd done this exact routine every morning for the past five years or something.

The sheer domesticity of it speared me through the gut with visceral hunger, and not the stomach kind. I had to casually go up to my room on the pretense that I needed to find something.

And yeah, it was my logical brain. Because I was a raging torch for a woman who is just my friend, and is under my protection, and has minus ten interest in more. The only way I could calm the hell down was with upside down pull ups. Just to really punish myself. And also to get the blood flow going to my brain.

You'd say, *Miguel, you know your place, dude. Why do you keep punishing yourself?*

Because I can't help it. Because my damn cells vibrate when she's nearby. Because I'm in awe of her and I know I can be her rock. Because I'm in love, damn it.

So here I am, on the field for the *SPORTY* commercial shoot, wishing she'd just look my way once. It doesn't matter that everyone else has their attention on me—including my rowdy teammates—Audrey just keeps her focus on the director and the crew. I know it's her job, and I'll never interfere with it, but I feel like a teenager trying to catch the attention of his crush without having the cojones to verbally ask for it.

"Hey, Machado," Cade Starr, the pitcher we're riding our season upon, calls out from behind the crew where the rest of the team is gathered to watch the show. He brackets his mouth with his hands to really make sure I catch every word. "Looking buff out there, what's your secret?"

I glance down. To my surprise, my abs are showing. And I'm not even clenching.

Slowly, I look back up at him. "Hard work, man."

And by hard work, I mean the difficult task of behaving around a certain woman.

Lucky Rivera, the best shortstop I've ever seen, of course chimes in with, "Hard marriage work, ey?" He nudges the guy next to him.

The combined braincell of the Orlando Wild bursts into various forms of laughter, the dominant ones being guffaws and giggles. I was wrong when I thought I was acting all high school like. This is middle school.

"Stop acting like clowns," our captain barks, but this time the comedians are having way too much fun.

I twist my lips and tongue in a very specific way, passed down by my dad, and let out a whistle loud enough to echo around the field and pierce everybody's eardrums. All the attention returns to me.

"Make fun of me all you want but I will appreciate you not joking about my wife or making her feel uncomfortable, or there'll be consequences."

There's a beat of silence, where everyone looks at me like they're meeting me for the first time. It takes a while to realize that it's because I used a new voice. Dad voice, relaxed teammate voice, and heck, even tax prepping voice sound very different.

This was husband voice. The caged animal type that really conveys if you hurt my person, I will destroy your life.

And now Audrey's certainly looking at me—in a weird way. Like she got a glimpse of something she didn't want to see.

I run my hand down my face and drop my hands on my waist. "Sorry, I—"

"You're right, I went too far," Lucky says and turns to

Audrey. "I'm sorry, Audrey. I really didn't think before I spoke. I'll only focus on sock pranks."

The what?

As other guys join in—including Cade calling her *sugar* for some reason—Audrey just waves their remorse away, explaining, "It's okay, guys. I know none of you are malicious and all of you have too much testosterone to be fully rational."

That dig brings the mood, or the testosterone, back up. The guys go back to joking around about what has now become a tradition for the team: *SPORTY* coming over to photograph or film one of us, and how apparently I don't have enough baby oil rubbed up on me.

"It's fine," I try to argue, but the vultures aren't satisfied.

"No, our superstar needs to shine the brightest," Lucky fires back, cracking a grin that I now recognize too well. I don't know what sock pranks are, but I'm pretty sure what's coming next isn't that. "Can someone bring the baby oil?"

His best friend also smirks. "That's right, when it was my turn at this I got oiled up in every damn crevice. Same for you, right?"

That he asks to our captain, who answers in a nonchalant way with, "It's true."

I empty my lungs. It was super weird to have a random person from the crew try to do this, so I politely asked if I could just do it myself. But obviously I missed spots. I was counting on sweat saving the day. After all, we're standing in the middle of the open field, the sun blaring over us while we cook in a million degrees and a thousand percent humidity.

The same crew member from earlier comes over with a damn bottle of baby oil, but before she makes it a quarter of the way, Lucky finds his moment. "Wait, unlike the case of Starr and Kim, Machado here is married."

He says nothing further. Just lets the obvious meaning hang in the air.

"I can do it myself, I'm pretty flexible. You just have to tell me where I missed." I start for the oil girl, offering my hand out for the bottle.

"But what if something goes wrong-wrong?" Lucky asks, widening his eyes in the most earnest way.

Baseball players are notorious believers in luck, omens, jinxes, curses, and everything superstitious under the sun. As I've learned, one of this team's shticks is to not use any word that alludes to getting injured, to guard off from attracting that possibility. And never in the history of the team have we been closer to the World Series. It is especially important to prevent wrong-wrongs.

"Fine." I return the bottle to the crew member and brace myself.

"I got it."

We all turn in complete silence. Audrey's breaking through the line of filming staff and heading over…

Here?

I resist the instinctive urge to look around to confirm. Consciously, I know there's nothing but green behind me. Subconsciously, I can feel all my teammates's excitement at the unfolding scene. You'd think they're watching a telenovela being filmed, instead of the behind the scenes of a sports apparel commercial.

But sure enough, Audrey receives the oil bottle from the other girl and pops it open with calm and certainty. Complete unfazed. Unbothered. Bored, even.

"All right, let's start heading back to the gym," our captain barks in the quiet. There are some mild protests until he adds, "We've wasted enough time here and we have a World Series to qualify for. Let's move it."

Groans and complaints echo as he starts to herd the cats back inside, but fortunately some of the more rational guys join in the efforts. That's precisely when Audrey lands her warm, oiled up hands on my chest.

I jolt. She doesn't seem to pick up on it. Something distracts me from behind her, and it's Lucky giving me the most exaggerated wink.

Shit, so this was his little prank this time.

He figured out that I don't have platonic feelings for my fake wife and is now making me suffer.

Meanwhile, the filming crew is busy setting up the equipment—cameras at different angles, reflectors, microphones, and stuff I don't even know how to name. They're professionals and don't pay a lick of attention to us, which gives me the wrong feeling like Audrey and I are alone. While she rubs baby oil on my exposed skin.

I wonder if she can tell I'm sweating with the effort to not moan.

"Is this making you uncomfortable?" she asks all of a sudden, still in that casual tone of voice that betrays nothing.

The real answer is: yes. Like I've never been before. But only because I've never been at bigger risk of embarrassing myself in public.

Wait, is she noticing that?

I try to speak but a thick lump in my throat forces me to clear it first. "Why do you ask?"

"Well…" She trails off as her hands travel down my chest without bypassing the, uh, sensitive areas. "You looked really out of sorts with the idea of the crew member doing this, but it's not like this is any better."

Shit, it is. So much better. Too damn good.

I clench my jaw to keep down the noise of a feral raccoon in the dumpster of a fast food chain.

"I'm okay." The hell I am. "Thanks for stepping in." Hell yeah, I'll treasure this moment for the rest of my damn hungry single dad life.

"Don't worry, I'll be quick," she says while squeezing more oil onto her hands. She tucks the bottle under one of her arms, rubs up her hands to warm up the oil, and starts on my ribs.

I look up into the sky and nail my eyes into a cloud suspiciously shaped like a heart. *Yeah, I know*, I scream in my head.

"Are you okay, though?" I manage to ask.

"Hmm?"

"With the teasing and all that."

"Oh." She pauses. "Yep. Pretty sure this whole thing actually helped bystanders believe we're married." Another pause. "You acted like a very convincing husband too."

Therein lies the problem. I wasn't acting.

Even I surprised myself with how ready that threat was in my tongue.

She moves on to my back and I close my eyes in pure, tormented bliss. "I deserve an Oscar, huh?"

"You sure do," she whispers behind me.

Somehow I keep my shit together, even as she unknowingly touches some other sensitive areas. When she's done, the director asks me to do some basic stretching while they film to demonstrate the quality of the new *SPORTY* pants I'm modeling.

This time I'm the one who can't meet Audrey's watchful eye. And like every other time I've gotten my own damn mind deep in the gutter, I take it out on my hornball body with grueling exercise.

Except this time it's happening on cameras, and will soon be on everyone's screens.

CHAPTER 37
AUDREY

"Are you ready?" I ask once I've turned off my car, turning to Marty.

She's on the passenger seat, looking out at her school with a serious mien. Like instead of participating in a school event, she's psyching herself up to fulfill her obligation of jury duty.

The fact that there's no response from her is also an answer. I prod, "Nervous?"

"Yes," she admits, frowning even more, her eyebrows like thunder and her mouth shaped like downturned u. "I told you they don't like me. What if they make fun of my clothes in front of their very real moms?"

My shoulders droop a little. It's only been one week into the new school year, and Marty has met the rest of her classmates who weren't at summer school. Of course, the mean kids started treating her as if she was lazy or not smart—which are normally the reasons why kids land in summer school. On top of that, there's apparently one specific girl who declared to the class that Marty wearing so much black was weird.

Kiddo has had a really crappy time. It's almost criminal

that the mother and daughter tea party is so soon. I'd have loved for Marty to have more time to find her rightful place in the classroom—as the brightest bulb wrapped in black than anyone's ever seen.

However, she twists toward me with worried and watery eyes. "Pink was a bad idea. This whole thing was a bad idea. Can we go home? Get some ice cream? Not dance around this time?"

I can't help it, even when she's being a melodramatic ten-year-old, she makes me smile. Reaching over, I brush a wavy curl off her forehead. "Martina Jane Machado Smith." I use her full name but with a gentle tone. "I wish I had been like you when I was your age."

Her jaw drops.

"I wasn't a brave kid. I was too used to being ignored to even try standing up for myself. My brother was the only person who had my back, but he wasn't always around because he was older. I only learned how to sharpen my claws when he was gone, and I was nearly at college. But you're stronger than I was. You have a dad who would break the moon if you wanted a piece of it. And I may not be your real mom, but I'm here to put on the best performance of my life as if I was."

Marty's chin starts to tremble.

"Oh, sweetie. I didn't mean to—"

Then she tackles me. I land against the door with her bony arms squeezing the life out of me. "Thank you, thank you," she repeats in my ear over and over.

Chuckling, I hug her back. "You're absolutely welcome. It's an honor to be your fake mom today."

She pulls away, offering me a quite shy smile for the context. But I never figure out the reason behind it because she immediately says, "Let's do this." And then she jumps out of the car with renewed energy.

I scramble to match it. After clumsily gathering my things,

I step out of the car and find her right outside, waiting with the stance of a warrior. Chin high, watchful eyes, back straight. I copy her because I'm not about to ruin her highly anticipated day by acting like I don't belong, even though I sure as shit have no idea how to act like a mother. My own was never the best role model.

Marty nods at me. I return the gesture. We reach for the pockets of our gorgeous, thrifted dresses, and pull out our matching sunglasses. I don't normally need them, but we're going for full drama here.

I offer my hand to her and repeat, "Let's do it."

We walk calmly across the parking lot, Marty in her powder pink kitten heels, me in killer stilettos that are going to drastically reduce the life expectancy of my ankles. That time we went thrifting together with her dad, we found matching dresses to show off. They're apron shaped with ruffly sleeves, tight bodices, and the flowiest skirts that have ever flown. The tone is just a step up from a pastel pink, something lively and delicate that no one who knows us would ever associate with Marty and I.

But we're here to put on a show, and there were no better outfits for it than this.

Some heads turn to us as we join the stream of people walking into the school. The teacher who checks us in gives me a funny look, like she's never seen a large chested woman in a tight dress before. Or as if I had a responsibility to hide them so that no one has to notice them.

Joke's on her, I like to dress this way because I have no hips to speak of. I feel more feminine this way, and in turn more confident. One day Marty will also find her own way of feeling like a million bucks, and if I could, I'd make it so she never develops any insecurities in the first place.

I grab onto her smaller hand with both of mine, just trying to imbue every last bit of warmth in my chest into her.

Gah, I love this kid. It's gonna suck so bad when we have to part ways.

The gym has been converted into a DIY country club with balloons tied into the shapes of flowers as table centerpieces. They're covered in the cheap, paper tablecloths but in a cute lavender color that Rose would really approve of. There's a big speaker playing some violin music, and actual tea is being poured into actual cups.

Most of the plastic chairs are already taken by moms and their daughters, but even then it's easy to tell what the power dynamic is. There's a table in the middle with three very chirpy pairs, and every so often, girls and women from other tables turn to watch them and whisper.

"Are those the mean girls?" I ask Marty, casually pointing at the table.

She sighs. "Yeah. Those are Vivian, Reina, and Kelli with their moms."

"Perfect, let's go sit with them."

"What?" she hisses, grabbing my arm with both hands to stop me. "We can't do that, I'll be miserable."

"Or," I pronounce the word with much gusto, almost succeeding in rolling the r. "We make *them* miserable."

She blinks up at me.

I blink down at her.

Slowly, as if we shared the same braincell, we both smile at each other. And it's not the sweet kind, either.

We march over, our clicky-clacky shoes catching some eyes here and there, until one of the mean girls spots us. She nudges her mean girl friend, and their attention on us has the whole table zeroing in as we join.

I pull up the chair for Marty and she takes it with the grace of a princess. Following in her example, I join in next to her and only now do I remove my sunglasses. From the corner of my eye, Marty does the same.

"Um…" One of the mean girls does that annoying head tilt and the up and down scanning. It's like someone teaches every mean girl generation to do the same. "Why are you sitting with us?"

"Why wouldn't we? Clearly this is the table to be at," I respond, half annoyed and half glad that my rich brat voice has decided to wake up after years of being dormant.

Deep down, I knew that this is what it would take, and I'm not proud of myself for it. But I'll use it if it helps my kiddo.

One of the moms doesn't catch the bait. It's there in the way her eyebrows arch and her nose turns slightly up. "Excuse me, but this is a mother and daughter event only, and you are clearly not that child's mother."

Marty tenses, and I place my hand on her arm to calm her.

I delicately touch my chest with my free hand. "Goodness, that is offensive. Can't you see the uncanny resemblance between us?" Here I motion at our outfits, carbon copies of each other in different sizes.

The bat scoffs. "Please, you can't prove that you're related with your dresses. You couldn't look more different from each other."

Straight for Marty's jugular, I see. But years of enduring rich bullies for classmates trained me precisely for this moment—when it's not my own feelings the ones that matter, but those of the innocent girl in my charge.

Theatrically, I look at my left hand where the rings gleam like I polished them on purpose. "I guess anyone can wear wedding rings, but should I show you the marriage documents between Marty's father and I? Would that please you?"

Ohh, that's my best sarcasm work to date. Concentrated saccharine drips from my words, but the sugar is laced with venom.

Wait, is this why Cade Starr has always called me *sugar*?

The adult bully snaps her mouth shut so hard, I'm sure her

teeth hurt. Meanwhile, the other woman next to her chimes in, "Is that so? I'm also not Reina's biological mom." She leans forward to cover the side of her mouth that Reina would see, and whispers, "She passed during the birth."

Somehow I hold back from a big reaction to that plot twist. But next to me, Marty gasps. "Really?"

The Reina girl looks away, her high ponytail shifting until it covers her face. Is that embarrassment I see painting her cheeks?

"Lisa, I've told you many times that we don't talk about that," the head honcho adult says sharply.

The third adult finally speaks, and her natural voice could break glass. "Right, it's for the good of the children. It's not good to remind them of such things. They're too delicate."

I, a grown little shit, pick up one of the teapots and pour some tea into Marty's cup, and then on mine. It actually smells pretty good, like something sweet and woodsy, and like this and the little cakes are the biggest splurge of the event.

"Hmm." My hum returns their attention to me. "Is that why your children have been making my daughter's life miserable, because they're so delicate and sheltered that they don't know right from wrong?"

It's almost like someone pressed the mute button on the auditorium.

I channel my best impression of my badass, reckless brother as I turn to Marty in the most unaffected way. "Sugar?"

"Yes, please." Somehow, Marty copies my uppity manners as she asks, "Strawberry shortcake or apple tart?"

"Apple tart, please," I respond in kind.

Then someone gasps in outrage. I brace for a fist fight or hair pulling, when actually, the head honcho mom turns sharply to her daughter. "Vivian, you did *what*?"

I tilt my head.

This isn't a plot twist I saw coming.

Her meanie-me shrinks a little. "It wasn't anything too bad. I just said her clothes were weird."

"Too bad implies that you know it was bad to some degree," her mother admonishes. "I didn't raise you to say things like that about others." Fascinating, when she was so quick to judge earlier. Almost like she doesn't consciously realize that she's the blueprint for her daughter.

"Besides, I think her dress is adorable," the second mom adds. "Hey Reina, should we wear pink next year?"

Reina shakes her head like she'd rather disappear.

Vivian's not done, though. She points at Marty. "*This* isn't the weird part. She wears black every day at school!"

The third kid, Kelli, jumps in. "Yeah, if you'd dressed like this we wouldn't have found you weird."

"If you don't like me at my black, you don't deserve me at my pink," Marty declares, folding her arms like a queen who has lost interest in her court jesters.

I bite my lips really hard so I don't burst out laughing.

Glass cracking mom lets out a laugh that unfortunately chafes in my ears, but she says, "I like this kid! She's got spunk."

And my chest puffs up like a preening mother hen. And my baby chick, Marty, lifts her chin and smiles so broadly, so genuinely, that I know this is the exact moment when she's found her place in the classroom.

*

Turns out the mothers of the mean girls aren't bad people. Head honcho just suffers from a case of female lawyer-itis, where she assumes that attacking first is the best defense every time because that's how she has survived. She actually apologized for her rude introduction, which I found kind of funny because it turns out that her name is Rudy.

They actually invited me for coffee one day. As if I was one of them.

Marty and Reina chatted a bit, and at the end of the day they saved each other's numbers on their phones. Vivian didn't exactly come around. She spent the whole thing sulking as she stuffed little cakes into her mouth. Kelli seems a bit ditzy, like she'll just go with the flow and with whomever is steering. There's no way she'll resist Marty's kickass charm, so I'm sure eventually they'll drag Vivian to make peace with Marty.

"How are you feeling?" I ask her as we walk out of the school, along with many other moms and daughters. The evening is still hot, but the August sun is starting to set earlier. It'll probably be dark by the time we get home.

"Ah. May. Zing!" Marty whisper-yells every syllable separately. "Did you see Vivian's face? Ooh, she was *so* annoyed. And Kelli wasn't making fun of me anymore. And did you see that Reina and I liked the same cakes? What should I text her? Should I just say hi, or like, send her a cool game?" She interrupts her own excited rant to gasp. "What if she likes BTS too?"

"Then you'll have no choice but to become best friends forever."

"Nah," she surprises me by saying, swinging our arms as our hands remain joined. "That's your spot. No one's gonna take it."

A little sound peeps out of my mouth. It's the mix of surprise and pain. Because that is so incredibly sweet, but I also know that she means it—she's said it twice already—and I don't deserve it. I won't be around forever. In fact, her dad and I should get a divorce the second my dad gives me my damn inheritance and signs a paper that formally removes my friends and I from his influence.

But Marty doesn't notice the agony that's twisting my gut. Her eyes squint at the distance. "Is that dad?"

My head whips forward.

At first I don't see what she's seeing, until some moms gasp and start murmuring. And then the path clears and I can see him.

Miguel Machado, in the flesh.

Walking toward us like a dream fantasy man come true, in a white, fitted button shirt that highlights his impossibly wide shoulders. The sleeve tightens dangerously around his thick bicep as he runs a hand through his hair. He's wearing some simple trousers I recognize and loafers, but the hard muscle of his thighs and calves make them remarkable. How are his legs so freaking straight when he's so tall and filled up?

And how dare he wear the *SPORTY* pants that I had to stoically watch him in as he filmed the ad? I've never had a more difficult time in my life than watching him show off his perfect, athletic body for a camera right after I felt him up.

But the part that's killing me the most right now is the Aviators that sit on his pretty face, obscuring his eyes from view and adding such an air of mystery that for a second, he doesn't seem like the Miguel I've come to know. Kind, playful, open, gentle.

This is the man version, not the dad. The one that makes my tongue so thick I can't even swallow. Whose skin is still printed on my hands from two wild opportunities to touch him. The one that makes my body feel hot, my knees buckle, my lips tingle, my hands itch. The *daddy* version.

The final form that doesn't allow me to keep pretending like I'm immune to him.

Why's he walking so damn slow? Or is my heart beating way too fast?

When he's close enough, his lips stretch into a smile I'm familiar with, one that is only reserved to the apple of his eye.

Miguel spreads his arms wide and bends to one knee. "Mi niña, ¿cómo te fue?"

My rudimentary Spanish skills allow me to get the gist, but the fact that his voice is even deeper in his mother tongue almost knocks me over.

Fortunately, he's very distracted by the fact that, for a change, Marty willingly complies and wraps her arms around his ribcage with enough strength to make him grunt.

"Dad, it was amazing! Audrey was amazing! *Everything* was amazing!"

Miguel laughs the proudest dad laugh I've ever heard, and picks her up for a twirl that normally she would grouch about. "That's fantastic, Marty. I'm so glad."

Gosh. I want to join them so bad. I want to be able to squeeze the tar out of the two of them. To tuck myself against his side. Kiss Marty's nose like I have a right.

I almost jump out of my skin when Miguel suddenly turns to me, fearing that he's read my mind.

Instead, he leans toward me to whisper, "We're being watched. What do we do?"

"Kiss me," I blurt out, not even flinching. And also not acting.

I just want his lips on mine. If that's all I can get, that's all I'll take.

But Miguel is the true MVP of this play. He smoothly brings me against him with the free arm and places a soft but firm peck on my lips, like a normal husband would everyday. My hands are on his chest, over his heart beating strong and steady—just like him.

Marty chuckles a little while her father still carries her, and that's how I know I'm toast.

CHAPTER 38
MIGUEL

"Miguel, how do you feel, coming into this first game of the postseason when you're about to break a historic record?" Steve Boateng, the face of the Orlando Wild broadcasting team, asks me minutes before the game starts.

The crowd is larger than ever and buzzing. Even though I'm not on social media anymore, I've caught whiff of the wild amount of talk about what potentially may happen today. Two home runs would tie me with Barry Bonds and his historic 2001 season, with seventy three home runs. An extra one would surpass it.

But people throughout my life have called me weird for many reasons, the main one being this: that I don't focus on these things. It's also why I don't do social media. I have no need to feel important or better than anyone else. All I want is to be better than I was yesterday, and I think that's what keeps me sane in this career.

With that as my north star, my answer to him is "Steve, the most incredible thing is seeing our home stadium fully packed with fans who are excited for the game. That really feeds the team, and I think we're about to make some magic tonight."

"And we are all really looking forward to it, thank you for joining us," Steve says with his unwavering anchor voice.

I nod and offer a smile for the camera. "Thank you for having me."

"Back to you, Greg," he says to the camera, shifting the transmission back to the studio.

After shaking his hand and the camerawoman's, I jog back to the dugout to gear up for a potential turn at bat. The game starts with us on the offense, and I'll be in the classic cleanup spot. Enough energy to power the whole state courses through my veins, and it's not so much for the home run record—after all, if I don't break it tonight, I might break it in tomorrow's game.

It's because my wife is watching from the clubhouse.

Er, my fake wife. The woman I have real feelings for.

I wish I didn't have this childish need to prove myself to her, but I can't help it. I want her to pick me, and I'm not above using a home run world record to achieve that.

When I arrive, McDonald, the hitting coach, brings me into the circle of players, managers, and staff members. Rob Beau, our manager, looks at each one of us before speaking. "We all know what's happening tonight. It's our first go at the postseason in a long time. Records could be broken tonight. There are more eyes on us than there's ever been. We could easily crumble like crackers with all this pressure, and certainly our rivals are banking on that."

Some expressions around me darken. Grudges are very much real in the world of baseball, and there are two teams that have earned that eternal distinction from this organization.

There's the New York Eagles, the team where our catcher's

brother plays. Everything I know from Logan is that his family is absolute garbage, and that his brother tried something on Rose in the middle of a game. And no one who messes with our people is gonna get a second chance.

And then there are the Denver Riders.

The crimes committed by Ben Williams are innumerable. From sabotaging Cade's career in every way he could. because he knew that otherwise the Cowboy was gonna gobble him up, to being an absolute piece of shit to Rose and Logan. I wasn't immune either. If a big change hadn't been necessary for my daughter, I'd still probably be playing in the Riders, slowly being consumed by Williams and his toxicity. Pretty sure I wouldn't have been about to break a historic record in that alternate reality.

Right now, we have to focus on the Texas Longhorns first, but it's looking very likely that the Eagles will come next, and maybe eventually the Riders. That's gonna be more exciting than what could happen tonight.

Beau continues, "But this is a team that doesn't give a shit about anyone else's expectations. We're here to play the game our way and on our terms. We're the Orlando Wild, the dark horse, the team that everyone underestimated, and we're going to shut them all up and make history together."

"That's right!" someone exclaims.

"For the pizza!" a second one shouts.

And then the whole dugout is roaring with "for the pizza!"

A laugh bursts from my chest. I make a mental note to suggest to Audrey that we should get sponsorship from a big pizza chain or something.

"Ready to rumble?" Lucky asks me as he walks out of the dugout, since he's our leadoff batter.

"Hell yeah, baby." We dab like five times and off he goes.

Low key, Lucky's my favorite player in the team. He's on the field the same way he acts off it—cheeky, a little wild, and one hundred percent on purpose. It's like the shortstop position was tailor made for him, having to react to wild plays with no warning, stretching his body like a damn gymnast, and then making an *oops* face for the camera as if every one of his feats was just a fluke.

He's the same as a batter. There's no better player to start us off with when it's our turn to bat.

I put on my protection pads while watching him in action. The ones really having a blast are the fans in the stands who get to eat popcorn for this. Dude swings at the very first ball with reckless abandon for a wild hit that sets the pace for the game.

Once Lucky's on base, the next at bats are also a carnival. Mike Brown takes a few more pitches, but he eventually makes it to base with the dirtiest bunt. It gets everyone booing but does the job, and no one will be able to wipe the grin off his face after this.

I wait on-deck as Logan steps up to the plate. Pretty sure he'd get offended if I tell him that he's of the exact same breed as Lucky. Both are devious and calculating, but while Lucky is very obvious about it, Logan is like a calm ocean with violent undertows under the surface. This guy's capable of batting a ball one half an inch inside of the foul line if he so pleases. I kinda wish I had that talent because it's so damn cool.

And entertaining. I practice some swings as he waits for a couple of pitches, still as a statue. The Longhorn starting pitcher is good, but not Cade Starr good, and the ball slips out of control just enough for Logan to clock it.

The clanging sound against the wooden bat is so satisfying, for a moment I'm sure it's gonna be a home run. Instead, two outfielders run like the loan sharks are behind them. The hit's long enough that it lets Lucky advance to third base, and suddenly it's bases loaded and my turn at bat.

Well, kinda wish I had worn ear plugs for this.

The audience is so hyped up that I can't even hear my walk up song. I wonder if Marty's watching along with Consuelo. This game will end too late into the night for them to be at the stadium, and Marty has school tomorrow and after that, a pajama party with her new friends.

As I do my little ritual on the plate, I catch Lucky's extensive lead. He'll basically score the second my bat hits a ball. Mike's is a bit more conservative but he's a good runner, so he can make up for it. Meanwhile, Logan is being Logan. He's right on top of the first baseman to narrow down the other guy's play area.

I cross myself and touch the crucifix and wedding band at my neck. This is such a good place to play at. It doesn't matter that it's a million degrees and a thousand percent humidity. The guys in this team are all quality people, and they introduced me to Audrey.

I hope she's watching.

Not because I'm gunning for a grand slam here, but because I'm thinking of her right now.

Finally in position, the pitcher shakes his head at the catcher a couple of times while the pitching clock runs. He throws at the last possible second—classic—and instinct kicks in. My head jerks back right in the nick of time. If I'd been slower, I'd have been hit in the face.

The umpire calls, "Ball!"

And that gets the whole stadium booing harder than with the bunt from earlier.

There's always a chance that pitchers will prefer to walk me than to deal with me face to face. Those are my least favorite. There's nothing entertaining about playing like a stinking coward. It would also be a really bad idea to do that right now, when we're in prime scoring position.

I settle in for the next pitch. This time there isn't any head shaking, and the pitcher throws quickly.

The ball breaks right at the last moment. I react before processing. But the break doesn't give enough warning. The ball slams into my side.

CHAPTER 39
AUDREY

, and a few other back office employees watching from the clubhouse, jump to our feet the second Miguel is hit. The difference between us is that I run to the dugout.

A mess of people blocks me right at the entrance. Franklin and the rest of the physical therapists team, including Hope, make their way through the players to go on the field. I don't know if everything is silent because it really is, or if all sound is drowned by the buzzing in my ears. I try to jump a little, see if I manage to get a clearer view, but of course I don't stand a chance among the sea of giants.

My sneakers make a horrible squeaky sound as I pivot back to the clubhouse. Now I'm the one elbowing my way through people to see the screen. The cameras are trained on Miguel's face, scrunched almost in anger. But I've seen him really angry before—every time Henry showed his face and grubby hands—and this is different. This is a mask of pain.

I'm going to freaking murder that pitcher.

Franklin and Hope get in the way of the cameras for a moment as they verbally assess Miguel. He's not a showboat in his pain like other players, who start jumping or rolling around to really milk the beanballs. Rather, Miguel is stoic by the plate other than how he sometimes shakes his head.

I only realize that the place was really silent until the audience starts booing again. The camera pans to the Longhorn pitcher, who looks completely stunned by what's happening. I don't know if he really intended to hit the best baseball player of our time, or if it was an accident. I'll murder him anyway, but after I make sure to check on Miguel.

The minutes after that pass excruciatingly slowly. Lucky scores our first run and the bases are still loaded, and now that the pitcher's caught in whatever his game was, we move through the batting order until eventually the inning finally freaking ends.

Then I take off for the dugout again.

"Make room, make room," someone's saying. The team moves like a school of fish, absorbing Miguel into the mass as the inning ends and blocking him from view.

He startles a little upon finding me there, waiting for him. Our eyes meet and it's like a conversation that happens in a single second. In my mind, I ask if he's fine, he responds that he is, and I don't believe him.

"Go back to your places, everyone," a clear voice cuts into the tense quiet. It's Logan with his team captain voice. "The game's still going."

"You heard the man, let's go." One of the managers starts shooing people off, players back to the dugout, staff members back to work. Even the back office folks get sent away on the off chance that anything they see may leak to the media.

He finally turns to me and stops cold. I fold my arms. "I'm not going anywhere."

"Uh, right, boss." He clears his throat, checks one last time that the only ones in the clubhouse are Miguel, Hope and her boss, and me, and returns to his place outside.

Franklin gets to work right away. "Garcia, we need the kit and the cooling pads."

"On it." She rushes to the trainers room.

Miguel is calm as he pulls up his jersey off his pants, but I don't miss the tiny flash of frown that appears on his face before it's gone. He works the tight undershirt off, exposing gleaming brown skin covering rippling muscles—and the bruise already forming at his ribs.

I fuss without making a sound, fluttering at a distance as Franklin digs his gloved hands in different places to check on the extent of the injury.

"Does this hurt?" he asks Miguel.

He answers honestly, "Yes, but like a five out of ten."

"What about here?"

"Nothing there."

Hope returns with a case that she splays open on the floor, reaching for a tub of something. Hanging off her shoulder is a long gel ice pack. She's so fortunate that she gets to do *something*. All I can do is watch and pray that this isn't a major injury, and also that I don't commit a felony after this.

"You're lucky that the ball hit your elbow pad first," Franklin says, getting the tub from Hope and opening it. "I do have to check in with Beau to see if he wants to bench you for the game, though."

Miguel sighs, throwing his head back and exposing his neck, like the prospect of not playing is more exhausting than that of playing with a fist-sized bruise on his ribs.

"I think he shouldn't play again tonight," I blurt out, calling their attention to me. Miguel's eyebrows rise. "For all it's worth, I mean. He's probably running on adrenaline right now. We need to see if the damage is actually worse than he feels right now."

"Exactly." Franklin finishes applying the ointment thing and wraps some sort of adhesive patch on top as if it was an open injury. "I'll bring the news from Beau in a second. Garcia, I trust you with the rest."

"Yes, sir," she says, already at work at wrapping the cold pack around his ribcage.

Miguel cooperates by raising his arms, but clearly he's not pleased by the development. "I really am fine. I once played with a broken clavicle and trust me, this doesn't feel anywhere near that."

"Miguel!" I bark, almost the same way that our All-Star catcher would. The two of them jump to attention. "You're always taking care of everyone else. Can you just let us take care of you for a damn second?"

Once Hope recovers from the shock, she snaps her mouth shut and her lips curl into a very Lucky-like smile. "That's right, Miguel. Let your friends and your wife worry about you, hmm?"

He clears his throat, Adam's apple bobbing hard. "Um, okay. Yes."

"Atta, boy." Hope pats his shoulder when she's done, like he's a good doggo. She tosses me a lopsided smirk as she heads back to the dugout, saying, "Tag, you're it."

I huff. I don't know what she means because I can't do anything for this man. Can't magically heal him. Or wave away his frustration. Or really commit murder as I'd prefer.

My arms squeeze so tight around my ribs that it starts to hurt.

"Give it to me straight, Machado. Are you pretending like you're okay or are you really okay?"

"Wow, last name basis, even." He has the nerve to smile. "I really am fine, though."

"I don't believe you."

"I know you don't. I *like* that you don't. It means you're really worried."

How dare his eyes and his smile soften like that, like he's

just watching a tiny kitten fumble around, and not like he genuinely gave me a fright.

"Of course I'm worried, you're our best player. Our entire postseason run hangs on you." Something flashes in his eyes that dulls him just a notch, enough for my chest to squeeze painfully. "Marty would also kill me if something happened to you, you know?"

It doesn't improve his mood. It's not like he's upset, exactly, more like pensive. Looking into my eyes like the answer to his questions is in there somewhere. He stuffs his hands in the pockets of his stark white pants, almost in a casual way. But there's nothing laid-back in the air around him. Rather, it's like I'm a pitcher and he's calculating what my next move will be.

Then he opens his mouth. "And you? How would you feel if something really happened to me?"

My breath hitches.

A million possibilities circle in my mind, too fast to grasp each one, but every one worse than the previous ones. All I know—all I can feel—is how my heart beats painfully and my body grows cold, colder than it's ever been. And I wish I could just walk up to him and melt into his chest, absorb his warmth, his strength, and know that he's not going anywhere.

But I don't know how to say any of this. I *do* know that I shouldn't. And as he waits, steps echo behind me and Franklin appears into the picture again. "Beau agrees that you're done for the night. Cool down and go home. We'll assess you again tomorrow."

Miguel turns his attention to the other guy. A muscle jumps at his jaw, until he nods. "Fine. I'll see you tomorrow." Franklin also bids him farewell with a pat on Miguel's shoulder.

My whole body is fluttering with nerves. I don't want to answer Miguel's question. If I admit how horrible I'd feel if something would truly happen to him, he may either freak out or be glad. I'm not ready for the consequences of each scenario. I'm not ready for things to change between us. I wish we could be like this forever, happy together but not together *enough* that all my fears and flaws will be exposed, and that I'll get attached to someone so precious that losing him would be like dying.

I'm not ready.

I'm just not ready.

My voice almost comes out as a sob while I turn around. "Take your time, I'll wait for you in the car."

But I'll have to face it. We came together to the facilities today. We'll drive home together, and the silence will only be filled in with the conversation I left hanging. I speed walk out of the clubhouse and then take off running to the admin building, as if I could outrun a truth that is about to be revealed.

What I feel for Miguel is something I didn't think I had the capacity to feel at all, and I've never been more scared in my life.

Because this isn't just something that would only affect my life, or his, but also his daughter, who has claimed me as her best friend and who deserves a much better one.

I'm just a broken shell of a woman, and all that leaks through the cracks is fear. Of being abandoned again. And worse, of letting them down.

Grabbing my stuff from my cubicle, I somehow manage to hold it together until I find Miguel's modest but trusty SUV in the parking lot. That's just like him, unassuming despite his greatness, so reliable that it robs my breath. *He* robs my breath. Somehow, he also took my heart.

"What am I gonna do?" I fully sob into the steering wheel once I'm safely alone inside the car.

My body heaves with great sobs. Somewhere in the back of my mind I know I'm being melodramatic, that nothing's happened. That I have no right to be acting this way, like I'm mourning something that hasn't come to pass. Like this was the most difficult moment of my entire life—not every time I was neglected or shunned by my parents, not when I lost my only brother, not when I was bullied by the other rich kids who didn't find me enough.

It's like I'm mourning the Audrey who could consistently close off her heart no matter what. Because the moment to really bare it is here. I can't run away from this conversation, not today or tomorrow, or the day after that. I have to be honest with Miguel.

And then I *have* to pick up the pieces.

By the time he joins me in the car, taking the passenger seat, I've already calmed down enough that I can drive. I wait until he straps in before getting us in motion. The radio is off, all that fills the silence is the engine and the dampened sound of traffic. Miguel is large enough that his left arm has no choice but to take up most of the space of the console between us. He's turned away to the window, watching the lights go by as I drive us through downtown.

"We need to talk," I say, finally breaking the silence. Even as my attention stays focused on the road, I feel him shift to watch my profile.

"I'm all ears," he says softly. His voice raises goosebumps on my skin, and I'm glad to be wearing a sweatshirt.

"I think…" I trail off, swallowing hard. "That we should stop this."

Miguel doesn't fill my pause with questions, but I gather my nerve to answer them anyway.

"It really struck me in there, at the clubhouse," I explain, my voice steady but only as strong as a whisper. "You deserve someone who genuinely worries for you, and puts you and Marty first. Right now, and if we continue playing this marriage game, I'm just getting in the way of that. We should… we should get a divorce. For real."

Still, he doesn't say anything. We're stopped at a red traffic light and I can't face him. I keep my eyes firmly on the license plate of the car in front of us.

"Marty's already settling into her new school with new friends, and Consuelo is there for her. But she deserves a proper mom. Someone who can be a good example to her, who even knows how to be a good mom. And you…" The light turns green, and I struggle to find my voice. It takes a few tries to finish with "you deserve *the world*."

He does. Gosh, Miguel deserves the absolute best. At least someone who can give him back as much as he gives. Someone mentally and emotionally healthy and confident and full of love. Someone who is entirely the opposite of me.

Finally he joins the conversation. "Is that what you meant back there? When you said you were just worried for our postseason?"

A stab of pain crosses my heart, breaking it in two halves.

My hands squeeze the steering wheel, keeping me from falling into a pit of my own making.

That's not what I meant at all. It was just a diversion. The depth of my own fear of losing him numbed my wits. And now it has become the perfect exit strategy so that I can protect him from myself.

But I will never treat him like he's just another player, some figure on TV that makes anchors and watchers lose their minds.

"Of course," I say, no longer managing to hold the wobble in my voice. "But we're friends, Miguel. I also care about what happens to you."

The words taste worse than candy infused vomit in my mouth. I've never hated myself more than in this moment.

"I see." He turns back out to the window and takes a moment. He sounds calm as he asks, "Do you want to divorce right away?"

"No!" I exclaim, unable to hide the truth for a quick

second. I clear my throat. "After the postseason. I don't want to invite drama into it."

"Makes sense. That's the most important thing."

*No, it's not. It's you—*you. *Only you. And you're better off without me.*

My chin trembles. "Right." And that's the last word for the rest of the drive home.

CHAPTER 40
MIGUEL

t's the bottom of the ninth at the fourth game against the Longhorns. The past few days have been a slog between not playing, so the medical team could run all the exams they wanted—including measuring the diameter of my eyelashes and shit—and the weird dynamic at home.

Audrey and I can't seem to find a way to talk to each other anymore. Either I freeze when I find her suddenly in front of me, reaching for a cup or for the fridge or about to leave at the same time as me or…

She runs. Once, she almost slipped to near death in her rush toward the guest bedroom.

Marty has obviously picked up on the weirdness. She continues treating Audrey as usual, hanging out, joking, and spending time together. But my own daughter is ignoring me like she knows that deep down, I'm the one who screwed up.

She's right. I shouldn't have pressed Audrey for an answer. That was selfish of me. Maybe I really was loaded up on adrenaline and just used that as an excuse to satisfy my own craving for her. I could tell that I screwed up the second I asked with how Audrey immediately shut down. The concern wiped off her face, and every line carefully turned to reflect absolutely nothing. Not even annoyance.

I finally made her be done with me.

And I can't stop agonizing about it, because if I could turn back time I'd do the same damn thing anyway. I would ask her for a crumble of hope, for permission to want her. I would've still been unable to keep it bottled up any longer.

The consequences are that I'm now on the outfield at the bottom of the ninth inning, we're about to sweep the Longhorns in two more strikes, the crowd is riled up and already celebrating with horns and whistles and a million voices, and all I feel is an anvil is perched on my shoulders.

The Longhorn batter hits off Josh Thomason, who is closing for the game. The hit is long, high enough that it could be dangerous. My feet take off, eyes still on the ball as it flies in the dark sky. I know the exact point it's going to land at, and my legs act like springs when I'm right at the spot.

But I jump a little too high.

The ball bounces off my glove on the wrong side. I'm cursing in more than two languages in my mind. I waste further time rolling to a stop on the grass, but luck finds me anyway because the ball isn't far. Landing on my feet, I pick it up and take a deep breath. I'm glad I'm not mic'ed up for the big word that comes out of my mouth as I throw.

It's a whole damn cannon. Lucky intercepts it right in time to tag out the runner from second. He throws to home with all he's got and—

"Two outs! Game over!"

The whole place comes down in wild cheering.

I stand there, breathing hard, soaked in sweat through my uniform, kinda shocked that my error didn't cost any runs for the team. If those two runners had scored, we'd be looking at a game five. I could've screwed it all up for everyone just because I'm feeling like a failure in my private life.

"Guys, I'm sorry," I say once we're in the clubhouse. It kills the celebratory vibe. Removing my hat, I wipe the sweat off my face with my forearm and say, "I was in my head and that error could've cost us."

You'd think Beau would be the one to reprimand me here, and he would be right to. Instead, he just keeps chugging some more of the electrolyte drink from Henry Vos's company.

The one who picks up the baton is Logan. "Why were you in your head? Are you actually hurt?" He points his chin toward my ribs, which further entices the attention of the whole team.

Everyone's eyes are on me, waiting to see if this moment will mark the last celebration of the team this year.

Conscious of the weight of every second I don't respond, I take a deep breath and decide to just spill the beans, all of them. In a way that would make Marty cringe herself into a black hole.

"I'm in love with Audrey, but she doesn't return the feeling and she asked me for a divorce."

The first part surprises no one. The second part, though… that one gets jaws dropping, throats gasping, eyes bulging, mouths spluttering. Even the team manager and his crew aren't immune. Even the trainers are at a loss for words.

"But you just got married like, yesterday!" O'Brian exclaims.

"Yeah, what did you do to screw up so early?" asks Fernandez.

The three guys who are in the know are looking at me like *this*—and not breaking the record set by Barry Bonds earlier tonight—is what I have completely shocked them with.

Lucky murmurs, "No way."

As the noise increases, I raise my hands while still holding the cap, and manage to quiet them down. "We got married just to help her out of a situation, okay? Divorcing wouldn't be a big deal, it's just…"

"That you love her," Cade states like it's the most obvious thing in the world.

"And that you don't think she loves you back." Lucky gives me something like a side eye, even though he's squared up in front of me.

From between a couple of players, Otto Berger—a physical therapist—asks, "Why are we talking about this instead of doing the postgame cooldown?"

"Shhh," one of the players next to him hisses. "Can't you see one of our own needs therapy right now?"

"Yeah, but not of the physical kind. Or at least not one you can provide, my dude," someone else adds with a chuckle.

Logan folds his arms, his pads creaking against the strain. "The question here is, do you know that she doesn't feel the same, or do you think she doesn't?"

"Oooh," someone whispers.

I realize my mouth has been hanging open and close it. My eyes lower to the floor, a massive art piece of the team's purple logo with a green alligator.

"It's pretty obvious." I frown at the gator. "After the bean-ball, I asked her if she cared about me and she said that she cared about what getting injured could mean for the team."

Mierda, it hurts even more to say it out loud.

"And that was it?" our captain asks in a completely offhanded way. I look up sharply. "You just assumed from that point forward?"

My eyebrows scrunch in confusion. "I mean, she asked for a divorce after that. What else could be happening?"

He sighs hard enough that his throat vibrates, almost like a growl. "After everything you saw me go through, didn't you learn the lesson that you have to have a clear conversation with women? That we can't read each other's minds?"

Cade raises his paw. "And is that all you said or did you also explain your feelings in full?"

"I…" My mouth opens and closes. "I did not."

Berger explodes. "Ugh, just go and talk to her so we can cooldown once and for all."

"Shut up, Berger," someone yells from the back.

However, as weird as it is to be talking about my fee-fees in front of the whole team, including the managers and everyone else who is part of the player support team… I needed this.

I needed a reset. Something to get me out of my funk and back into thinking more clearly. Nothing worth having comes easy and I didn't even try hard. I've never told Audrey that I'm in love with her, that I want to be her rock, that she's the one who was meant to join my family—no one else. That I don't want to lose her. That I want her in my bed every night. During the day too.

My baseball cap falls to the floor and I reach for my head, running my hands all over my face and hair. I grunt, "You're right. I need to tell her—"

"Damn right," Lucky interrupts.

"—Right now," I finish.

Silence, but not the tense kind. The one that permeates the air right before a game.

I drop my hands and sure enough, each one of my teammates looks like adrenaline has hit their central processing system. The series is over, and yet they're even more amped up than when the game was about to start.

"Let's go." Lucky pumps his fist in the air. More voices join him.

I square my shoulders and pivot for the door. "Let's do this."

CHAPTER 41
AUDREY

You know what's really awkward? Having an emotional breakdown and needing your girls in the middle of the postseason. They should be down there with the boys, doing the amazing work that no one does better than Hope and Rose.

Instead, they asked for the day off to join me in the WAGs section for a little intervention.

I spent nearly the whole game avoiding it, as if voicing my thoughts is going to make them feel more real than they already are, until Hope threatened me with bodily harm. Coming from her, that threat is more than credible. So I took a record-breaking chug of my soda, and once the sugar rush kicked in I spilled the beans.

The result is the two of them screaming, "*Divorce?*"

Luckily, or not really, the crowd goes absolutely bananas because the weirdest thing has happened. Miguel, who would still be a fan favorite if he wasn't a slugger, makes an error when trying to catch a fly ball on the outfield.

I jump to my feet, leaning forward like that will get me to see the expression on his face. "Shit, *shit*. This is my fault, isn't it? I messed up his game. He's gonna start a bad streak because of m—"

"Don't even say that!" Rose grabs me by the shoulders and sits me back down. She gets all up in my grill. "Now, start talking before I decide to help Hope beat you up."

Our other friend harrumphs. "Thank you."

The breath that leaves my lungs melts me down into the chair, and I hang my head. Of all the emotions that have tumbled around my belly since I brought up the D-word, shame is one of the largest.

How dare I get him involved in such a wild scheme, and then turn around and try to get out of it when it's convenient for me?

In turn, that also confirms that it was the right move *for him*. I only know how to be selfish and take, take, take. But what have I given him other than headaches and maybe even this error? Miguel's mentality is so elite that this seldom happens, and as far as I'm aware, I'm the only person in his life that has disturbed his peace the past few months. Even bruised ribs wouldn't do this to him.

When I finally explain all of this aloud to my friends, the expressions on their faces tell me they've never heard anything quite as absurd. I feel it in my bones, too—there's that shame again.

"Audrey, I'm going to say this with a lot of love." Rose grabs my hand in between hers, and stares at me with her unfathomable eyes. "Are you out of your damn mind?"

"I'll give you the benefit of the doubt in one thing," Hope chimes in, setting her arm on the backs of our chairs to turn to me. "Love makes us lose our logic often, ask me how I know. And all of this that you're saying"—she motions at me with her free hand—"is illogic, because you're in love with the man and his daughter, and you're afraid that it seems too good to be true."

"Yes." I frown. "I explained it very logically, though."

She ignores me. "But… have you stopped to think that maybe it seems too good to be true because you're just used to shitty love?"

"Or no love at all," Rose adds.

"I mean, it's true that I've been single a very long time but…"

My voice trails off because something clicks all of a sudden. Shitty love is more what I'm familiar with. My parents's version of love was very shitty, gold leaf gilding around neglect. My brother's love was short lived. The few guys I dated never even loved me in the first place.

I look at the two of them, in turns since they're sitting on my sides. The only real love I've known so far has been from my friends. It's why I'd do anything for them.

And then Miguel came along, and the only way I was able to recognize that there was something special about him, was because I had already experienced it with my friends.

"Hope, look," Rose whispers, her eyes as wide as they can be.

"Oh, shit." Hope stares at me. "I don't think I've ever seen this."

My chin trembles and I sniff. After wiping the tears off my face, I grumble, "Yeah, I'm doing a lot of this crying thing lately."

"My word, our frosty sugar is melting." Rose smiles with zero mockery behind it. She almost looks motherly, like she's proud of me.

Meanwhile, Hope hands me some napkins. "I'm here for not bottling things up so, can you tell us what you're thinking while you keep crying?"

That tears a little laugh out of me. It's hard. It takes a lot of false starts and a few more sniffles, but I manage to somewhat outline what I've just figured out. As result, both of them throw themselves at me and squeeze the tar out of me.

"Can't—breathe," I gasp out.

"Ugh, I'm so proud of you," says Rose.

"I *knew* that my own meltdowns would help you some day." Hope squeezes harder.

"Ack!"

It takes much wriggling to get them off me, and Rose is casually dabbing at her eyes as if neither of us could tell why she has the need.

"So basically, you're selling yourself short because you're scared of real intimacy with a man who is basically tailor made for you, so you threw big words around and now you're sad that they worked?"

I wish I could hide from Rose cracking the code that makes me the way I am, but I can't. Not with the two of them blocking all my exits. The game is done and the fact that the whole stadium is celebrating with all their lungs still doesn't provide enough cover.

"Yeah, I guess so," I admit in what sounds like a mumble, but is actually a whole scream.

Many WAGs start making for the exits. Even though this is a private section, there are enough relatives of the players that it makes the process slow. I stay firmly in my chair by virtue of Rose and Hope doing the same.

"What's the plan now?" the latter asks when the noise has quieted down a couple of notches. "Like, do you really wanna proceed with this divorce or not?"

"How can I not?" I massage my temples, ignoring the WAGs making their way out. "Let's say that I grow an extra pair of ovaries and I go tell him that I have feelings for him I'd like to explore. How would that even work when we're married under a farce?"

"Very easy. Men are simple creatures." Rose shrugs. "Mine

is obsessed with the shape of my bottom. Leggings are enough to lower his defenses."

Hope snorts a little. "And mine is fixated with my thighs. It doesn't matter what I'm wearing, he's drooling about them regardless."

I ponder for a moment. "I don't know if there's a part of me that Miguel's into."

"You're kidding, right?"

"I can't believe what I'm hearing."

"What?" I ask, completely left out of their conversation.

"Those."

"*That.*"

The two of them point at my chest. I look down at it, currently encased by an Orlando Wild jersey with the number 3 at the back. I'm still channeling my best wife impression until the last second so Miguel doesn't feel embarrassed.

"No, trust me. He never looks at them."

"Just because the guy is respectful doesn't mean that he's not dreaming inside of that testosterone riddled brain of his," Rose says with a shake of her head, curls bouncing all over.

"I mean, he didn't make a whole kid by himself." Hope gifts me with a deadpan stare. "Are you sure he's never showed any particular interest before?"

"Oh." The night of my dad's cocktail party flashes in front of my eyes. Heat starts creeping up my neck, and I know I'm going to start looking like a white and pink Dalmatian soon. "There was one time…"

"Oh yeah?"

"Hmm?"

They make me smile a little. It's like they were waiting for the tables to turn all this time.

"Please don't tell Logan but Miguel and I made out in his Maserati."

"You *what?*"

Hope starts laughing like Santa Claus.

"It was a weird night, okay? We were both stressed out and got caught in the rain. Anyway, long story short, he was very much into my legs."

Rose cocks an eyebrow. "Was he kissing your legs or how did this even happen?"

I clear my throat. Twice. "No, I was um… sitting on his lap."

Gasps. Looks of outrage.

Hope starts with "I'm going to need all of the—" but can't finish because there's a heck of a lot of noise all of a sudden. Almost as if every WAG and family member who vacated the premises was coming back at the same time.

The three of us turn around and…

Of all things I was expecting, nowhere among them was Miguel freaking Machado in the flesh, walking down the stands in his dirty uniform and no cap on his head, hair messy, skin glowing with sweat, and eyes fully trained on me, with the whole damn team tagging along behind him.

"What's happening?" I whisper. The girls respond different versions of *I don't know*, but they sound amused where I'm confused.

We follow their journey until it stops, and that's only when Miguel is standing in front of me. He leans forward, both hands propping him up against the backrest of the chair in the row below mine. The other boys are all over, spilling into the stands around us for reasons I don't understand.

"W-What's going on?" I ask, looking around.

"Audrey." My name coming out of Miguel's mouth never ceases to stop my brain function, and I focus on him. He's the only interesting one in this crowd, anyway. A drop of sweat trickles down from his temple, caressing his incredible jaw, until it finds that chin I'd still love to bite.

Oh snap. He just said something and I was too busy eating him up to register it.

"Sorry, what was that?"

He swallows hard but doesn't lose his patience. "I want a chance."

Someone stifles a squeal.

Not me, I'm too busy letting flies into my open mouth.

"I know it's probably very crappy of me to ask for one when I promised I was just your friend, but…" He runs a hand through his damp hair, messing it up even more. "That's the one promise I won't be able to keep. I want you, and not in a very friendly way."

Turns out my jaw had the capacity to drop even more.

Miguel smiles a little, uncertain—maybe shy. He's never been more beautiful than at this moment, not even when his shirt was splayed open before my eyes and my hands.

Pretty sure I'm self combusting now.

"So, I… I want to propose a new deal," he says more firmly. Someone in the crowd tells him that he's got this. But Miguel's focus is still only on me. "Take all the space you need to think about this—us, and if we win the World Series, you'll go out on a date with me."

Silence.

I mean, aside from the fans that are still loitering in the stands.

"A proper date," he continues, "Just you and I, no one else to judge, really getting to know each other and considering a future together. And if we lose—"

"Dude, don't even say the L-word!" one of the guys shouts.

"Shut up, let him finish," another one says.

"—Then you decide. Whatever you want, I'll do it. If you want to divorce the very next day, we will do that. If you want more time to think, consider it done." There's no wavering in him, like he's sure this is the right course of action.

"That's a big bet. Are you sure you want to play it?" I whisper, looking up at him as if he wasn't the best professional baseball player of our time.

As if he wasn't the one guy who can make all of this happen even with bruised ribs, thrown off by an annoying, insecure woman, and with the weight of the whole team on his very wide shoulders.

"Yes, I am," he responds firmly and extends his hand toward me. "Deal?"

If my heart wasn't trying to claw its way out of my chest, I'd suspect this is all a dream. That there's no way this man—this wonderful, kind, and sweet man—would basically be staking his career on me.

I blink up at him. "This is absolutely wild, you know?"

"Yeah, I know. It's been a big hit with the whole team, though." His grin is almost contagious, or would be if I wasn't feeling like I'm underwater.

"So the whole team knows?" I question.

Lots of people clear their throats and make whistling noises that don't fool me.

So this is why the whole freaking team joined in. Not only they know what's happened between Miguel and I, but they're being his wingmen. Some of them weren't very fond of the idea of someone of Miguel's caliber joining the team and hogging all the attention at first, but he's won over even those haters. That's how special he is.

I'd be a complete fool to not bet on him.

Slowly, I rise to my feet and clasp my cold hand in his big, hot one. "Deal."

Cheers break out all around.

CHAPTER 42
MIGUEL

"Isn't this so poetic?" Lucky Rivera asks. He's got his forearms up against the barrier. Beside him is Cade, then Logan, and me. We're all chewing gum and probably look like cows.

The Cowboy mumbles, "Hmm?"

"That we're up against the Eagles and then it'll be the Riders," the Boricua shortstop says.

Our batter connects with the ball and it sets the diamond in motion. The runner on first takes off, and the Eagles focus on him rather than the batter. We're tied and they clearly don't want us to score before our batting lineup rotates back to the top. I'd do the same if I was them, especially being at the bottom of the eighth on game seven. Whoever wins this one gets the ticket for the big, big show.

Lava courses through my veins at the thought of it. It's funny because on the one hand, I'd also have been one step away from the World Series if I'd stayed in Denver, but that possibility would've been so much emptier. Marty would still be in a bad place in school, and there would be no Audrey in the picture. Also, none of these cows.

"Save that for after we win this game," Logan grunts.

But Lucky doesn't leave it alone. "Shouldn't you be the second most excited about getting this bag?"

"The second?" the Cowboy asks before blowing a huge bubble with his gum.

"Yeah, I mean grumps over there is about to get sweet, sweet revenge on his estranged weirdo of a brother, and our softie over there is gonna save his marriage."

The three of them turn to me and my eyebrows rise. "I'm the softie?"

"Yes."

"No doubt."

"Uh huh."

Touching the crucifix and wedding band at my neck, I face forward just as the Eagles manager and a handful of players are surrounding their pitcher to strategize. Lewis Kim, the pitcher and mastermind of that whole team, appears to be screaming at his catcher. I'm sure that's gonna work out great.

"It's not about saving a fake marriage," I muse, chewing on cinnamon gum with all my might. "I just want a chance to love her openly and for real."

Heck of a lot of silence on the barrier. Turns out the three original stooges are looking at me like I'm a raccoon in a zoo cage.

"What?"

"Damn." Cade drawls out the word with gusto. "This really isn't for the pizza anymore."

"What?" I repeat, now even more confused.

"You used the big L-word," Logan translates and if he wasn't such a master at the art of a poker face, I'd confirm whether he's smirking on the inside. "Have you told her already?"

"Of course not. I don't want to spook her."

This is followed by various sounds of agreement to that.

"But you do love her?" Lucky insists, his eyes wide like a cartoon.

The unbelievable thing is that… yeah, I do.

I don't even know how or when it happened. It'd be easy to say that it happened with every moment Audrey brought my daughter out of her shell, or even since the first hint that she was someone who could change my life while she wrestled with her mailbox, and ended up delivering a wild hit to my eye. Everything Audrey has done has marked me one way or another, my body, my mind, my soul. She's made me laugh, woken up my deepest instincts, made me hungrier than I've ever been for a woman.

There's so much more about her that I don't know. That I crave to know. There's still so much of her life for her to walk, and I'm sure I can be the right companion for her. That Marty and I can be her family.

And I desperately need her to want all that.

I swallow hard. Yeah, I'm in love, a'ight.

"Look at his face," our captain says drily. "I bet he's writing a romance novel in his head."

"Well, he is the one who most helped you draft your letter to Rose," Cade casually tosses out there. Somehow I had forgotten about that.

"Clearly it's our turn to help you back," Lucky says, pulling away from the fence. "So, watch me score a run for your happy ending, old man."

I scrunch up my face. "Since when am I an old man?"

"Since you're married and with a child." He laughs before leaving us to get on-deck.

"That guy's never gonna be serious, is he?" I ask in awe, even though the answer is clear.

Logan just shakes his head, sighs, and heads over to the cubbies to get his batting gear. A heavy paw falls on my shoulder, and it's from Cade Starr. He's already done pitching for the night, but no one would fault him for wanting to watch the show from the front row.

"Personally," he says while a grin creeps up on his face. "I think it's a much nobler cause to play for love than for pizza, or revenge, or socks. But don't tell the guys that I said that."

The snort that comes out of my mouth transforms into an incredulous laugh. "Thanks?"

These guys are a rollercoaster, but somehow in just a few months they've had my back more than any other teammates before.

I don't know if it's something about the weather, the beware alligator signs that can be found in the most random places, or the no state tax, or simply that Rob Beau and the Orlando Wild organization have a great eye for choosing guys that will really become a unit. But for a change, I don't feel like the whole game is on my shoulders, and that all of us are joined by one purpose.

"Get the girl, dawg," one of the guys says as I make my way out of the dugout to stand on-deck.

"You got this." This one pats my butt with his glove.

"We're rooting for you."

"Don't forget to invite us to the real wedding."

I can't help but cracking a smile.

There's always uncertainty in this game. The wind can blow too hard all of a sudden and carry a ball in the wrong direction. Someone may slide weird to base and break a toe that won't let him run anymore. A pitcher may hit you on the damn ribs because too much sweat made the ball slip from his hand.

But there's one thing I know. Even if I break my toes, my knees, my ribs, or have to do it in the middle of a hurricane… I'll keep on playing for a chance with the woman of my dreams. And no one's getting in my way.

When my walk up song starts playing, it's no longer about one niña bonita who lives in my heart. Now there are two.

CHAPTER 43
AUDREY

My friend Camila, who works at *SPORTY*, texts me to say that she'll come to Orlando in December for a conference. It's going to be great to catch up, especially after so much has happened, but right now I can't fathom the concept of tomorrow. Let alone two months away.

Game four of the World Series is tonight—Orlando Wild versus Denver Riders. And against all odds and predictions…

We're about to win the whole show.

This is the single most important moment in our team history. We'd never made it farther into a season than we have this year. Hell, everyone had already written us off the second Spring Training started. But now, not only are we the new favorites to win it all, but we're also the top trending sports team on the internet. People can't stop talking about our dark horse race, about how our standout players have carried us through to this moment, or about the wild acquisition that turbo charged us during the season.

Yet, none of that matters to me right now because *this* is the single most important moment of my life. I just don't know if that moment ends tonight or stretches for three more games.

I sure as shit hope that it's tonight, if only so I can stop pretending like I'm strong and independent and mature, and just run into Miguel's arms because there's no longer any risk that I'll throw him off his game.

Gosh, he's got me so down bad.

My phone buzzes in my hand again, and I check right away, thinking that it's another text from Camila. But no. I stare at the words on the screen with a block of ice sliding down my throat.

FATHER

Come to my office immediately

"What's wrong?" Marty asks next to me, her hand deep in a caramel popcorn bucket. "You look like something's wrong, so don't lie."

I expel the air in my lungs. "It's just my dad."

Her little face scrunches up. "He's mean, isn't he?" Once I nod, she adds, "Then ignore him."

How do I explain that when I did that for a few years, he just maneuvered me into a harder corner?

"It's okay. It'll be quick." I give her a one-armed hug that she returns as though routine. From above her head, I glance at Consuelo and say, "Call me if anything happens, please."

Anything could be an issue with Marty and Consuelo sitting at the WAGs section, even though now the whole team and no doubt their significant others know that I'm not legitimately Miguel's WAG. Or the game starting before I manage to return. Or Miguel's beef cakes looking otherworldly in his white uniform pants.

Maybe not that last one. Even though I sure don't wanna miss it.

As I'm shuffling down the row, I hear an obnoxious voice say, "Ugh, look at her. She's not even a real WAG."

Another person shushes the top mean girl, who somehow

found herself married to the pretty nice guy that is Mike Brown. "Careful, she's still the owner's daughter."

The comments sound snide and certainly spark the heat of irritation in my chest, but they're not lies. I have no right to get upset at truths that I withheld and have finally come out.

Of course, the internet is also abuzz about that. Some of Miguel's most ardent fans have argued that the fact that he didn't hit any home runs in the previous series is because of the mess I put him in, and that I'm shameless for using him that way.

Joke's on them because I am nothing but full of shame. And of longing for him.

Staff members have become nicer to me instead. I get greetings and smiles as I make my way through the corridors, away from the general public that would boo the lights out of me. I don't know if it's because of the little tidbit about who my biological father is, or if it's because they're privy to the deal Miguel and I made. After all, that's also made the rounds through the company intranet.

Dad's assistant is still a stuck up snob of a little man, though. I actually appreciate the stability of his character. What I don't appreciate is what seeing him means.

I try to not sneer at the double doors leading to my father's office. Why is he even here when his team's about to fight for the big W out there? Shouldn't he at least be at the owner's box?

Turns out I failed, and I have to carefully wipe the annoyance off my face before walking in. Except, instead of finding only my dad inside, there's also Henry Vos. And that tells me this is gonna be much worse than I anticipated.

I have enough neurons to stay near the door, though, and still I wish I wasn't anywhere near Henry Vos. Sealing the door shut behind me feels ominous.

Thankfully we're also nowhere near Miguel's sight. I'm

sure seeing this junk of a human being would turn his stomach, worse than having heaps of candy and proceeding to have a vigorous dance off.

My dad's frowning at me. "Audrey, come over here," he demands from behind his desk, but Henry stands beside him as if he was Dad's son.

"I'm good here," I offer in a caustic way that I can tell he doesn't like by the way his twirly mustache curves. "Whatever this is, can it wait? I have to get back to watch my husband's game."

Henry barks an unwelcoming laugh. "Still pretending? Breaking news, baby, the ruse is up. I gathered enough evidence of your marriage to that clown being a fraud, and I've just shown every last bit of it to your father."

The block of ice that had slid to my gut not only stayed there, but is now expanding toward my limbs. I wish I wasn't wearing Miguel's jersey with the number three emblazoned at the back, and instead was wrapped up in my comfy pajamas and under a fluffy blanket, and that this whole scene was just a Kdrama playing on my TV screen.

Alas, Henry's face is still painted with the glee of a villain who just won, and Dad's is full of disappointment.

"Is this all true, Audrey?" the latter asks, his voice rasping with how low and angry it is.

Henry cuts me off before I can even make a sound. "Don't try to deny it. I have witness statements from a few players and even a WAG, and plenty of footage."

A WAG, huh? I bet it was Amber, trying to get back at me for not playing her game. And she did seem oddly interested in my affairs.

"Is that the one you got after hiring a PI to spy on our private life?" I snap, absolutely out of shits to give. He's cornered me against a wall, thinking I was going to coil up and whimper.

No, I'm going to fight. With every tooth and nail until I bleed, because this is no longer about me. This is about Miguel and Marty's safety against these entitled rich men.

Slowly, my father turns his chair toward the younger man. "You did what?"

I blink for a solid few seconds. That tone of voice from my dad awakens the sleeper cells of my childhood traumas. He used to exercise that voice whenever he found out about Mom's latest indiscretions, or whenever he caught Adam sneaking in alcohol so he could knock himself asleep and not hear the drama anymore. And also when I disappointed him, which was any time I did anything but acting like a doll.

I had never seen him use that tone on anyone outside of his so-called family, though.

That's also probably why Henry doesn't realize the danger he's in, and fully steps into the trap. "I had no other choice. I knew there was something weird about Audrey marrying some random guy she just met, especially when I've faced years of rejection from her."

"Yeah, because hitting on me at my brother's funeral sure was going to be a great start to a relationship between us," I deadpan with tragic sharpness.

Dad's face whips toward me but he says nothing, and Henry resumes spewing bullshit out of his pie hole.

"I did it for your own sake. To protect you from the vultures around you, like that gold digger from a backwater country you call your husband."

My fists tighten and now I really regret being so far, because I can't introduce them to Henry's face. Heat spreads across my chest and my face, and for the first time I don't give a shit about how terrible that makes me look.

"Don't you dare insult Miguel. Your whole damn self doesn't even compare to his pinky toe."

"See?" Henry looks at my dad while pointing at me. "This

is what happens when you don't keep a tight rein. Now your estate is going to fall into the hands of that overpaid clown."

"Is that all you care about?" Henry and I snap our focus to my father. He pushes away from the desk and rises slowly to face the other jerk. "All your concerns seem to be around my daughter's inheritance and not about her. Shouldn't you, as a man who professes to have loved her since your youth, be more worried about *her* than her riches?"

I choke.

Henry steps further in the manure. "Of course I want to protect her! That's why I'm doing all of this. With this, we can have the marriage annulled and—"

"And then what? What would happen after that?" I ask, still coughing.

Henry's eyes flash with every disgusting thought in his sick brain, and for the first time I realize that this isn't just about putting his grubby hands on whatever Dad intends to pass down to me, but also on me.

Like maybe the fact that he couldn't stop himself from coming onto me while I was in mourning was more about me than money. That he desired me even when I was just a teenage girl and he was already an adult.

Bile rises up my throat. I manage to keep it down somehow. "I'm not yours, Henry. Never have been, and never will be."

"Then are you his?" He makes a disgusted face, like we're talking about the different consistencies of poop instead. "Did you already give yourself to him like a filthy—"

"Enough!" my dad screams loud enough for his voice to echo against the marble walls.

Still shaking with anger, I lift my chin and say, "No, I am my own, and what I do is none of your damn business."

"That's right," Dad says, and that's even more shocking than him screaming. "There is absolutely no way in hell I'll give you my daughter after all of this has been revealed."

"What?" Henry takes a step back, his good rich guy façade finally crumbling before the older man. "But I just—We made a deal, Charlie."

"Mr. Cox for you, and when did we sign a damn contract?" Dad asks, the same brand of sarcasm as mine dripping from his words. "I just wanted my daughter to be set up comfortably for life. I thought you'd be a good candidate for that, but clearly I was wrong about that. And about many other things in my life."

My jaw unhinges.

Behind my back, I reach for one arm to pinch my skin. The jolt of pain tells me that I am, indeed, not dreaming.

"But you approved of me," Henry says, echoing the same language Dad used that set me off on this strange path. "You didn't approve of that Machado clown or whatever. *Me.* I was your chosen candidate."

"Who said I didn't approve of Machado?" Dad gives out his villain Santa laugh, the one that comes out every time he nabs a deal and smashes his competition. "I'm the one who negotiated his trade into our team, because I heard Audrey say that he was probably the best player of this generation."

"What?" I'm not sure I even finish the sentence before a memory slams into the forefront of my mind.

Last year, after our season ended as early as usual, Dad sat in for a PR meeting that I was leading. It was all about how we should turn the team's image around not just for fans, but also to attract top talent.

"Who knows?" I said dryly, not quite believing myself enough to be firm. "We might even be able to acquire someone of Miguel Machado's caliber, who's the best player of our generation."

I stumble backward until my back hits the closed door. My heart is about to explode. My legs itch. I wish I could run—just freaking teleport right next to Miguel and wrap myself around him to make sure that he's real, that he has been existing in my life for the past five months. That my sarcastic wishful thinking really came true.

And more importantly, so I can stop hiding my all consuming feelings for him.

"I even introduced them myself," Dad says, probably referring to the fancy party where Miguel and I danced for the first time, not knowing that Miguel was wearing makeup to hide the black eye I had already introduced myself with. "That's how much I approved of him."

Henry snaps and yells back. "Then why did you bring me here?"

"Because I didn't imagine that they'd get together. I was just trying to make my daughter happy," Dad admits.

"They're not—"

"We are." Both men turn to me. "Or we will be, after the team wins tonight. I'm going to march into that field and claim my husband in front of the entire world."

Dad's bushy eyebrows twitch. "But you'll keep it PG for the cameras, right?"

I mull it over for a moment and fold my arms. "PG13. I haven't been waiting for this moment for so long for it to end with a bland kiss."

And then the strangest thing happens. My father, who has never cared about anything but his businesses and himself… starts laughing.

It's not even a mildly amused sound, but great guffaws that leave him breathless, turning his face the same mottled red and white that mine does.

"Are you two out of your damn minds?" Henry's voice cracks not just because his anger is so great, but because it's finally clicked that he was never one team with my dad. He was and is on his own.

"If that's the definition of what being in love with someone else is like, sure." I shrug.

Dad wipes his face with a handkerchief that costs about as much as a used car, and releases a satisfied sigh. "That's it, that's all I wanted. For you to be happy, Audrey. I know I didn't exactly go about it the right way, but I didn't want to make the same mistake with you like I did with your brother. I just—I wanted to give you everything you deserve, and I didn't know another way to do it."

I steel myself, but there's no fighting back the tangle of mixed emotions in my chest. There's still a lot of anger and resentment toward him, but deep inside there's a tiny box that looks like something out of a dollhouse, and it cracks open to filter out hope. Hope that my father and I might still be a family—a broken and misshapen one, but one nonetheless. Hope that he might care about me after all.

All of it comes trickling out of my eyes.

Dad's smiling at me. "Now, go watch your husband win the World Series while I get rid of this fool."

I wipe my face, because for the first time in over a decade, I want to offer a genuine smile to him. "Thanks, Dad."

I slip out of the office, ready to start a new life.

CHAPTER 44
MIGUEL

"My only question is…" Logan sighs like a long suffering father herding a gaggle of his kids through one of the amusement parks. "Why did they have to be *these* socks?"

He unfurls a pair of white knee-height socks that would blend with our uniform pants, if it wasn't for the tiny alligator legs peeking at the top from under our knees.

"Listen, suckers. Every time I've given you prank socks throughout the season, y'all have gone on to play like some damn machines." Lucky motions at Cade and Logan. "Now we need the whole team to do the same." He pauses for a shrug. "And also, marketing thinks these will sell like cakes and I'll get royalties, so…"

That causes a bunch of people in the clubhouse to laugh. The cheek of this guy is unmatched, and that reminds me of something.

I'm sitting by my locker, also working up the matching socks before I finish getting dressed. "A lot of people told me that I should expect you to sock prank me as a welcome to the team, and it never happened. What the hell, man? Do you have some beef against me?"

The Boricua turns around with an innocent look on his face. "No, I know you, and you'd have just laughed along with me, which isn't as impactful. I have socks for your wife, though."

Cade blows a raspberry. "Good luck getting sugar to wear those without her ripping your head off."

"Our victory depends on it," Lucky explains in absolute seriousness. You wouldn't think we're on game four against the Denver Riders, and on the verge of winning the whole thing.

Honestly, the Eagles were a bigger challenge and took us all the way to a difficult game seven. But the Riders are getting off their horses. They have a grand total of no wins, and this might all be over tonight.

No one who lives and breathes baseball could imagine this before the season started. The Orlando Wild wasn't dead last in the previous one, but it was just a few places removed. And when Ben Williams, their best pitcher, ditched the team for Colorado, everyone wrote the Wild off. Which is pretty absurd when Logan Kim stayed on the team all along, and Lucky Rivera is one of the best shortstops. And sure, Cade Starr wasn't really in the radar, but it only took a little bit of spotlight and a lotta bit of no Williams for Cade to become an unstoppable monster.

The three of them are the brains, the brawn, and the heart of this team. I know they alone would've taken the team pretty damn far into the postseason.

Then I came along.

Everyone thought I lost my senses for making this move, but I could see what these guys were building—and I knew Marty would fir in better around here. It wasn't a hard decision.

And now here I am, dressing up for what is possibly the last game of the season, my heart beating a thousand miles per hour, not letting myself consider this done and won so I don't jinx shit, but desperately wanting it to be so that I can finally ask Audrey out.

But even though I've broken my home run record and some, I haven't smacked a single ball out of the park this series.

Like, I'm playing at my max. I'm not making errors and no ball goes by me. My hits are solid and nasty, making the Riders fielders scramble for their lives while our wildlings score.

No home runs, though. It shouldn't matter but it does. It makes me wonder if—

Cállate, I scream to my brain.

Worse is how everyone is thinking the exact same thing. The new team motto has become for the marriage and not for the pizza. And it's like I'm choking.

No, I'm not. I grit my teeth as I finish rolling up one sock all the way. The team winning is more important than any individual heroics.

Lucky checks his phone and announces, "She should be getting her own pair of socks right about now."

I wanna see it. I'm sure Audrey will make such a sour expression that it'll disprove Cade's nickname for her. But also because as amusing as that part would be, her legs are killer and will still look amazing even when wearing these silly things.

Would Marty like them? I'm fifty-fifty on that. She's settled into herself a lot, but I feel like if gator socks come from me she'd yuck the heck out of them, whereas if they come from Audrey she'd be all on board. Funny how that's panned out.

I send a prayer up above that I do get to see *that*.

I'm only starting to work the second sock up my ankle when there's some sort of commotion. Those of us who are farther from the door crane our necks to see what's happening.

"Is there a fight or somethin'?" Cade stands up to try to peek between the heads.

"Excuse me," McDonald's voice rings above the murmurs because we're used to hitting the pause button whenever the coaches raise their voices. "You can't be in here, we're gonna have to escort you out."

Call me nosy, but I also stand on my tippy toes to see who's getting served with that speech. And of all people I possibly could've expected—fans, unauthorized journos, the tooth fairy—the last one was Henry Vos.

"The hell is that piece of shit doing here?" I mumble.

"Let me through or I'll air every piece of dirty laundry Miguel Machado has!"

"Dude, we all know that he's in a prefab marriage and that he eats too many carbs. What other laundry does squeaky-clean here have?" Lucky shouts back.

I rub my barely ridged stomach directly, since I haven't finished dressing yet. It's true that I'm one of the most carb heavy guys in the team. Not my fault that Venezuelan cuisine is comprised of fried dough.

"He's trying to steal the team!"

That settles everyone down. One by one, all pairs of eyes turn to me. In the process, the view between the unhinged rich guy and I opens up. He points at me too late to really stress his accusation, only making it more awkward.

I point at myself. "Me? How?"

"Don't act all innocent. Tell everyone how you married Audrey for her fortune."

Logan grunts. "You do know that Machado is rich too, right?" That logic goes completely ignored.

"*You.*" Henry What's-His-Problem Vos is so full of bullshit that it must be up to his throat now, with how hard it is for him to get the words out. "You knew that the team was in Audrey's trust. That's why you seduced her."

My eyebrows would take off like airplanes if they could. "I'm sorry, *what?*"

"Yeah, dude doesn't know how to flirt, forget about seducing," Lucky argues back.

"Uh, excuse me, but I'm a pretty good dancer," I return.

"Guys, I don't think that's the point." Cade laughs, which is what reminds me of the absurdity of this situation.

Clearing my throat, I squeeze my way between my also nosy teammates and speak directly to the damn jerkface. "Anyway… No, I had no idea about that when we got married. But I find it very curious that you did know that."

"Yeah… sus," one of the guys says from the back.

Another one asks, "Wait, does that mean that Machado's wife is the new owner of the team?"

"Future owner, I think," a third clarifies.

"Oh, cool. I like a woman on top."

A round of chuckles.

I snap my mouth shut because, thanks, I really needed the reminder of Audrey on my lap running her hands down my bare chest while in the middle of a jam packed clubhouse. I have to run my hand down my face so I can wipe it off the hunger that always rears itself every time I think of her.

"Please, you fools. How can you possibly trust your future to a blonde woman, who knows nothing about baseball, and lets herself be taken advantage of by an opportunistic clown who only knows how to swing a stick?"

This…

This is probably the worst thing this asshole could've said in a room full of clowns who also swing sticks.

"And what makes you think that you know more baseball than Audrey, blondie?" I step into his grill, pointing out the fact that he looks like he bleaches his hair daily. "The fact that you have a twig between your legs?"

"Ooohh."

"Burn!"

"Yeah, a twig might even be too generous."

McDonald rolls his eyes behind Vos, probably regretting every choice that led him to this moment. "All right, that's enough bullshit. Security's on the way and you need to leave the clubhouse right now."

"No." Vos pulls at his suit jacket like somehow that beefs him up or something. "Don't you know who I am? I will have anyone who touches me fired."

"Under whose authority?"

Another guy heckles, "The State of Self-Delusion?"

"That's a good one."

"Listen." I balance my weight on one leg. "Even if I wasn't in the picture, Audrey's not marrying you and giving you the team, if that's what you wanted all along."

One by one my teammates quiet down. Even the staff observes this guy like they can't believe a venomous centipede somehow managed to walk into the clubhouse right before such an important game.

Beau's voice rings out in the silence. "Who the hell let this damn fool in?"

"Not me."

"Me neither."

The guys keep passing the buck until finally, the only one who can't deny it is Otto Berger, one of the physical therapists. "What? I thought it was the person delivering the refilled coolers."

Cade removes his cap and wipes his forehead. "Dude, if I could I'd fire *you*."

Shaking my head, I say, "Expect to hear from my lawyers again tomorrow." And turn around to finish dressing.

But that's when all hell breaks loose.

With a roar, the self-entitled prick tries something that gets everyone jumping into action. Too late I turn to watch out, and his damn heel slams against my ribs. Same side where I got beanballed.

"Oof." Air comes out of my mouth.

"Get him!"

"I claim his teeth!" Lucky screams.

"No, I got this. Time to return the favor." Logan gets in my way, cracking his knuckles.

The coaches are already grabbing the intruder and are shouting orders all across the room. This is when security finally barges in, and I catch Beau telling them to press charges for assaulting one of the players. This is gonna get him banned for life from our facilities and from every one of our games, which is great.

I breathe hard, more out of confusion than anything. Between the guys, staff, and security, they swallow Henry Vos up and drag him out, screaming his lungs out. Regaling everyone around him with obscenities and defamations that are building my case against him with no effort on my part.

"You okay?" someone asks me.

I turn and almost jump in my skin. I've never seen Lucky Rivera this serious, almost like I'm talking to a completely different person.

"Yeah. I'm good."

"You sure?" He looks down.

I do too, and this is when it clocks with me that I'm holding my side. And that it's throbbing.

Slowly, I ease into a casual stance and say, "This won't be an issue unless we make it one."

He gets it. I don't need to spell it out. It's not that I want to protect my ego or some useless crap like that. But any sign that this mess rattled me could shake the team's confidence, and that's the last thing we need tonight.

And the last one *I* need. I'm not letting that creep ruin my chances of taking Audrey out on a date. That honor only belongs to her.

Lucky gives me a solemn nod, and I get it too. This stays between us, but he's gonna be watching me. We dab and return to our places to finish suiting up for the game. No one else peeps even a twitch from my face, even though the throbbing is starting to get more annoying.

CHAPTER 45
AUDREY

never in my life wondered what it feels like to have different types of bugs on your skin, yet as of tonight I have the answer.

There are ants in my legs. Not *on* them. Pretty sure what's coursing through my veins isn't blood—it's freaking ants. They especially like to concentrate in my calves. No matter how hard I shake them, they don't get off.

Meanwhile, my arms are being bitten by mosquitoes, the literal ones. You'd think the suckers would all be dead in the middle of October, but we're still in peak hurricane season, and I guess they also love baseball. I smack one directly on my arm but when I lift my hand, all I see is the red of my skin and no quashed bugger in sight.

My chest is full of spiders, though. I know those aren't bugs, but right now I can't think of anything else that has so many legs. It's like they're line dancing inside of me to a tune only they know.

Or actually, to Miguel's walk up song.

"Here we go," mumbles Hope beside me, leaning forward

so far that she almost falls onto the person sitting in front of her.

"Let's do this, c'mon." Rose claps non stop and continues repeating herself.

They're freaking out just as badly as I am. Normally they'd be down there doing their kickass jobs, but they're only human. And of the special kind that are deeply invested in the success and happiness of the men they love—official members of the WAGs club.

Shit, so am I. I already have planned out the route I need to take to the field once the guys win. Miguel will find me in a second. I'll be the woman in the MACHADO 3 jersey and the weird alligator socks rolled up over my jeans.

"This is gonna have a happy ending, right?" Marty asks me while chewing on popcorn with her mouth open. Beside her, Consuelo's hands are joined in prayer.

The only response I offer is a smile, because I'm not going to be the one who makes the team lose by jinxing them with my own damn mouth.

Yes, they're gonna win. I know it in my bones. I feel it in my soul. I just can't wait for reality to catch up with what I already know.

So I can kiss the daylights out of that man and tell him that I don't really want to get divorced, as outrageous as that sounds.

The place is absolutely packed to the rafters and everyone's buzzing—not just because it's BOGO for beer at the concessions. There has been incessant yammering online about whether Miguel's in a slump. After breaking the historical league record of home runs, it's kinda odd that he hasn't knocked at least one out of the park in the course of this series, even considering how the Riders have been fumbling the bag so hard.

Even then, there isn't a single person in this stadium that doesn't know that Miguel is capable of greatness even with a bunt. The Orlando Wild fans know it, the Denver Riders do too—and are also extremely unhappy with finding themselves on the other side of Miguel's genius. Every single broadcast professional and staff knows it. The newborn babies in attendance know it.

And I sure as hell do.

Miguel *is* magic. He's everything that is good and worthy in this messed up world, and the most unbelievable part is how the world doesn't affect him. Life and its difficulties haven't sharpened his edges, like juggling an elite professional athletic career and being a single dad would to anyone. Or like all the slander online would mess with anyone.

If he hasn't hit a home run it's simply *because*. He doesn't owe anyone anything. No matter what, he's still taking the team toward victory.

They're gonna win, I say in my mind. *They're gonna make history and I'm kissing him tonight.*

Miguel doesn't swing for the first pitch, which isn't surprising. He's an observant batter. That brilliant brain of his calculates outcomes at a speed that mere mortals like us can't even fathom. But when he doesn't swing at a strike, it gets an alarm going in my mind.

"What's happening?" I mutter, and the bugs make me smack Hope several times. "Hope, am I overreacting?"

Her eyes narrow. We're not close enough to catch every detail on the field, but we're not baseball nerds for nothing. "This is just his second at bat. Lucky's the only runner on base. He doesn't really need to exert himself."

The third pitch gets him swinging.

And missing by a mile.

After a quiet moment, Hope admits, "Okay, that's not entirely normal for him."

"You don't think…" Rose leaves the question hanging, also not daring to vocalize something that might cast bad luck on the team.

"No," Hope and I say in unison, because this is how we negate what we're all fearing. Miguel's not in a slump. Everyone has a lackluster at bat every so often. I *am* going to bury my fingers in his sweaty hair and claim his mouth for my own.

"What?" Marty asks, her eyes widening. "*What?* Is my dad okay?"

People in the audience start booing, and we all snap back to attention.

There is absolutely no stinking way that Wild fans are the ones booing our cleanup hitter, which can only mean one thing. The Riders fans are catching up onto what we're fearing. Miguel isn't playing his usual.

But then comes the fourth pitch and he connects.

I jump to my feet, barely registering that I'm not the only one. The ball flies like a rocket. I push onto my tiptoes. Miguel takes off for first base. The outfielders start running toward the same area, close to our side. Lucky's dashing to second. My ears are roaring. I cram the word *please* some five hundred times in a single second. The ball crashes against the fence— on the inside. It's not a home run, but the outfielders are scrambling.

And then there's silence.

Complete, and utter lack of sound.

My heart stops. There's no air in my lungs. My eyes run to Miguel. But my worst fear doesn't happen—he's on first base, not bleeding from anywhere. And he's looking ahead of him, still as a statue.

One of the girls gasps. I can't tell who. Because now I'm seeing what happened.

My second biggest fear *has* happened. One of our guys is

hurt.

It's Lucky, and his leg is out of shape at the knee.

I drop the popcorn I forgot I was even holding. Before anyone wakes up from the nightmare, I say, "We need to go, Lucky will need us."

Screw nerves and jinxes, we have to go to our friend.

CHAPTER 46
MIGUEL

t's hard not to feel some type of way when someone like Lucky Rivera gets a potential career ending injury on a decisive game like this, where the result can dictate the rest of the series.

Especially when it happened during one of your plays.

The logical part of me keeps trying to explain how it wasn't my fault. I didn't bat the ball into his knee, nor was I the overly excited baseman who got in his way too early, making him slide off the wrong direction. I also wasn't the base itself that caught his shoe at a weird angle and ensured the snap of Lucky's knee.

I sure watched the whole thing unfold… after I was the one who set that play in motion.

These things happen in the game of baseball. It looks very easy and low contact compared to something like hockey or rugby. But freak accidents can happen anyway, with long lasting impacts. Or worse. A pitch to the wrong spot of the head can kill. An accidental collision can incapacitate. And people in the stands are also not always safe. We all know this. We practice to prevent this. We hone our bodies to our own peak to be more flexible and stronger.

It's still a roundhouse kick to the solar plexus when it happens. Makes a guy wonder when his turn will come.

So after that inning I made a big error that got a run for the Riders. Then our relief shortstop made another one. And that set a chain of events in motion that has taken us right into this moment.

Bottom of the ninth. Our last chance at bat.

We're trailing four to one, with two runners on base.

Our captain is next at bat, and then it's my turn.

No one knows that my side's really bothering me. It's why the hit that led to Lucky's injury wasn't a home run.

Right now we're on a time out, huddling around the on-deck area with Beau, McDonald, Logan, a base coach and at least five other players. Beau wants us to go for broke, be as aggressive as caged wild animals that are hungry. A few of us glance down at our alligator feet socks. I bet Lucky's screaming the same at us from the medical ward.

"No wussing out," Beau says with more calm than I'd have in his position. "We haven't come this far to crumble like cookies. Our rivals out there are hoping and praying that we do, so how the hell are we gonna give them that satisfaction?"

"Who are we?" the base coach shouts above the noise in the stadium.

"The Wild!" all of us scream in unison.

Logan takes a single step forward, it brings him into the middle of our messy circle. He turns slowly, staring at each of us in the eye and stopping when he faces me. "Lucky would get so angry at us if we screw this up now."

My shoulders slump a little. "Yeah…"

"Did he just use Rivera's first name?" someone whispers.

"We can't afford going into another game where he won't play," our captain continues, "because that would piss him off even more. We have to finish this tonight to make it worth it."

My eyebrows climb. I hadn't thought about that aspect,

even though it rings as true as the earth being round. I've just been focused on how shitty it would be to lose because his injury rattled us—me especially—when the real nightmare for him would be to watch us lose like damn fools.

Coño, seré pendejo.

I smack my cheeks hard enough that everyone's attention turns to me. Even better, all the capacity for pain in my body now concentrates on my face. My mind hasn't been clearer all night than at this moment.

"Get on base, Logan," I command as if I was the boss of this operation.

"Only if you get enough of us home to salvage this," he retorts with a sharp look in his eyes.

Three runs would tie this. If I can hit the ball nasty enough to frazzle the fielders, I can get the next guys at bat to come up. Scoring a run of my own would be even better.

"For Lucky," I say, putting my paw in the air.

Logan smashes his over mine. "And for your marriage."

"And for the pizza." We turn just as surprised to see that Cade came out of the dugout for this, even while he's half undressed and cooling his shoulder. "What? I've also worked hard, I deserve a few slices."

"For the pizza!"

"And the socks!"

"And for a sixteen-hour-long nap!"

Snorting, I shake my head. The circle begins dissipating and, for the first time since I've met him, Logan Kim shoots me a Lucky-style grin before heading to the batter's box. Shit has hit the fan when our grump of a captain starts looking like our favorite class clown.

But this team is more than stereotypes. They're brothers, warriors, and strategists. I haven't met a single Orlando Wild player who doesn't think at least two steps ahead, some even as far as ten. Logan holds that record, and I have no doubt that this guy's gonna make something happen during his at bat.

I crouch, holding myself up with the bat. My heart beats so furiously, it's almost like every fiber's screaming. My whole body tingles and burns. The last time I felt like this was when I was kissing Audrey.

While I watch Logan bait the pitcher with balls and fouls, I practice some breathing exercises and kind affirmations to myself.

"Your daughter's gonna be so embarrassed if you swing and miss like a pee wee," I mutter to myself. "Audrey's gonna reconsider giving the time of the day to such a loser. The internet will rip you apart. The team's gonna trade you to the worst one in the majors. Or even send you down to minors. *SPORTY* is definitely not gonna air that ad where you act like a big shot."

I know what's gonna happen the second the ball leaves from the pitcher's hand. I rise back on my feet. Logan's front foot stomps the dirt hard. The voices in the crowd get louder. I give the bat with the doughnut one last warmup swing.

Clank!

"Damn." I watch the ball launch like a rocket from Logan's bat, and it's so beautiful that I can't help copying the Lucky grin. "What a reliable jerk. Anxiety," I say to myself, "I can't let you make these guys lose."

Tossing the heavy bat, I pick up the regulation one and wait.

Logan reaches the base before the fielders can make sense of his hit. Our other two runners have advanced.

"How the turns table," I mumble in my dad joke voice. My walk up song starts playing and I no longer see the look of disappointment in my mind's Marty version. She's telling me that I better not hold back. "I won't," I tell her. Reaching for the chain at my neck, I lift up the pendants and bring them to my lips.

The fate of the whole team isn't on my shoulders. There are three runners on base hungry for glory, who will do whatever it takes to achieve it. Dozens of men are in the dugout and in the clubhouse, sending me all their fighting spirit. There's one in particular who is probably doing the same, via quite a few strong words in a strong Boricua accent. My parents and the rest of my family back home are watching on TV, which might or not be hooked to the family car if this catches them in the middle of a blackout. They, too, sacrificed everything so that I could have this moment.

And my girls are in the stands. I know that no matter what happens, they're going to be my soft landing place. This is all for them.

The first pitch curves inside, far out of the strike zone. The umpire calls for one anyway, but I'm not bothered. Life gives you more chances than you realize.

Next, the pitcher shakes his head. And again. Running down the pitch clock. Finally he throws. I can practically see the trajectory of the pitch in the air.

"Ball!"

People start booing, but my blood roars even stronger in my ears. I check my stance—and move a little closer to the catcher.

Okay, a lot.

"Don't blame me if you get hit," the guy says before crouching down.

It would suck if I get beanballed again. One run is not enough to win. The baserunners would have to work even harder. The Riders will only be too happy. Ben Williams would feel like the king of the world.

Ain't no way.

I'm going big so that everyone can come home, even if I break in the process.

The hairs at the back of my neck stand up. My arms flex. My hips start rotating as the ball launches. My brain zeroes in. It's like everything else fades away—except for the ball. I can see each red seam. The spin changes. A cutter. As if I didn't practice with Cade Starr everyday. Every part of my body acts. I twist in tune with the violent centrifuge. The percussion point of the ball has never sounded clearer. It's the only sound that filters through.

The ball explodes out of the bat. The wood stick keeps going into an arch. So does the ball—into the night sky.

"Eso es," I tell myself with complete chill, as if I was watching the play from the comfort of my living room.

I drop the bat, and the thud snaps me awake.

The stadium is going down. Thousands of voices screaming. Blowing whistles. Vuvuzelas? Damn, that was a pretty wild hit, huh?

I start making my way to first base as the ball disappears behind the stadium screen. The Riders outfielder closest to it melts against the wall in defeat.

So, a grand slam… Surely this makes up for how bad I played tonight.

The base coaches follow me as I circle the diamond, stepping on each base like this is just a drill. The Orlando Wild dugout empties, a gaggle of men turning into children as I approach the home plate—and jump firmly on it.

We win, five to three.

And as someone douses me with icy sports drink, I realize that I have earned the biggest reward of my life.

I get to ask Audrey out now.

CHAPTER 47
AUDREY

"Thank you for using your nepo-baby powers," Lucky says from his bed, loopy as all get out on the pain meds he had to be put on so he could hold out for the end of the game, instead of going to the hospital right away.

Reckless? Yes.

Understandable? Abso-freaking-lutely.

Besides, our staff is top notch. The only thing they can't do is surgery, but we're equipped with everything that's necessary to contain his injury and keep him at ease.

Even then, we're all around him careful not to cause any more damage. Consuelo fluffs his pillow and pats him on the head like he's her long lost child. In his state, the gesture makes him smile like a pampered little kid. On the other hand, Rose is wiping the sweat off his face, and Hope is making sure that his injured leg is tied well enough so that no sudden movements can affect it.

Meanwhile, I'm holding his gigantic hand in between mine. I'm not a very touchy feely person, but if I was in his place I think I'd want someone to hold my hand. Even better, hold *me*.

A song that at this point all of us recognize like the back of our hands starts playing. We all slow down and turn our full attention to the TV screen. It's large enough that I almost feel like I'm there on the field, watching Miguel walk up from the on-deck circle.

Wow.

Goosebumps break all over my body. The noise in the stadium is so strident that it practically makes the walls vibrate —and that's not through the TV. It's like the whole world knows how important this at bat is for the team. And for me.

Lucky realizes that I'm muttering something over and over. The word *please*. And now he's the one squeezing my hand. "It's gon' be fine. That man is yours already."

I snap my mouth shut with a loud clacking sound. One of my friends is snickering.

"It's true." Marty nods at me. "Dad's been moping around the house ever since you moved back to yours."

I duck my face, but since I made the mistake of braiding my hair tonight, it's not currently available to fall like a curtain and hide whatever expression I'm making.

"Just for the record," I explain, "I don't want the team to win just for my own sake."

"Sure."

"Uh huh."

"I'm loopy but not enough to believe that lie."

"Besides, what's wrong with that? I do want you to become my mom." Marty shrugs. If she wasn't on the other side of the clinic bed I'd squish her against me.

"Strike!"

We all turn back to the screen. "Shit, I missed it." I grunt at myself.

It's the ninth inning and we're trailing pretty badly. I need to watch every single second, convey every ounce of my energy to him. I'll be happy to never be able to plug a USB cable right the first time, never match socks, get lost every time I drive to a new place, and find my pillow a tad too warm every night. All I want is for Miguel to shine—and shut up everyone who's been talking crap about his performance tonight.

"Please," the word slips out.

Then Lucky joins. "Please."

And next thing I know, we're all please-pleasing as the next pitch comes.

"Ball!"

The booing takes me by surprise. Are our fans doing this to Miguel? I will ban them all from the damn stadium if so.

Until I remember that there are plenty of Denver fans in attendance, and also that pitching such a clear and cowardly ball to someone like Miguel is an affront against the sport. I'd boo as well if I wasn't busy praying with my simple word.

Our own voices rise once more as the pitcher prepares for the third pitch. A little voice in my head says that this is it, three time's the charm.

Then the ball is launched. We lean forward, even Lucky. He lets go of my hand to prop himself up. We're all quiet as the camera pans into the ball, flying into the dark sky as if it had wings of its own.

Lucky starts shaking.

"Shit, are you hurt? Should we call someone?" I all but screech.

Instead, he launches a fist in the air and shouts, "¡Así es!"

Then the camera returns to Miguel. Only when I see him start to trot at leisurely pace toward first base is when my brain catches up.

It was a home run.

No, a grand slam. We had full bases.

"Oh my wow." I stumble. I have no idea when I stood up, but my knees shake and I start going down. My friends are screaming and crying and jumping around. Lucky is fortunately tied to the bed because otherwise he'd topple right over.

And I'm on the floor, sitting stunned. Trapped in a reality in between life as of a moment ago versus now.

The Orlando Wild. The dark horse. The un-historic team… well, not anymore. We just took it all. We're in the history books now.

And Miguel's smile on the screen does me in.

I start bawling like a baby, my face buried in my hands. I don't even understand why—I should be freaking ecstatic, jumping around like my friends are. But my chest is being stung by the invisible stab of mourning.

Adam would've loved this moment. In an alternative reality, we'd be celebrating like fools, smashing our hands together and screeching in joy. But that wasn't meant to be.

Just like the previous version of me wasn't meant to endure for the rest of my life.

Tonight I'm saying goodbye to the Audrey that tucked herself away from the world, who would rather be alone and cold than risk getting attached and hurt again. As of tonight, I promise to myself that I will live with no reservations.

Someone grunts above me and a big hand grabs onto my arm. "Get up, woman. Time to go get your man."

I emerge with a gasp and let him help me up. Placing a kiss on his forehead, I say, "Thank you, Lucky. For everything."

He leans back on the pillow. "Make sure the camera captures you and your husband."

"But like, don't make it too embarrassing." Marty cringes a sort of smile.

Chuckling, Consuelo shoos me off with a wink. "Do what you want, I'll distract Marty over here."

"Let's go!" Rose elongates the last word, and with that it gets the three of us going.

The route I had mapped in my head from the family

section to the field is no longer necessary. Since coming to keep Lucky company in the team clinic, we have a much shorter commute through the medical wing, then the clubhouse, and straight out of the dugout.

All three of us run with joined hands even as we rush through the tunnel. But once we hit the dugout and our attention shifts solely on finding our boys among the celebrating mass of people on the field, we have no choice but to let go.

"Godspeed, soldiers," Hope says.

Rose nods. "You too. And don't forget that kids are watching."

"It's okay, I'm in PR. I know how to write a good apology." The laughter that comes out of my chest is brand new, never before released into the wild. My friends echo it as we split up.

My eyes jump through every face, my heart thumping at a furious pace against my temple. Every limb trembles with pent up energy, my feet shuffling around to get a better view of the players and staff spread around the diamond. Streamers and confetti in our colors rain down from the stands, and sprays of various drinks explode like geysers between the players.

And then I find him.

Miguel is surrounded by his teammates, his uniform soaking through and sticking to him like a second skin. His face is split in absolute joy, eyes shining like the stadium lights, his smile so unabashed that I get a glimpse of how he must've looked like as a boy.

And then he finds me.

Amid the commotion and glee all around him, somehow my presence is a magnet that has him turning his head clear toward me. I take a step forward that is too timid, too heavy, like my legs are caught in quick sand. Miguel starts making his way between his teammates.

Thomason, who was a fantastic closer for this game, gets

the attention of the players around. "Guys, guys. Watch out! It's time for romance!"

I crack a laugh. Gosh, I love these silly geese. Or silly gators, considering they're all wearing Lucky's socks.

If anything, Miguel's smile grows positively more beautiful as his teammates start clearing a path for him. Finally my legs start cooperating, there's no cell in my body that can wait any longer.

I'm not the athlete here, but I run—harder than I ever have, my thighs burning and the balls of my feet digging into the green. Miguel blinks in surprise and now he's the one in quicksand, because he can't seem to move.

I launch myself at him with all my might, in a feat I probably wouldn't be able to repeat if I wanted to. My arms wrap around his neck and my legs around his waist. In my haste, his cap gets knocked off and I'm finally kissing him. A whimper escapes from my throat, a recognition that I'd denied this moment to both of us for far too long.

Miguel takes a deep breath even as I devour his mouth, those massive and hot hands splaying across my butt so I don't fall. Or maybe just because. I squeeze him even harder, delving deeper into his delicious mouth with my tongue, trying to make up for lost time in a single kiss. I release one hand to press it against his jaw, loving the way it works so hard to savor me as well.

A myriad of voices bounce all around us and dazed, I pull back just a little, enough to find nearly the whole team jumping around us.

"Ack!"

Of course, I should've expected to be doused with a cold drink. My muscles tighten and I squeeze harder onto Miguel— All-Star, single dad, my fake husband, my real love.

He laughs into my neck, chasing away the cold with his breath.

"I don't want to get divorced!" I all but shout over his head. In case he didn't hear me, I lean back again, still hanging off him and knowing he won't ever let me fall. "I don't want to lose you. I don't want to screw up our chance just because I'm always afraid. I like you way, *way* too much—more than I dare to say right now—and I also like who I have become since I've met you. I want to learn what being a family is like with Marty and you, and I don't care what anyone says but—I want to stay with you."

I'm holding his face, kind of squishing it. There's a touch of gold in his eyes under the blaring stadium lights, and they search all over my face. *Please* continues to repeat in my mind, never have I wanted anything more than I want a lifetime with him.

"Hey Audrey?" Miguel asks softly.

"Yes?" I bite my lip and it catches his attention for a solid moment.

He swallows hard and forces himself to meet my eyes once more. "I also have something to say."

"What's that?" My lower lip trembles. I have to use the rest of my willpower to not trap it between my teeth again.

This joyful man gets a glint in his eyes, and next thing he's squeezing my cheeks a bit harder. Not the ones on my face.

"Turns out I have to disappoint you—"

"What?" I screech.

"—Because I can't just be your friend. I want to be that and more. Your lover, your rock, your refuge."

"You do?" I ask with a thread of voice.

And finally, this friggin' man breaks into a grin. "Yeah, we might've gotten fake married, but I really fell in love with you."

The fireworks explode in my chest, and laughing, I lean down to claim his lips as mine. Forever.

CHAPTER 48
MIGUEL

After the ceremony and the trophies, and pictures that are going to be etched in the eternity of sports, the real party begins in the clubhouse.

Here is where we get showered with beverages of higher alcoholic degrees—and that includes Lucky. It might not have been a good idea to send him off to the hospital smelling like a bar, but he laughed even harder than anyone else as he was being carted into the back of a private ambulance.

The WAGs have joined in, and it's great to see every couple in jubilation together and all. But all I want is a moment alone with Audrey.

I don't know what she is—my girlfriend or wife or something different—but in a deeper language, the kind that one can only feel in the gut, I know she's my soul. With her I'm complete.

Her smaller hand is in mine, and I jerk my head toward the door, which makes some drops of who knows what land on my face. Her lips, pink and swollen, form a quiet *yes* that I know more than hear. The drunk singing has started, and it would be impossible to have a real conversation here.

Audrey's the one who tugs at my arm toward the exit, and I follow her. Deliriously, even. This is just the beginning of us walking together for the rest of our lives.

The corridors in the staff building are still lit up but empty. Everyone who earns a paycheck from the Wild organization is crammed into the clubhouse. Our steps echo and Audrey doesn't let go of my arm for a second, not even while we climb some stairs that start looking familiar, or when she shoulders a metal door open into the night.

The wind seems to cradle us into the outdoors. Automatic lights come on and finally I recognize where we are. It's the terrace over the staff entrance, where we once officially became friends.

Audrey whirls around to face me, her mouth opening to speak. And I can't help myself, I cover it with my own, now fully free to show how much I hunger for her. Moaning and holding her tight isn't enough, and I bury my hands in her wet and messy hair. A sound comes out of her that makes my blood boil, and my heart tries to claw into her chest.

"Miguel," she groans my name, nearly decimating me on the spot. "Miguel… Miguel…"

"Audrey," I rasp out against her lips, caressing them with mine while I try to catch my breath. "You make me wild."

"So do you." Her feminine laugh sets me even further ablaze.

My head is spinning. I've wanted this moment so much, so damn hard, that I'm afraid of myself. Of this feeling that is swallowing me up right here, right now.

Leaning my forehead on hers softly, I draw in a ragged breath and open my eyes. "I wanted you to know something."

"Wait," she pants hard. "Why are you still able to think?"

I laugh. "Trust me, I *am* about to lose my mind."

"Oh, okay." She offers the sweetest, most lethal smile. I can't wait to wake up to it every morning.

I kiss it. Gently. But I can't pull away for the longest time. Her hands run up my chest, one of them resting over my booming heart. Not to be outdone, I bring her flush against me by her waist.

"You've never been my hard place," I mutter against her lips, my tongue running against them for a quick taste. "You're my soft place, my sweetness, my joy, and I officially want to ask you out on a date."

"Just one?" She looks up at me, brushing my hair away from my forehead. "Because I want at least a million."

"Deal," I respond, palming the curve of her lower back like it's the only anchor I have to reality. "Then let's have our first one."

"Now?"

"Yes." It's a damn shame that I have to let go of her for even one second, but it's only to ask for her hand. "Dance with me."

Audrey throws her head back for a laugh, the untidy braid falling off her shoulder. "But there's no music!"

And that's when I hear it, a soft pitter patter all around us, the gentlest of sounds that transports me to the stormy night that brought down my carefully built resolve of just being her friend. I smile as the first cold drops hit my shoulders.

"Look at that, the heavens are giving us a little waltz. Let's dance in the rain, mi vida."

She draws in a breath, and her chin trembles. Her eyes are bright, though, two gleaming jewels that bore into me like only she can see me—the real me, with all my virtues and my flaws.

Her delicate hand falls on mine, and the other one finds my shoulder. "I have two left feet," she jokes, barely containing her happiness from breaking out on her face.

"Don't worry, just follow me." I find her lips again, and slowly, we start our first real date, dancing in the rain.

EPILOGUE

DECEMBER

"Audrey Machado," my dad says, bushy eyebrows nearly meeting, his mustache arched in discontent. "Would you leave some of that cake for Martina?"

"It's Marty, Gramps. Besides, I kinda want cheese instead," she fires back as she brings a big square of gouda into her mouth.

"Does anyone want more coffee or tea?" Consuelo asks, holding a thermos up for view. At first she wasn't too fond of the idea of lowering to sit on a mat that's spread over the cold grass of a public garden in the middle of Orlando.

But it's Christmas, the gardens are decorated with cheerful lights, and it simply is a delight to experience.

Also, I happen to be sitting against Miguel, my back flush to his chest, his arms around me infusing me with all his heat. I don't even feel the chilly breeze of the evening in his cocoon.

I snuggle deeper against him as I continue chewing. "It's not a cake, Dad. It's an apple tart and you heard Marty, she wants cheese."

"Hmph." He turns to Consuelo, lifting his travel mug. "I can take more coffee, thank you."

Miguel's chest vibrates against me. "Mi vida, I think your dad may have wanted some tart for himself."

"Did not," Dad answers with the same dignity that has enveloped him all his life, even taking a sip of his topped coffee. But then he says, "Fine. Maybe. Apples are my favorite fruit, after all."

My chest twists. I didn't know this about him. But then again, I didn't know that he's been sober for years, and that early on in that journey is when he decided to buy the Orlando Wild team, where I already worked at, as part of his plan to slowly create an actual relationship with me.

I probably will never understand him, especially that penchant he has of using his might rather than speaking his mind clearly, but we've been finding some common ground the past couple of months. Small things like this one, liking the same fruit.

"Fine," I parrot, stretching to offer the remaining half of the tart to him.

He accepts it gracefully. "Thank you." And gobbles the whole thing up in a single bite.

I grunt. "Greedy old man."

"Cranky old daughter," he returns while chewing with none of the manners he'd typically employ.

Miguel chuckles. "I guess it's good to know that this dad and daughter type of dynamic lasts forever."

"But I'm not old," Marty grumps, skewering more cheese cubes on the plate and this time, popping in a grape too.

Sighing, I hug Miguel's arms tighter around me.

So this is love, a little tea party in a crisp Christmas evening with my family, watching the holiday lights shine brighter as the sun dims in the sky, not a single person around to distract from this precious moment that I've managed to earn after so much heartache.

"Wait a second." I sit up to attention, sweeping a glance all around us. "Why is there no one else here?"

Silence.

And knowing looks.

I fold my arms. "Who paid an exorbitant amount of money to rent this whole freaking park for the evening, and clearly needs a lecture on financial responsibility?"

Dad's hands come up. "Don't look at me, I'm just here for the ride."

Scooting, I make enough distance between us to turn toward Miguel, but the scolding dies on my lips.

He's sitting there, his thick and oddly very straight legs wrapped in the *SPORTY* pants that made his ad go massively viral, and a simple flannel and jacket that somehow make his shoulders look infinite. His full lips are turned in a playful smile, eyes dancing with lights in a way that will never stop making my heart flutter.

"I didn't rent the whole thing. The staff recognized me when I called and offered a few private hours for free. I do plan to make a healthy donation to help with operations after this, though."

"Good." I fold my arms, nodding. "That sounds more reasonable."

"You're not going to ask why he even did it in the first place?" my father wonders, almost confused at my lack of sharpness.

Marty shushes him and whispers, "Hold on, here comes the best part."

"What would that be?" I ask, turning to her for any sort of hint. But then Consuelo points forward with her lips, in that uniquely Latin American fashion, and I bring back my attention to Miguel.

And the shiny thing in his hand.

My eyes widen and I lean closer, even changing angle to really make sense of what it is.

A ring. Gold. With a large oval rock in my favorite color.

Actually, in the exact shade of my irises.

My mouth opens.

"I know that we're already married on paper," Miguel says, not missing a beat. Either he rehearsed this or he's never been surer than in this moment. "And I also know that some people may think it's too soon."

My dad coughs.

Miguel bites his lips to hold back laughter, and he clears his throat before continuing. "But the simple truth is that I love you, Marty loves you, Consuelo loves you, I think your dad does too—"

"Hey!"

"—And out of all of us, I'm the one who absolutely can't wait to spend the rest of our lives together—to be one, and to have the right to love you more than anyone else under the sky."

I'm so engrossed in him that I startle when my hands come to my mouth.

"So… Audrey Machado Winters Cox—"

"Why is my last name third?" Dad complains, and it falls into the cracks because then Miguel says words I never expected to hear directed at me on purpose.

"Would you marry me?"

His eyebrows pinch a little, almost like he's growing shier with every second I spend in utter silence. What he doesn't know is that he's robbed me of words, that all I can accomplish is to stay still, rather than throwing myself at him and scandalizing our family.

Slowly, I lower my hands down to my lap and busy them with squeezing my cable knit dress. I fill my lungs with the scent of cinnamon and tea, sweet little tarts, damp grass, and magic with a touch of cedar.

"Miguel."

"Audrey?"

I lift up my eyes. "Yes, I will marry you again—and for real this time."

Joy spreads on his face and I let myself loose. I throw myself at him and somehow manage to land a wild hit on his hand that sends the ring flying. As the other three scramble to search for it in the grass, I gently bite Miguel's chin and he bursts out laughing until the world around us fades away.

THE END

*

*Thank you for reading **Wild Hit**! I hope you can take a brief moment to leave a review on Amazon here.*

*Stay tuned for **Cheerfoul**, the second book in the SPORTY Christmas series featuring our favorite Boricua, Lucky, and his very lucky lady! It will come out in December this year.*

Here are my other works if you're craving more closed door sports romance:

*Sign up to my newsletter here to get my free volleyball novella, **Set Me Up** and be the first to find out what's next from me.*

*The St. Cloud Hockey Series, **Faceoff** (rivals to lovers), **Overtime** (grumpy x sunshine), and **Shutout** (childhood friends to strangers to lovers) is complete and can be found here.*

And of course, you can find the full Wild Baseball Romance series right here.

Happy reading!

MORE FROM THE AUTHOR

Upcoming Soccer Romance Series · Book 1* ·
Wild Baseball Romance · Wild Pitch · Wild Catch · Wild Hit ·
St. Cloud Hockey Series · Faceoff · Overtime · Shutout ·
SPORTY **Christmas Romance** · Mistlefoe · Cheerfoul · Book 3* ·
Volleyball Romance Novella · Set Me Up** · Set Me Up 2* ·

*Coming soon.
**Newsletter exclusive.

*

Find my closed door romantasy, paranormal, and sci-fi romance books as **MC Loyal**.

GLOSSARY OF SPANISH VOCABS

Chapter 2

- Pero: but.
- Vamos (see also Chapter 8): let's go/let's do this.

Chapter 4

- Mi Niña Bonita (see also Chapter 24, 30, 42): my pretty girl.
- Arepa (see also Chapter 10): arepa is one of the national dishes of Venezuela and has no English translation. It's a corn flour "bread" that can be filled with basically anything.

Chapter 6

- Mi Niña Bonita by Chino y Nacho: the song "My Pretty Girl" by the singers Chino and Nacho.

Chapter 10

- Chiquita: little girl.

Chapter 12

- Mierda (see also Chapters 14, 16, 20, 40): crap/shit.

Chapter 13

- Mondongo: traditional Venezuelan soup that is basically everything but the kitchen sink.
- Mija: short for "mi hija," my daughter.

Chapter 14

- Uno, dos, tres: one, two, three.

Chapter 16

- Estoy en problemas: I'm in trouble.
- Mi niña: my girl.

Chapter 18

- Cabrones (see also Chapter 20): equivalent to "assholes."
- Chanclas: the flip flops every Latino kid gets Olympically acquainted with.

Chapter 20

- Amigos: friends.
- Bailar pegao: colloquial way of saying dancing very close.
- Cacique: a famous brand of Venezuelan rum.

- El papá de los helados: extremely niche joke about the guy who went on to Venezuelan Who Wants to Be a Millionaire and answered "the daddy of ice creams" instead of the very well known lyrics of a massively popular Mexican song.
- Dura: Puerto Rican way of saying a woman is hot.

Chapter 21

- Mucho macho: much manly.

Chapter 22

- Coño: big word used in Venezuela for many contexts, surprise, anger, frustration, etc.

Chapter 26

- Eso no, pendejo: not that, fool.
- Mi vida (see also Chapter 48, Epilogue): my life.

Chapter 28

- Bueno: good/fine.

Chapter 30

- No bueno: not good in bad Spanish grammar.

Chapter 32

- Mierda, y más mierda: crap/shit, and more crap/shit.

Chapter 34

- Joropo: Venezuelan folklore music.
- Toy Contento: I'm happy in bad Spanish grammar.
- Prima: female cousin.
- No te hagas ilusiones, papá: don't get ideas, dad. — Extra note: in certain contexts, "dad" is a way of referring to men, whether they're fathers or not, unrelated to attraction level.

Chapter 36

- Cojones: men's dangly bits.

Chapter 37

- Mi niña, ¿cómo te fue?: my daughter/child, how did it go?

Chapter 44

- Cállate: shut up.

Chapter 46

- Coño, seré pendejo: damn, I must be a fool.
- Eso es: that's right.

Chapter 47

- ¡Así es!: that's right! (Yes, a different *that's right*, lol).

ACKNOWLEDGMENTS

Tamagotchi were a huge thing back in My Youth™. The collective attention was sucked in by a tiny, pixelated pet that would die if you stopped paying attention to it for five minutes.

But I never wanted one, because it'd make it harder to watch my afternoon anime.

So you can imagine the level of outrage kid-me felt every time I'd come home from school, and instead of finding my beloved anime playing on TV, there was…

Baseball.

Yep, the sport that was so intertwined into the lingo and culture of my home country, that people didn't know they were speaking In Baseball in day to day conversations. If someone was in a pinch they were in 3-2. And if someone had done something amazing? They knocked it out of the park.

If all that wasn't annoying enough, my dad *loved* baseball.

He used to play it growing up and had a lot of stories to share about it (according to the family legend, he taught one of his neighborhood buddies how to pitch, and that kid went on to become a major leaguer). So he'd tune in to said baseball games, reminding me of the joy I lost that afternoon (yes, I'm melodramatic that way. Why do you think I write books?).

One day, after years of whining from my side, I encountered the anime Touch by Adachi Mitsuru.

A. Baseball. Romance. Anime.

And I didn't hate it. Like not at all. Like not one bit.

I did hate the male gazey-ness about it, though, and since

then I had the idea of one day writing my own… but for the female gaze (aw yeah).

I only decided to finally go for it in 2017, right after my dad was first diagnosed with cancer.

I became fully determined to write my take on baseball romance. I could feel the clock ticking, and I wanted to allow myself to love something he did while he was still here. It was my way of coping with what my family was going through.

The first baseball romance I wrote was a YA that I posted on Wattpad in 2018. Even though my writing has evolved a lot, it's still one of the best stories I've ever written. And I was determined to see it published and in my hands.

I signed up with it to two author mentoring programs, one with fellow Wattpaders that same year. Two years later, I signed up for another one from the traditional publishing industry called Write Mentor, and got accepted into it. I queried the cleaned up book. I got partial and full requests.

And then I got the rejections.

"Sports romance isn't a thing in the market."

"I don't know how to sell this."

"I'm not a fan of baseball, so I can't relate."

"Query me again with a new manuscript."

What didn't matter to the publishing machine at that point, is that my dad had already died the year before.

In 2019, when he was still going through treatment, we were talking on the phone once and he tried to give me some baseball advice for my book.

"No thanks, Dad. I don't need it because I already finished writing the book."

Yeah, that's what I said. I've regretted it since.

I had heard so many of his baseball stories growing up that somehow I convinced myself there wouldn't be any new ones. But what if I missed out on new memories? Why the hell did I value my own time more than his during that conversation?

Those were all the feelings I was querying and getting rejected with. I had to mourn again when it became clear that the book wouldn't happen, and I didn't think I had it in me to come back to baseball romance.

Until much later. And many other books later.

By that point I'd already made baseball an important part of characters in other books. I was in a better place mentally and emotionally—and I'd also consumed copious amounts of baseball anime and manga by that point.

That's how this series was born. From not wanting to join the Tamagotchi life, to losing my dad.

I've been writing it for roughly a year, and it has rewired my mind completely. I'm able to contain both grief and joy for the sport. When I watch a game, I no longer wonder what my dad would've thought of that play. I *know* he would've had a blast with it, and I share that joy with him *now*.

This series is no longer about making it up to him. It's about celebrating who he was, what made him happy, and all the encouragement he gave to my writing dreams—even when it was too early. It's about finding happiness after loss, about not giving up and believing in myself.

So, thank you, Dad. I know you're supporting my plays from heaven with the Lord. This one's for you.

ABOUT THE AUTHOR

Mari Loyal was born and raised in Venezuela, a baseball country that only cared about another sport, football soccer, every four years. As such, she decided to make hockey her whole personality because she had to make a point of being different. These days she no longer suffers from Not Like Other Girls syndrome and is very happy to be in the sports romance fandom. She writes closed door romance with a Latin American flair and an abundance of cinnamon rolls heroes. She also enjoys eating cinnamon rolls (the confections), in her spare time.

Find her:

Website & Newsletter mariloyal.com
Instagram mariloyalauthor
Threads mariloyalauthor